BADGER

Other Titles by C. M. McKenna

WRITING AS CARA MCKENNA

Hard Time
Her Best Laid Plans
Unbound
After Hours
Curio
Convenient Strangers
Don't Call Her Angel
Skin Game
Dirty Thirty
Ready and Willing
Willing Victim
Off Limits
Ruin Me
Brazen

THE DESERT DOGS SERIES

Lay It Down
Give It All
Drive It Deep

THE CURIO VIGNETTES SERIES

Coercion
Craving
Reversal
Confession
Exposure

THE SHIVAREE SERIES

Backwoods
Shivaree
Getaway

WRITING AS MEG MAGUIRE

Wild Holiday Nights
Thank You for Riding
The Wedding Fling
Headstrong
Trespass
The Reluctant Nude
Caught on Camera

THE WILINSKI'S SERIES

All or Nothing
Going the Distance
Takedown

C.M. McKENNA

BADGER

Brain Mill Press · Green Bay, Wisconsin

Published in the United States by Brain Mill Press.
ISBN 978-1-942083-03-0
EPUB ISBN 978-1-942083-04-7
MOBI ISBN 978-1-942083-08-5
PDF ISBN 978-1-942083-09-2

Cover illustration and interior art © 2015 by Grace Mutuku.
Cover design by Book Beautiful.
Interior design by Williams Writing, Editing & Design.

Interested in reading more from Brain Mill Press?
Join our mailing list at www.brainmillpress.com.

My name is Adrian Birch, and I'm nobody.

Don't mind me. Carry on doing your somebody things. I'll just be over here, taking up as little space as possible. No, really. I like it this way. This is how it's always been.

The best way to explain my childhood would be to have you imagine a kid's painting. Picture a rainbow—red, orange, yellow, green, blue, purple. Add some grass if you want, a big-ass happy sun. Now add a small, muddy blob in the lower right, a toadstool or a rock. That's me. The rainbow is my sister, Amanda. You look at our family and you see the blinding, beautiful rainbow and go, "Wow, just look at that!" Then you spot the blob and say, "Oh, did your brush drip? Never mind, we'll cover that with a fridge magnet."

I wasn't a bad kid. Never a troublemaker, not much of a drama. But if you opened up Amanda's paint box, you had all the original ovals of colors, vibrant as the day you bought it. Open mine, and you'd find a drab spectrum of brownish gray, everything blended together and no chance of a rainbow.

My sister's default is wide-eyed joy and possibility, and mine is a sort of involuntary gloom—not one I wallow or revel in, but not one I've ever been able to kick, either.

Amanda and I are fraternal twins, and our eggs were as different as Fabergé and scrambled. Amanda is fair and pink-cheeked, with irises like gems cut out of the pure blue sky. Whereas I'm thin and dark, with what my mother calls "gypsy eyes," probably to try to make me feel mysterious or interesting. Hangover eyes. A bit squinty, their edges the color of a ripe bruise.

I was a deferring pregnancy, a wispy shadow hiding behind Amanda's robust fetus that my parents didn't even discover was a second daughter until nearly the third trimester. A uterine wallflower, that was me. Amanda burst forth screaming and vital, and I slipped quietly into the world behind her, never one to want a fuss made.

I stayed that way through high school, the invisible girl. Not odd enough to mock, not ugly or fat, just so remarkably unremarkable that I simply blinked out right before your eyes, blending into the wall, where I liked to be.

The only point in my life when I could've been described as anything resembling dynamic would've been the not-quite two years I spent addicted to Vicodin. For the middle portion of that period, I moved back in with my parents so they could keep an eye on me. Or keep an eye on the wild animal they'd invited to inhabit their house, sleepwalking through her days, hungry and snarling when the fleeting pacifism of chemical hibernation wore off.

When I came down off those suckers and wanted more . . .
I was ballsy. I was fearless. I was dumb as shit, and I stole
anything that wasn't nailed down.

My record could be worse—could be breaking and
entering instead of mere shoplifting—but it still doesn't
impress potential employers. A little over a year ago I was
caught stealing from a department store, the same week
I turned twenty-six. It was for the best. It was my third
such offense, and I got sent to a women's correctional
facility for a month. While I was there I went through a
sadistic but supervised withdrawal, came out clean, and
was granted a "scholarship" to rehab, then to a sober living
home for six months. Now I live by myself in a shadier
corner of Jamaica Plain, my little overpriced rented sanc-
tuary just west of Boston.

I was really lucky, in some ways. Job searching with a
criminal record sucks, but hey, my mom's talking to me
again. And I'm no longer banned from family gatherings,
as I was the year after I sold Amanda's engagement ring
to a guy loitering outside the Sullivan Square subway
station. I stole it off the sink while she was showering at
my parents' house the morning after Thanksgiving, two
years ago. Eighty bucks that half-carat solitaire earned me,
which kept me happy and thoughtless for maybe twenty
hours. Eighty bucks that basically amounted to me taking
a shit in a chocolate box and handing it to my beloved
twin, my greatest defender.

Fucking Vicodin.

But I don't like dwelling on all that. Those were an ugly
couple years, a possession. "Adrian's Mr. Hyde period,"
Amanda calls it with a dismissive wave of her hand. I never

got her ring back, and her fiancé had to buy a replacement. I don't think he's forgiven me, but Amanda has. She's way too good to me. Someday I'm going to make it up to them and hand over the thousand bucks the ring was worth.

If I ever find a goddamn job.

2

The very first time I saw the Badger, it was a drizzly Wednesday in late September, and I was bleeding from my chin and arm.

I'd been hit by a car—a Jaguar sedan, I think, a streak of gleaming gunmetal—which sprang like a sucker punch from a backstreet parking lot. I'd been crossing the wide alley on a shortcut to Downtown Crossing following a disheartening job interview, my third in two weeks.

A hot bolt of pain as my right wrist broke, a scraping burn as I hit the pavement. It was mid-afternoon, but there was no one off the beaten path to witness it. No one but the Badger.

I remember my ChapStick rolling from my purse all the way to the far sidewalk like it had someplace better to be. I remember staggering to Summer Street, where of course no one acknowledged my injuries or expressed any concern. This was Boston, after all, iciest of New

England icy, eyes forward, don't engage lest you're accosted by a crazy person or a survey taker or a tourist in need of assistance with the spiderweb our forefathers passed off as urban planning. A blur blew past from the side street where I'd been hit, flying in the direction of the Jag, and someone shouted, "Dude, it's the Badger!"

I fumbled left-handed in my purse for my phone, since no one else seemed poised to dial 9-1-1 to get the bleeding girl a fucking ambulance.

° ° °

They called him the Badger because he was rabid and aggressive, black and gray.

They called him the Badger, but I thought he made a far better pigeon. He swooped out of no place and disturbed people on busy city streets, peppered clothes and cars with white paintballs like combat-grade bird shit. Black and gray on top from a striped hoodie, faded orange sneakers on his feet. People said he was dirty and feral, an urban transient. People loved or hated him, just like a pigeon.

Me, I like pigeons.

The Badger rode an old yellow Schwinn, faster than a bike messenger on meth. Which was exactly what I imagined he was, at first. He shot between the slow-moving cars on Summer, tugging something at his lower back. I found out later it was a U-shaped bike lock, one of those big steel numbers that hipster couriers somehow manage to stash in the back pockets of their too-tight jeans. I heard the crack when the Badger sank that thing into the maybe-a-Jaguar's rear window, another as he whacked the driver's-side mirror clean off. I read later on a Boston crime blog he got the windshield as well, then disappeared in the direction of the Common.

But when all that happened I was leaning against a building and stammering my whereabouts to a dispatcher. Soon the approaching wails of my rescuers drowned out the Jag's alarm and the honking of the cars around it. As I was helped into the ambulance, police sirens came and went. Soon I was heading to the hospital, and my hero was long gone in the opposite direction.

And for a brief time I forgot about the Badger, because all I could think was, *Who in the fuck is going to hire a writer with a broken wrist?*

3

As I sat in the back of the ambulance, an EMT fussing over the blood and grit ground into my chin, freshly fractured bone shrieking in my dominant wrist, I thought, *They'll give you something for the pain. You're supposed to tell them not to, but you won't.*

It was a relief, like the universe was giving me a sign, a hall pass, a nudge in the direction of Easy Street.

Then I remembered those seconds—the hum of chain and spokes, the scrape of rubber on asphalt as the Badger flew past to avenge me. A gray blur on two skinny wheels, a man seeming as elementally fearless and angry as I was meek. My fantasy involving an orange prescription bottle dissipated, whipped away in the suction of his slipstream.

As we pulled into Mass General, I thought, *I've just got to meet him.*

o o o

Once I was back home in my tiny apartment with my wrist in a cast and six stitches in my chin—prescription soundly refused, clap for me—my research began in earnest.

I'd heard of the Badger, but only in passing. I thought I'd read a fluff piece about him in the *Metro* once, or eavesdropped on people discussing him on the subway. I knew he was a bit infamous and unsavory, but for what, I couldn't have told you.

Once I began investigating, most of what I could glean came from a single website, *BostonBadgerWatch.com*. It was a blog people sent their "Badger sightings" to—grainy cell phone pictures and written reports, the odd snatch of shaky video.

As best I could tell, he was like a bargain-basement Batman.

The website was a little over a year old, and it seemed the Badger had gone rogue about a year before that, right around the time I—or rather, my Mr. Hyde self—was busy selling my sister's ring for pill money.

Everyone agreed that whoever he was and whatever his deal might be, the Badger was definitely on something. Crack or speed or glue, or some special recipe he whipped up in his secret lair.

But basically, he was a menace on a bike. He probably didn't make Boston any safer. The opposite, really. He just made it more *fair*.

He fought violence with violence. If you dinged a pedestrian or cyclist with your car, he'd smash your mirrors off with his U-lock. But if it was something less heinous, you'd just get balled—run a red light or splash somebody with dirty puddle water, and he'd nail your window with a white pellet shot from a Glock-style paintball pistol. Harass or intimidate somebody on the street, or generally be a dick in any way to your fellow man and get caught—*thwack!* Big white bird-shitty splatter all over your nice new coat.

Given what a dramaphobe I was, you can see why I'd find the Badger both terrifying and hugely compelling. I hate a scene, and he was a human scene. He was everything I wasn't and couldn't ever be, not outside of opiate withdrawal.

Of course that time I spent being a fearless fuckup . . . it was merely another flavor of cowardice, just me trying to get out of my head, silence all its anxious whispering. I still did that, I'm sad to admit, but now when I needed to feel The Nothing, I just drank a measured dose of Nyquil and went to bed at nine thirty. It was pathetic, but legal and cheap. I guess it was technically abuse, since I didn't have the flu, but hey, it was a step up.

I hadn't always wanted to hide and sleep. For almost all the time I was in college, I came alive in my understated way. I had a pulse. I went to art school, because that's what you do when you grow up being praised for your drawings. Amanda got praised for everything else, and with good reason, but drawing was *mine*. The absolute only thing that distinguished me from my twin for the better.

I studied illustration here in Boston, and you know what? I was goddamn good at it. I was among the best in my class, my specialty these crazy-intricate interior scenes collaged out of tiny slivers of X-Acto-cut paper, which I'd embellish with hand-stitching. I also took to writing unsettling vignettes and taught myself bookbinding, and I created a series of rather exceptional little volumes as my degree project and graduated with honors. For a while, I'd really felt like someone special, with something to share. Like the thing in the sunshine in front of the shadow, for a change.

But fine art and publishing are not industries for the deferring, and with the assignment-based sense of purpose that college offered behind me, I misplaced my compass.

I was a good writer, and one of my professors helped me get an entry-level gig penning copy for an ad agency her husband worked for. I hated that place, but I'd liked the somebodyhood that a job title gave me. I stayed there until I had a violent back spasm, when I was informed that Vicodin addiction had an opening that just might be a perfect fit for me.

During my time in the correctional facility, I'd felt awake and alive for a little while. I hadn't had much choice, once detox did its thing.

I'd started drawing again to fill the sleepless nights, and all the women in my ward treated me like da Vinci. I was writing, too, and when I got out I'd felt like someone again. I'd taken a menial job as a grocery-store stock girl while I was in sober living in a dumpier corner of Back Bay, thinking it would give me endless hours to brainstorm and meditate on where my art was trying to lead me. But in the end it had just left me exhausted and glassy-eyed, fingertips cracked and itchy from dust, and my fire died all over.

And that brings us to the present.

I needed a real job, because the supermarket had laid

me off three weeks earlier and the first of the month was looming. If I couldn't pay my rent, I'd have to move back in with my parents in Lincoln, and I knew I wouldn't be able to do that and not start looking for the next pill, the next great escape. If I was going to be miserable at a job, I might as well try to get a decent salary and health insurance while I was at it, so I'd been looking for in-house copywriting gigs. But again, there's my record. That permanent smear of dog shit on my heel, its stink lingering well after I'd get led back to the elevators and told to have a lovely day, we'll be in touch if you're the right candidate.

○   ○   ○

I hadn't even seen the Badger's face, but with every scrap of information I uncovered, I felt more and more as though he and I were two halves, polarized and separated. And the more I learned, the more sharply I ached to be near him. I wanted to feel and hear the magnetic *click* as I snapped tight against him, to someone *like* him. To someone so unlike myself. I wanted to see his face and hear his voice and touch his skin, as surely as zealous Catholic school-girls secretly want to bone Jesus.

According to Boston Badger Watch, he'd never been caught. Thanks to the coke or crystal meth or whatever secret sauce kept him going, he escaped through alleys, under overpasses, sometimes on foot up fire escapes, and allegedly even down subway tunnels and storm drains . . . though some of the stories did smack of embellishment.

One BBW report claimed the Badger saw a business-man flick a lit cigarette on a homeless guy who was panhandling at Downtown Crossing. Could have been vindictive, or it could have been that this jerk hadn't registered the homeless man's existence any more than he might a sack of garbage. But *flick* went the cigarette, and *pop* went the Glock, and apparently the paintball hit the business-douche square in the back of the head and knocked his toupee off. I grinned when I read that one, because I felt silent and invisible in this city, too.

The Badger was a huge hit with the local homeless population, and there was a special "Badger Spotting" section in the *Spare Change* homeless-run newspaper. Most people seemed to think he was a transient himself. One thing was for sure—he had issues. Major issues. You'd think that would've put me off, but it didn't. I wanted to find out myself if he was for real.

And for the first time in ages, I wanted to create.

After I'd exhausted the Internet's disappointingly meager Badger knowledge, I stayed up late obsessively stitching the shapes of bicycle wheels and gears onto an old scrap of muslin. Awkward work using only one clumsy set of fingers, my right hand reduced to a fleshy pin cushion. But awkward felt beautiful in the moment, and being awake felt better than sleep, which it hadn't in months. I brainstormed a million crappy strategies for finding the Badger, none of them viable. And real-life worries beckoned me with the dawn.

o   o   o

After my run-in with the Jag, I needed a paycheck worse than ever. I'd never gotten around to signing up for health insurance, and though I was broke enough that my ER visit got reduced to twelve hundred dollars from four thousand, that was still twelve hundred bucks more than I had. It was time to settle for freelance.

Maybe I could write a local color article about my run-in with Boston's infamous Badger. That might not sell for much, but if I could actually meet the guy? I could be Lois Lane. If Lois were a former klepto painkiller addict and Superman a tweaker on a ten-speed.

It was worth a shot, and most important of all, it validated my new obsession. The Badger had also been the only witness to my hit-and-run. Was there any chance he'd remember the guy's plate number? Who fucking knew. Plus, considering how many assault warrants he surely had, it didn't seem likely he'd volunteer to testify for me.

Then there was the little matter of even finding him.

Some enterprising nerd had taken the time to create a Badger-spotting interactive map on the BBW site, with virtual pins marking all the places he'd been seen. Some corridors were more clustered than others—certain stretches of Tremont Street, various hot spots downtown, dots all along Mass Ave. I also found a post from a guy who claimed that he saw the Badger all the time, late at night while walking across the Longfellow Bridge after his bartending shift. He said the Badger had glided past him on dozens of occasions, bound for Cambridge. He'd never seen the Badger do anything exciting, but right around two thirty or three in the morning, there he'd go with his stripes and his Schwinn.

The Badger didn't respond to people yelling at him, I'd read.

Didn't answer to his nickname or make eye contact.

He only engaged to mete out his crude brand of justice via U-lock and paintball, so if I was going to stand a chance at interacting with him, I'd have to be either the perpetrator or the victim. After mulling it over through the weekend, I decided to be both.

o o o

Late Monday night, I made it to the Charles/MGH stop on one of the evening's last trains and walked halfway across the Longfellow Bridge to a spot bathed in streetlight.

I knew I had a good hour or more to wait, and as I stood before the ledge, cold autumn air whipping my hair around, I imagined falling in love with the Badger.

I'd had a few relationships, though no grand romances. In college I'd had a boyfriend I wanted so desperately to love, I'd scared him away. Once he was gone, I'd found I didn't really miss him, only the idea of him. I'd felt sad to realize I hadn't loved him, and ripped-off that my heart wasn't broken. I've always wanted to be in love. Companionable or passionate or train-wreck tragic, I'm not choosy. Just real and inspiring. Yet another chemical escape to this junkie.

The bars closed and the city quieted, more still and calm than I'd known Boston could get.

After nearly two hours, after thousands of glances over my shoulder at the Cambridge-bound lane, I finally spotted an approaching cyclist. My stomach lurched, a strange tug more solid and purposeful than nausea, one that seemed to tell me, *He's close.* The magnet-click I'd fantasized about.

My limbs had grown stiff and cold, my bad wrist moaning low and plaintive beneath my skin. I got into position on my knees on the bridge's wide concrete railing—dangerous and stupid in itself with only one working hand. Adrenaline locked my joints as I stood.

I stared at the water, eyes glued to the shushing black waves. I ran through what I'd tell any non-Badger passerby who confronted me.

No, I'm fine, thanks, I'd say in my best well-adjusted voice. *Sorry to scare you. A friend of mine committed suicide here last year. Sometimes I just like to come here and remember her. Yes, very sad. Thanks for stopping, though.* A corny lie and bad karma, but I didn't want the cops called. And I didn't want anyone to worry. No one except the Badger.

I heard the bicycle approach, then slow. I stood with held breath, anticipating words but not receiving any. There was a scuff and a clatter, soft footsteps, a huff. Then the Badger was standing beside me on the concrete ledge, staring down at the water with his hands in the pockets of his hoodie. I felt as if I was standing next to a celebrity, an angel, my grubby cut-rate Christ.

His voice rang unnaturally loud in the crisp fall air, a not-quite-echo bouncing up from the water. A tired voice, a bit deep, a bit flat. "How's it look?"

"Cold," I said, watching the waves.

In my periphery, the Badger nodded. "Does look cold."

Unsure what to say, I kept mum.

"I don't really feel like going in after you."

I turned to face him, wishing I could tell what color his eyes were in the yellow streetlight, or how old he was. His hood was up. His skin was pale, stubble dark, and he was attractive in a broody, Eastern European way.

Heavy eyelids and strong bone structure. Not handsome, but sort of sexy . . . if danger and angst turn you on. He was a local, too, ignoring the Rs on the ends of words, banishing the Gs from his gerunds.

I looked to his chest, his hoodie half-unzipped so I could see the thick leather strap of his pistol holster.

"I'm not really going to jump," I finally said.

"Yeah, I could tell."

"Oh?"

"Nah. You're not dead yet. Not dead in the face." He circled his own face with his hand. "You're just a cry for help, waiting for somebody to come by and plead with you not to do it. Want me to plead?"

Embarrassed, I shook my head and fumbled to the sidewalk. Badger jumped down to join me, sneakers slapping asphalt.

I smiled sheepishly. "You're right. I was never planning to jump." I held up my right hand with its cast. "Do you remember me?"

"No."

"Oh. Well, my name's Adrian—"

"Good for you. You must get called first during attendance."

Okay, fine. No small talk. "A few days ago, I got hit by a car in Downtown Crossing, and you smashed the guy's windows."

"Sounds like something I'd do."

"I wanted to find you, to say thanks. Do you not even remember it?" How could that be, when it was among the most dynamic events of my life?

"Sorry, no clue who you are."

"So I guess you didn't catch the plate number, then."

His smile was faint and wry, bereft of apology. So much for my witness, my outside chance at recouping my medical expenses. As if that was really why I'd come here.

"Well, thank you, anyhow." I took a deep breath and blurted, "I think it's really great, what you do. Helping people you don't even know. I was hoping to maybe . . . find out more about you, I guess."

His smile tweaked to a smirk, the gesture carving a parenthesis beside one corner of his lips.

"Would that be okay? If we met for a drink or a coffee—"

"Sorry to wake you up from whatever Robin Hood wet dream you've been fingering yourself over, but I don't do that stuff to help anybody."

My hopeful balloon deflated with a doleful sputter. "Pardon?"

His bike was lying against the curb, and he righted it, holding the handlebars. "What I do, I do out of hate, not humanity. Because punishing assholes gets me off—not saving victims. And actually all this . . ." He cast his gaze around us. "This isn't doing a fucking thing for me. So if you're not going to jump, I'd just as soon be home in bed."

Home. Well, there was one question answered.

Face burning, I shook my head. "No, I'm not jumping."

"Great." He slung a leg over his crossbar. Face utterly unchanged, the Badger drew his infamous Glock from inside his hoodie, took aim, and shot me in the thigh from five feet.

"Ow, Jesus!" White paint exploded across my favorite jeans, and a bolt of exquisite pain promised a welt.

"That's for wasting my time," he said, replacing the

pistol. "I'm too fucking tired for false alarms, so next time have the decency to jump."

My slack mouth produced no words. I watched him glide away, silent and passive once more. As ever.

I glanced at my palm, streaked with white from where I'd grabbed my leg. Looked and felt just like when a bird shits on your hair. You pray it's a raindrop, but it never is.

Fuck you too, Badger.

I don't know what I'd expected would happen. That we'd wind up sitting on the ledge until the sun rose over the Charles River, Badger and I locked in deep and meaningful conversation? Some outlier fuckup bond cementing us as soul mates? In the end, the T had stopped running, so I walked to Kendall Square and withdrew the last of my savings at an ATM, flagged a cab to take me home to Jamaica Plain.

I stayed up the rest of the night typing angry poetry with my left hand, and though it wasn't very good—the sort of woeful laments I'd penned after any number of Tori Amos benders when I was fifteen—it felt better than a shot of Nyquil. Being awake still held more appeal than the promise of artificial sleep, which couldn't be discounted.

I didn't know what I'd been expecting, but he hadn't

been it. It was my fault he'd disappointed me, not his. What was I smoking, that I'd wondered if he might just be in the market for the love of a good woman?

Yet I wanted to know more. I could admit I was still hung up on the Badger, despite his being an asshole. Despite him assaulting me.

But no way in hell was I going after him again.

∘ ∘ ∘

On Thursday evenings, I always tried to go to a Narcotics Anonymous meeting.

I was ten months sober—if you don't count the cough syrup—which is still a dangerous stage to be in. I attended a group that met in the basement of an ugly concrete church downtown, because that was where the really down-and-out people went. People who'd done some really fucked-up shit that made my eight-Vicodin-a-day habit look like cutesy-poo chocoholism.

I didn't mind sharing with these people, because here, in this group, I was the Amanda—the youngest and most together-seeming person in the room. Once a week, down in that basement, I was the rainbow among toadstools.

I arrived on time and took a seat on a cold metal folding chair at one end of the horseshoe, exchanging nervous smiles with familiar faces. There were about twenty of us this evening. The basement was chilly and the pipes rattled now and then, but the cinderblock walls were painted periwinkle blue, and something about that reminded me of my grade school, of possibility and potential. I sat up straighter when I was down there, proud to report I'd done my homework.

The meeting got underway, and just as Jimmy the recovering heroin addict was admitting to a recent temptation on the heels of a chaotic breakup, the door swung in with a creak.

My heart stopped.

No one did much aside from look annoyed that someone had come in late, because it wasn't the Badger—not officially. No striped hoodie, no yellow bike, no Glock. But I knew that face now, better than just about anyone could claim to.

His gaze grabbed mine, and there it was—that magnet-feeling I'd thought I invented, so strong I was surprised my chair didn't start moving, scraping across the linoleum, dragging me to him. He kept that tension strung between us for each step and second it took him to walk to an empty seat on the other side of the circle and plunk down next to Deb the former speedballer.

His stare told me he was here for me.

Then again, he sure did seem the type to have a drug problem. *Could* have been an innocent coincidence. Maybe that stare was telling me, *Well, look who it fucking is. Fancy meeting you here.*

"So I get home and she's gone, all her stuff and some of mine." Jimmy sighed, agitated. "And I want to use so bad . . . Then God intervenes, you know? 'Cause who do I get a call from but Andy." He nudged his sponsor, sitting beside him. "And he said he got some feeling, like we gotta talk, and I think to myself, Jimmy, he's right, you gotta talk. You gotta talk *bad*. This is a sign." He stopped and looked around, letting the rest of us know it was time to nod sagely and feel grateful for our sobriety.

"Thank you, Jimmy," said Mandy, the meeting's leader. She turned to me next. "Would you like to share?"

I'd gotten pretty okay at this the past few months, but the Badger wasn't normally in the room. But fine, whatever. Let him hear. He'd shot me in the leg and suggested I find the balls to toss myself into the Charles River—he couldn't humble me much worse than he already had.

I cleared my throat, toying with the strap of my purse. "Hi, my name is Adrian." I waved limply as everyone except the Badger chanted, "Hi, Adrian."

"I'm ten months sober from Vicodin," I went on. "It's been hard, because I'm trying to find a job, and that's really frustrating because I have a record, and I'm not sure how I'll pay my October rent. I also got hit by a car on Friday." I held up my cast. "And Tylenol sort of sucks, you know?"

A few people laughed, several smiled and nodded knowingly, and I relaxed a little.

"But I was good—when I got to the hospital I told them, 'Don't give me any narcotics.' So life's sort of shitty at the moment, but not as shitty as when I was using the pills, and at least I didn't ask for a prescription. Um, thanks."

"Thank *you*," Mandy said, and moved on to the next person.

There were ten or more people between me and the Badger, and he stared at me for the entire fifteen minutes it took Mandy to reach his seat. It wasn't a threatening look—not quite. But it was freaky-intense, and I didn't like it one bit. I wondered if it was revenge for what he saw as my jerking him around on the bridge.

Finally, Mandy turned to the Badger. "Would you like to share?"

Though it wasn't protocol, he stood, chair squeaking against the tile. "My name's Ronaldo," he said, and I'd never doubted someone's name more thoroughly in my entire life.

"Hi, Ronaldo," the circle chorused. Everyone but me.

"I used to be addicted to crack, but now I'm not," he said, speaking quickly and without much emotion. Not sarcastic—bored. "That's it." He sat, and Mandy thanked him.

I'd hated him a bit when he'd left me on that bridge, but right then I *really* hated him. I hadn't realized until that moment that I'd grown fond and protective of my group, and I wanted to sock him in the nose for standing up and lying to them. I'm sure we addicts lie all the time to each other, but that was different. I think.

The final person shared, and Mandy told us to take five and grab a coffee or go up for a smoke before that evening's speaker was due to start.

I really didn't need a coffee—my blood was already boiling. Though the weird thing was, it felt good. I rarely let myself register intense emotions, and hating the Badger felt pretty amazing, almost like I was high. Inappropriate as that was, given the setting.

I shouldered my bag and got in line for the carafes, ignoring the Badger with all my might. I sensed him standing beside me as I stirred sugar into my coffee, tangible as a draft. I felt him behind me as I returned to my chair. I crossed my legs, having forgotten the welt on my thigh, and swore under my breath. The Badger sat next to me, leaning close, saying nothing.

After an excruciating minute's silence, I cracked. "What?"

"*Hiii*, Adrian," he mocked, a one-man NA circle. "Vicodin, huh?"

I raised my chin to glare at him. "So what? And like your name's really Ronaldo. Like you were ever addicted to crack."

He shrugged.

"Did you follow me down here?"

"Yup."

Good God. How long had he tailed me? Had he simply spotted me coming out of Park Street Station, or was it more premeditated than that? Did this freak know where I lived? Too many questions, so I went with, "Why?"

"Why'd you pretend you were going to jump off a bridge?"

Sure, fine. We just wanted each other's attention. "Well, congratulations," I murmured. "You're making me really uncomfortable. Are we even now?"

"We were even when I shot you. Now we're just in the same room, having a coffee."

I shook my head, flustered. His magnet was too close to mine. My needle spun madly, pointing nowhere.

His eyes were blue. Dark, lonely blue, like the Atlantic on a cloudy day. That night, with his trademarks gone, he could have been any guy in his late twenties, early thirties. Overdue for a shave, with short brown hair, spiky from the rain streaking the basement's high half-windows. His T-shirt was still damp, dark along the shoulders.

The Badger set his coffee on the floor. "You got a pen?"

Leery, I dug in my purse and handed him a fine-tip

Sharpie. I gasped as he grabbed my right forearm, tugging it across my body toward him. He pulled the cap off with his teeth and began writing on my cast.

"What are you doing?" I barely whispered it, though I ought to have made a scene. This room was one of few places where I might've felt able to, but I didn't. And sure, in part because I wanted to know what he was writing. He finished and let my arm go. On my cast was scrawled an address in Somerville and a time—ten thirty.

He capped the pen. "If you want some of your questions answered. And bring cash." He stood and tossed my Sharpie into my open purse, abandoned his coffee and headed for the door.

Once he'd disappeared, I stared at his black letters, no clue what to do. The meeting recommenced, and Tina shared a long story about getting sky-high and ruining her daughter's wedding before finding a new sense of purpose rehabilitating greyhounds. I took in perhaps every fiftieth thought she shared, clapped with polite appreciation when she was done, shuffled out into the night amid a flurry of tired goodbyes.

5

It was five after ten, just enough time to get to Somerville.

And of course I went. You know I went.

There was no stronger object to draw me away, keep me in place. The Badger's pull propelled me down the wonky Park Street steps, through the plastic jaws of the turnstile, down to the Red Line platform. Through the tunnels, up to the surface, across the Charles, past the spot where I'd stood on the bridge railing, then back down into the earth through Cambridge, all the way to Davis Square. All those stops, all those doors that parted and chimed and invited me to change my mind . . . No chance.

I got to the address a minute or two late, jogging more to minimize how rained-on I was getting than to be punctual. It was an all-night diner, which surprised me. I'd been expecting something more sinister. I looked for the Badger's bicycle on the sidewalk. Nothing.

As I opened the door, a slap of *what-the-fuck-are-you-doing?* nailed me across the face, but I shuffled inside, scanning the stools and tables. No Badger. Rather than wisely take that as a sign I ought to turn around, I sat in an empty booth and studied the laminated menu, like maybe the description of the eggs Benedict would tell me why in the hell I'd come here.

Before the door even swung in, I knew he'd come. My body prickled. I was facing the end of the restaurant. I couldn't see him, but I *felt* him. Felt every footstep until he passed me and slid onto the opposite bench. He looked me over with his Russian assassin's eyes, blue irises hiding in the shadows of his languid lids.

"Hey," I said stupidly.

"Hey."

"I brought all the cash I have, which is only about thirty bucks. I'm not sure how much you had in mind."

He glanced at the menu. "That's fine. I only want toast."

"Pardon?"

He met my gaze again. "This place doesn't take cards, but that's fine. I'm a cheap date."

"Oh. I thought you wanted me to pay you, to talk or something."

His eyes narrowed. "You a reporter?"

I shook my head. I wouldn't tell him I'd wanted to write about him only a few days ago. I didn't want that anymore. He had far too many dimensions, far too much to try to capture in something so dumb as a local color piece. And it wasn't worth the couple hundred bucks I might get paid if such a thing would only piss him off.

"So," he said. "I was a dick to you the other night."

I gave a little start. "Um, yeah. You were. And this evening."

"But you were worse," the Badger said. "Threatening suicide's a pretty shitty thing to do to a stranger."

"I know. But it was the only way I could think of to get you to talk to me."

"I don't like being jerked around." He said it slowly, then paused, glancing at our hands or the table between us. "But here I am, so I guess it worked. Congratulations."

I smiled tightly. "What should I call you?"

"You don't like Ronaldo?"

"I don't think that's your name any more than 'the Badger' is." I looked to the center of his chest, to a diagonal stripe of dryness bisecting a V of damp cotton. He'd been wearing his hoodie and holster, but where he'd ditched them I couldn't guess. A phone booth, maybe, if he really was a hero. Or in his top-secret Badger Cave.

"Call me whatever you feel like. But I don't hand out my name to random girls off the street."

"You think I'm a cop?"

"I don't know who the hell you are, except maybe somebody who's going to pick up this check, in exchange for wasting my time the other night. But no, I don't think you're a cop."

"Definitely not. I'm a writer," I said. "An unemployed copywriter. Not a journalist or anything. What do . . . What *are* you?"

He leaned forward and I did the same, and the conversation turned hushed and strange and intimate, a conspiracy gelling across the Formica.

"I'm a guy on a bike with impulse-control issues and a

lot of warrants." His lowered voice was the first taste of discretion I'd yet witnessed from him.

"Were you ever something else?"

A waiter interrupted us and took Badger's order for toast and a cup of coffee, mine for scrambled eggs and decaf.

"What's your deal?" I asked when we were alone again.

He smiled, more tired than amused. "Exactly what you see."

"Why do you . . ." I sighed, feeling ridiculous, afloat in a vat of questions. "I don't even know why I care. Or why I did that stupid thing on the bridge. But you're more different from me than anybody I've ever heard of. I guess I want to understand you. Or figure out what the heck you are, and what you do, and why you do it. What's going on in your head that lets you do it, because I'm sure as hell missing it."

He shook his head. "That's all backward. It's whatever you've got in *your* head that *keeps* you from doing stuff. That's what *I'm* missing. That filter. That little secretary's desk your thoughts and reactions pass over before somebody stamps them 'approved' or 'denied' and either lets you get on with them or changes your mind. I'm missing the 'denied' stamp."

"Oh."

Our coffees arrived, and I pondered that idea as I shook a sugar packet.

"I get that, a little," I said, stirring my coffee. "When I was addicted to painkillers, I'd get like that when I came down. Do you . . . Are you on something?"

"What do you think?"

"I think maybe, yeah." I squinted at him. There was lucidity there, a glimmer of presence I'd never caught in the eyes of still-intoxicated women as they arrived at the correctional facility. "Well, maybe not. I don't know."

"I don't need anything like that. If there's anything I need, it's probably heroin, and I'm not rich or stupid enough to take that shit up."

I nodded, believing him. "Most of the Internet thinks you're on meth."

"Internet's a fucking retard," Badger said. "All it cares about is shopping and porn and videos of cats falling off shit."

I laughed. "That's true. So all the stuff you do . . ." I leaned in close again, and he did the same. I watched his mouth as I spoke. "What makes you do it? All the stuff with your bike lock and the paintballs?"

"What made you keep swallowing those pills?"

I frowned. "Well, at first it was because I felt anxious and depressed. But then later it was the chemical dependence making me do it."

"It's a bit of both, with me," Badger said. "I do it to shut my brain up. And I do it because I can't *not* do it. My body's no good at processing adrenaline."

"Mine, either. But it makes me go all shaky and mute. I guess it does the opposite to you. You said you're in it to get back at the assholes, not to help the victims?"

He nodded. "When I see something that pisses me off, it's like . . ." His gaze jumped all over, as if the words he wanted might be scrawled on the walls or windows. "It's like hell opens up inside my head. Then I chase, and I do something to even the score, and cold blue water fills my skull. All the anger goes *hissss*." He closed his eyes as though meditating, wriggling fingers miming dispersion. "Just steam. And I can breathe again."

I smiled. "You've got problems."

His eyes popped open. "Maybe. But I've also got fixes."

"Temporary ones."

"Only kind there are, cupcake."

"What's . . . Okay, no offense, but what's *wrong* with you? Is there a diagnosis or anything?"

"I've got faulty wiring." He tapped his temple. "Apparently it's called an explosive disorder, if you can believe that shit." His slapped his palms to the tabletop. "Kaboom!"

Diners seated at the counter turned to glance at us, making my cheeks heat. "Indeed."

"I have a really nasty temper, and no restraint. I've basically got no impulse control, so I do whatever I feel like, the second I feel it. I'm also into really fucked-up sex."

I blinked. "Oh."

"Plus, since I got no impulse control, I tell girls I just met that I'm into really fucked-up sex."

"You don't say."

"I'm a fucking mess," he said, with the delivery of someone remarking about the weather, like, shrug, *What can you do?* "I can't hold down a job, since I always lose my rag and flip out on my boss or a customer or a coworker. But since I started doing what I have been, people give me money. Some random person will flag me down and thank me, and shove a couple twenties in my hand. I actually make more now than I ever did at a real job. Not that I was ever an investment banker or anything."

I dropped my voice even lower. "And you won't tell me

your name, huh? I won't blab it to anybody. I like what you do. I'd never want you to get caught."

"No offense, but considering how we met, I don't have much reason to believe you're not batshit."

I nodded. "That's fair. How old are you, then? Or where did you grow up? Anything."

"Grew up all over Boston and the South Shore."

"Okay. And your parents are from here?"

"My mom was a mail-order bride," he said.

My head gave an involuntary shake. "Wait. Really?" Something about the way he said it . . . I didn't believe him. Though it did explain how strikingly *Russian* he looked.

"What about you?" he asked. "What's your deal?"

Our food arrived, and I leaned into the padded seat back, our conspiracy ruined by the introduction of the mundane—toast and eggs and jam packets.

"I grew up in Lincoln," I said. "Then I moved here to go to MassArt. I live in Jamaica Plain now, this tiny place above a laundromat. It's kind of a shithole, but I don't want roommates, and it's what I can afford. Where do you live? Like in a church belfry or an abandoned cannery or something?"

He smirked and oh shit, he was sexy. Goddamn it. And I'd gotten so good at hating him in the last few days.

"I rent an attic apartment from my grandmother, not too far from here. On Sundays I let her cook for me, and we play canasta 'til her fingers start hurting."

I believed him this time, more than about his mail-order-bride mother. But he was very tough to get a handle on, his delivery neither snarky nor deadpan nor sincere. I bet pathological liars share a continuum with people with impulse- and rage-control issues, so I decided to take what he told me with a very generous dose of salt.

"So what does your grandma call you?"

"Isaac."

His attention was on his toast, and I let the name settle between us. It might be another lie, but he looked like an Isaac, I decided, with his interesting, haunted eyes. Maybe his supposed mail-order-bride mother was a Russian Jew. All I had to go on was mythology, but it was better than nothing.

We ate without speaking for a time, and though I still didn't have much of a clue who was sharing my booth, I suspected I liked him again. I admired him, at least, and no longer worried he was a tweaker. Not one who fed off chemicals not naturally occurring in his brain, anyhow. His own cranial meth lab, prone to frequent explosion. I felt proud to have intrigued him enough to be invited here, and just a little disappointed I couldn't brag to anyone about it. Not that I had many people to brag to.

I leaned in to whisper, "Does your grandma know about the whole Badger thing?"

"My grandmother's a shut-in who thinks the Internet is a fad, same as cell phones and homosexuality. So no. She's not on top of the rumors. She thinks I'm an accountant."

"*What?*"

He shrugged. "I just told her that 'cause it's the kind of job she'd approve of. And she pretends to believe me, and everybody's happy."

"Right."

Badger popped the last of his toast in his mouth and

dusted the crumbs from his palms. "Well," he mumbled, chewing, "thanks for dinner, Adrian."

"You're going now?"

He drained the still-steaming coffee from his mug and stood. "Yeah. I got shitheads to shoot. I'll see you around."

"Okay. See you. Ride safe."

"Enjoy your life."

And he was gone again.

6

And so that was it—my brief and nonexistent love affair with Boston's worst and only vigilante.

You'd think I'd be disappointed it ended like that, me dismissed with a few scraps of secrecy—and those few tidbits likely lies—but I wasn't. I felt special that he'd deemed me interesting enough to share a meal with, even if I'd had to pay the tab. Interesting enough to tease, and to inhabit a space with for a while.

Friday passed quietly, and I applied for about ten jobs, nine that I knew I'd hate if I got them and one that was too good for me, a dream gig writing promo copy for my favorite art museum. They wanted a senior writer though, so I was dead in the water. But I was feeling oddly positive and hopeful and, frankly, *what-the-fuck? go-for-it*-ish, so I hit SEND. The best thing that could happen would be a miracle, and I'd wake up with a salary in the high fifties, almost twice as much as I'd made at the ad agency.

The worst case, I'd simply wake up, as always. For once I needed excuses to talk myself into *not* taking chances, instead of the opposite.

My stitched chin was healing, itchy and ugly but not painful. My welt had faded to a green bruise. My broken wrist was a moody thing, sometimes shrieking madly, or moaning softly, or muttering with restless discontent. I monitored its swings, waiting for the urge. Waiting for hungry, opportunistic mechanisms in my brain to suggest this was exactly what painkillers were invented for, so it couldn't be abuse. Somehow, those urges never rose above a whiny murmur.

It was gorgeous on Saturday, and I sat on the bench outside the laundromat my apartment resided above. I closed my eyes and hugged my purse to my middle, feeling the cool breeze on my skin, the warm morning sun on my face. I breathed in that comforting dryer-sheet scent mixed with the best smell there is—autumn. Some strange guy whistled at me as he passed, but I just smiled. I was dressed up special, and I'd take whatever compliments I earned.

Amanda pulled up in her perky little Jetta, getting out so we could hug before our journey began.

"Hey, sister."

"Hey, womb-mate." I squeezed her tight, loving that perfumey whiff of her hair, loving her eyes as we parted, bluer than the cloudless autumn sky. I loved her so much. So much more than I loved myself.

"You look great," she said as we got into the car.

"Oh, yeah?" I glanced at my skirt and boots. "I figured I should look presentable, since you'll be in ball gowns all day."

Amanda's first wedding dress search. I'd been dreading this, before. Since I attached so much guilt to the first engagement ring, every other thing to do with her wedding —with anyone's wedding—felt awful by association. I winced at ads for diamonds and dresses, burned bright red when I spotted couples having their announcement pictures taken in the Public Garden. I was like that with *The Lord of the Rings*, too. I'd overheard my dad telling my mom I reminded him of Gollum when I was on the pills. Now whenever I thought about hobbits or wizards or Ian McKellen I cringed, picturing myself as a slimy, pitiful, ring-snatching wretch. Cringed because I knew he'd been spot-on.

"No ball gowns," Amanda said, turning us onto Centre Street. "Not my style. Is that what you were picturing?"

I shrugged. Lovely Amanda, lovely wedding, lovely white dress to wear as she starts the next phase of her lovely life. "Something bridey, is what I pictured."

"I've been looking online. I think I want a strapless dress, but not a big poofy one. No train. Fitted on top but maybe sort of swishy in the skirt. I'll know it when I see it. That's what everyone says, anyhow." She squinted at me, smiling. "And what I said before—you do look good, and not just because you're dressed up. You look really healthy."

I made a face, surprised. "Oh. Well, good."

"How's the job search coming?"

I laughed. "Let's focus on beautiful frilly things today, thank you. But it's okay. I'm doing my best."

"And that's all you *can* do," she chimed, the second half of our mom's favorite adage. Amanda flipped on the radio and we headed for the highway.

"What's that on your cast?" she asked, pointing to Badger's scrawl.

"Oh, uh. I was meeting a friend for dinner and didn't have any paper."

"That's nice. Have I met—"

"I don't know why you need to go all the way to New Haven for a dress," I blurted.

"It's cheaper than Boston. Plus, it's fun to get away for a day. Like a mission." She bobbed her eyebrows at me, meaning all the "missions" we'd gone on in the woods behind our house, growing up. To uncover the buried treasure we convinced our dad to hide for us, to save an invisible lost puppy, to rescue a wounded unicorn or slay a dragon—Oh, damn it. Goddamn you, Tolkien.

"So what else is going on?" she asked.

Badger, seated before me at the diner, flipped like a View-Master slide across my brain. Precisely when I'd dropped the "the" from his title, I wasn't sure. Halfway through my scrambled eggs at the diner, maybe. "Not much. What about you guys?"

She groaned, though her smile was huge and warm. "Wedding, wedding, wedding. Ten months sounds like forever, until you start making lists."

"What exactly are you subjecting *me* to, dress-wise?" I was going to be maid of honor, and our younger cousin and Amanda's two best friends from college would be bridesmaids.

"I found this place with a really nice selection of white party dresses, and I think I'm going to let you pick your own styles and get fitted, then the store will dye them all the same color."

"That's a pretty cool idea. What color?"

"Not sure. I need your help with that, oh artistic one. Plum, maybe? Or, like, deep marine blue? Some color that'll look good on the guys' ties and vests. That's your first duty as my maid of honor. Well, after helping me live through this trip."

I perked at the assignment, and I was not one to perk. Certainly not over wedding plans. I really wasn't feeling like myself, but that only meant I was feeling happier than usual.

We chatted about her many nuptial projects as we drove, we sang along to the radio, we grabbed lunch at Denny's on the outskirts of Hartford and got to New Haven in the early afternoon.

My sister looked like an angel in every gown she put on, even the corny sequined one she tried just for a laugh. We knew the second she'd found the right dress, because we both started crying when she came out of the changing room. I sobbed like I never had in my life—like a mother, blubbering and overwrought and happy and pure *my-baby's-all-grown-up*. Amanda got measured and paid in full on the spot, and was told her lovely dress for her lovely wedding would be ready around Christmas. Lovely.

We drove back in high spirits and ate dinner in JP before she had to head home to Woburn. I floated up the steps to my apartment, buoyed by an easy, external happiness undampened by my oft-gloomy mental forecast. There'd be no need for Nyquil tonight, none at all.

I decided to make a pot of tea and flip through my old Pantone swatch books, picking color candidates for the bridal party dresses while I was still in the mood to embrace my sisterly assignment.

As the water heated, I unpacked my purse. There was a message on my phone from a Boston number I didn't recognize. My stomach soured, and I imagined it was the hospital calling about my bill or a fresh confirmation from one of the more courteous places I'd interviewed at, letting me know they'd decided to go with another candidate . . . and on a Saturday, too. I must have *really* disappointed somebody to inspire them to reject me outside normal business hours.

I dialed my voicemail, hovering my cast over the steam of the warming kettle.

"You have one. New. Message. Message one."

"Hi, Adrian. This is Carol DeWitt."

Oh my God. Oh my God. It was the art museum. The steam burned my shaking fingers and I switched off the stove. I stumbled to my tiny dining area and sat.

". . . impressed with your credentials, though we really are looking for someone with seven or more years' experience."

My heart sank, posture crumpling.

"However—"

However?

"We're also seeking a mid-level writer to work with our design department on exhibit and catalog materials. Full-time, in-house. I took a look at your portfolio link, and your work is beautiful. It also looks like you're familiar with the programs our art department uses, which is a big plus. I'd love to fast-track your résumé for the mid-level position, if you're interested. It's not listed officially yet, so I'm not positive about the salary. If you're interested, give me a call back when you have the chance, and I could arrange an interview with our communications director. My number is—"

I scrambled for a pen, scrawling in childish left-hand digits on a takeout menu. I listened again to confirm the number, and to confirm the message had even been real.

Fast-track? Me?

And she'd called on a Saturday?

My heart pounded as I set my phone down. I felt jittery and paranoid, but pleasantly so. I paced around the kitchen, blinking madly. I wanted to call Amanda, but she'd be driving. Plus, I was afraid. The opportunity felt like spun glass, delicate and improbable, and I was afraid to do anything to jinx it, to bump it, to wreck it. And I couldn't get my hopes up. It wasn't an offer, only an invitation to interview. Still, it felt . . . good. Why was everything feeling so good lately? And why did good feel so terrifying?

Eventually I quit pacing long enough to make my tea. I turned on the TV to quiet my racing brain and flipped through color swatches for Amanda's big day. I flipped and flipped and flipped, and I tore out sample chips for nearly every color there was, far more than was useful. Because you know what? Every damn color looked beautiful. The whole fucking rainbow.

7

I called the museum back on Monday morning, and I chatted with Carol DeWitt for nearly thirty minutes. Twenty-eight minutes and forty seconds, my phone said.

Carol was awfully nice, and her son had graduated from MassArt two years behind me. By the time the call ended, I felt like we really had a rapport. And more importantly, I had an interview the following afternoon with the head of the communications department.

I went downstairs and did laundry so my best interview outfit would be ready. The nice Korean lady who does the pressing asked why I seemed so happy, and I told her. She ironed crisp creases into my trousers and dress shirt and didn't even charge me, just wished me luck. Later that day, I brought her a bottle of the iced tea she was always drinking, to say thanks.

Since Carol had seemed so jazzed about my illustration work, I dusted off my portfolio and got it reorganized. I trimmed my hair, plucked my eyebrows, shaped my nails. As I was buffing my dress shoes at the edge of the bed, a segment on the evening news snapped my head up.

"The Badger strikes again," announced a young reporter with a wry smile. He was standing on a street corner, rush-hour walkers and shoppers passing behind him.

"Whether you love or hate him, Boston's vigilante cyclist made another appearance today. I'm told an SUV paused for a two-way stop right here on Newbury Street but didn't wait for a group of pedestrians in the crosswalk to have their turn. Witnesses say a man on a bicycle sped out of nowhere, passing the SUV to shoot its windshield with paintballs. The SUV braked, but collided with a parked car. Both vehicles incurred minor damage, and no one was hurt. The cyclist disappeared down a side street."

The scene switched to on-the-spot interviews, the first with two college-aged guys. *"I think the Badger's awesome,"* one said. *"I mean, the police aren't down here, making things safe for people."* His buddy added, *"He's cool, man. He cares about stuff, and actually bothers to do something about it. The cops are just pissed he's making them look bad."*

The scene changed again, to a well-dressed woman holding her young child's hand. *"Sure, some people didn't get to cross the street when they should've been allowed to. But so what? What if that SUV had hit a person, not an empty car? It's dangerous. It's selfish, juvenile behavior. He's no better than a driver with road rage."*

Next, an older man in a satin Patriots jacket. *"The Badger's good. He's got that old-school Boston spirit. Balls. I think he should run for mayor. He'd get stuff done, you know? He'd have my vote, anyhow."*

Again, the smiling anchor. *"And the debate rages on. Back to you, Kathleen."*

My heart raced, because in a way, they were talking about my secret. My acquaintance, if not my friend. I knew the well-dressed lady had a point, but really, I wanted to live in a world with the Badger in it. Not because he made anything better or worse, just because it was a more interesting place to call home.

I wondered what Amanda might think of him, if he made the news in Woburn. She'd probably think he was a menace. I imagined him sitting next to me at her wedding, dressed in his hoodie. Then I imagined introducing him to my parents and laughed aloud.

I shut off the TV. I needed groceries and dinner and a good night's sleep. Tomorrow was a big day, and I wasn't going to fuck it up.

8

I didn't fuck it up.

Before my interview, I went over Badger's writing on my cast with Wite-Out, missing it when it disappeared beneath the second coat. The only real evidence I had that he existed, that we'd spoken . . . Still, I liked knowing it was there, undercover. It felt secret and intimate, like a tattoo no one knew about.

When the time came on Tuesday afternoon, I was charming and smart-sounding, and not only did I seem to impress the guy who interviewed me at the museum, Carol DeWitt popped in halfway through and made me seem even more interesting and competent. I told them up front about the scuff on my record and was given the impression they didn't have any major misgivings, but of course that was for Human Resources to decide. I left in good spirits, confident I'd be offered a second interview.

But I wasn't.

I was offered a *job*.

A job with health benefits and vacation days, with a real title and business cards and a starting salary of forty-two thousand, with a raise likely after six months!

I went back to the museum on Thursday and filled out HR forms and took a pee test without fear. Proudly, even. I received two calls inviting me to interview at other places, jobs I'd applied for knowing I'd only ever take them if I was truly desperate. I phoned both back to politely decline, dancing as I spoke.

I'd be starting at the museum in just under three weeks. I might have to beg my landlord for an extension on my rent, depending on when my first paycheck came through, but I could let him know ahead of time, forward him my job offer e-mail as assurance. He was a flexible guy, and he told me all the time I was his tidiest tenant.

I floated for the rest of the week. While I waited for the HR packet I was going to receive, outlining the museum's policies and benefits, I actively transformed into the New Me. I went window shopping, even bought a couple items on my credit card to bolster my meager business-casual wardrobe. I wore them around the house, the way I used to dress up in my new fall school clothes in August, sweltering but excited by What Was to Come. I called and e-mailed the few people I hadn't burned bridges with, to share the good news. I told my NA group on Thursday, beaming. I bought a business card case, for crying out loud.

The following Friday in the late afternoon, I was walking down State Street, meandering from Quincy Market toward the stores near the Common, on a mission for a blazer. My phone buzzed at my hip, and I slid it from my pocket. I knew it was from the museum by the middle digits.

"Adrian Birch," I said brightly.

"Hello, Miss Birch. This is Teresa Shaw." I'd met Teresa briefly—she worked in the HR department. She'd brought me a cup of coffee while I'd been filling out forms. Someday we might share a hearty laugh at the museum Christmas party.

"Hi, Teresa. What can I do for you?"

"Well, I'm afraid I'm calling you with some bad news."

I stopped walking to lean against a bike rack. Bad news, like I'd messed up a form and had to resubmit it? Like they'd told me the wrong salary? Like I couldn't start when I'd thought?

"Okay."

"I'm afraid your drug test came up positive."

Silence from my head, from my mouth. Heaviness in my body, like gravity was sucking my heart into my toes. Finally, "What?"

"Your drug test came up positive. I'm awfully sorry, but our policy is very strict on matters like this."

"Positive for what?"

"I'm not privy to that information, only the results."

"I don't understand. I don't use any drugs. I used to—" *Shut up shut up shut up!* "I don't understand," I repeated, numb. Everyone at NA had assured me ten months clean was enough. Everyone. Definitely enough to pass a piss test, plenty even for a hair follicle test, and I'd only had the former. "Can I take another one? It has to be a mistake."

"You can talk to the head of HR, but I won't lie—they're likely to be really hard-line on this, especially in light of your criminal record. But I'm happy to give you the number."

Yeah, fucking thanks. I wouldn't be able to talk to anyone until Monday. Not with only a few minutes before close-of-business to calm myself enough to be able to communicate. I took the number down and said thanks, my voice eerily, creepily cheerful, though I supposed that beat crying, as professionalism went.

The call had come at ten to five on Friday, and I knew, I just fucking *knew* she'd been putting it off. How many days had they made me waste, still believing everything was going to be okay? Letting me think it was cool to go shopping? To get my hopes up? To let myself feel so good and so fucking worthy, for the first time in years?

Heaving hijacked my chest, the start of hyperventilation. I moved to sit on the edge of a concrete construction barrier, forcing slow, shallow inhalations. The world grew faint, a movie watched through a pinhole, flat and tiny, monotone. Tourists passed, following a guy dressed as Paul Revere. Cars honked. Pigeons ticked by on their clockwork legs. There was a whir, a click, a squeak, and a pair of orange sneakers stopped before me.

I looked up, and Badger was as fuzzy and far off as everything else, faded like a photocopy. He stared at my face like he was reading a newspaper headline, interested but separate. After a few moments, he wheeled his bike around and leaned it against the wall behind the barrier, and he sat next to me.

"Hiii, Adrian."

I said "Hi" back, but it was warped by a hiccup, swallowed in a dry sob.

"You look like shit."

I laughed, then another sob, but the world was coming back into focus, more saturated and in stereo. "Thanks. What are you doing here?"

"Friday rush hour in the Financial District? All-you-can-shoot asshole buffet. What are *you* doing here? Crying your eyes out?"

"About to," I admitted.

"How come?"

"I got a job offer, a really great one." My voice broke, and the tears began rolling. "Then I just got a call that I fucking lost it, because I failed my drug test."

"You relapse?"

"No. I don't know what happened. I might as well relapse now, if I stay clean for ten months and it still doesn't matter. Fuck!" I pounded the concrete at my side, the most publically enraged I've ever been, sober. So. Fucking. Sober. Maybe I could keep pounding it until I broke my other wrist, keep pounding until I had a prescription tucked in my purse.

A silver sedan pulled up in a line of cars at the red light, and the window lowered. A young guy yelled, "The Badger! You fucking rock, man!"

Badger gave him the finger. "Suck me."

"Jeez, fuck you too, you dick."

His former admirer disappeared as the light turned green, and Badger spoke quietly to me. "How close are you really, to a relapse?"

"I dunno. What have you got?"

"Something better than pills, if you want it."

I didn't know what he meant, but his offer gave me

direction—momentum, if only in following him, in getting away from the ugly place I'd led myself to.

"Get on." He stood and wheeled his bike around, patting the bars and holding the frame still.

I don't know why I did it. I don't know why I didn't hesitate, except maybe that doing something stupid and scary and dangerous couldn't possibly make me feel worse than sitting on that Jersey barrier, successful people with briefcases and job titles streaming by. I shimmied my butt onto the middle of his handlebars, and in a breath we were moving.

I wobbled and clung to the tops of his drop bars for dear life. He pedaled standing to see over my shoulder. I swore a lot. People yelled at us, cheerful stuff from Badger's fans, plus a few threats to call the cops. I found my balance as we entered the Common, squeaked and yelped as he dodged people and dogs, shrieked as we popped out on Beacon Street and banged a sharp right at Charles, heading for the bridge.

Over the river, past the spot where we first spoke, where he'd shot me. Through Kendall and over to Mass Ave. My purse flapped in the wind, bumping his arm.

In Central Square we passed a teenage thug-wannabe who dropped a candy bar wrapper. Before it even fluttered to the ground, Badger shot him in the ass, white shittiness all over the embellished back pocket of his pristine oversized jeans. His cussing faded behind us.

I wondered who people thought I was. Badger's sidekick, his girlfriend? His figurehead? His kidnapping victim, perhaps, face surely white with terror from the ride, streaked with tears. I heard distant sirens, but either they weren't meant for us or we got away, and before long they, too, faded to nothing, along with the bustle of Harvard Square, then Porter, then Davis.

We rode for a long time, and somewhere past Alewife Station I lost track of where we might be. We rode until the streets turned suburban and the streetlights blinked on, and the houses grew farther apart. Until my bony butt felt bruised, my knuckles cold and stiff, my wrist wailing. We slowed and cruised through a vast park as the sun was officially dying for the day, and I had no clue where we were. Lexington? Farther? We glided along a paved walkway beside a river, a path winding through a stretch of woods.

Badger slowed us to a stop. I hopped from the handlebars onto rickety legs, extremities dead from the cold and the fearful clenching. He wheeled his bike down to the river's edge beside an old stone bridge straight out of a fairytale. I followed.

There was no troll underneath, just a cobblestone ledge with tufts of dry fall grass in the cracks. Just privacy and coolness and the echoing white noise of the river.

Badger laid his bike in the shadows then took a seat himself, his back against the wall. I sat beside him.

I was jacked on more adrenaline than I could ever remember feeling. My face was icy from the wind, tears streaking hot trails down my cheeks.

We were quiet for a long time, as my panic dried up and my breathing deepened. The urgency of my misery receded, swept away in the current, bound for the next town.

"Where are we?" My question was magnified by the stone and water and the growing darkness.

"Winchester, maybe. I'm not really sure."

"You come here a lot?"

"Not a lot. Just sometimes. Is it doing anything for you?"

It felt how I imagined one of those sensory-deprivation pods might. You can't escape your own thoughts, but you feel sort of okay about it. Your head feels manageable. "Yeah, I think it's helping. Thank you."

"You want me to hold you or something?" Badger asked.

"Um, I dunno. Maybe."

He spread his legs wide, inviting me to sit between them. I did, liking the feel of his chest behind my back, his arms as they wrapped around mine. I was pinned, but it felt nice. Badger was a straitjacket, filling me with a beautiful sense of containment and surrender. I leaned my head against his shoulder and breathed out, out, out. He smelled faintly of cigarettes, but mostly just of himself—his clothes and skin and hair, human and vital. I hadn't been close to a man this way in ages, and I'd forgotten how personal that was, breathing someone in.

My butt wasn't far from his crotch, my boobs within easy groping distance, but I didn't worry he was taking me there. I felt more like a wounded animal he'd picked up and deigned to soothe. Plus, frankly, I wouldn't have minded him trying to get sexual with me.

"You still want to relapse?" he asked, that growly voice just behind my ear.

"I don't *want* to want to, but yeah, I feel itchy for it. If I had anything at home, I'd probably use . . . But since I don't, and don't know where to get any, and I'm too sober and chickenshit to go out looking, I won't."

"That's something."

After a couple minutes, I melted against him. Not gooey, not romantic . . . just the softening of two bodies where heat sealed them together.

I cleared my sticky throat. "Does it seem weird to you, that you found me right when I needed somebody to?"

"I dunno. Maybe. But other times . . ." He trailed off.

"What?"

"That night you had your addicts' meeting, I found you by mistake then, too. When I see you, I get this weird tug inside me, this pressure. Almost like I need to take a piss—"

I laughed. "Oh, great."

"Just this funny feeling, like this hook in my guts is dragging me toward something. Only I don't know it's you until . . . there you are."

"I get that, too. Like a magnet."

"I don't know why, but I feel calm around you. And I don't feel that much."

"I have been called a downer before," I joked.

Badger gave me a squeeze.

"I find you kind of exciting," I told him. "Normally I hate that—feeling anything intense."

"Maybe we're twins. Except I got all the speedy genes, and you got the downer genes."

"I already have a twin. I'm pretty sure my mom would've told me if there'd been a third person in there."

I thought about my family, of having to tell them my awesome job was gone—pissed away with a positive result for who-knew-what. Shame stabbed me in the middle, with a chaser of injustice, because goddamn it, I *was* clean. Those two other interviews I could have had, dismissed with such cocky triumph . . . I still had the job offer, on paper. At least I could use that to get a couple weeks' extension on my rent. But I could be right back in this position a month from now. Easily. And I needed groceries, means to pay my bills . . .

I was crying again, and Badger shifted behind me as a ragged sob set my shoulders trembling.

"What's up? Why're you leaking this time?"

"I need money."

"Don't we all."

"I need seven-fifty for rent, twelve hundred for my medical bills, another thousand I owe my sister's fiancé." I groaned. "What the fuck have I done to my life?"

"Better to fuck up your own life than someone else's."

For a long time we said nothing, and the tears and the rushing water washed my panic away. The air felt cool on my ankles, but Badger's body was warm and reassuring. I listened to his breathing, feeling his exhalations against my neck. *I could die here*, I thought. In the nicest sense. I could've died here, and it would've been the best I'd felt in ages. Not high and euphoric like when I got offered that job, but a true, simple, sober easiness, even sitting amid the refuse of my reality. A contentedness in simply being.

Maybe by osmosis, I could absorb some of Badger's ballsiness. I didn't know if he liked movies, but if we ever went to a theater, he sure as hell wouldn't hesitate to stand and tell the annoying, gossipy girls behind us to shut the fuck up already. I couldn't. I couldn't even manage an over-the-shoulder glare, a *shhhh*. But I'd like to, someday.

I'd love to tell someone to shut the fuck up instead of just marinating in mute, seething resentment.

I heard him lick his lips. "Your hair smells good." It wasn't a flirtation, merely a remark.

"Thanks."

"Smells like . . . pink."

I smiled at that. "I think it's supposed to be strawberry-kiwi."

I wished . . . Oh crap, I wished for lots of things, none of them bright ideas. I wished he'd kiss my ear. His mouth was so close, he could. He just could. But in the end, what good would it do? It wouldn't bring back my job offer or pay my rent. It wouldn't fix anything. It'd be another distraction, giving me permission to throw my hands up and shout "Fuck it!" at my problems until the thrill wore off and I woke to find things even worse than I'd left them.

I sighed. "I feel like such a loser."

"Why?"

"Because of how badly I messed my life up. And it's not like I had the hardest life."

"That's what drugs do. It's nothing personal."

"Oh?"

"Drugs are like fire. If you're dry, or if maybe there's already gasoline on you, and you end up in the path . . ." I felt him shrug, the gesture squeezing me tighter. "You just go up. Sometimes you or somebody else manages to put you out, and you stay out of the path. But some people, because of their circumstances and their aptitude, they just burn. And if you burned once, you want to burn again—you're primed for it."

"Huh."

"Some people won't catch, no matter how close they stand. It's not fair, but that's how it is. You just burn, cupcake. Sorry."

"Thanks, I guess."

"You're not a loser. You just need to maybe get better at running when you smell the smoke."

"It still sucks." I gave a gross, wet sniffle, but Badger just held the cuff of his sleeve in front of my face. I laughed and took the invitation, dabbing my nose on it. "Thanks."

After a minute's silent tear-oozing, I asked, "Were you ever an addict?"

"Long time ago. Now I just dig conflict."

I nodded, bumping his cheek with my head. "Sorry."

I felt something against my hair—maybe a kiss, or maybe nothing at all. A wishful thought. "Don't worry about it," he murmured.

"What do you want to do with your life?"

"I'm already doing it."

"Well, what do you think people should do with their own lives? How do you know you're doing what you're supposed to?"

After a pause, he said, "I know 'cause it's what I'm good at. You do what you're good at, and what you enjoy. Do that for as long as you can, then find something else, or die."

"What I'm good at doesn't pay very well."

"How long'd you spend doing it?"

I thought about it, realizing I'd never really done much illustration outside of college, just the odd burst, and never with the intent to make a serious go at selling anything. "Not very long."

"Then what the fuck do you know about it?" There was no judgment in his question.

"You're probably right."

"Fucking right, I'm right."

"But anyhow, it's not a field known for being lucrative."

"Well, you'd be a retard to know what you love doing, and what you're good at, and not do it. That's how you wake up as a stockbroker or a realtor or an alcoholic house-wife."

Depressing as his wisdom was, it cheered me. Did I really want to write copy for other people's art exhibits, at the end of the day? Maybe. Maybe for a while, until the time came for someone to do the same for my work . . . But not really. I just wanted to *be* somebody, labeled by what I was contributing, not what I was recovering from.

After ten minutes, Badger broke our silence. "You live in JP, you said?"

"Yeah."

"Want a ride back there?"

I shifted from cheek to cheek, ass still sore from the first half of our commute. My butt said, *Let's find a commuter rail station*, but you know my mouth's answer. "Yeah, okay. Can we go slower, since it's dark out?"

"As long as the cops don't spot us, sure. Slow as you want."

We made it to our feet, and Badger wheeled his bike up the embankment, me at his heels. The world beyond the bridge was still and quiet. It couldn't have been later than eight, but it felt like three in the morning. It felt like something must have come and wiped everybody out, just him and me left, nobody I owed money to. Nobody to disappoint. Then there was a curt honk—someone locking their car, somewhere in the distance. The human race went on. I went on, for better or for worse.

Badger rode us back, slow and quiet, nothing like the trip out. It was still scary, because he had no lights and there were plenty of cars on the roads, but more anonymous. Plus, I knew where he was taking me. As we passed through Arlington, my butt and wrist piped up to say I should ask to just be left at the T, to make the rest of the journey the safe, comfortable, familiar way. But the rest of me vetoed the idea.

We rode through Cambridge on the back streets, took Memorial Drive across the river and slipped through the alleys and parking lots of the Fenway. I wondered if Badger would come up to my apartment if I invited him.

I wondered if I might make us a pot of tea, and maybe we'd wind up on my bed, since there's no couch, and maybe we'd kiss. We could roll around on my covers, and I could feel him above me. I could inspire something better than pity in him—affection or lust. Maybe we could feel that ultimate magnet-snap, the sharpest of tugs in our middles if we fucked. Or maybe that would wreck it all. Maybe sex would depolarize us, and that'd be the last I ever saw of him, the last I thought of him. No more pull, no more hook-in-the-guts.

We made it to JP without incident, not a single pause for vengeance or even a word spoken until I told him which streets to take. We glided into the laundromat's parking lot, and I nearly collapsed when my soles hit the ground, my calves numb with pooled blood.

"Thank you," I said. Badger straddled his crossbar, and I

touched his arm. "Thanks for taking me out there, and for bringing me home. And for caring, if that's what it was."

He shrugged. "Glad you didn't jump, this time."

"Me, too."

"And you're not gonna jump, when you go inside?"

I shook my head. "All I've got up there is Nyquil. And now I'm too tired to want even that."

"Good."

I chewed my lip, glancing up at the dark window of my bedroom. "Are you hungry? Do you want to come in for something to eat?"

He smiled, and it told me everything I needed to know. He knew what I meant, what I really wanted, but he didn't want the same thing. "Nah. My shift's not done yet."

I nodded, working hard to hold the tears inside. "Keep Boston safe."

"Fuck that."

"Keep Boston's assholes nervous, then."

"Will do."

I took a deep breath, then jumped as a motorcycle blasted to life at an intersection. "Maybe I'll see you around."

"Maybe. This town's got a lot of bridges."

I nodded, lips opening and closing, so ready to say something but not knowing what it might be. Finally, Badger spoke for me.

"Go inside, dummy."

I smiled like a dope and gave him a final wave as I headed to the side entrance and unlocked the door. I grabbed my mail and trudged up the steps, entered my kitchen and flipped on the light. I crossed to the bedroom and knelt on the mattress, twisting my blinds open. Badger was still standing there astride his bike. Our eyes locked. I yanked the cord and hoisted the blinds. For a minute we just stared at each other, faces blank, my heart tight and achy. Finally he looked to the road, looked back at me, put a foot to a pedal, and rode away.

9

The moment my eyes opened, I remembered everything—losing the job I'd become so infatuated with, the dreamlike journey that followed.

I also remembered what Badger had said, about people waking up in careers they weren't meant for.

Easy for him to say. Not everyone can get handed wads of cash just for cruising around on a bike assaulting assholes.

Still, I wanted him to be right. His philosophy seemed too simple for this complicated world, but we could all use a bit more simplicity.

I rolled out of bed, realizing I didn't feel as awful as I might have expected. I didn't want to use. I just wanted time to speed up, so I could reawaken three weeks from now, when the pain—in my wrist and pride alike—would be officially faded. When I'd know what might happen with my rent and my life, the rashlike uncertainty of the present cleared up.

I made a pot of coffee and went online, and you know what?

It was the fucking Nyquil.

Retard though it may be, the Internet solved my riddle. Cough syrup has ingredients that can cause false positives for methadone. Perfect, since I was born looking like a heroin addict. Very corroborating. But now I could fight for myself, for my chance. I could call HR on Monday and explain the mistake, say I had a cold, beg for a second test. It'd be out of my system in a couple days, tops.

But would I call? Did I really want that? To be someone who worked somewhere with fucking *HR* to answer to?

Kind of, yeah. I wanted to keep my apartment, and maybe be able to afford a better one someday. I wanted my parents to admire me and have faith in my trajectory. I wanted to pay my future brother-in-law back. I sure as fuck didn't want twenty weathered faces beaming a circle of pity at me on Thursday night at NA when they found out their little hope-mascot had failed her drug test.

So I'd call on Monday, because what was the worst that could happen? They'd say no, flat-out no, and I wouldn't be any worse off than I was now, just a bit more officially humiliated. I wouldn't get my hopes up, though. I'd apply for more jobs, maybe e-mail the places whose interviews I'd declined and see if the positions were still open.

Inspiration struck. I set my laptop aside and stood from the bed, marched to the bathroom and grabbed the Nyquil from the cabinet. Down the drain. No, down the toilet.

I emptied it, swished water in the bottle until the red syrup turned pink, turned clear. I flushed the toilet and gave the swirling, cherry-stinking water the finger, went to the kitchen, and chucked the bottle in the recycling bin. I took it out again, tossed it on the floor and stomped on it, then threw it away for good.

I'd had rebellious outbursts like this before, with the Vicodin. Twice I'd fed pills to my parents' garbage disposal, spat down the drain after them as I flipped the switch and listened to them grind, my body gripped by a great and unholy anger. It felt good in the moment, like slapping your pimp, I imagined. But goddamn, he hits back hard. *Hard.* Knocks you to the ground, and suddenly you're begging to be taken back, you sorry, you won't do no wrong never again, Big Daddy.

I took the train into the city and returned all the clothes I could from my spree, all but a sweater whose tag I'd recovered from the trash stained with soy sauce or tea. My pride couldn't handle the stammering it would've taken to explain that to a clerk. But the other splurges I recouped, including the business card holder. It was a bit like the eighth step—my least favorite of the dozen. Admitting the wrongs I'd done to my credit card balance and trying to make amends.

I grabbed job applications from a few stores downtown. I swore I'd go after any gig that would have me, just to make my rent. Every time I heard the whir or squeak of a bicycle, I jerked my head, seeking those familiar stripes but never finding them. I hadn't felt the pull, so I should have known as much.

While I was out, I noticed graffiti tags for the Badger,

but I knew he hadn't done them. He wouldn't advertise. But he had groupies, that's for sure. I was surely among the worst, seeing as how I'd been ready to spread for him, right before he called me a dummy and sent me to bed alone.

I wound up walking all the way back to Jamaica Plain in the tinny autumn sunshine, tote packed with applications I collected along the way.

At CVS, I bought a Halloween-sized bag of mini Milky Ways, then went home and poured myself into the job applications, insurance against the disappointment that might come when I called the museum on Monday. My left-handed writing was so awful, I ended up finding most of the forms online and filling them in that way, so the stores and restaurants wouldn't think I was a drunk or a kindergartener. I threw hooks in the pond, so many you couldn't see the water by the time I went to bed, and I did the same on Sunday morning.

For hours at a time, I forgot about Badger.

I forgot about him right up until I heard my bell at ten-thirty on Sunday night and felt that old lurch yanking me from my warm covers, until I thumped down the stairs and found him on my doorstep, blood all over his palms.

10

"Of course I didn't kill somebody. Jesus, what's wrong with you?" Badger wiped his hands on his jeans, looking annoyed.

"Then why's there blood all over you?"

"'Cause I just left half my palms all over Huntington Ave."

I hugged myself against the breeze and looked to his bike, propped outside my building, front wheel twisted like a taco shell. "How did you get here?"

"I walked."

"Were you hit by a car?"

"You gonna invite me in or what?"

"Sorry." I flattened myself against the mailboxes, and Badger carried his bicycle up the steps so I could lock the door behind us.

The Badger was in my kitchen, and it was like suddenly having a real badger in there, like, *Oh shit, this can't be good.*

He leaned his bike against my cheap wire shelves and crouched to assess its injuries.

"So were you hit by a car?"

He shook his head, squinting at something. "Wheel found the train tracks. Road found my hands."

"Ouch. Do you need medical attention?" Jeez, what did he do when he *did* need medical attention? Maybe he had a secret wallet full of actual ID someplace and just went to the doctor like any normal person. Or maybe he lined up with the homeless people at the free mobile clinic. Maybe it didn't come up. I mean, Batman never went to the hospital, right?

Badger stood. "I just need to get cleaned up."

"Sure. You can use my bathroom. Oh, take your shoes off, please. The bedroom's carpeted." I felt dumb, asking that—asking this remarkably rude man to respect my housekeeping rules.

But he toed off his sneakers and left them by the door. I got the weirdest thrill as he unzipped his infamous hoodie and draped it over a chair, as he unbuckled the leather holster strapped across his chest. It felt absurdly profound. Like he was de-Badgering himself before my privileged eyes, shedding his skin, exposing Isaac or Ronaldo or whoever the fuck he really was. He hung the holster and its pistol on my doorknob, suddenly just a guy in black socks and a faded navy T-shirt in my little kitchen.

Well, not *just* a guy.

I led him through the bedroom, past the droning TV to my bathroom.

"There's rubbing alcohol in the cabinet, and I've got Band-Aids around here someplace . . ." I rooted in the plastic drawers beside the toilet, finding only a couple too-small bandages rattling around in their box. "Hmm."

"It's fine. You got a dark towel?"

"Yeah." I went back to my bedroom and grabbed him a purple one from the closet. The Badger's blood was going to be on my towel. Odd.

I loitered at the threshold as he soaped and rinsed his palms, dried blood washing away to reveal injuries slightly less disgusting than I'd feared. But he'd need to wrap them. Once he'd splashed his scrapes with alcohol, I devised the world's most ghetto Ace bandaging, duct-taping folded paper towels to Badger's palms. It looked profoundly pathetic. Nearly as pathetic as the *zing* I felt, touching him. Helping him, as homely as my nursing efforts were. Again, a flash of that dopey romanticism, as if my tending to his wounds would endear me to him, imprint me on his scabby black heart the way he was stamped on my soft, bruised one.

"Thanks."

"Not my best work, but you're welcome."

He shrugged. "Whatever keeps me from bleeding to death on the walk home."

"Would you like to stay for a while and see how they hold up? Replace them before you head back? Oh God, that'll suck—holding your handlebars all that way. Ouch."

He flexed his hands, testing my handiwork. "Pain doesn't bother me."

"Would you like some tea?" I rolled my eyes at myself for asking. Of course the Badger didn't want any *tea*.

"Yeah, sure."

"Oh. Okay. Uh, make yourself at home." I pointed to the only place in my room to sit—the bed. Then I ran away to hide in the kitchen, away from all the scary, exciting possibilities that sprouted from the concept of Badger-on-my-bed. The scariest of all being that maybe he really did only want tea and a chance to stop bleeding. I glanced at my ensemble, my pajama pants and a threadbare T-shirt from a Police concert my dad had gone to when I was too young to have any clue what "put on the red light" meant. No bra. Not that I needed a bra—a couple eye patches would've sufficed.

When I came back in with two steaming mugs, I wanted to freeze the world. Or at the very least take a photo. The Badger was on my bed with his back against the wall and his legs stretched across my mattress, watching my TV with a blank expression on his fascinating face. Gingerly, I crossed the mattress on my knees and set the steaming cups on the windowsill. I sat cross-legged, leaving a few inches between our thighs.

I noticed something I hadn't at the diner, the last time I'd seen him sans hoodie. In the dim light of my reading lamp, I could make out a tidy ribbon of raised lines along the outside of his left arm, like he was the most OCD, perfectionist self-mutilator in the world. Clean and uniform, an inch wide, perfectly parallel, as though he'd held a comb to his skin and drawn a razor between the teeth. It made me feel close to him—this proof that he, like me, sometimes did stupid shit to himself in the privacy of some lonely room, somewhere. It reminded me of my art, the obsessive strokes of my X-Acto blade cleaving paper, and the calm it brought me to get lost in the slices, the ritual, the repetition.

I kept my eyes on the lines as I spoke. "Your scars are really . . ."

He looked to the spot. "Meticulous?"

"Yes, exactly."

He shrugged, turning back to the TV. "If you're going to do something, may as well do a good job."

"You do that a lot?"

"No. Not since I started shooting people."

"Huh." I studied it a while longer, since my scrutiny didn't seem to bother him. And because, well, he had really nice arms. He was quite nice all over, from what his T-shirt was telling me. I guess spending eight or twelve or twenty hours a day on a bike will do that to a man, burn away all the softness. Oh fuck, what must his *calves* look like?

Touch me, I thought. *Push me down and jam your knees between mine. I won't stop you.*

But I wouldn't ask him, either.

I blew on my hot tea, barely aware of what was on TV —some stupid crime drama. I had a real, live fugitive on my bed. Top that, television. I had a criminal on my bed, and I'd fixed his wounds, kind of. I'd made him tea. I was useful and nurturing and complicit. And sure, horny. But that shouldn't detract from the goodness of my charity, just because I wanted to bone my patient. I'm sure Florence Nightingale felt that now and then, when she'd been busy blotting the forehead of some hot, vulnerable soldier. Badger's war wasn't quite the Crimean, but he was still a one-man militia. My casualty. My patient.

I sipped my tea and fantasized about pressing my hot lips to his cooler ones.

It was hard to imagine Badger simply making out with me. Kissing seemed far too subtle a gesture for a man of extremes, one whose baseline was speed and retaliation. Then I remembered him holding me under the bridge and thought, *Like I have the first fucking clue what he's capable of.*

We watched TV without speaking for a long time. The show ended and a new one started, and our companionable silence steadily turned pointed and awkward. I wondered why I wanted him so much, when he'd never even admitted he liked me, never told me I was pretty, never laughed at anything I'd said. It was like the Vicodin, I guessed. I wanted it for how it made me feel, regardless of how little it cared for me. *Do whatever you want—just give me the bliss.*

"How are your hands?" I asked. "Do you need fresh paper towels?"

He looked right at my face, expression tired. "I didn't need to come here."

My throat tightened. "No?"

He shook his head. "I didn't need to get patched up that bad, not bad enough to walk all the way down here in the opposite direction of where I live. I coulda gone home and my grandma would've done the job. Without the duct tape."

"Oh."

"I just wanted an excuse," he said, gaze dropping to the strip of bedspread between us. "To come over."

My heart sped, a drunk hummingbird banging around inside my ribs. "You didn't need an excuse." My voice was soft and condemning. I wanted to kiss him. I wanted to be kissed *by* him, and I didn't care anymore if he knew it, or if he'd mock me. "Why'd you need to come over?"

"To feel that calm again, I guess."

"Do you feel it now?"

"Yeah." After a long pause he asked, "What d'you think it is we're supposed to be doing?"

"What do you mean?"

"I mean whatever this suction is that keeps bringing us together—what's it want us to do?"

Marry me, tonight. Let me bear your stripey, violent babies. "I'm not sure. I just know I feel better after I run into you. Like the world isn't as bad as it usually is."

"You think we're supposed to fuck or something?"

I swallowed. "I dunno." *Let's try and find out.*

He stared at my mouth. "I don't think we're supposed to fuck."

"No?"

He shook his head. "But I'll kiss you, if you feel like kissing me."

I wanted to know why on earth we shouldn't screw, but the offer of kissing placated me. "I'd like that."

He scooted closer, and I did the same, turning toward him. I shut my eyes as he leaned in, and I huffed a tiny breath as his palm touched my cheek. Warmth from his fingers. Dry, scratchy weirdness from my sad first aid. He pressed his cool lips to my tea-heated ones, and it felt just how I'd guessed. My body clicked with recognition as our two halves snapped together at the mouth.

Badger could whip a pistol from his jacket and vandalize a human quick as he might blink, but he didn't kiss that way. Not reckless at all. Not impulsive. Downright cautious, in fact, each sweep and press and nip of his lips intentional and exploratory. It felt like when the doctor had gingerly pressed my arm, searching for fractures. Apparently Badger didn't find anything of concern, though, and when his mouth asked for more, I gave it. I'd expected his kiss to be as filthy and coarse and selfish as his justice, but I'd take this, too. Take it gladly.

His tongue stroked mine in firm sweeps, and I felt something I never had while kissing anyone . . . like he was telling me things. Like I was learning as much as I might from talking to him. My palm was hot from holding the mug, his face cool against my skin. His stubble was soft, his jaw hard. He tasted like black coffee behind the Earl Grey. No wonder he made me jittery.

I rubbed his hard arm with the fingers of my cast-clad hand, feeling the texture his cutting had left, uniform and velvety as corduroy. Then I slid my hand under his T-shirt sleeve, and my fingertips found the pit on his left shoulder. I freed my mouth to ask, "Why do you have a smallpox scar? Were you born abroad?"

"It's a cigarette burn."

I took my hand away, and we caught our breath.

"You had a shitty childhood, didn't you?" I asked.

"Prize-winningly shitty."

His damage was all so much more tangible than mine, so tactile. Like the darkest scenes from his life were stamped in Braille across his skin. I wanted to touch him for hours, for days, as long as it took to teach myself to translate his scars.

I tugged at his shoulder, and we lay together on our

sides. We kissed forever, until I knew his mouth the way I knew vanilla ice cream or a Granny Smith apple, its precise smell and texture and flavor. He had the most wonderful lips, as soft as his eyes and body were hard. He made me a good kisser in return, because my caution was gone, swallowed utterly by need. I didn't have to try with him, I only had to *be*.

The kissing tapered off, then stopped completely, and an aspect of fooling around I'd never experienced before took over, a touching that had nothing to do with sex. I stared at his eyes as my fingers recorded his brows, his ears, his nose, his chin, the thump of his heart beneath my palm. He stroked my ribs and waist, hand glancing my breast but feeling nothing like a grope. We were animals, trying to figure each other out, wrap our heads around the weird connection we shared, perhaps in preparation for our bodies taking things to the next logical level.

I tugged at the hem of his shirt, and he peeled it up his body and tossed it aside. The Badger's shirt, on my floor. Huh.

I let him see how I studied him, not caring if I looked nervous or perverted or laughably eager.

He was pale, veins like blue lightning streaking from his inner elbow to his wrist. I traced them, ran my palm up his arm, over his throat, across his chest and stomach. He wasn't skinny, exactly, not emaciated, but so lean I could witness anatomy at work in each breath that tensed his abdomen, each small but unmissable flex as he moved. He looked like what I'd thought he was at first—a tweaker. I wanted to watch this body as we fucked, see it drawn tight as a spring, see him clench and shudder and finally relax, a heap of muscle and sinew cast beside me on my mattress, spent. Calm.

Though calm was what he was already. Not horny, not as far as I could tell. His breaths were steady and slow, formerly ominous eyes soft and reverent as I explored him. With a final stroke of his striated cutting scars, I took us back to kissing.

He let me lead, but it felt good. He wasn't lazy or indifferent, merely accessible. I was making him as calm as he was making me crazy.

The more we kissed, the hotter I got, my blood pumping hard with some chemical I'd never felt before, like sexual adrenaline. I held his face tighter, wishing his touch would turn aggressive, too. But it didn't. Was he deferring? Was he letting me keep the lead and set the pace, afraid of upsetting my delicate emotional balance? God, I hoped not. If I'd wanted that, I would've recruited a different man for the job.

When I edged closer, he took my hint, sliding a hard thigh between mine. The last time I'd been with a guy had been awful—I barely remembered it. In fact, I remembered the pills he gave me with more clarity than any feature on his face, or his name, certainly his dick. I'd been too out of it to be traumatized. I'd fucked for the Vicodin, not the pleasure or the connection. I'd been a whore that night, an open cunt hungry only for the chemical bliss, oblivious to the mean body plowing my limp one.

But that hadn't been me. That violation, if I chose to admit it hurt, was no more personal than someone keying my car. I'd felt nothing outside the warm mist in my skull.

But with Badger, it all got turned inside out. My body wanted his for the chaos it made me feel.

We were a mess, with only the one functional hand between us. Perfect, though, because we weren't meant to be tidy. We were always meant to fumble into this, to get where we were going in spite of the injuries. To thrash upstream against the awkwardness, not to be swept up in ease, or logic, or anything resembling a good idea.

I slid my palm down his front, over his chest and stomach, the buckle of his belt, and cupped his crotch. He wasn't hard yet, but I kneaded him as we kissed, eager to feel the most feral part of this feral man come growling to life from what I was doing.

But after what must have been two minutes' spirited fondling, nothing. My excitement withered to worry as he moved my hand away, settling it on his hip.

I freed my mouth to ask, "What am I doing wrong?"

"Not enough," he whispered, lips against mine.

"What?"

"You're doing everything right, and that's the problem."

I pulled back, frowning my confusion.

Badger sighed. "This is all nice. Which is great if you're into 'nice,' and I'm not."

"Oh." I must have been the portrait of abject disappointment, because he laughed. He took my good hand and rubbed my knuckles.

"Listen. You're as cute as a kitten taking a shit on a moonbeam, but a crush doesn't get me hard. Kissing doesn't get me hard. *Pleasure* doesn't get me hard."

"What does?"

"Conflict. *Pain.* Takes a lot for me to feel anything. Except rage—I'm real good at rage. But everything else . . ." He shrugged against the pillow, looking pensive a moment before saying, "You're a nice girl."

I sighed. "Too nice."

"Too nice to let me talk you into fisting me with no lube."

I blinked. "Correct. Very perceptive."

He made a face like, *Well, there you have it.*

"Is that really what it takes, for you?" I hoped I didn't sound as desperate as I felt, though it was so incredibly stupid. Why on earth did I have a crush on this man? We were compatible in exactly zero ways outside of our basic plumbing.

"Takes pain," he said. "Pain I need inflicted on me, not necessarily the other way around, but I'm guessing you don't have that in you. And I don't want to be the guy who traumatized you, pressuring you to go there. So don't worry about it—it's just a cock."

If only it felt so simple to me. "So who do you need, then? Some freaky cutter girl?"

"It's so adorable that you don't think you're freaky."

I rolled my eyes.

"I just need somebody who's not afraid of what I need. But I get that what I need is sort of terrifying, so I know it's not going to come along very often. I'm not that bothered about sex, really."

"Why'd you even kiss me, then?"

"I like kissing you. It's nice . . . like lying in the sun. Like eating a cookie. It's not going to get me hard, but that doesn't mean it's not, you know. Pleasant."

I frowned.

"What?"

"I wanted it to do more, I guess." Fucking unfair that what was getting me hotter than I'd been in ages was doing absolutely nothing for him. I wasn't even sure which of us was being cheated. I only knew I didn't want to be the Badger's goddamn cookie or sunbeam. I wanted to make him *feel* something. Something way better than "nice." I stared at his mouth, anger burning in my cheeks.

He ran his finger up and down between my eyebrows, tracing the line that forms when I scowl. "Why in the hell do you like me so much?" he asked.

"I don't know. You make me feel stuff. Stuff I'm not used to feeling."

"Like your pain pills?"

I shook my head. "Nothing like that. I took those to *not* feel stuff. I don't know what it is with you, because usually I'm afraid of feeling intense things. Like, you see someone being harassed on the subway or something, and you get that spike in your blood, and you—*you* do what you do. Me, I just want to disappear. I hate how my body feels when there's conflict happening. It hurts. Physically. But whatever you make me feel, it doesn't feel like that." I'd never had any interest in uppers, but I bet coke felt like that. Exhilarating. Addictive.

"Well, I like kissing you. Makes me feel content."

I sighed again. "Content. Great."

"You got any idea how exotic *content* feels to me? I feel content for, like, two seconds a day, for maybe two breaths right before I fall asleep. Content's like euphoria for me, like fucking El Dorado. I don't care if it doesn't give me a hard-on."

"I do."

He slumped, nostrils flaring. "Give it up. The kind of sex you probably want doesn't do shit for me. And the kind I want will land you in therapy. Best I can tell, kissing's better than not kissing, but if it's not what you want anymore, then let's just quit that, too. And if you're all hot and bothered and horny, tell me how to get you off—I'm happy to oblige. Just don't expect me to feel the same way."

I rolled onto my back with a huff.

Badger leaned in close. "Lemme make you come."

"No. It'll feel weird, knowing you're not getting anything from it. Not anything except, like, the satisfaction of solving a jigsaw puzzle or something."

"Why do we both have to feel the same thing at the same time?"

"Because that's how it's supposed to work."

"For a girl who says she's afraid of conflict, you sure fucking argue a lot."

After a moment, I smiled at that. "Only with you."

"Lemme kiss you. If you get all worked up I'll shove my hand down the front of your pants and get you off, okay? Is that really so fucking awful?"

"Fine. Fine to the kissing, at least."

He was right—content was a rare sensation for me, too. There was nothing wrong with plain old nice, I supposed. I turned onto my side, angst fading as he put his fingertips to my jaw. It did feel good, knowing I was giving him something he wasn't used to. Felt more personal than lust, in its quiet way.

He offered more of those slow, deep, surprising kisses, and I enjoyed the heat when it returned. Badger was in his sunbeam. I was right back in my pressure cooker, hot and agitated. Let us both enjoy whatever we felt.

I imagined the things he couldn't give me—hungry sounds rumbling from his throat, the impatient, pushy thrust of his erection against my thigh. I imagined his body, and how he might look naked. How he might look aroused. His tongue teased mine, sensual . . . though goddamn, I wanted more than that. I wanted the sex equivalent of his U-lock spiderwebbing a windshield. I wanted to be wrecked, shattered. I wanted *Badger*, the impulsive, angry asshole, not this pleasurable but tame creature—

Oh, fuck.

Maybe I wanted what he did. Maybe.

For another minute we kissed, my curiosity and fear fighting over which was going to drive. I envisioned his body again, his face leering down at mine. I imagined him horny and needy and rough, and I bit him.

I bit him hard. Not enough to break the skin of his lip, but *hard*, and I held on. His breath hissed as his body tensed. My teeth released his flesh, and we opened our eyes at the same time. He did nothing aside from breathe and stare, waiting until I brought my mouth back to his. Another minute's kissing, and I found the balls to bite again. I was rewarded with a groan and the tightening of his hand against my side.

"Harder," he murmured, a tiny, pleading gasp of a word.

As scared as I was to hurt someone, I was equally eager to please him. The instincts clashed, and I felt a bone-deep bolt of that Badger-feeling, that hot, scary chemical rush that the mere idea of him gave me. I'd felt it before, dozens of times now, but that was a prescribed dosage, a pill. This time it was a whole fucking bottle, cooked in a spoon and shot into my vein, don't even bother with the cotton ball or a fresh needle.

My lips quivered as I obeyed. I bit him hard, hard, *hard,* and I tasted blood.

He gasped a soft "Yeah."

The flavor matched his noises, elementally animal, so natural but so wrong. When I let his lip go, he took my bad hand, the one tucked between his ribs and the mattress. He led it to his neck and coaxed my fingers into claws, pressing my nails hard to his skin. I ignored the twinge it triggered. When he began to kiss me, it was all different. Not just the wrongness of the blood I tasted, but Badger himself. He kissed me roughly, so much nicer than *content.* The harder I dug my nails into his throat, the deeper his tongue swept, the louder his moans, the more agitated his energy.

He grabbed my other hand and dragged it down between our bodies. He cupped it over his cock, and fucking hell, he was hard. I pressed my thumbnail into his jugular, and he forced my other hand, mashing my palm against his erection in sloppy strokes.

"You on the rag?" he muttered. On the *rag.*

"No."

He didn't make a noise of relief, causing me to wonder if maybe, just maybe, he was disappointed by my answer. Wouldn't really shock me, the creepy-ass carnivore. Christ almighty, who in the hell was in my bed? And why did I want him here so badly?

His kisses were so exactly what I needed from him.

Deep and filthy, like his voice and words, threatening like his eyes and his build and his ethics. I clawed his skin, tasted his blood. I fantasized about how hard he must fuck when he was rabid like this. Fantasized that I might discover myself capable of being whatever sick bitch he needed.

He pushed my hand aside and fumbled with his belt and fly. My breath caught as he wrapped my fingers around his bare cock. Hard. Big. So hot it might blister the skin off my good hand. I began to stroke him, a slow drag of my palm up and down the underside of his shaft.

"Tight."

I clasped him, making the pulls as mean as I dared.

"Rough," he whispered. "Real rough, like you fucking hate it."

I did my best, and when my strokes weren't harsh enough, he clamped his duct-tapey hand over mine and showed me how tight he wanted it. Scary-tight. Tighter than I'd have dared, worried about doing permanent damage. His eyes were squeezed shut, head pushed deep into the pillow and teeth bared, pink from his own blood. What was he imagining? Maybe nothing. Maybe he was just *feeling*. I was afraid of him, as much as I was fascinated. I was miles outside my comfort zone, but wasn't that exactly what drew me to this man? Still, my intuition wasn't happy. He was riding the edge of what was too much for me, and he wasn't exactly famous for his self-restraint.

"I'm scared," I murmured.

His hand on mine slowed. "Of what?"

"All this. But I don't know if I actually want to stop. I don't know what I want."

He cleared his throat, hand going still. "Well, I wanna err on the side of not traumatizing you."

"Yeah, me too."

He let my hand go. I kept touching him, praying my lighter, sensual caresses might surprise him, keep him hard. Convert him to my safer, meeker breed of sex. But he was wilting half a minute after I took the pain away. I let him go, disappointed. Pissed. Angry at myself, angry at him.

He replaced his dick and zipped his jeans. "Lemme get you off," he said.

"I can't now. I'm too frustrated."

He sighed, then lowered his face to my throat. His steaming breaths slowed my racing, angry heart, and before long I simply felt tired. We lay that way for ages, maybe an hour, though neither of us fell asleep.

Finally breaking the silence, I spoke against his temple. "You're welcome to crash here." Translation: *You're welcome to stay the night with me, in my bed, since I haven't got a couch.*

"Can't. If I'm not around when my grandmother wakes up she'll assume I'm dead."

"Oh. You can't call her?"

"I don't know her number."

I narrowed my eyes. It could have meant anything. It could have been true, that Badger really didn't know the phone number of the place he lived, the only family he seemed to have. Could have been a tactless man's tactful way of saying, *No, I don't want to crash here.*

"Okay," I said. "How will you get home?"

"Walk."

"Jeez. That's a long way. You could take an early train.

They start running at, like, five." Translation: *Stay. Stay in my bed. Please?*

"Not taking that bike on a train. That's like me walking around with a broken leg, begging to get arrested. Might as well lock myself in a holding cell."

"Oh, right."

"Thanks anyway."

Don't go. Don't leave me here, not knowing how to feel.

He climbed over me to leave the bed. I sat up, hugging my knees and watching. I'd been touching and kissing him for maybe two hours, yet he looked all at once like a stranger again, a raw, fascinating body I had no recollection of either calming or arousing. As he tugged his shirt over his head, I looked to his swollen lower lip and the pink scratches on his neck, stumped that I could have given him those marks. I would've guessed I'd feel some sick, possessive pride about it, but I didn't. I felt as impersonal as a razor blade or cigarette, just another handy implement, willing to scar him. The only thing special about me was the way I calmed him. An arbitrary talent, like we were extraordinary together through no fault of intention or affection, as profound yet impersonal as a bone marrow match. But I wouldn't cry until he left.

"How are your hands?"

He flexed them. "They're good."

"Need fresh paper towels?"

He shook his head, and my usefulness reached its official conclusion.

"Okay." I got up and followed him into the kitchen, watched him re-Badger himself. Leaning in the doorway, I faked weary apathy while he took the bent wheel off his bicycle and stood on either half, flattening it somewhat, yanking out the popped spokes. He reattached it and pushed the bike back and forward, seeming to deem it good enough to roll home. He got his shoes back on, and my heart began to pound, idiot that it was, wondering if we might kiss each other good-night. He stepped to me, arms crossed over his chest, seeming very tall. And very distant.

"Thanks again."

"No problem."

"I guess I'll see you around," he said.

Maybe. Maybe, if our pull wasn't ruined. But right then, he felt far away. We'd swapped too many ions or atoms or however the fuck magnets worked, bodies rendered neutral, our two halves falling dead away.

"Try to not show up bleeding next time," I teased.

He smiled, that rare gesture warming me around the edges. "No guarantees."

I walked to the door and pulled it wide, preceded him down to the foyer to hold the downstairs doors open as he carried his bike through. He dug a plastic lighter and a bent cigarette from his pocket and managed to light the thing without setting my paper towels on fire.

"Walk safe," I said.

He blew smoke off toward the street. "You take care." Those standard Boston-guy parting words, spoken in that perfectly homely accent. It reminded me that he'd come from here. That he'd come from *somewhere*. That he'd walked through this dark city to find me, to *seek* me, and that I meant something to him, even if neither of us had the faintest clue what that something might be.

He glanced over his shoulder. "Now quit fucking drawing me across town with your weird-ass magnet voodoo."

"Out of my control."

He looked away, walking out of the parking lot's glow into the dark en route to the next wash of streetlight. En route to Somerville. Six miles? Eight? Perhaps two hours' walk with nothing but the scuff of his shoes and the tick of his chain for companionship . . .

I locked the door behind me and rubbed the cold from my bare arms in the kitchen, checking the microwave clock. Two hours from now, it'd be three a.m. I was exhausted already, eager for sleep and its blessed oblivion. And yet I'd stay up with Badger—in consciousness if not proximity—until he was safe in whatever secret place he called home.

11

The museum's HR department gave me the runaround.

I called them on Monday morning at ten sharp to explain my false positive. The man I spoke to promised to relay my request for a second drug test to the person in charge of such matters, and they'd get back to me. I knew in my gut they'd get back to me as soon as they'd filled the position, the perfect polite excuse to dismiss "that shoplifter girl" or however they surely referred to me in shorthand around the break room.

I rang the two places who'd offered me interviews, the ones I'd cockily turned down. One job was taken, but the other was still open. I was passed off by an assistant to the owner-slash-founder-slash-manager, Lani, and we chatted for maybe twenty minutes.

She was one of the more annoying people I'd talked to in a while. It sounds like a snap judgment, but there was something unmistakably disingenuous about the way she spoke . . . like she pitied you, but also distrusted you, while simultaneously kissing your ass. I had no clue what to make of her, but if she was interested in employing me, I'd give her a shot.

The company was small—just a handful of employees in the States—and it designed and marketed super-upscale cosmetics and moisturizers and natural age-defying treatments, that kind of crap. It was all manufactured in Israel, somewhere exceedingly kosher. The job this annoying Lani woman was looking to fill was for a copywriter who'd be penning ad materials, press releases, product descriptions, and so forth. Making Dead Sea salt scrub sound as though it wasn't tainted with the skin flakes and mucus and discreetly passed urine of a thousand buoyant daily tourists.

My hope came and went in waves, like nausea, visceral and unnerving. But the call went well, and the job came with a perfectly passable salary in the low thirties and health benefits. I accepted a fresh offer to interview the following afternoon.

No one else called me back all day—not a single one of the stores or restaurants or cafés I'd so indiscriminately sprayed with applications. They could probably smell my desperation. And it wasn't like a convicted shoplifter had any business pursuing retail.

I dented my karma, ringing my landlord with my heart in my throat, prepared to pass off my now flatlined museum job offer as proof I was a safe gamble, just in need of an extension on my October rent. But he said he didn't need the proof, just pay October and November together, on time. He assured me I was his best tenant. Having encountered most of them, I didn't doubt it. Though it's not a great credit to him that the lying, unemployed, recovering addict with the criminal record is the shining star in his stable of renters.

On Tuesday I was torn between hope and dread as I prepared for my interview with the cosmetics place. Attempting to look the part, I put on makeup and wore my smartest outfit—creased black slacks and the one sweater I hadn't been able to return, with a chunky necklace and pointy flats—a look I hoped might trick someone into thinking I was sassy and urbane.

The company's headquarters was in Brookline, not far from the movie theater. I got there a half hour early and wandered around, admiring the shops and restaurants. I let myself fantasize that I'd get the job, and maybe I'd even like it. Maybe it'd be my springboard to an exciting, overpaid career in advertising. Maybe I'd surprise myself and wake up in a nice apartment like the ones around here, with bay windows and hardwood floors. Maybe I'd learn how to order a latte with confidence and walk in heels. Who knew? Being who I was hadn't gotten me all that far in life. Maybe experimenting with being someone else was a better alternative. Or at least faking it for eight hours a day. That's what everybody else did, wasn't it?

The office was on the second floor of an unassuming yellow-brick building, one that screamed "insurance broker." Flanking the entryway were display windows showcasing soaps and oils and bath bombs, the company name and website etched elegantly on the glass. Nice-looking stuff, and they had a slick website and a single boutique on Newbury Street. If I managed to land the gig, it'd look good on my résumé, if nothing else.

The receptionist buzzed me up and said Lani would be a couple minutes.

Magazines fanned across the coffee table. One was in Hebrew, with a dewy-faced woman of nondescript ethnicity seeming to inhale rapturously, a perfect tuft of wheatgrass cupped in front of her nose. I unearthed a copy of *Allure* from beneath it and boned up on celebrity skin-care tips.

"Adrian?"

I snapped to attention as Lani appeared from a hallway. "Yes."

"Come on in." She beckoned me to follow her.

I was in awe of her ass, packed into a snug houndstooth tweed skirt suit but unmistakably firm for a woman of middle age. I could have followed her with my eyes closed, no problem, her sharp, powdery-smelling perfume impossible to lose track of.

She held out an arm, inviting me to precede her into a three-dimensional spread from a West Elm catalog.

I sat as she closed the door before rounding her tasteful, modern desk with its tasteful, slim vase full of tasteful, leafy bamboo stalks.

"Thank you for coming in," Lani said.

"Thank you for offering the interview again."

She dismissed the thought with a wave of her French-manicured hand, the gesture looking like a charade for *graciousness*.

"So tell me—have you tried our products before?"

"I haven't. Not yet." Their site's cheapest offering, a four-ounce jar of body lotion, literally cost as much as my weekly grocery budget.

"Oh, you *must*. We really do make the best stuff there is. A hundred percent natural. You know who swears by our night cream? Meryl Streep." Lani shot me a look, like God Himself was in her fan club.

"That's very exciting."

"On your way out, be sure to ask Dana for a sample set. Sixty-dollar value." She sat up straight. "But anyway, let's talk marketing. You worked for an ad agency, correct?"

I nodded. "I wrote copy for all sorts of products."

"Great." She leaned over to roll open a drawer and plunked a glass bottle with a nifty green atomizer pump before me on the desk. "Tell me how you'd word a tagline for this."

Shit, pop quiz. I picked it up and read the plain white label, clearly just a mock-up for a new product—cucumber and red chili body mist. Fuck *me*. "Let's see. Who's your targeted demographic?"

Lani perked right up, like I'd uttered a magic word. "Our current customer base is largely well-off women, forty-five to sixty-five, but I'm curious to hear how you might describe this product to attract a buyer closer to your own age."

"Oh, okay. Maybe something like . . . 'Soothe your mind and awaken your senses'? Like a mix of the two fragrances. Play up the contrast between the cool and the spicy? That might make a fun product name, actually, just 'cool' and then a plus sign, you know, instead of 'and,' and 'spicy.' Cool and spicy." I was on a roll! A big-ass bullshit roll.

"A plus sign . . ." She grabbed a notepad and wrote down the name I'd suggested, with a plus sign in the middle.

"Or like . . ." I put out my hand, and she gave me the pad and a pen. I sketched a couple ideas, my still-mending wrist giving a shriek of alarm as my fingers worked. I wrote the words lowercase in my best impression of Futura, thin and modern. I wrote them with the plus sign, then with a big, light ampersand behind them, then "cool" right-side-up and "spicy" underneath it, upside-down. I handed back the pad. "Something creative and clean," I said, suddenly tempted by my own snake oil.

"Clean" must have been another secret word of Lani's, because her eyes lit up. "I like these. I like these a lot. I could see a whole line in this vein."

I nodded, realizing I was actually enthused, too. "A series of scents, all based on contradictions, like spicy and cool, light and dark, mellow and vibrant . . . You could call the line something like, I don't know . . . 'Contrapposto,' or 'Versus,' or 'Polarity.'" Ah, polarity, a concept I'd become so preoccupied with myself of late. No wonder I was riffing like a Madison Avenue wunderkind. "Something for a spontaneous, modern woman who wants to feel like she can be everything, even opposites." Oh God, I could slap myself. But whomever I was channeling, keep her coming.

For a long moment, Lani stared at me with her mouth open, blinking. I got nervous, until it became clear she was doing a pantomime of delighted shock. "I *love* the way you think," she announced.

"Oh, good."

"Do you have any graphic design skills?"

"Yes, a little. I know Photoshop and Illustrator."

"If I hired you, would you be able to mock these sorts of ideas up in one of those programs? With the right fonts and colors? Liaise with the package design firm we use in New York?"

"Oh, sure. No problem." But would I be able to demand the salary bump I'd deserve for such a modification of the original job description? No way in hell.

"Here," she said, rooting through her drawer. "Let's try another one."

∘ ∘ ∘

All told, I gave Lani nearly two hours' free product concept brainstorming. If I didn't get a second interview, I'd be mightily pissed off. Yet I was confident I'd knocked her Talbots stockings clean off. And I felt so smart and validated by the time I left with my paper shopping bag full of free stuff, I actually *wanted* the job, despite knowing I'd soon enough find it soul-sucking, find Lani suffocating, and find myself still mocking things up at eight o'clock at night.

But a job's a job. And I wanted this one, just another contradiction to add to the list. Plus, she hadn't actually made me fill out a formal job application, which meant I'd dodged having to come clean about my record.

I got home around five thirty, barely surviving an

interminable and inexplicable train stoppage between Ruggles and Roxbury Crossing, one that left the grumpy horde on the verge of mutiny and possible cannibalism, taking the shine off my professional triumph.

I limped the four blocks to the laundromat, trying to appease a growing blister. Among the junk awaiting me in my mailbox was a rather dreary postcard from a publication company I'd interviewed at three weeks earlier, officially informing me I was a loser.

To hell with them. Lani liked me. I dropped the card in the recycling bin under the boxes.

As I went to slide my key into the door to the stairs, I noticed something alarming. The knob was gone. The wood was splintered.

Blood rushed north to throb in my temples, making it hard to know what I was supposed to be doing.

Someone had broken into my building. Someone could still *be* in my building, possibly wielding an implement bad-ass enough to smash the knob off my door. Heart thumping in my throat, I went inside the laundromat and meekly approached the sweet old Korean lady.

"Yes, hello, miss. How you today?"

"Um, fine. Do you know anything about the apartments being broken into?"

"Something broken in you apartment?"

"No, someone seems to have *broken into* my apartment. Did you hear anything?"

"I no know nothing about apartments."

"No, of course not. Sorry."

Flustered, I went to the bank of slippery plastic chairs by the front window and dialed 9-1-1. The cops arrived pretty damn quick, and while they went upstairs to investigate, I prayed my apartment was untouched. That if anyone had been burgled, it was that noisy asshole from the third floor. Not me. I didn't own anything worth—

Oh, fuck.

Not my laptop. *Anything* but my laptop.

It had the past four years of my life on it—my digital portfolio, electronic reams of writing projects, photos from before the Vicodin days, ones I'd always meant to have printed. It had dozens of different résumé versions, contact lists, long letters of apology I'd written to family members but not yet mustered the balls to deliver.

The cops came back down.

"Which unit are you?"

I gripped the handle of my paper bag, praying. "2B. The second floor, to the right."

"Yeah, you've been broken into."

"Oh, fuck."

He nodded sagely. "Gonna need you to go up and see what's missing. Then we'll have you fill out a report."

My apartment was trashed. All the cupboards flung open, pots and pans on the linoleum, fridge and freezer doors swung wide. A jar had been thrown or dropped, and it reeked of vinegar, pickle spears and glass everywhere. My laptop was gone—no shock—and my DVD player. My alarm clock, too, which pissed me off intensely. What in the fuck did burglars care about waking up on time?

The bathroom had been ripped apart, but the only thing they'd taken was my ibuprofen. I'd kept them in an old Altoids tin, so they must have looked like something exciting. That was when I started crying, because

I remembered every family event I'd gone to during the more functional days of my active addiction, every relative's medicine cabinet I'd pawed through, the lame shit I'd taken—sleeping pills, daytime flu caplets, my aunt's boyfriend's leftover Oxycontin from his knee surgery. Maybe I'd been robbed by myself. By the person I might have stayed if I hadn't gotten busted trying to shoplift a six-hundred-dollar handbag.

I filled out reports and talked to a couple different cops, and while they were taking photos, something terrible occurred to me.

Could Badger have done this?

It wasn't his MO. He was a hero, sort of. Not a villain, not to me, anyway. But he knew where I lived. He'd *just* been here. Could a U-lock take out a doorknob?

"Did any of the other units get robbed?" I asked.

The officer nodded. "Both on this floor."

The relief this statement triggered morphed in an instant, dropping into my gut as guilt. But it wasn't him. Or at least, the theft hadn't been personal, exclusive to me.

At some point during all the chaos, my landlord was contacted, and he arranged for a locksmith to secure the apartments, though the inside foyer door was pretty solidly fucked, and he'd have to come back the next day to fix that. I was handed a new set of keys and given some direct police lines to call if anything happened.

It all took ages, but it passed in what seemed like a few rapid breaths. When the cops left, I felt abandoned. Ditched at the scene of a crime, left to fend for myself. And let's be honest—self-sufficiency wasn't one of my strengths.

No less than thirty times, I picked up my phone, so close to calling my parents or Amanda so I'd have someone to cry to. But every time I had their numbers cued up, my finger hovering over the CALL button, I couldn't do it. They wouldn't believe me. They'd think I was making it up as a ploy to ask for more money. Or worse—they'd believe there was a break-in but worry I was the perpetrator. Or some unsavory friend of mine, like I'd brought this on myself.

I fretted for ages as I reassembled my bathroom and bedroom. The kitchen was the worst of all the rooms, and I couldn't imagine for the life of me what they'd been looking for amid my shelves and cabinets. What did people in my shady neighborhood hide in their freezers? In their broiler drawers?

As I stooped to pick up a frying pan, my heart broke open. I held my face as the tears escaped, and I felt like, *yes,* this was my restitution. I'd made so many people feel this violated and blindsided and disrespected, of course I'd had this coming to me. I sat among the Tupperware lids and utensils and cans of soup and glass shards, and I sobbed until my body felt parched and brittle, my eyelids packed with cotton. I shivered and hugged my knees, wishing I had someone to hug the rest of me.

I could call Amanda. With my safety freshly trampled and the foyer door busted, I wouldn't sleep. She'd drive the forty minutes from Woburn and bring me home with her, let me whimper and honk my snotty nose into her silky, lotiony name-brand tissues. I could sleep in her little guest room and feel safe, if misplaced. But in the morning I'd have to talk to Derek, her fiancé. I'd have to tell him what had happened and worry I sounded like I was lying. I'd have to worry that he didn't believe me, because frankly, he probably wouldn't. When had I ever given him reason to? I'd have to rush back here anyway, to prove I wasn't after their charity, so why bother running away even for the night?

At long last, I dragged my butt off the floor, put on my coat, and headed back downtown.

There was a Tuesday night NA meeting I'd attended once or twice in a community center in Brookline. The Sox were in the playoffs and had a home game that evening, so rather than put myself through the torture of braving the Green Line past Kenmore, I took the bus to Brigham Circle and walked the rest.

It was a late meeting, and I only recognized one woman in the whole group. I looked incredibly guilty, with my puffy red eyes and my shaky hands, but I explained what had happened, and the sympathy felt good. A couple attendees hugged me during the break, reminding me that for better or worse, these were my people. And lonely as it felt, they offered a kind of anonymous, unconditional goodwill that my family couldn't be expected to. The unconditional love of my fellow fuckups.

It was late when I got out, pushing eleven.

Not late enough for what I needed to do.

I wound up wandering for another couple hours, then buying a coffee at a 7-Eleven and drinking it on a bench near the Coolidge Corner stop. I watched laughing college kids mill past and jumped at the sporadic honking of cars declaring the fresh triumph of Red Sox Nation. No one asked me for change, which was just as well. I found it impossible to ever tell anyone no, thinking a dollar was a small price to pay to avoid angering a stranger. But these days a dollar really did mean something to me. Right then, a dollar was the warm cup in my hands, the cost of a scrap of comfort.

I know part of the reason I was sitting on that bench was because I wanted a hit. A little taste. I wanted that pull, and I wanted a sign that when I needed him, he'd show up, called to me by some psychic Badger signal that lit up in our connected brains. But it didn't come.

The baseball fans were heading outbound, so I took the train back toward the city, mercifully quiet. I got off at Park Street, thinking I'd take the secret shortcut to the Forest Hills platform, stand still until the doors arrived to swallow me, and be taken home . . .

But I banged a left. Up the stairs to the street, past the church where my Thursday meetings happened. I crossed to the Common—something I'd never normally do. Well-lit though it was, people get rowdy that time of night. People talk too loudly, make too many sudden movements, shout things I worry might be aimed at me.

Fuck it.

Unmolested, I made a beeline for Charles Street. At long last, Badger-gravity had me in its pull. It led me across the street and onto the Longfellow Bridge. My heart was thumping, yet I felt serene. I wasn't fighting it, just going where the pull told me. I stopped at the same stretch of railing where I'd first met him, but tonight I faced the road, not the water. It would be a long wait. If he didn't show, the trains wouldn't be running, and I didn't have enough for a cab. Not even close. I'd be fucked, stuck waiting for five a.m., for the T to wake up, or stuck walking all the way home, an hour and a half's journey on my blistered feet through not-the-nicest neighborhoods. But it couldn't feel worse than twiddling my thumbs back in my ravaged little ex-sanctuary. Some anonymous asshole had shot a hole through my safe place's head and skull-fucked the security right out of it.

I hugged myself against the cold, shifting from foot to foot as one or the other grew achy. When noisy groups or large men approached, I pretended to get a phone call. I squinted into the distance, as though a car were about to pull over and pick me up. As though I were someone with somewhere to be, with someone who cared enough to take me there.

One o'clock arrived. Two and two thirty. My joints hurt from the cold, and my eyes hurt from the crying and the caffeine and the bright streetlights punching through the darkness. They hurt from staring toward the oncoming lane, scanning for Badger. I monitored my body for any sign of the pull, but there was nothing now, just the sourness of my stomach, pickled in coffee and fear.

I spaced out. The world felt trippy, like someone had applied a Photoshop filter and made the edges blurry and distressed.

In the distance, a shape grew.

I could see his legs, rhythmic up-and-down, his white face half-swallowed by his hood. I felt the blessed pull, that wrenching suction like you get in an elevator, gravity yanking me toward him. I crossed to the edge of the sidewalk, still hugging myself. Badger slowed. He braked, straddling his crossbar, staring at me. He looked as tired as I felt, and just as unsurprised that we'd found each other again.

"Take me somewhere," I said. "Anywhere."

12

The ride was a fever dream. A stream of streetlights and cars and storefronts, until the familiar faded somewhere past Davis Square.

"Shut your eyes." The first words Badger had spoken to me since we'd parted after fooling around that past Sunday.

I did as he asked, and he cupped a cold palm over my eyes lest I peek. We sped this way and that down streets whose names I clearly wasn't meant to see. I felt us mount a hill, then we came to a stop that nearly pitched me from the handlebars. I hopped to the ground before a handsome house at the end of a cul-de-sac, an old three-story stone number with a mansard roof and tall windows, chimney and ivy and a wrought iron fence, all that stately jazz.

Badger put a finger to his lips, and I nodded.

I followed as he opened a gate and wheeled his bike down the skinny side yard, waited as he deposited it in a toolshed and padlocked the door. He led me to a fire-escape-style set of stairs, and we climbed one, two, three flights to the top, where he unlocked the back door.

He flipped on a dim light, and I peered around, surprised.

Nicely decorated, if old-fashioned—lampshades with fringe on them, heavy-framed paintings, grandfather clock. The only evidence I saw of Badger was the bed in the corner of the room, heaped with covers and screaming "single male" in its chaos. But the rest of the room . . . Hell, I guessed he really did have a grandma after all. How about that?

Then again, he could be squatting. For all I knew, the old lady was downstairs, three years mummified, and Badger was about to pull a Norman Bates on me, maybe prop a curly white wig on his head and offer me some cyanide tea.

He waved a hand toward his bed. "Get comfortable. Just try to not break anything. Apparently all this ugly shit is valuable."

"Your grandma's downstairs? Should we be quiet?"

"She's on the first floor, so no, you're fine."

I draped my coat over an easy chair and sat on the edge of his mattress, pushing off my shoes.

"So," he said, unzipping his hoodie by the door. My heart raced, addict that it was. "Looks like you wanted me bad enough to come looking. What's up?"

"My apartment got burgled."

He dropped his jacket from his shoulders and unbuck-led his holster. "Sorry, cupcake. That sucks. What'd they take?"

"Mainly my laptop. It wasn't new or nice or anything,

but it had my portfolio on it, all my résumé files and music and photos . . ." I stopped. Dry sobs rose, and I held them inside, terrified they'd escape from my throat in a shriek and rip me in two. "And my alarm clock," I added lamely. "Though who the fuck knows why."

"Don't waste your time trying to decipher the logic."

I nodded. "Yeah. Who knows what I stole when I was fucked-up."

He crouched to unlace his sneakers, and I ran my hand over his green cotton bedspread, listened to the soft pulse of the grandfather clock. So this was where he slept every night. His den. How odd . . . and comforting. I longed to see his shower, verify he owned things as dull and personal as shampoo and deodorant. That he really was human, and that he really must have a heart behind all the scar tissue, one I might have some snowball's chance at touching.

He could kiss me for hours tonight. I wouldn't ask for anything more. Just to feel another human's warm body, feel welcome somewhere. Invited someplace.

He crossed the creaky hardwood and took a seat on the floor at my feet, bracketing my ankles between his. "You smell like pickles."

"I know. Sorry. They ransacked my cupboards."

"So. You're all freaked out?"

"Yeah. Someone sort of fixed the locks, but only sort of. Not properly until tomorrow morning. And I can't get the idea out of my head that whoever did it might come back." Okay, so maybe that was a fib. But it was a great excuse for coming after him.

"You know who it was?"

"No clue. I'm assuming it's just random. I *hope* it's just random. The only people who might hate me . . ." I laughed weakly. "Well, in those cases, I'm the one most likely to be burgling somebody. It, um . . . It wasn't you, right? Sorry to even ask."

He shrugged. "If I'm not the most suspicious person you know, you've got some real fucked-up acquaintances."

I smiled at that, relieved I hadn't insulted him.

"But nah, wasn't me. Only thing you have that I want is this weird-ass *whatever* we got between us. And you keep giving me that for free."

I nodded. "I didn't really think it was you."

"So what exactly do you need from me?"

"A place to sleep?"

"Alone?"

I pursed my lips. "No, not really."

"Good, 'cause I'm exhausted, and I don't feel like crashing on a couch. You need the can?"

"Yeah, that'd be good."

He stood, and I followed him down a short hall and past a set of steps to a cramped little bathroom with a shower stall almost comically close to the sink. Once alone, I splashed my face above the soap-scummy sink and used the toilet, snooped in his nearly empty medicine cabinet. Razor blades and rubbing alcohol. *Oh, Badger.*

When I got back to the main room, he was lying sideways across the bed, staring at the ceiling.

I sat on the end of the mattress. "Bathroom's all yours."

"You need something to sleep in?" he asked, sitting up. "You look awful dolled-up."

"Oh, yeah. I had a job interview this afternoon."

"I'll find you a shirt." He went to a mahogany dresser and tossed me a soft old tee before disappearing in the direction of the bathroom.

I changed and assembled his covers before slipping beneath them. I'd kept my panties on, but I shifted my bare legs around under the comforter—under Badger's comforter—and listened to the water run and the old pipes thump. I felt a lovely mix of things, sexy and safe and excited, a bit protected, a bit privileged to be in the Badger Cave. Er, Badger Attic. I wished I'd never have to leave, since there wasn't really much to go back to now. Familiar clothes and books, but little else. The familiar hadn't been feeling all that great lately, anyhow.

Badger returned and switched off the light, though I could still see him pretty well from the street- or moonlight coming through the tall, wavery dormer windows.

"It must be really pretty when it's snowing," I said as he lay on top of the covers beside me.

"I guess."

I tried to imagine him sitting before a Christmas tree with his mysterious grandmother. Or perhaps a menorah, if he really was an Isaac.

"How'd your interview go?" he asked, gaze on the window.

"Pretty well. But I'll hate the job, if I take it. Which I will, if they offer, since it pays okay and has benefits. But it's so not me. Though thanks for asking."

He turned, and I smelled mint when he spoke. "You feel like kissing?"

"Sure."

He wrestled with his side of the covers, crawling underneath. We came together with less caution than before, his clothed leg sliding between my naked ones as I welcomed his tongue, deep. His palms were unbandaged, and his scratchy cuts rasped my cheek, creepy but insanely intimate. My lovely feelings morphed, their edges sharpening until comfort turned to hunger, safety to curiosity. I slipped my good hand beneath his shirt and dragged my nails down his skin, the scrape like a match head sparking against the box, his leg twitching between my thighs.

"I freaked you out last time," he muttered.

"I'll tell you when it's too much."

"When you're ready to give me blue balls, you mean."

I smiled at him. "Thought you liked pain."

My heart leapt at his smirk—I'd made him smile, on purpose this time.

As we fooled around, I savaged his throat with my nails. His breaths grew harsh and deep, and I ran my good hand down his side, over his hip, finding him hard again.

"Is it enough, my nails?"

"For now."

"Would it be enough if we wanted to . . . you know? If you have condoms."

"Probably not. The nails, I mean. Condoms, yeah, no problem."

"What would you need to stay hard?"

"You think you could hit me?"

"Hit you how?"

He pushed the covers down and reached between us, shifting his hips, drawing his belt from his jeans. He folded the leather in half and handed it to me.

"Whoa. I don't know. Like, your back?"

"Back, ass, legs, whatever."

"Hard?"

"Hard as you can handle," he said.

"I can try."

"Do you *want* to try?"

I gave it a few seconds' serious, careful thought. "Yeah, I do."

He nodded. Then he left the bed, heading for the other side of the room to a small bureau. He fished what I thought was a crumpled wad of bills from his jeans pocket and shoved them in a drawer, then opened another, and another. It seemed to take him forever to figure out where he'd last stashed his condoms, which made me deeply, dangerously happy. Whatever was about to happen was rare for him, too.

He came back, tossing some wrapped packets on the table beside the bed. He peeled away his shirt. His lean body looked ethereal in the low, bluish light. He opened his fly and pushed his jeans to the ground, then sat at the edge of the bed, facing away to brush the grit from his soles. I could see the lash marks on his back, faint, shiny streaks in the ambient light. I sat up to trace one.

"Are these from sex or from . . . earlier? When you were younger?"

"Both, probably. Plenty from myself, too."

I let my hand drop, feeling sad.

He joined me back inside the covers, his energy quieting my anxiety. At my coaxing, he got on top, his knees between mine, and lowered to his elbows to kiss me. I raked my nails across his scalp and breathed him in, his sweat from a long day's vigilantism. He changed as my touch grew harsher, and then his hips shifted, erection brushing my thigh. He groaned into my mouth.

"This doesn't happen for you often, does it?" I asked.

"Hardly ever. You?"

"It's been a long time. I haven't felt very good about myself since I got sober. Haven't really been in the mood to date. Haven't really felt qualified to be that way with anybody yet."

"What are you into?"

"I want to feel whatever that thing is we share," I said. "That chaotic feeling you give me, the sex version of that."

"Keep hurting me, and I'll do my best."

I had a vision of toiling in an old-timey locomotive, tossing shovelfuls of coal into a blackened furnace at breakneck speed, racing to keep Badger stoked and hard. Sex with him was going to prove an exhausting, stressful pursuit, but I also suspected that it might be exactly what I needed. Sex I couldn't help but be present for and active in, the opposite of a limp, passive body, just along for the ride.

I ditched the shirt he'd lent me. He leaned back, bucking the covers from us, and we got our underwear kicked away. He lowered, soft cock warm against my mound.

"Get me hard."

I clawed at his ribs with both hands, my nervous energy turning to pure sexual curiosity as he began to thrust against me. I felt him grow stiffer with each stroke, like my punishing hands were wired directly to his cock. That scrape, scrape, scrape of the match against the strike strip, spark, spark, spark. It sparked in me, too, my pussy turning impatient and wet and goddamn angry. The horn-iest I'd felt in ages. He leaned over to grab a condom. I kept clawing as he got it open, scared to lose him. I held my breath as he rolled the rubber down his erection, that acrid latex smell just exactly perfect, ugly and intrusive.

"Belt," he muttered, and nodded to where it lay on a pillow.

I took it, folded it in half with the buckle in my clumsy left fist. "Which . . . end?"

"Business end, if you can handle it."

"Maybe. But maybe not to start."

"Fine."

I took a few deep breaths, each one doing nothing to calm me, just hoisting the diving board higher and higher.

"Do it," he whispered.

My hand shook and tensed three times or more before I actually managed to hit him. It was a lame strike, as was the second. "Sorry, I'm right-handed—"

"Here." He grabbed the leather from me and leaned back, whipping it over his shoulder to land on his back with an authoritative crack that seized my fists and jaw. He lashed himself a half-dozen times, moans growing deeper with each strike, cock growing bigger. He seemed almost to be getting drunk on the act, his lids heavy, mouth slack. He handed back the belt and angled his cock, pushing inside. It was no perfect magnet-click, more a pleasurable intrusion, but after a few testing, impatient thrusts, my body welcomed him. I had a couple seconds to revel, to enjoy how big he felt, to process the gloating, petty shock that holy hell, I was fucking the Badger.

"Hit me."

I gave him a whap, my best so far. The next was even harder, landing with a smart snap.

"Fuck. Good. Keep doing that."

I found a rhythm, and though it was satisfying as a challenge, it wasn't getting me anywhere near as aroused as him. Plus, it was rough, knowing he was basically having sex with the pain. I was giving it to him, sure, and he'd invited me to do this with him, *to* him. Still, a compliment about my body wouldn't go astray. Something to let me know it mattered that it was *me* here with him. That I was wanted, not merely willing.

It was hot, though, in its wrong-ass, fucked-up way. But there was no way I'd be coming from this—too distracting, too new, just plain too hard to get off with my right hand still in traction, *if* I found the balls to touch myself in front of him. Fine, though. Getting Badger off was a fascinating enough goal, worthy of my concentration.

I'd never come while having sex. And yes, I was one of those horrible women who faked it, too meek to make demands or risk hurting a guy's ego, letting him know it wasn't working for me. But I wouldn't fake it with Badger. He seemed far too lost in his own masochistic pleasure to care, anyhow. This was no more an equitable romance than two animals rutting. It had nothing to do with fairness or feminism or anything pretty.

I whipped him hard, earning a gasp and a quickening of his graceless, hammering hips. I toyed with a couple ideas—slapping him, spitting at him, pulling him down by the neck and biting his lip open again.

But not yet.

If this really was a rare thing for him, surely we'd have

more chances. Surely he'd want me, truly *want me*, after all this.

Oh, bad thought, Adrian. Terribly, terribly bad. Feigning a proclivity for sadism had to top even orgasm-fakery on the continuum of Stupid Shit to Do to Keep a Man.

But I kept lashing, and Badger kept fucking. He was a frantic, groaning, perfect sex-wreck, nothing like the calm and sleepy man I'd kissed on my bed. He was a beast, charging toward release, and though I felt incidental—though I knew my only distinction was being here with my legs spread and willing to do as he asked—the privilege of simply doing this with Badger was intoxicating.

Suck on it, Lois Lane.

Through the grunts and gasps, he croaked, "I'm close."

I replied in the most appropriate-seeming way, whipping his lower back with a gorgeous strike.

"Fuck. Get on top of me." Not a request. He was rolling over, grabbing at my thighs and waist, pulling me down as his cock jabbed my thigh, demanding entrance. I got him inside, and he shoved the belt back into my hand.

"Fuck me hard."

Thank goodness he hadn't said *Fuck me well*, because it was a mess. I'm bad at cowgirl at the best of times, plus my rhythm was screwy from my trying to belt his chest, afraid of hitting his face. He pumped up into me, our paces so hopelessly frenetic it felt like fighting.

He bucked and moaned and swore. "I'm gonna come. So fucking hard."

"Good—"

"Choke me."

I froze. "What?"

I dropped the belt as he grabbed my wrist. He cupped my palm to his throat, other hand grasping my arm, hauling me down so my weight was on his windpipe.

"Stop!"

He was stronger than me. Strong enough to clamp my hand there for innumerable, terrifying seconds, until his eyes rolled back, whites prevailing as his body bucked. His grip went slack enough for me to yank my hand away. It had taken seconds, seconds that felt like an hour, a horrifying, helpless hour. I sucked shallow, ugly breaths, on the brink of hyperventilation.

The moment his irises dropped and met mine and I saw his consciousness return, I slapped him.

"Thanks."

Fuck, *fucking* masochists. You can't even hit them.

"That got me close. Really close."

"Don't *ever* do that again."

Badger grinned, still dozy from his brush with death. "You're so fucking cute when you're pissed off."

"Asshole." I stood and found my panties and slacks, yanking both up my legs. I nearly put my bra on inside-out, pissed at my hands for being so flustered. Pissed at my heart for having been dumb enough to bring me here. Pissed at whatever part of me had enjoyed it at first, tricking me for a short time into thinking we were in any way compatible. That he wasn't the shithead I already knew him to be.

He sat at the edge of the bed. "Adrian."

I glared at him. "Do you have *any* idea how dangerous that is?"

"You have any idea how little I care about what's dangerous?"

"I'm not worried about you, jackass. You die, making me do that to you, and I have to carry that shit around with me the rest of my life. Some of that life possibly spent in jail for manslaughter."

"Jesus, chill out."

"Fuck you." I crouched, searching for my socks in our jumble of clothes. He grabbed my good wrist, but I yanked it away.

"I'm sorry," he said.

"Never thought you'd do apologies." I found a sock.

"Me, neither. But hey, stop for a second."

I did, but only to glare at him.

"I thought you seemed okay with the rough stuff. I didn't know that was too far. It felt right, in the moment."

"It's really dangerous." Rusty nails shot from my eyes into his. "Like, people accidentally die from that. People accidentally *kill* other people doing that."

I saw annoyance pass over his face, saw him tempted to tell me to chill out again, calm down, quit being a scoldy, spastic bitch. But he swallowed those things and sighed, repeating, "I'm sorry."

I shook my head, resuming my search, but limply.

"Come on. Come up here." This time I let him grab my arm. I flopped back against the rumpled bedclothes, because where else did I have to go? He pulled me into a hug, kissing my forehead. "I won't ever do that again," he murmured.

"You've got no impulse control."

A hot breath hissed against my temple. "No, I don't."

"So you can't make that promise."

"I dunno. Maybe not."

"Do you know what it's called when you force somebody to do something they don't want to, sex-wise?"

His expression shifted, eyes softening, brows drawing together.

"I hope if you'd seen some guy doing that to some girl, you'd have whacked him in the teeth with your stupid bike lock. He'd deserve it."

He didn't reply. I sighed and stared up at the ceiling. Oh God, why was I there? Why was I falling for a man who, for all I knew, was one jerk-off session away from being discovered dead with a belt around his neck?

Maybe because he made me capable of feeling as pissed off as I did now, and actually being able to express it. I felt gross. I felt pierced, oozing thick, rancid anger, but it was far better than festering, keeping it inside as usual.

"Did you hate every single thing we did?" he asked quietly.

I pondered it. "No. I was okay with trying all that stuff, right up until the choking. I liked some of it, turning you on like that. Though the choreography's pretty demanding. I don't think I'd ever be able to come if I'm also trying to hit you with a belt."

"I'll get you off now, if you want."

I shot him a look. *If you think I can come after that, you're a fucking moron.*

"Well, if we wind up like this again," he said, "we'll figure it out. We'll only do stuff with me tied down, maybe, so I can't go berserk on you."

"Don't get your hopes up. Trust me."

Badger pulled back and pursed his lips, worry narrowing his eyes.

"What?"

"Did I just traumatize you?"

I took a massive, stilted breath and blew it out before I replied. "I dunno."

My answer seemed to unnerve him more. He rose to sit beside me. I did the same, hugging the covers to my chest. He was the naked one, not me, but it felt like the opposite.

"When I was a kid," he said slowly, "I had some pretty fucked-up shit done to me."

I nodded.

"I hope I didn't just fuck you up, the way I got fucked up."

"Not that badly, I don't think. Not permanently. I'm just angry. You made me do something that scared the crap out of me, and I couldn't stop you. It's an awful, helpless feeling."

"I know it is."

I stared at his shoulder, rubbed the knob of bone there with my thumb. "But whatever you had done to you, this probably wasn't that bad. You just scared me. I'll probably be mad for a day or a week, but not forever. You didn't scar me, you just sort of . . . bruised me. It'll fade."

"I hope so."

I rubbed his thigh. "It will. It's already starting to. Just don't ever do it again."

"You know how you said you didn't think I did apologies?"

I nodded.

"I didn't think you did fuck-yous."

True, I didn't do fuck-yous, not out loud. I didn't defend

myself normally, not like I just had. I didn't slap people. Sober Adrian didn't. Then again, I couldn't truthfully say I felt sober when I was with Badger. And even though he'd just forced me to choke him into unconsciousness, who did I want to be with more than this fucked-up man?

"I would've gotten you off," he said quietly. "I care about getting you off."

"Not much of a ladies-first policy," I murmured. It was a hypocritical jab, since I didn't make it a point to stand up for my own sexual rights. Yet I wasn't faking my annoyance. This might've been the only man in the world I felt comfortable making demands of. Strange, when his personality seemed to be everything confrontational and callous that frightened me so much.

"Does it even matter that it's me here, smacking you with a belt?" I asked. "Or would anybody have done?"

"Of course it matters. It matters way more that you're even here in the first place. I'm not exactly in a position to take people home."

"But did you want to have sex with me? Was it about *me* at all, or was it about the pain?" I sounded needy and girly and pathetic, but fuck it. I could sound any damn way I pleased.

"Course I wanted to have sex with you."

"As long as I was smacking you around."

He backed away enough to look me in the face. "I can't help that. I can't change what gets me hard any more than I can erase my ugly scars or any of the worse shit that's been done inside my head."

His stare was too intense. I cast my gaze lower, studying his stubbly chin.

"I would if I could, trust me," he went on. "I'd cut my hand off if it meant I could wake up tomorrow and be able to get off just jerking to porn or messing around with a girl, just screwing like anybody else. But I can't. And if you're not into what I need, that's fine. I never expected you to come this far with me. But don't make this into some big pile of evidence that I don't like you. I *do* like you. And I don't like anybody, usually."

"Oh."

"So sorry if I can't get a fucking hard-on staring at your tits. The fact that I want to even be in a bed with you, doing nothing . . . It's plenty for me."

"That's nice, I suppose."

A quiet, heavy breath answered me. "I know you're probably getting a body complex or some shit like that, thinking you're not hot enough. Like if you looked different, you'd fix the wiring in my dick."

"I'm trying not to think that way."

"Just don't bother. And I won't give myself some complex about how you'd like me more if I could get hard whenever you wanted me to. Because you're way too nice, and I bet you'd hate for me to think that."

I nodded.

"We suck, as a couple," he said. "If that's what we are."

My heart froze, shocked he'd suggest it. Shocked and euphoric. Even *I* hadn't been ready to think such a thing, and I had it pretty damn bad for him.

"But I'm okay with us sucking," he went on. "I got no problem with you thinking, 'Shit, this guy's such a bad fucking idea.' I got no designs on being normal. I'm never gonna be normal."

"Me, either." I could blend and assimilate, unlike Badger, but I wasn't someone whose default would ever be happiness and optimism. He had a point. Why fight it? Why keep buying into that myth that the right person will show up and fix all your problems, fill your cracks and chips and make you whole? I was with the wrong person, right now—societally wrong, and wrong for me in every logical way. But he sure was teaching me a fuck of a lot about myself.

"So you don't think there's some woman out there, some right woman who'd transcend all your fucked-up-ness and, like, I dunno . . ." I trailed off, knowing how dumb it sounded, and how wrong it was.

"Far as I can tell," he said, "that woman's you."

I blinked. "Oh."

Badger rolled onto his back, gesturing before him, framing some invisible scene. "I ride around all day, and human beings are like objects to me. Objects that are either totally neutral, or else they piss me off. Except you." He shot me a glance. "You do that thing, whatever this weirdness is that keeps bringing us together. I dunno how to describe it, except, like, I'm riding around and everyone and everything is either in black and white or bright, angry red, everyone blurry and 2-D, there to be ignored or attacked. Except you. I'm riding around in fuzzy, flat monochrome, then there's you, all in color, in focus, in like, five dimensions. I'm sorry that doesn't mean you magically fix my dick. But how's that? That make you feel special at all?"

I was blushing, face hot with pleasure and surprise. He was so, so forgiven for making me choke him. I was way too easy with this man, but it couldn't be helped. "Yeah, that makes me feel special."

"Good. It should."

It was the closest I'd felt to him since we'd sat beneath the bridge. It was the closest I'd felt to anyone in a long, long time. I pulled at his side, and he turned, letting me kiss him. A selfish part of me did wish he was simpler, that he was like any guy, able to come from a boring old blow job, much as I hated giving those. But I might not feel all these things if he was simple. Doing what he needed was a price I was willing to pay, at least for a while. Long enough to find out if I could afford a romance with this man, or if I just wasn't strong enough to offer him what he needed in bed. Or heck—maybe slapping a guy around was just the therapy this meek, mousy girl required.

I freed my mouth. "I'd like to keep messing around with you. But you can't make me do stuff, like before. You can ask for anything you want, and I'll think about doing it, just . . ."

"I know."

"Can you promise that? Or does your brain just take whatever it wants, at a certain point?"

"Nobody can ever promise anything to anybody." He went quiet, thinking. "I haven't fucked in a long time. And I know you think maybe it's the pain that gets me hot, but it's not. It's a million times better, what we did, than anything I can do by myself. It's been forever since I've had a chance to be that way, so long I forgot how fucking good it feels. And I crossed a line with you. So I *hope* I can promise not to do anything like that again. But I'm not honestly in my right mind when I'm fucking.

If I was in my right mind, I wouldn't be hard. And I'd be lying if I said I was in control."

"That's scary."

"It's the truth. It's all I got."

"I know." I kissed his chin, a wholly thoughtless gesture.

He kissed my forehead. "And I meant what I said—if we want to keep fucking around, you can tie me down. I like that shit. Tie me down and give me a slap now and then and go nuts on my dick. I like feeling used."

"I'm not used to being aggressive that way . . . But I'll give it a shot. Sometime." Not tonight, though. I wasn't up to the challenge.

"Deal."

He kissed me, and I kissed him back. We kissed for ages, and soon enough the light changed with the arriving dawn. My body knew it was six in the morning, but my brain was as juiced as ever.

"I gotta go downstairs and have breakfast with my grandma, so she knows I'm not dead," Badger said. "You wanna come? If not, I'll be back up in a half hour."

"Jeez . . . No, I'm not ready to meet your grandma, I don't think. No offense."

A smirk. "What the fuck made you think you stand any chance of offending me?" He got up, and I flinched at the marks I'd left all over his back.

He forewent underwear, tugging yesterday's jeans up his legs and pulling on a T-shirt. "Feel free to use the shower. She won't care that you're up here."

"Will she be offended that I'm not coming down for breakfast?"

"Nah. We're real autonomous."

"Okay."

"I'll bring you up some coffee."

"Thanks. What time do you . . . you know. Start your patrol or whatever?"

"What time do you have to leave?" he asked.

"Um, not any time, today. I don't have anything planned."

"Then let's take the fucking day off."

"Oh, okay."

He disappeared into the hall, and I listened to him thumping down two flights.

Wow. The Badger wanted to play hooky and hang out with me. All day. I didn't know what that might entail, but I was game. I braved the morning chill and headed for the shower to prepare for whatever the day was going to throw at me.

13

After I'd showered and dressed, Badger came back upstairs with a mug of black coffee and a giant, too-perfect-to-be-homemade blueberry muffin. We chatted while I ate, and then we promptly fell asleep, waking again around eleven thirty.

His apartment was different in the daylight, all the eeriness gone. It looked like what it was, a generous attic full of outdated but tasteful furnishings, worn but not neglected. It was surely incidental, as much to his taste as a belfry is to a bat's. But it was his home, and here I was inside it.

I sat up, finger-combing the slept-on mess of my formerly damp hair. I felt him watching me and found his sinister eyes sleepy, face placid.

"How's your hand?" he asked, tapping my cast.

"Feels all right. I have an appointment tomorrow, for

an X-ray, to see if I can switch to a brace. What did you want to do today?"

"Don't care. What about you?"

"I don't care, either," I said. "Do you have any hobbies aside from cycling and shooting litterers? And masochism?"

"Not especially."

"Maybe we could just go for a walk. Incognito. Do you like Mount Auburn Cemetery? I like to get over there at least once while the leaves are still changing."

"Yeah, we can do that, spooky girl."

I smirked. "Are you going to make me close my eyes again when we leave here?"

Badger shrugged. "Nah. Be kinda rude to fuck you, then act like you don't get to know where I live."

Ah, chivalry.

We got dressed for the cold and clomped down the outside steps, waded through the soggy fallen leaves in the backyard. It smelled like fall, to the nth degree. I thought I ought to tell Lani to get her fragrance technicians working on the formula.

We headed down Badger's quiet residential street, and the day felt surreal in its normalness. It felt like I was simply out with a friend, wandering around in the overcast coolness. We got on the subway at Davis. It was odd to see Badger do something as normal and upstanding as pull a T card from his wallet and go through the plastic gates. We rode side by side a couple stops to Harvard Square, not speaking.

He had on a different jacket, a plain black zip-up, different sneakers, and of course he'd left the holster and bike behind. Even just having his hood down, he looked like a different guy. I wondered which was the costume, to him—Badger or Isaac.

As blurry as things between us had become the last few days, it wasn't a romantic outing. We didn't hold hands. We bought our own coffees from Peet's and loitered around the square, people-watching. His eyes were restless, and I wondered how many offenses he saw that he deemed ball-worthy, if only he'd been suited up.

Our knees barely touched on the bus ride to Mount Auburn. Still, as we wandered all over the gorgeous cemetery, I felt closer to him than I'd felt to anyone since before my Vicodin possession. I felt equal to him in my up-fuckery, and it was pleasant and comforting, meandering around, our clothes growing heavy in the day's drizzly mist, shoes soaked from the wet grass, toes stiff. We trudged up the tower's corkscrew of stone steps to the top, and I bet we stood there staring out over Cambridge and Boston and all the fall-colored treetops for forty-five minutes, until I got so chilled and clammy I was shaking. Even then I didn't want to go back down to earth.

Another bus ride—soggier than the way out—back to Harvard Square, then the subway out to Davis. As we walked in the general direction of Medford, toward his neighborhood, I managed to ask, "How long are we hanging out today?"

He shrugged. "Till you're sick of me."

If I hadn't been so thoroughly damp and cold, the words would've had me blushing with happiness. "Does your grandma have a dryer?"

"Sure."

So strange it was, picturing Badger doing laundry.

Another scrap of his mystique fell away, but I liked who lay underneath. Maybe the real Badger wasn't the guy on the bike, the one seemingly fueled by anger and vengeance. His shell was genuine, but the more I talked to him, the more I realized his motivations weren't as black-and-white as they seemed. The vigilante stuff wasn't a mission. It was a tic. A compulsion, involuntary and distasteful as scab picking or nail biting. Like cutting. It was how his anxiety made itself an outlet, same as my pill habit, my antisocial hibernation spells. He was very human behind all the animal mannerisms. Very human and very, very screwed up.

And I was very, very much in danger of falling in love with him.

Or at least falling in love *toward* him. He didn't seem capable of reflecting such a sentiment, merely absorbing it. Our moments of tenderness aside, he was a cold man. Cold and apart, and possessing a unique, lonely view of our city, like that tower on the hill overlooking Mount Auburn.

We made it back to his grandma's house around four, just as the sky turned dark and opened up. Too bad, too—the storm would knock all the ripened leaves to the ground, strip the trees to their skeletons by morning, and hello, New England winter.

We trudged up the slippery back steps and ditched our shoes inside the door.

"Gimme your clothes," he said.

I stripped, keeping my bra and panties on—they'd dry soon enough. Badger did the same, changing into fresh jeans before disappearing shirtless down the stairs with our wet clothes. I wondered if his grandma would see him, and if so, did she even notice his scars anymore? His corduroy cutting scars, the cigarette burn, and the fresh marks I'd given him—the red stripes on his back and the fading cut on his lip? What must she think of the unseen woman upstairs, abusing her grandson? *I'm not an evil, crazy bitch*, I told her telepathically. *I'm a deferring, cringing coward. Don't hate me.*

Badger returned shortly and switched on a lamp to combat the gloom.

"So is your grandma your mom's mom or your dad's?"

"I don't know who my dad is."

"Oh. Well, did she move here after your mom did?" I asked, paying lip service to his old mail-order bride story. "Or together?"

He selected a T-shirt from his dresser and pulled it on. "My mom was a contortionist with a traveling circus."

I felt my eyes narrow. "Your mom was a mail-order bride, *and* she traveled with a circus?" It was possible. It was *just* possible, if she'd been, like, a child acrobat in Russia or the Ukraine or someplace, escaped to the States in her late teens. I might be woefully, even *willfully* naive at times, but I wasn't an idiot.

Badger didn't answer my question, just tossed me a flannel shirt and a pair of boxer shorts. My already cloudy vision of his mother blew away to nothingness, a big question mark floating in its place. But fine, let him have his lies.

"Unless you want to be stuck with me again tonight, I better leave by eight," I said, buttoning the shirt up my front.

He shrugged. "Leave whenever you feel like it."

I glanced at the rain hammering the drafty windows, such a handy excuse to overstay my welcome, to avoid confronting my violated apartment and the skunk-stench of insecurity the burglars had sprayed across every surface. "Would it be too much if I crashed here again?"

He gave me a look, then beckoned me with a curled finger. I padded barefoot across the cold floorboards.

"I like having you here," he murmured.

"Okay, good."

"And I'm not one of those guys who knows how to overthink crap like this and start worrying if you're clingy or in love with me or something, or what my homoerotic frat brothers are going to make of you."

"Right."

"So knock yourself out. It's nicer having you in my bed than it is sleeping alone."

"Good."

His reassurance was an equal mix of impersonal and validating. I'd take it. I mean, I wouldn't waste time waiting for something more.

He put a hand to my side and coaxed me to join him as he wandered to the edge of the bed. It felt so unlike him, so normal. Tender. A happy shiver tiptoed up my back.

"I'll grab your clothes and find us some dinner in a couple hours," he said, sitting on the mattress. "You wanna kiss until then?"

Yes yes yes. "Yeah, okay."

We got under the covers, the soft sheets and his jeans feeling like heaven against my clammy skin. We kissed and kissed and kissed, deep and slow and in no rush to get anywhere. And for a long time, there was no place I wanted to be except right here, in this madman's bed.

Our chilled bodies warmed, and the goose bumps peppering his arms smoothed, leaving only the raised texture of his damage. He felt tight and minimal. Just muscle and skin and tendons and heat, a man stripped to his essentials. How a man might feel, rescued after a year of surviving on a desert island, all the softness and civility of the Western world melted from his bones in the sun.

I stroked his back and throat, his chest and stomach and sides. Once again I was horny as hell, Badger lost to his blissful contentedness. I grazed his naked torso, remembering how he'd looked, worked up. As feral as I'd hoped for. Exactly as advertised, if a bit too much, in the end. But up until the choking . . . perfect. I ran my nails down his ribs, light, then harder. He moaned softly against my mouth.

"You trying to start something?" he muttered.

"Yeah, probably."

"Want me to get you off?"

"Um, you can try."

"Okay. Be easier to try if you tell me what makes you come."

"Oh, uh . . ."

"Is it really fucked or something?" he asked, expression brightening.

"No, no. I've just never tried to explain it to anybody before."

"You want my fingers or my mouth or what?"

"Fingers, I guess."

"Cool. Just tell me what to do."

Easier said than done. But as he settled behind me and wound an arm around my waist, mouth at the back of my neck, my worries faded. He slid his hand between my legs, touching me through the boxers and my panties. I lost my breath, from both the suddenness of this intimacy and just how good it felt. Two fingertips stroked firmly at the seam of my lips, the pad of his hand rubbing my clit.

"You need me to talk nasty to you?" he asked.

"Uh, no." God knew what freaky monologue that might invite. "But your breathing sounds nice."

"Want me to moan and shit?"

I stifled a laugh at the sheer Badgeriness of his wording. "Sure."

Oh Christ, what a brilliant idea it turned out to be. I should have known a shameless man like this one wouldn't have made it cheesy or fake-sounding or embarrassing. He sounded just like he did when I hurt him, only without the stress of inspiring it. It sounded like pure sex in my ear, that low, mean pitch of his voice, those harsh breaths. I cupped my palm over his hand to feel his knuckles dance as he touched me.

"You can . . . you know, under my panties," I mumbled.

"Sure."

He slid his hand beneath the fabric, his fingertips cool on my overheated sex, asphalt-scarred palm rough against my softness. I closed my eyes and inhaled the smell of him, let his noises fill my head. I imagined him above me, in my own bed, just fucking. That raw, ropy body, these moans and grunts, and his cock, hard and easy. In my mind he needed nothing more than what I did. The closer he came to release in my head, the closer I edged against his stroking fingers. "Inside me," I mumbled.

Two fingers parted my lips and dipped between them. Fuck, I wanted to whisper his name. But "Badger" didn't feel right, and "Isaac" could so easily be a lie. I settled for swearing instead.

"You close?" he asked.

I nodded. I shut my eyes tighter, conjuring the scene I'd been enjoying. His soft, filthy sounds returned, and heat tingled in my feet, always a giveaway. Oh, wow. Oh *wow*, I was going to be given an orgasm by someone who wasn't me. *Oh . . . wow.*

In my mind, he came. And against the callused pad of his finger, I came. It was fast and harsh, and I had to grasp his wrist to still him. We lay frozen for half a minute before I melted against his chest, my breathing loud in the quiet room, drowned out only by the occasional rattle of the windows.

The haze of my orgasm dissipated, but my desire didn't. I twisted around to face him, and we kissed—my light, grateful pace to start, but soon enough, deep and dirty.

I'd made him come in my head. I'd kill to make him come for real. No wait, bad—I wouldn't kill. Poor choice of words, given the choking debacle. But my orgasm had made me greedy and curious, and I'd see what I was capable of. I scraped my nails down his throat, earning a shiver, a hitch in his breath. I bit his lip right on the cut I'd left there. He groaned.

I kept biting him, leaving my good hand free to cup him. I moved my teeth to his ear, rubbed him through his jeans. I felt him stirring against my palm, but not blazing to violent life. I wondered if I had it in me to belt him again . . . The idea made me feel small. I tried a new tack, squeezing him tightly, tighter than I felt okay with, surely a fraction as cruel as he'd prefer. Still, he grew stiffer.

I heard him swallow. "That'll get me going, but it's not gonna take me all the way. Not unless you can make it meaner."

"I want to get you off," I muttered. "But I don't think I can do that much harder, not without upsetting myself."

"There's one way I know of how you can get me off without hurting me, but it's royally fucked-up."

I sighed. "Shock."

"And I'm not gonna freak you out for a stupid orgasm, so let's just quit now. If my balls get any bluer, they'll drop off."

"Is it really worse than choking you, the other thing?"

"It is and it isn't. It's not dangerous, but it's pretty fuck-ing sick."

I mulled it over. "I probably wouldn't be here if I wasn't a little bit intrigued by your damage," I admitted. "Tell me what it is, and I'll decide if I'm up for it."

After a moment's consideration, he stood and stripped. As fascinating as I found his body, it looked stark and threatening with the sex we might be about to explore such a vast, black unknown.

He returned to the bed, crawling on his knees, drop-ping forward to hug one of the pillows, pressing the side of his face into it. "Touch me," he said, the order muffled.

"How?"

"Just touch me. Everywhere, down there. Doesn't have

to be rough—just fuck around. And if I make any noise, shush me. Or tell me to shut up. Or slap me if you have it in you, but shushing's fine."

"Oh. All right."

I told myself I didn't know what this was about, but my constricted heart knew better.

His knees were planted wide, and I knelt, straddling one of his calves. I touched his back first, tracing his shiny, flat scars and the red ribbons I'd branded on him, my better efforts with his belt. *He likes this,* I reminded myself. As impossible and sad as that fact was to me.

Badger was silent, eyes shut tight. One of his hands was visible, strangling the corner of the pillow. His body looked so strong, even as it pleaded to be exploited.

I ran my palm over his ass, his hip. I focused on the tiny private details of him, the blue of his veins, the odd freckle, the fine, pale hairs glowing in the warm lamplight. Anything to keep me rooted in the man I was touching, firmly separate from the fantasy I feared he was indulging.

I stroked his ass, eliciting a shiver, a tiny jolt and a soft noise. *You're turning him on. That's all that matters.* I wouldn't judge a woman for indulging a rape fantasy, would I? Was this so much worse? I slid my hand between his legs, stroking his inner thigh, knuckles brushing his balls. He sucked in a breath. As I cupped him, he let go a wheezy grunt.

"Shhh," I hissed. I felt as scared as he sounded, but I'd done it. I'd made the noise he'd asked for.

I fondled his balls, stomach clenching. It felt as if I was appraising him, like livestock. But this was what he wanted, or close to it. Icy-cold objectification. I held his hip with my bad hand, sliding the other deeper to feel his cock. He was heavy and warm, not quite hard but on the way there. He was turned on, and I wasn't hurting him, not physically. This was progress. This was *okay*. Wasn't it?

I weighed his cock in my palm and triggered another soft, sharp, fearful sound.

I managed to whisper, "Shut up."

He shifted, widening his stance.

I knew what he wanted. I *hated* what he wanted. I limited my exploration to his cock and balls and the crease of his uppermost thigh, shushed him when he made noises. I could see it as he got hotter. I saw it in his tensing, tightening muscles and the faint shaking of his legs, unmistakable sexual excitement. I tried to focus on what *I* wanted—to make him come, give him release and relief. To hear how he'd sound as he got there, to witness his expression in the wake of orgasm and hopefully find him dozy and tranquilized because of me. Because I'd been brave enough to do this.

Still, was I helping him or fucking his head up more, scratching some sick groove even deeper onto his sexual psyche? Or was I thinking too damn hard about it when this was only sex? Fuck, I wasn't built for role-playing. But I wasn't built for Badger, either—not made-to-order, anyhow. If I wanted him, I had to suck it up and go places, ugly places, root around in the dark through the cobwebs and insect hulls, trusting there was a reward hidden in this creepy mess.

A deep groan hauled me out of my head and back into the present. "Shhh," I hissed.

He whimpered, sniffed loudly through his nose. I slid

my hand to his ass, running my thumb between his cheeks. He gasped, and I shushed him again, feeling sick.

I heard him mutter a single syllable. "Bad."

"Shut up." Another wave of nausea. Disgust at this act, but also disgust at my cowardice, my judgment. I wanted to be what he needed, so, so badly. I touched him everywhere, just as he'd asked, focusing only on his reactions, his obvious excitement. His cock was beyond hard, and I gave it a squeeze, triggering a thrash and a moan. He'd caught me off guard, and when I didn't shush him, he seemed to do the job for me, his whisper sharp in the dim, cool room.

"You shut your fucking mouth like a good boy."

My fingers froze until I willed them to move.

Fucking hell, it was scary. As scary as smacking him with a belt, knowing he was fantasizing about being molested. Far scarier to wonder if he was getting off from the *memory* of being molested.

I did as he asked, screaming a mantra inside my head, *It's what he wants, it's what he wants,* though not nearly loud enough to block out the sounds of his whispered self-admonishments, the hiss of my own obedient shushing. It couldn't have taken more than two minutes before he was trembling and straining at the doorstep of release, but Jesus, it felt like an eternity.

He bucked, his jerking body too frantic for my hand to follow. He ground his cock against my palm, his groans crescendoed, and he came with a fearful, pitiful sound, pleasure wrapped in terror.

I backed off and sat cross-legged, patiently faking calm. Still on his hands and knees, he gulped deep breaths. I watched his ribs clench and swell like fisting fingers. He'd cupped himself when he came, and he dropped back to his knees and reached for his jettisoned shorts, wiping his palm.

When he lay back against the pillows, I did the same.

I had no clue what to say to him. We'd gone somewhere dark together . . . though only one of us had taken pleasure from it. Only one of us had wanted or enjoyed that. I'd fantasized a lot in the last couple weeks about what it might be like to make this man come. None of my guesses had looked *anything* like that.

We were quiet a long time, and I felt his energy shift as he came down from his orgasm, from panting disbelief to something heavier. Regret, maybe, or remorse. For which one of us, I couldn't guess.

I listened to us breathing for ages, until it quieted enough to reveal the hush of the wind and rain, the pulse of the clock. I found the voice to murmur, "I don't think I can do that again."

"Did I fuck you up?"

"No . . . No, not permanently. But it doesn't feel good, knowing you're thinking about . . . You know."

"Just another kind of ugly. A different sort of pain." He licked his bottom lip, tongue worrying a fresh cut I'd left there.

"Why does it get you off, do you think? Such awful stuff?"

He sat up, and I did the same, hugging the covers.

He shrugged. "It's just how you get wired when you're young. You run across your dad's *Playboy* stash at nine and presto, you're a tits man. Glance up your babysitter's skirt by mistake, and white cotton panties get burned onto your libido for the rest of your life. Some little girls get fucked with, and they grow up hating themselves because they have to fantasize about being held down by a guy to have a fucking orgasm."

"I guess."

"Did you know that the vast majority of child molesters were molested themselves?"

I nodded. "I've heard that."

"Sometimes it just imprints, that early development shit. The thing that fucked you up the most just comes back. It just equals sex, in your head. Me, I'm just fucking over the moon I'm fucked-up the way I am. That I got no desire whatsoever to be the perpetrator."

"Just the victim."

Another shrug. "Take it or leave it. I never said I wasn't fucking sick."

"Is it like therapy for you, reenacting it?"

"Nah, it's not fucking therapy. It's just the fucked-up, disgusting thing that gets me off."

I frowned deeply, achingly sad for him. But it wasn't like the scenarios I conjured while masturbating were populated by gentle, seductive men making slow, candlelit love to me. Nothing as ugly as Badger's footage, but nothing that'd sell perfume, either, that was for sure.

He sighed. "Sex has never had anything to do with feeling good, to me. Not happy, you know? Sex was always terrifying and lopsided, all about one person getting hurt and the other doing the hurting."

"Huh."

"So now I'm stuck with that, with getting hard from feeling real shitty stuff. Thinking about shitty stuff. But whatever. It's only thoughts."

"That's so . . . God, I don't know."

He made a noise, too harsh to call a sigh. "Well, it's not something I can change about myself. And you asked to get me off, so don't bother making me feel like a shit when I *fucking* warned you." He was agitated suddenly—agitated in a way I hadn't seen before. A shaking in his arms, tension in his face instead of the usual stony control. I'd hit a nerve, a ragged one.

"I'm not trying to make you feel bad. I'm just trying to figure out how *I* feel about it."

He stared past me at the wall, and I saw him calming, anger leaving as quickly as it had come.

"Sorry," I murmured.

He closed his eyes, breathing deeply for a few moments. "Don't be sorry. Just don't take it lightly when I warn you something's probably gonna freak you out."

"I won't." *Not after that. No sirree.*

"I got messed up enough as a kid from this shit. It'd piss me off to know it just ricocheted and hit you, too."

"No, it didn't. I just want to understand."

"Understand me, or what happened to me?"

"I dunno. Both. Since it seems like it was pretty . . . formative."

He took a long, deep breath and closed his eyes. "When I was about six, this guy I was staying with gave me some pill he said was candy. Made me warm and spacey, all trippy."

My stomach curled in on itself, dreading whatever was coming.

"He fucked me with a handgun, you know, to loosen me up—"

"Oh my God."

"He said it was loaded. And he held that stinking barrel to the side of my face the whole time he—"

"Oh, stop! Stop, stop, stop." I covered my ears, tears stinging my eyes. When his mouth closed, I dropped my hands. "I can't hear that. It's too upsetting."

"That's like two percent of what I've got for you, if you want to understand me. And what I had done to me."

"I guess maybe I don't want to know."

"Yeah, I guess not." He reclined, staring at the ceiling with his hands laced atop his stomach.

"Not yet. I don't know. I'm sorry."

"That's fine. It's ugly shit, and I got tons of it. When I was little, really little, I was a fucking puppy. Anybody who'd pay me attention, I was in love with them. Follow them anywhere. Then you get kicked enough, you get neglected enough . . . You get fucked with and screwed with enough, and you figure out how to bite. I got real good at biting by the time I was ten, twelve, fourteen. I was rabid. You fucking look at me and I'd bite. I'd rip your fucking hand off, just in case you planned on putting it someplace I didn't want it to be."

"I'm sure."

"But before that . . . You get that done to you when you're young, with nobody around to protect you, you just get this victim stink on you. Like this carrion stench that hits the wind, draws people to you, the ones who like that stuff. I'm not special, the way I got fucked-up."

"It's still incredibly sad. And hard to hear."

"Don't ask, then."

"I won't."

"You hungry or anything?" he asked through a sigh.

"No, not really. Maybe later." Maybe never, I felt so queasy. "How do you . . ."

"How do I what?"

"How do you even function, with all those memories in your head?"

"You think I'm functional? That's hilarious."

"Well, Jesus, I dunno. I'm a mess, and I had a pretty happy childhood. Or a safe one, at least."

"It's not a contest," Badger said. "And there's no minimum requirement for how shitty you had to be treated as a kid to qualify to be a fucked-up adult. Plus, as fuckups go, you're not that bad, cupcake. A pill habit's a trip to the candy store to some people."

"I know." As I lay back down, I conjured the faces from my NA meeting, the ones who'd hit bottoms so infinitely deeper and harder than I'd had to before they'd turned things around. Prison had been plenty to scare me, given how little I'd been traumatized before then. But some people in my group had lost homes, children, marriages, careers, the respect of everyone they knew, struck people with their cars, and that still hadn't been enough to get some of them clean, especially if they'd grown up surrounded by that kind of chaos. And for someone like Badger . . . What in heaven's name could rock bottom look like when *that* was your childhood? What reality was worse than getting raped with a fucking handgun? Murder? Suicide? How was it that he *didn't* have a drug problem, for crying out loud?

"A pill habit's no worse than what most people have done," he said. "You're just stuck with your dirty laundry waving around in the open because of your record. But plenty of people fuck up worse than you did. They just have the luxury of keeping it to themselves."

I turned over, impulsively stroking his hair and face with my good hand. I couldn't comfort him any better than I might a wild animal, it seemed. I'd try, though, even if it meant getting scratched or bitten.

"Still don't know why you like me," he muttered.

"Sometimes I don't," I said. "Sometimes I think you're a colossal asshole."

He smirked.

"Thanks for making me come," I said. "I wouldn't have had the guts to ask you to."

"Shit, if I could come from something as simple as getting fingered and having somebody breathe on me, I'd be asking strangers on the bus for it."

I smiled, shaking my head.

"Maybe I can figure out some way of hurting myself," he said, "where I can still do that to you, but stay hard enough to fuck you at the same time."

I laughed, finding his proposal sweetly ridiculous. "That's so romantic."

"I mean it. I don't know how, since usually when I get off, I'm whacking the hell out of myself with a belt or an extension cord."

I flinched.

"But I'll figure something out, so maybe I can get what I need and you're not stuck doing shit to me, too distracted or disgusted to come. If you still want us to be like that, I mean."

"You're on."

I imagined such a thing, him actually finding a way to get there. It'd be my first orgasm while having intercourse, if we succeeded. Then I'd definitely fall in love with him. Better hope we fail, in that case. I was already too far gone as it was.

14

"Hey. Cupcake."

I roused at a shaking of my shoulder and promptly turned over and mumbled, "Yeah, pigeon." I woke properly as I registered what I'd said. Glancing around Badger's dim lair, I found it was morning again, early morning.

"Pigeon? What kind of fucked-up dream are you having?"

I sat up and combed my fingers through my hair. "Sorry. I don't know why I called you that."

"Oh, you were addressing me?" The cock of an eyebrow, overdone offense.

"Yeah. You've always reminded me of a pigeon."

"Thanks. I can't think of any more disgusting possible animal to remind someone of."

"They're nicer than *badgers*. Plus, you know, you're gray and black, you splatter people with white stuff . . . and anyway, I like pigeons."

He climbed on top of me, straddling my hips and

pressing his warm chest to mine, arms sliding under my back. "Would you do this with a pigeon?"

I shook my head, staring into his eyes. We'd accomplished very little after my non-victory in making him come—just eaten sandwiches and lay in his bed, talking about nothing, asleep by ten. It'd been nice. Just being with someone. The awful things I'd felt from molesting him had faded in the face of whatever strange, calming chemistry we created together. I'd fallen asleep with his arm slung over my waist from behind, his deep exhalations tickling my neck.

He kissed me—a soft press of his lips to my forehead, then my nose. "I like pigeons, too." He shifted to the side, leaving my skin cold but my heart awfully warm and happy.

"I gotta leave soon," he announced, standing from the bed. I watched his lean muscles flexing, his belt marks—shiny and red alike—seeming to dance as he pulled a T-shirt down his trunk. They reminded me of wings, diagonal lashes of feathers. "Gotta punch the clock."

"And shoot the wicked."

"And you have a doctor's appointment."

"Oh, I do." But it wasn't until one. I had plenty of time to get home and change.

"Come down for breakfast," he said. "Otherwise my grandma's going to think I'm hiding you from her, and she'll bitch at me for being rude to one or both of you."

"Oh, um. Okay."

He'd brought my clothes up from the dryer when he'd found us dinner, and after I used the bathroom I changed into the same outfit I'd worn to interview with Lani. Odd.

So much had happened since I'd met her in Brookline. I'd been burgled. I'd spent a night and then a whole day with the Badger, been briefly traumatized twice to varying degrees, swapped orgasms, spent another night. All that without a change of underwear or socks.

My nerves hummed as I followed him downstairs, through an elegant sitting room and down a final carpeted set of steps to a front parlor. We took a left through a dining area, and I smelled bacon.

Badger's grandma had her back to us when we entered the kitchen, busy at the stove, curly gray hair held back in a wooden clip.

"Morning," she said absently.

"We got a guest," Badger said.

She turned and studied me a second. "Indeed we do. Good morning."

"This is Adrian," he said. "Adrian, this is Barbara."

I crossed the tile to shake her warm, bony hand. "Nice to meet you."

"Indeed. How do you like your eggs?" If her name weren't enough proof, her utter absence of any hint of a foreign accent answered the old mail-order-bride-mother question.

"Whatever's easy," I said.

"Scrambled it is." She turned back to the stove, leaving me with an impression that was equal parts maternal and cranky.

Badger filled three mugs from a coffeemaker and carried them to a smaller table than the dining room boasted —cozier, with a pretty view of a narrow side garden. I took a seat, fussing with my nails.

"You need help?" he asked his grandma.

"Just an extra place, for your guest."

He fetched me a plate and silverware and a juice glass. "Thanks."

He pulled out a chair, sitting close to me, filling me with confusion and pleasure.

"It's going to be in the thirties tonight," his grandma said, turning bacon rashers over. "Wear a sweater under your jacket."

"Okay."

"I left the grocery list next to the mail pile. We're nearly out of milk. Don't forget."

"I never forget."

"That's because I'm so studious about nagging you." She said it without a hint of playfulness, shooting him a look.

I tried to picture how such a chore would work. He'd have to come home, change out of his Badger uniform, walk to the store, walk home again, get back into his getup for the second shift . . . ?

No one spoke for a while, and it made me nervous.

"Um, thanks for breakfast," I said dumbly. I felt like I was ten, not twenty-seven.

"It's no problem," Barbara said curtly, with a little huff, irritation or maybe just exhaustion. Button-up sweater and clunky old-lady shoes aside, she wasn't much of a charmer. Then again, neither was her grandson. Plus, she of all people must have known what a shitty childhood he'd had. Maybe she was just cagey and protective of him where female guests were concerned.

"Okay, help yourselves." She shuffled to the table with her own food, and I followed Badger to the stove, plate in hand. Breakfast—especially fried, diner-style breakfast—was a rare treat for me. I usually gulped tea or coffee on my way out the door, unless there was something special going on. I supposed this was kind of special, accidentally meeting my crazy not-a-boyfriend's seemingly only family. We returned to the table with full plates.

Barbara was already picking at her eggs and had the newspaper spread beside her, open to the puzzles section. She tapped the tip of a mechanical pencil against the Jumble, looking likely to ignore us. It was all very weird, me trapped between a stranger and a man not known for his ability to make pleasant small talk.

"The meter guy's supposed to come by today," Badger said.

"I know that." She scribbled an answer with a coo of triumph.

"So don't ignore the doorbell. And you know we got a guest," he added. "I don't think that's happened. Ever. Maybe we ought to pretend to be good at entertaining people."

She raised her eyes to gaze at him, then me. "Right. So, Adrian. What do you do?"

"I'm a writer. And an illustrator." Though I used to list those vocations in reverse order, once upon an optimistic time.

"Not much money in that, is there?"

"Um, not a ton. But I'm a copywriter, not a novelist or a poet or anything."

She turned back to her puzzle. "Not a drunk, then."

"Um, no." Not an active one. I'd probably be *great* at alcoholism, if I gave it the old college try. Thank goodness

I didn't care for the taste. "Your house is really beautiful. How long have you lived here?"

"Fifty-five years," she said, looking up. Her eyes were blue, like Badger's, but paler. Skeptical instead of dangerous.

"Wow."

"Raised six kids inside these walls. Four sons, two daughters. Ingrates, every last one of them."

"Huh. Was, um . . ." I trailed off. I couldn't ask if *Badger's* mom was among them, nor did I trust asking about *Isaac's* lineage, lest I look like an idiot for not knowing the real first name of the man I was having violent sex with, up in this crabby old woman's well-appointed attic.

"What did you do?" I asked instead. "Did you have a career?"

"Wife and mother. Most exhausting, unappreciated careers there are. Forty-six years with the same man, then he up and dies on me on Christmas morning. Typical Harold, leaving me to do all the cleanup by myself. Never saw the point of a real tree. Too much hassle, all those needles."

"You're being a real downer," Badger said through a mouthful of toast.

"I'm out of practice," she said, waving her fork dismissively and going back to the Jumble. "She's your guest. You be charming to her. I made breakfast."

I glanced at Badger, but he shrugged, seeming to imply that she was like this twenty-four-seven. "When do you hear about your interview?" he asked me.

"Not sure. Soon, I hope. And actually, I should turn my phone on. They may have called me back, for all I know."

"You hope they say yes, even though it'll suck?"

"Don't say 'suck,'" Barbara murmured, scribbling. "It's crass."

I nodded. "Um, yeah, I do. Aside from just the paycheck and the insurance, I could use the structure, probably."

"So maybe I'll ride by and you'll be all dressed up?"

"Yeah, maybe. If you ever get out to Brookline."

He made a face. "Not much. People there don't piss me off as much as I like."

"Don't say 'piss,'" Barbara cut in, still not looking up.

"People there don't urinate me off as much," Badger corrected dryly.

"Don't be smart."

"I better get ready to leave," he said, and popped the last piece of bacon in his mouth. "You got everything you need from upstairs?" he asked me.

"Everything but my purse."

"I'll grab it. You can just meet me out front in, like, five minutes, if you want to finish your coffee."

I didn't. I wanted to go with him and escape his cranky grandma, but I nodded politely. "Cool."

He carried his dish to the sink, then let us be, clomping around above en route to the attic. I ate my eggs slowly, hoping I could use them to occupy my mouth and thus avoid conversation for the next five minutes.

A sigh drew my gaze off my plate, and I looked up as Barbara's rheumy eyes narrowed. "So. Are you Isaac's girlfriend?"

Oh ho, so he really *was* an Isaac. "Um, I don't know, actually."

"I see." Her wry look lingered, a glimmer of hopeful approval warming its edges, if I wasn't mistaken.

"We're not really at that stage. You know, putting names on things."

Another sigh. "Kids."

"How, um, how old is Isaac, exactly?"

She cocked her head to the side. "I don't rightly know."

"You don't?"

"Neither do you, it sounds like."

"Aren't you his grandma?"

She laughed, another taste of warmth, like maybe that sourpuss act was something she played up when he was around. Like maybe she liked him more than she cared to admit, or maybe because a more kindly approach didn't jibe with him.

"No, I'm not his grandma. I don't know why he calls me that. I'm just his landlady. Not that I'm not fond of him. He's a nice young man, if a bit excitable."

I relaxed a little. "Do you know his last name?"

"Sorry, dear. All I know is that he pays me in cash and doesn't give me any trouble. Once, some kid tried to break into the house, and Isaac hit him with a pipe and he ran off."

"Whoa."

"I like having him around. Like a guard dog. And I think he likes me. He lets me cook for him, now that all my ungrateful children have moved away and forgotten about me."

"How did you meet him? He just applied for the apartment?"

"Oh my, no. I never wanted a tenant. He used to deliver my groceries."

I nearly spit out my coffee, so shocked by the proof that Badger really had held a normal job. "Did he?"

"Yes. Came twice a week on his bicycle and delivered my food from the store, helped me put the heavier things away. And one week I didn't answer the door, because I'd passed out, you see. It was July, and very hot, and I'd passed out at the kitchen table. And he knew I was a bit of a shut-in, and he broke into my house and found me slumped over my Sudoku book and called an ambulance."

"Wow."

"And after that, I always invited him in for coffee and a snack when he came by, and eventually I asked if he needed a place to stay, because he always looked awfully rough. Like no one ever taught him how to feed himself. He still looks that way, frankly, but it's not *my* fault. At least I get a good breakfast into him."

"Huh."

"He's a quiet tenant. I like having him here, in case something happens to me. None of my selfish, idiot children will do the job, after all."

"Ah." As interesting as it was to hear all this, it was also frustrating. I'd hoped that meeting this woman would offer some proof that Badger—Isaac—was a real person, one with a childhood outside of the horror stories, a social security number, the trappings of a past.

A job, though. That was something.

"If I had to guess," she said, "I'd say he's maybe thirty. But you young people all just blend together, at my age."

"Do you know what he does during the day?"

She pursed her papery lips. The way her gaze shifted to

the window told me I was being lied to—though about what, I wasn't sure. "I couldn't tell you. But I very much doubt he's an accountant, if that's what he fed you. He disappears on his bicycle after breakfast, dressed like a hoodlum, and then I don't see him 'til the next morning, except on Sundays, for dinner. I don't make it my business what he does when he's out."

"I see."

"He's a lonely young man, and I'm a lonely old crank, but together we're both half as lonely as we might otherwise be."

"Have you heard of the Badger?"

"Not my concern," she said brusquely, getting unsteadily to her feet. "The Mexican who does my landscaping can worry about that. Now finish your coffee. You oughtn't keep a man waiting."

15

It was a strange day. Badger was in uniform, so we had to say our goodbyes on his street, lest we get spotted together and I wind up harangued by curious witnesses once he took off. Or worse, cops.

We didn't kiss. We stood nearly toe to toe, and he said something like, "I guess I'll see you when I see you," and I agreed. Then he rode off, and I headed for Davis to start the long train ride back to JP.

When I emerged from the Green Street stop, I finally switched on my phone. I had four messages. One from Amanda saying hello, and did I get her e-mail? Oops. The second from a cell phone store, of all miserable things. Me, trying to sell stuff to strangers and deal with their dissatisfaction? What on earth had I been smoking? The third from my landlord, telling me my copy of the key to the interior door was in my mailbox, and finally a message from Lani, from three o'clock the previous afternoon.

"Adrian, hello. It's Lani Weiss. Just wanted to tell you what a fun time I had chatting with you on Tuesday. I'd love to invite you in for a second interview. Tomorrow afternoon or Friday first thing are best for me. Give me a call."

Right, well. That was good news.

I called as I walked home and set up an appointment for the following morning, feeling pretty damn good about myself. Kind of. Everything at the moment felt uncertain and not ideal—my job prospects, my medical prospects, my living situation, my steadily weirdening romantic entanglement. It all seemed very sloppy, all these developments I was attached to even as I knew they weren't taking me in quite the right direction in the grand scheme of things. Oh, well. A direction, period, and one not aimed toward a prescription bottle, was progress.

It did suck, being back in my ravaged apartment. I'd only been gone a day and a half, but it felt foreign. Bigger somehow. The appliances looked wrong, like I couldn't recall ever having used them before. Maybe the miracle of achieving an orgasm by someone else's hand had scrambled my brain. That, or any of the other ridiculousness I'd undertaken in the interest of having some semblance of a sex life.

I switched on the TV—which had proven too small or outmoded to bother stealing, unlike the DVD player —and turned up the volume, drowning out my brain's negative chatter. Before I even took a pee, I tackled the mess. Within an hour the place was looking pretty much normal again, except without my "roommate," my laptop, my connection to the outside world.

Still, when I left at noon, my apartment was my own

again, just a bit more brine-stinking. And if I got the job in Brookline, the second I paid my rent and bills I'd buy myself a decent computer. A shiny new Mac, maybe, if the financing was fair. Maybe that was for the best. My old one was full of ghosts, straddling my past and present and the ugly in-between. Full of some other girl's letters and art, artifacts I'd do well to replace. Good riddance.

The doctor's appointment was a mixed bag. I was sick to my stomach in the waiting room, knowing even with my down-and-outer's subsidized billing I was still shooting another massive hole in my already mangled credit. But on the positive side, they took off my cast and proclaimed me nearly healed. I left with a lightweight plastic brace on my hand, with Velcro so I could take it off to shower. When the nurse tossed my plaster cast in the wastebasket, I almost asked to keep it. Somewhere under the Wite-Out patch job was Badger's handwriting, his invitation to the diner. The closest I'd surely ever come to a love letter from that man. But I let it go. *Forward, Adrian.*

Having the itchy, stinky cast gone made me feel like I'd shed far more than half a pound of plaster. I took the long way home, swinging by the library and catching up on e-mail.

Most of it was spam from the job sites, and there were some wedding-related links from Amanda, asking my opinion about invitations and colors. I dutifully explored and replied, though my enthusiasm was limp. My romance looked so unlike hers. Then again, I wouldn't swap my non-thing with Badger or Isaac or whoever for her real-life, grown-up relationship with Derek. Not in a million years, not for a million dollars. The life she'd made for herself was turning out so pretty, so picture-perfect, so functional inside and out . . . I didn't envy her. I was happy for her, but I wouldn't be happy *being* her. It made me feel better, accepting that. And it made me miss Badger.

Not enough to go after him, though. Not anytime soon. He'd been kind to hang out with me, take me in, take a day off to keep my sorry ass company. I'd leave the next move up to him. And I'd lie to myself about how badly I hoped he'd come after me.

But all that said, I bought condoms on my way home.

I skipped my NA meeting for two reasons, each as lame as it was legit. Firstly, I didn't want to admit I was re-unemployed to the group, in case Lani hired me and I could save face. And secondly, because Badger could show up at my place while I was out. I didn't beat myself up about skipping, because even though I was sitting around in my freshly violated apartment, I had no interest in using. I wasn't above a meeting, certainly, but it didn't feel reckless, letting this one slide.

My second interview with Lani went great. In fact, it really amounted to ten minutes of chatting and her showing me new comps from the design firm and asking my supposedly expert, supposedly sassy twenty-something opinion. Then she announced she wanted to offer me the job. I made a bunch of surprised noises, feeling her out, waiting for certain word-bombs to drop and decimate me—*background check, drug test*—but nope. I seemed to be in the clear. I accepted the job, and we decided I'd start on Monday at nine a.m.

And just like that, I was employed.

I felt different on the way home. I didn't feel all Mary Tyler Moore. I didn't swing my handbag around, eyes on the clouds, ebullient with my modest success, my latest do-over. But the sky seemed a bit brighter, and I could take a deep breath—deep enough for it to catch in the bottom of my lungs for the first time in what felt like ages.

I didn't go nuts like when the museum had hired me. Instead of a new wardrobe, I bought a four-dollar, hard-to-pronounce coffee and drank it as I walked down Beacon Street, foregoing the T in favor of the October sunshine. My phone buzzed in my pocket as I passed the St. Mary's stop, and I juggled my coffee and purse in one hand to fish it out, smiling as I checked the screen and hit TALK.

"Hey, womb-mate."

"Hey, sister."

"What's up?"

"Mom wants to do family dinner on Sunday," Amanda said. "Pot roast. Yum yum."

"Ooh . . . Well, works for me, if it's earlyish. I should get home by ten, probably. I, um. I start a new job on Monday morning."

A squeak, a gasp. "Really? Oh my God, that's awesome! Why didn't you tell me?"

"Because I accepted it about twenty minutes ago, and there's a hot cup of coffee in my hand?"

"Oh, wow. Where?"

"At this place . . . I don't even know what to call it. A cosmetics company? This place that designs and sells crazy-upscale bath products. So expect lots of 'invigorating' crap this Christmas."

"Wow, that's cool."

I headed for a bench. "It's, um . . . The day-to-day job is fine, and I think I'll be good at it, the writing. But my boss is a little nuts. Not psycho nuts, but sort of former-housewife-turned-Martha Stewart-entrepreneurial nuts. I have a feeling I'll be micromanaged all day long and probably get roped into working late a lot. But it's not like I have that many personal engagements." I pictured Badger, standing naked beside his bed in the lamplight.

"Well, that's *great*. Congratulations! Insurance and all that?"

"Yeah, Blue Cross, even. And an okay salary. And a *lot* of vacation days, since my boss is Jewish. Actually, I think she thinks *I'm* Jewish."

A happy cellular sigh warmed my ear. "This is such great news. Save it for dinner, to tell Mom and Dad in person. And I'll try really hard not to tell Derek."

It was so sweet, or perhaps naive, that she thought something so marginally, minimally upstanding as employment would bolster my worthiness in her fiancé's estimation.

"Yeah. It'll be nice to have good news to share. Do you know what time dinner's going to be? I'll have to check the commuter rail schedule."

"That's why I was calling—I was going to tell you I'll pick you up. I've got an appointment in Boston to go over my invitations that afternoon at the printing place, so I'll just swing by and take you."

"Oh, great." I knew in my heart she'd very likely rearranged said appointment upon hearing about dinner, just so she could give me a ride. How funny that we'd been born within five minutes of each other, yet one of us was so unmistakably the mother in our pair.

"My appointment's at four, and if I had to guess, I'd say expect me at five."

"Perfect," I said.

Another wistful sigh. "Congratulations, Ade. I'm really proud of you."

Crap, I was tearing up. "Thanks," I mumbled, heat scorching my cheeks.

"I'll see you Sunday."

"Love you. See you soon."

"Love you, too."

We hung up, and I felt humbled on top of the relief. Happy but vulnerable. I sipped my coffee on the bench for a long time, imagining how I'd word it when I told my family my best news in . . . Jeez, when had I landed that job with the ad firm? Nearly four years ago. Damn. And finally, some news that didn't involve a nice round number of days sober. News that I'd accomplished something good, not merely resisted doing something heinous.

I remembered the laptop I'd been fantasizing about buying once my rent and everything was paid and bumped it down the list. It might be ambitious, but maybe I could write Amanda and Derek a check for the pilfered engagement ring by Christmas, finally shoot that yappy little guilt-dog between its eyes.

I drained my coffee and crossed to the T stop. Time to head home. Time to . . . well, I wasn't sure what. Time to buy groceries, to laze about and wrap my head around the fact that I had a job.

Once all those things were done, I felt calm. I felt calm

until about ten o'clock, when I became all too aware of the time. With no alarm clock to glance at, I caught myself checking my phone's screen. First only during the commercials of the shows I was half-watching, then during the shows themselves. When it struck eleven, my brain came out with it.

Badger will be off duty in four hours.

No, don't think that. Bad.

Don't stay up, dressed and lucid until three a.m. just in case he comes by.

I eyed the bedside table, picturing the condoms inside. Like I wasn't already hoping he'd show. He hadn't shown the night before, but then we'd seen each other that morning. Not that he was remotely likely to adhere to manly conventions about how eager one was allowed to appear to one's love interest.

I wished the pull were stronger now, in the wake of the sex. In the wake of meeting his cranky makeshift grandmother, in the wake of making him come, indulging his totally fucked kinks and not having a complete mental breakdown in the process. I tried to remember what words he'd used when he'd said he wasn't sure whether we were a couple or not. I was pretty sure he'd used the word 'couple.' *Oh, stop it.* I'd swapped art for pills, pills for Nyquil, Nyquil for Badger. *Quit swapping. Quit craving.*

I split the difference in the end. At eleven thirty I changed into pajamas but reapplied deodorant and left my mascara and eye shadow on. Like I was a character on a soap opera. *Oh yes, I always look this put together when I'm sleeping.*

He didn't show, though.

I fell asleep with the TV on and woke at four, knowing he wouldn't be coming but too tired to bother washing my face. I switched off the voices and pulled the covers over myself. Alone, but all right.

16

The weekend arrived with the dawn, as it tends to do for people with jobs. I now had a job, so when I woke on Saturday, I was thrilled to realize that I, too, could get excited about what day of the week it was. They no longer all blended into one long, unstructured shrug-fest.

What to do . . . Maybe figure out a Halloween costume, so if my parents invited me to Lincoln for our semiofficial get-together appeasing trick-or-treaters, I'd look the part. That might be fun. I half-wished I could go as the Badger, but maybe one person in a hundred would get the reference out in the 'burbs. Picturing it, I remembered my best costume from childhood—white-and-black striped pajamas with a prisoner number below one shoulder and a plastic ball my dad had spray painted black, along with the chain that had attached it to my ankle. I wondered if he'd stumbled across that memory himself since my stint as a real-life inmate. Fucking hell, why did that costume have to be the self-fulfilling one? Why couldn't I have grown up and become a ladybug or Sarah from *Labyrinth*?

I'd better think of something cheerful to dress as this year. None of the things I was built for, either—no zombie bride, not anything gaunt or haunted-looking. Something happy. Maybe I'd go as the Old Adrian. No, wait, *something happy*, I teased myself, rolling my eyes.

I got caffeinated and puttered for a couple hours, then walked a few blocks to Boomerangs, JP's funky little thrift store, seeking inspiration. I found it in the form of a long, spangly black dress with a deep vee in both the front and back. If I could find some satin gloves and a feathery thing for my head, I could be a sort of glamorous flapper-type woman. It'd be nice to dress as something feminine, now that I actually felt womanly again. Thanks, Badger.

I bought the dress for fifteen bucks, plus another five for a big, fake onyx ring to wear over one of my gloves, should I find any. There was an alien, pleasant bounce in my step as I walked home, making a list in my head of what I needed to complete the costume. On my way, I picked up really delicious, really disgusting Chinese takeout in celebration of landing the job.

When I got home I did some sketches, getting grease smears on my pad from the crab rangoons. The brainstorming consumed me in a way I hadn't experienced since those little projects I'd done when I'd first become so obsessed with the Badger.

I was wearing the dress, auditioning shoes from my closet, when my doorbell rang. I had no idea what time it was. Nine? That was too early, surely. Wasn't it?

I jogged through the kitchen, hiking my ridiculous

sequined skirt up to my knees, and padded barefoot down the stairs, finding Badger beyond the glass of the front door. To make matters more embarrassing, I'd been playing with makeup, my eyes ringed in black liner. Blushing, I pulled the door open.

My body in its slinky ensemble tensed at the cold. "Hello."

He eyed me, my dress, my naked feet. "Jesus, where the fuck are you off to?"

"Nowhere. I was just working on my Halloween costume." I posed half-assedly. "Ta-da."

He blinked.

"Is everything okay?" I glanced at his bike, which looked as uninjured as its owner.

"Yeah. Just thought I'd swing by and see if you were home."

Oh, how my heart danced. "I am. Come on up, if you want."

I flattened myself against the wall, holding the door so he could carry his bike up.

"I've got plenty of leftover Chinese food," I said, shutting the apartment door behind me. "If you're hungry."

"Maybe later."

Ooh, *later.* Swoon.

Badger reached in his jeans' back pocket, then handed me a folded piece of paper. I flattened it, and on it was him. Sort of. A police drawing of a white guy in a striped hoodie, looking ominous. Cheekbones were about right, but the eyes were way off. I read the text. "Five thousand dollars? Whoa. You're officially wanted." Was I proud or scared?

"I know. Five grand for anything that leads to my arrest.

Probably something less for tips and info. Quick cash, cupcake."

I lowered the paper to stare at his real face. "What? No way. I'd never rat on you, not for any amount of money."

"Why not? Give 'em something harmless. That I live in Somerville or something. My first name. Might fix your financial problems for a little while."

I shook my head. "No chance. I'd rather lose my apartment than be a snitch."

His nostrils flared, eyes rolling with annoyance.

"Don't look like that. You actually want me to talk to the cops about you?"

He shrugged. "Closest I can come to handing you a big wad of cash."

"Well, that's sweet . . . but no." I passed the paper back. "I'm pathetic and desperate and broke, but I've got ethics." Sort of fucked-up Badgery ethics, but stronger and clearer than they'd ever felt before. "I also just got a job. That one I'll hate. I'm okay now, money-wise. Or I will be, in a few months. Not that that would change my answer."

"All right. Just thought I'd let you know."

"Um, thank you." I was a little insulted he thought I'd do such a thing, but overanalyzing what went on in that head was such a pointless exercise.

He was in full Badger regalia, leather holster peering from between two rows of zipper teeth. I also noticed something pale pink strung through his belt loop—a rag or a piece of clothing. I pointed. "What's that?"

"Dish towel. I got an idea about how maybe we can, you know. Fuck."

"Oh. Okay." What exactly would I have to do with this towel? Smother him? Had he brought chloroform as well?

"If you still want that," he added. Was it just me, or did he seem shy?

"Yeah, I still want that. What's your idea?"

"Change your clothes and put on a jacket and I'll show you."

I changed into jeans and a sweater while he sat on my bed, not quite watching but not not-watching my TV. I tried my best to ignore my nerves. I didn't know what to expect, but I'd give him the benefit of the doubt, not ask him questions. I was excited that he was even here. I'd focus on that instead of worrying why it was necessary for us to leave my apartment in order to fuck.

I got my shoes and jacket on in the kitchen, Badger loitering by the table while I did.

"Where are we going?"

"Not too far, I don't think." He drew the U-lock from his back pocket and set it on my counter.

"Do I need my T-Pass?"

"Nah."

I locked up, and when we reached the parking lot he looked around, seeming to pick a direction. He took my hand, of all shocking things, and we started toward Forest Hills.

"It's got to be someplace really quiet, with nobody around," he said. "Or someplace really busy or dangerous, where nobody'll be surprised by loud noises."

Crickets chirped in my head, and I frowned.

"I thought maybe we could use the arboretum."

"What kind of loud noises?" I asked, scared now. Loud sex noises?

He didn't reply, but his hand felt so nice I let him lead me. We passed a few people, mostly young, rowdyish types, but nobody hassled us or recognized Badger, not with his hood down and his bike gone. These kids probably didn't keep up with the local news, anyhow.

We got to the edge of the park in what felt like no time, and my anxiety tugged me in multiple directions. What noises was he trying to hide? Was I going to have sex in public? If so, did he have condoms? Would I be able to tell him no if I needed to? What sorts of unsavory characters might also be skulking around the Arnold Arboretum after dark, and were they creepier than us?

He led me into the woods, not seeming like he knew where he was going. He dropped my hand so we were free to shield our faces from whapping branches, and I mourned the loss of his heat. We hiked for five minutes to a soggy clearing, hurting for ambient streetlight.

"Good enough," he said. I could hear it better than I could see it when he unzipped his jacket.

"What exactly are we . . ." I trailed off as he withdrew his pistol and slapped the grip into my palm. "Oh. What?"

He dropped his jacket, unstrapped his holster, peeled off his shirt, and turned away, dropping the shed items on the ground.

I eyed his pale back in the scant light. "What am I doing?"

"Shoot me. Four, five times. From where you're standing."
"With paintballs?"

"Of course with paintballs, dummy. Why? You got a crossbow stashed in your panties or something?"

I sighed noisily at his tone.

"C'mon. Right in the back."

The pain part I understood. The rest . . . Was I supposed to be blowing off steam or something? Or did he think this was somehow easier for me than whacking him with a belt? Would this keep him hard long enough for us to fuck on the damp forest floor?

"I can hear you thinking, cupcake. Just shoot me."

"I'll try. Is the safety on, or . . . ?"

"You think I bother with the safety?"

I held the Glock the way I guessed I was supposed to, unnerved by how heavy it was, how much like an actual gun it felt. I'd seen a couple pistols in real life, left on bad people's coffee tables in shitty apartments I'd found myself in, searching for Vicodin. But I'd never touched one. I'd certainly never shot anyone, and paintballs felt as scary as bullets to this violence virgin.

"Let's go," he said, waving an impatient hand. "It's fucking freezing out here."

"Don't bully me," I said, too quiet to sound very stern. But I'd said it, which was something. Really something.

I steadied my breath. I took aim, murmuring "Okay" as a warning, and with a fearful heart, I squeezed the trigger.

The shot was loud. Not as loud as a real gun, I didn't think, but enough for me to fear the cops might be getting called. Loud enough for me to suddenly realize this must be illegal and to wonder if I'd get caught and wreck my chances with Lani.

"Good job. Three more," Badger said, sounding pleasantly pained. His breathing was heavy now. I could hear it from ten paces.

I stared at the white burst I'd left on his shoulder blade, bright despite the darkness, feeling vaguely proud of my marksmanship. No time to think, as my head was already fabricating phantom siren wails. I took aim and shot him again, dead center.

"Fuck. Shit, you're good at—"

Another shot, another swear. I had to admit, assaulting him was fun. Payback for the discomfort I'd undergone to please him, and for the welt he'd left on my thigh with this very gun—

Oh, wait. Okay. I got it. I got what we were doing here.

I squeezed off a fourth shot, hitting him right in the armpit.

"Shit. Good work. That was—fuck!"

I'd given him a fifth shot, for good measure. I felt like twirling the pistol on my finger, but knowing my luck, I'd shoot my own eyeball out. I held it by the warm barrel instead.

He pulled the towel from his belt loop and walked up to me, holding it out. I got the paint thoroughly smeared and dried, if not actually cleaned off, and he deemed it good enough and replaced his clothes. He sucked a mean breath as he shrugged into his jacket, his holster strap clearly finding one of the bumps.

We aimed ourselves toward civilization, me alert and paranoid, listening for warnings, scanning every car that passed along the Arborway for police lights. I attempted to engage Badger in conversation to take my mind off my delusions.

"Well, that was a first for me," I said.

"You're a natural."

I let the compliment bounce around my chest. "Maybe I should get a garter derringer for my costume, then. Do you do your . . . patrol, I guess, any differently on Halloween? Do you go up to Salem or anything? Where the real chaos is?"

"I take Halloween off."

"Really? It's such a drinking holiday now. All those annoying people, just asking to get paintballed."

"Not my scene."

"Do you hand out candy with your grandma?" I teased.

"Nope. She hates kids, anyhow. They remind her of her ungrateful grandchildren."

I smirked. "Does she count you among them?"

"I know you know," he said. "That she's not really my grandmother."

I held my tongue, unsure if he was upset about that fact.

"She keeps the lights off all night on Halloween," he concluded after a brief silence.

"Do you get to scare the shit out of anyone who eggs or TPs her house?"

"I just stay in my room."

"Oh." I let it go, since he was being evasive. And he'd told me plenty of horrible stuff with no hesitation, no filter, so if he didn't want to share, he must really not want to share.

"I loved Halloween when I was a little kid," I said. "I

liked being scared, especially from the horror movies they play that time of year, and the specials. Especially the Garfield special. But I think that went away the same time I started getting nauseous on carnival rides. Now scared is, like, the last thing I want to feel."

"I can't remember the last time I felt scared." His voice sounded far away.

"No, I bet you can't. Not with your hobbies."

"I think scared was probably the only thing I *did* feel, from when I was five until I was eight or nine. I think I must have just used it up. Or sealed it over. Then when the scab fell off when I was twelve or so, there just wasn't any fear left in me. Like it had fermented to rage inside me someplace, under the crust." He dug in his pants pocket, coming out with a cigarette and a lighter.

I frowned. "You don't even feel scared of, like, stupid stuff? Like snakes or loud noises or heights?"

I sensed him shaking his head in my periphery, heard and smelled it as he lit his cigarette and blew the first drag behind him.

"I got triggers, I guess," he said. "There's certain things I *think* I'm supposed to be afraid of, except like I said, it's all rage now. Those suck, since usually when the rage kicks in, it's a person who's pissed me off, so, easy—shoot them. But when it's an object or a smell or a sound, it short-circuits something, and I'll have a little mental breakdown, with no one to attack. Like a boiling pot with the lid on too tight to let the steam out."

"Can I ask what sorts of things trigger you?"

He took another drag. "It all goes back to the shit I went

through when I was little, when I was getting bounced around to a different house every six months."

"Ah."

"Froot Loops," he said. "That's a bad one."

My instinct was to laugh, but I stifled it, knowing it wasn't just rude—it was naive, because some awful explanation was surely coming. "Really?"

"Oh, yeah. If I smell that combination of milk and fake fruit flavor . . . Sherbet does it. Sometimes yogurt. I smell that, and my mind just goes blood red."

"Because of something that happened to you?"

"The first guy that fucked with me, if I got Froot Loops for breakfast, I knew some bad shit was going to happen later that day. Took my kid brain maybe four times to figure out that if I was getting a treat in the morning for being a good boy, I'd be paying for it by the time I went to bed that night."

My belly clenched. "That's awful." I'd definitely never look at Froot Loops the same way again.

"Masks freak me the fuck out, too."

We crossed the street and passed a small group of teens, an annoying reminder that he and I weren't the only people on earth. One of them asked Badger, "You got any more smokes, dude?"

"No, I don't. Thanks for offering." He extended an empty hand, but the kids just looked perplexed, then walked on.

"That's why you hate Halloween?" I asked once their voices faded. "Masks?"

"Oh, yeah. Doesn't matter what it's a mask of, either.

Just have to see that creepy-ass gap between the eye-holes and the person's actual eyes, and I start shaking, wanting to hurt somebody. And it's not like the cereal, since there's a person behind every mask. I don't want to risk attacking some poor little kid dressed as Spiderman or some shit."

"Do you think you really would?"

He shrugged. "I never have, but it's not a chance I'm willing to take. I don't trust myself any more than you probably trust me. After the choking and all that."

I'm sure I *shouldn't* have trusted him as much as I did, but oh well. "Can I ask why masks make you that way? Or maybe I don't want to know."

"Maybe not."

I took a deep breath. "What happened?"

"I don't remember a ton of it, but somewhere out there, there's probably still an old-school videotape of me getting raped by a fifty-year-old man wearing a kid's Kermit the Frog mask. You know, for anonymity. *His* anonymity, anyhow. Since who gave a shit about mine?" His voice had gone liquid-nitrogen cold, turning me brittle. "Or maybe there's, like, a hundred copies of it. Maybe I'm on the fucking Internet by now."

"Jesus, that's . . . Shit, that's creepy."

"Yeah, it is. Ruined the Muppets for me. And Halloween in general." He took a final drag, then snuffed his butt out on the ground.

Why *Kermit?* He was always my favorite. And why were we talking about this terrible stuff when the entire point of the evening had presumably been so we could have sex? I sure as hell wasn't in the mood. Still, I wanted to hear everything. I wanted to know this man, even if it meant carrying around this sickening knowledge. Plus, I hoped maybe it helped him, made his burden a little lighter. Or maybe I still just wanted to feel special.

"The people who did all that awful stuff to you," I said after a couple blocks' silence. "Are they still around? Did you get anyone locked up?"

"I didn't, no. I had nobody to tell. I didn't know telling was even an option. It was just the world I lived in. And by the time I was twelve or thirteen and puberty and hormones turned me from a traumatized little kid into a walking rage bomb, and I knew I should've done something, it was too late."

"Why, because of statutes or whatever?"

"Nah. Two of the three guys who'd done shit to me were dead by then. One of lung cancer, one of being a fat old alcoholic cunt. Oh yeah, that's another thing I can't fucking handle—smelling liquor on anyone's breath."

"What about the third guy?"

"He was in prison, for doing what he did to me to some other kid."

"Oh, good. That he got caught, I mean."

"I always hated his wife even more than him. He was the third guy who got to me, and compared to the first two, he was a walk in the park. Plus, by then I didn't expect anything from men except that they'd try to fuck with me. He was par for the course. But women I still trusted. Except this guy's wife totally knew what he was up to, but she pretended she didn't. She walked in on shit two or three times, just turned around like she'd forgotten something in another room."

"Did you ever confront her?"

"Yeah. When I was about fourteen and heard he'd got put away, I went over there. I don't even know why. Maybe I wanted to know if she'd apologize to me. Maybe to cuss her out. I dunno. I asked her about him getting sent away, and she got all pale and shaky and said she couldn't believe anyone could have done that to him, lied and said he was a pedophile. And I got pissed and said something like, 'You knew he did that to me. You *knew*,' and she just, like, broke. She didn't admit it, but it was like something in her head split open, like whatever denial looks like in your brain, a wall or whatever, it just crumbled. She told me to leave or she'd call the cops, and I think she'd given me a glass of water or soda or something, and I know I smashed it on her floor and yelled a bunch of shit, who knows what."

"Yikes."

"And I was so fucking angry. She'd been my foster mom, was all I could keep thinking. She'd asked somebody if she could take care of me. Maybe just for a check, but she'd fucking *asked* for me. I'd never had a good mother figure, ever, but I knew moms were supposed to just be like, the shit, you know? That's how they were on TV and in movies."

"Right."

"I was way angrier at her for not being a good substitute mom than I was at her husband for being what I figured all men were—sick fuckers. So I went back that night and spray painted the front of her white house with black paint. I think I wrote, 'I let my husband fuck little boys' in letters about two feet tall, right across the door and the windows and everything. I ended up going to juvie for that, but it was worth it."

We turned down my street and crossed the laundromat parking lot. "Was that your first act as a vigilante?"

As I unlocked the door, I watched his face in the foyer's yellow light. His expression told me he'd never thought about it before.

"Maybe," he said quietly. "That just might've been the first time I realized how good it felt to punish people."

17

Upstairs, I tossed my coat over a chair in my now too-warm apartment and looked to Badger. To Isaac.

"You still want me here?" he asked, toying with his zipper pull.

I nodded.

He shed his jacket. "I better use your shower so I don't get paint on your sheets."

Right, of course. I'd been so drunk from the conversation, I'd forgotten the circumstances of our entire outing. "Go for it."

He did, calling to me after the water had been running for a minute or two. I left the bed and TV and went to the bathroom. "Yeah?"

"I get it all?" he asked me, tugging the shower curtain open.

His body looked as threatening as ever in the bright lights. The lashes I'd given him were gone, but five perfect welts glowed angry and red, two on his shoulder blade, on the back of his bicep, just to the right of his spine, and one at the base of his neck. I rubbed at a few patches of lingering white paint, marveling at the bizarreness of our courtship. I touched the lump at the center of his back, just a faint graze. He sucked a harsh breath through his teeth.

"Good?" I asked.

"Yeah, perfect. Nice job."

He turned around, and I beat a hasty retreat, uncomfortable with his full-frontalness while I was still dressed. He didn't give a shit, but I did. After what he'd shared, I wanted to run from anything that smelled even faintly of his objectification.

Soon he joined me on the bed in his jeans and T-shirt, hair wet, feet bare. He looked like somebody's boyfriend, just then. Like a normal man, if a bit meaner than the average guy. *He might be* my *boyfriend*, I thought. The label felt wrong, like calling a duck you toss bread at your pet. But he was my lover, at any rate. That was a technical fact, and I bet some really weird, delusional Boston girls would be jealous of me for it.

Sitting cross-legged at the edge of the mattress, he seemed to watch the news that was droning. I scooted forward, and impulsively, I stroked his hair. It felt so intimate, I would've cried if I'd kept doing it. I dried my palm on the bedspread.

"How do they feel?" I asked.

"Not bad, right now. But they'll do the job if you're okay with touching them." He turned to look me in the face.

"How hard?"

"Not very. That's the point."

"I know."

"So, you wanna try?"

I nodded. "Just need to pee."

I excused myself to use the toilet and brush my teeth and wipe away my ridiculous eye makeup. I wasn't afraid of what he wanted this time. It was blissfully simple, in theory. If anything, I was afraid it'd go *well*. So well I'd get pushed over the line separating Misguided Infatuation from Official Gonerdom. But better to feel stuff than to avoid it or squish it all down or medicate it. I'd learned that lesson a million times over.

When I left the bathroom, I found he'd shut off the TV and overhead light, so there was just my little forty-watt reading lamp glowing, warming his edges. He watched as I ditched my jeans and top, and I watched him in turn.

He was trying to seduce me. Or rather, he was trying to make himself into what I wanted, or what we both assumed I wanted. I could sense that this all meant something to him, and that he cared how it went. I upgraded him to boyfriend in my head, since he really did deserve it, going to all this trouble. Opening up to me, if that was what our conversation had been for him. He seemed softer tonight, and I forgave him the bullying in the woods. I took a seat beside him and rubbed his lower back, away from the minefield of welts.

I'd been thinking about him the last couple days. Thinking about him a *lot*, because of all the scary sex crap. In moments of anger and irritation, I'd fantasized about telling him what I sometimes felt was true—that his vigilante shtick was actually pretty cowardly. He didn't confront bullies, he just hit-and-ran them. But after mulling it over, I'd decided it wasn't cowardly. It was fitting. Badger's justice was impersonal and thoughtless and selfish, exactly like the crimes he avenged. He was karma on a bike. He was perfect.

I'd thought about his creepy kinks, too. At first I'd marveled what a divide it was, him being so aggressive outside, so victimized in bed. I thought it must be his release, letting himself be hurt and abused, giving himself over . . .

But no, again.

Of the two of us, I was by *far* the more put-upon person when his masochism was being indulged. Even lost in some awful abuse memory or fantasy, he was in control. He was on top. He was always steering, propelling us, me just clamped to his handlebars, trying desperately not to fall off. Me shooting him in the back, but him ordering me to. If anything, his sex-pain thing was just him getting a boner from being in control. Made sense, since he clearly spent his formative years feeling helpless.

He shot strangers for being rude, defaced their vehicles when they didn't stop for pedestrians. What, if anything, might he have done to the men who'd hurt him, if he'd had the chance? Would the third guy ever get out of prison and *give* him the chance? What on earth must Badger's justice look like when it *was* personal? I stroked his back, wondering what this man was capable of but knowing I'd probably be happier not finding out.

"What are you thinking about?" he asked.

"Lots of stuff. Lots of nothing."

"You worried about what's about to happen?"

"No." I was eager to escape from my head, frankly. Escape into my body and his, where things were simple. Relatively speaking.

He shuffled around to face me, drawing my legs over his crossed ones. Leaning close, he pressed his forehead to mine. I made my head very quiet, trying to hear his thoughts.

I sensed he was going to say something, only he didn't. It seemed he was waiting for me to initiate. I kissed his temple, missing his usual smell, replaced by my soap. I kissed his jaw. I kissed his neck and let my hand slip from his shoulder down his back, palm drifting lightly over two welts there.

His body hitched, followed by a pained *Mmmm*. A satisfied noise, like he'd had his back cracked by a chiropractor.

"You're such a weird man," I murmured.

"Too weird?"

I backed away to glance at the two of us and around the bed. "Apparently not," I said with a little smile.

"What d'you think we are?"

I shrugged, pretending the question had never occurred to me, let alone consumed me on occasion. "Lovers, I guess. What about you?"

"I dunno."

I pressed my lips to his cheek again to hide whatever emotion my face might give away. I didn't want an "I dunno." I wanted a label so very, very desperately.

"I think you're like my insulin or something," he said quietly.

"Oh?" I asked his temple.

"Yeah. I spend so much time on the brink of . . . something. Like I'm going through my life in the middle of a big, slow-mo mental breakdown. Like my body's constantly in a crisis, every second I'm awake. Then we hang out—not even hook up, just this sort of sitting around and kissing shit—and you're like a dose of something I'm missing, and I feel all . . . manageable. After."

"Oh." I liked that much more than my worrisome drug analogy. I'd much rather be fixing Badger's damage than simply papering over it. "Am I like your antidote?"

"Maybe. You cure me of myself, for a little while at a time. Except from the sex stuff."

"Yeah. But that seems like a pretty big crack to patch up. I'm not *that* magical."

"Nah. But you'll do."

We stared at each other. His eyes were dark in the dimness, too dark a shade of blue to have a name. Our faces came together so slowly, I wasn't sure who kissed whom. I held his jaw, liking the brush of his nose against mine. Liking him in spite of all the ways he upset me, or maybe because of them, because I probably needed to be shaken up more often.

For a while it was mere lips. Then I tilted my head, and he did as the gesture asked, kissing me deeper. Before long we lay down on our sides, Badger's breath catching as he lowered himself, eyes narrowing in a series of winces. I let him slide his clothed leg between my bare ones, let him kiss me for ages. I could feel him drifting away into Placid Badgerland. I circled my fingertips where I knew a welt to be, awaiting the go-ahead, that he was okay leaving the bliss behind for the darker stuff.

"Do it," he whispered.

My fingers zeroed in on the lump. I gave it the gentlest press through his T-shirt, but the effect was instantaneous. He bucked like I'd shocked him.

"Does it feel how you'd hoped?" I asked.

"Fuck, yes."

I licked my lips, then drew my nail across the spot, slow and light. He made a long, spastic noise—his pleasure, anyone else's torture.

"Good," he muttered.

"It's easy. I could do this to you by mistake, barely meaning to. Is it, you know . . . working for you?"

He pushed his leg further between mine, until I felt him through his jeans, unmistakably hard.

"Why don't you take your clothes off?" I asked.

"Sure."

When he lay down again, I put my hand to his neck, then yanked it back, my skin so much chillier than his. "Sorry."

"For what?"

"My hands are always so cold. And my feet." I pressed one playfully to his ankle.

"Yeah, 'cause I hate discomfort."

"Oh, right." I put my palm back on his bare skin. We kissed some more, and I made him wait a full minute before I touched a welt, long enough that I felt his erection go soft against the crease that joined my thigh and hip. I ran my hand over a bump and pressed.

It was *awesome*.

Like a button that sent blood flooding into his dick. If we'd done this the first time we'd fucked around, it would've freaked me out, but having gone through the horrible stuff . . . This was easy. Stalking out into the dark woods with a firearm wasn't ideal as foreplay went, but still. This was nothing.

We kissed and rubbed against each other, and I turned it into a Pavlovian mindfuck experiment. Every time he did something that felt good to me, I gave him a press. Our own screwy feedback loop.

He urged me onto my back and got his legs between mine, his cock lined up against the crotch of my undies. That earned him a nice mean scrape of my nails.

"Fuck."

"Oh, good."

"You know," he panted, "it's not just the pain. It's that you put those there."

I circled one with my fingertips.

"That's so fucking hot, that you did that to me."

I stroked the spot, a motion that to me, the giver, felt like a gentle massage, but to him stung hard as a belt slapping home.

He groaned, swore through gritted teeth. "Fuck, that's good."

"Good. It's easy. It's way easier for me."

"Great."

"Even easier if you had a silencer for that thing, so we could do the prep in my bathtub, instead of a public park."

"Yeah, sure." He wasn't really listening, and I couldn't

blame him. I was rubbing a bruise probably more erogenous to him than a clit.

"Can I . . . Should I call you Isaac?" I asked.

"No. Not during sex. Not this kind of sex. It'll cross my circuits."

"Okay."

"But other times, as long as there's not a cop standing right there, sure. Go crazy."

"And it is actually your name, isn't it?" I asked with a little smile.

He cracked one himself, a rare sight that made me woozy. "Yeah, that's my name."

I ran my hands up and down his back, idly wondering what his last name was. Wondering what I might find if I could Google him, what criminal record he might have from the decade and a half between coming into his rage and becoming the Badger, before he'd discovered the violent hobby that let him sleep at night. Like so many details about him, I decided I probably didn't want to know. I had him exactly the way I needed him most. I shouldn't waste my energy thinking so hard.

I opened my legs wider, and he did exactly what I'd hoped, planting his knees and starting to thrust. The tease of him through my underwear was better than sex itself. The anticipation better than an orgasm by miles and miles. I mean, when did anyone actually fantasize about having an orgasm? You always fantasize about the stuff leading up to it. Maybe Badger was onto something with his pursuit of pain over pleasure. When I was super horny, I felt sort of pissed off down there, aggressive and a little angry. Felt awesome. I gave his welt another poke and watched him twitch.

He looked exactly how I'd imagined when I'd come the other night in his bed, from his fingers. That scary, fascinating body above mine, muscle and bone casting shadows from the reading lamp, those broody eyes, and fucking hell, his cock—hard.

"I want you," I muttered.

"You got condoms?"

"Yeah." I reached to open my bedside table drawer, got one ready while he wrestled my panties down my legs.

"I haven't been this hot in ages." His gaze bored straight through my eyes and brain, probably searing a hole in the pillow. "Except the other night, when I took you too far into what I like. So you need to tell me if I get too rough or creepy or intense, okay?"

"Sure." No guarantee that he'd stop, but I trusted that yes, this time I'd be able to tell him.

He reached for the condom, and I recorded the flex of his arms as he pinched the tip and slid it down his length. He lowered, bracing himself above me. I circled one of his welts—gently, teasing—then gave it a press, just to keep him stoked.

"Fuck."

He slid inside me, quick and deep, my body offering no resistance. He held there. I stopped torturing him, caught up in recording the moment. When I felt him wilting, I reached around and zapped the lump at the center of his back, and there he was, hard in an instant. Jumper cables.

"Gimme another hit."

I dug my nails into his tender skin, and he ground his body against mine, rough and dirty.

We spent a few minutes finding a messy rhythm, and I discovered the perfect strategy. I kept my left hand on his back—lightly, so when he withdrew from each thrust, it brought the welt right against my fingers, our two bodies a perpetual fucking machine. My right hand was free to do what I wanted it to, and what I wanted to do was touch myself and prove I could come while having sex. But what I wanted to do slightly more was *not* touch myself, since I'd never done that in front of anyone. Instead I watched our point of penetration, getting more and more wound up.

"How do I get you off?" he asked, so aroused it sounded like a threat of bodily harm.

"I could touch myself," I said.

"Do it."

Thank God for an order. I reached nervously between us, but the second I'd done it—been seen by another human being with my fingers on my clit—I got over myself.

My brace was off, my wrist only very faintly tender. I rubbed myself and watched him, watched the live, screwed-up porn I'd never even known I favored before this week. He propped himself on one arm and hovered the other hand above my breast, just glancing my nipple with his warm, raspy palm. *Zing zing zing* went my internal sex circuits, flashing and chiming like a pinball machine.

There wasn't a question that I'd come. The question suddenly became, how could I put off coming so this didn't have to end? Everything felt too good, looked too good. His moans sounded too good, his skin and our collective sex smelled too good. I came so hard, it didn't even feel nice—it hurt. But wasn't that poetry in itself?

He stilled above me, and as I floated down from my high I swept my palm idly across his back, keeping him hard. I was excited to watch him come and see him rip apart above me. Not before me on his knees, not beneath me with my hand clamped to his windpipe. Above me, the one in obvious control. Perhaps *far* above me . . .

Through my recuperative panting I said, "I'd like to . . . go down on you. If you're okay with that. Or do you not like people doing things—"

"You're thinking too hard again. If you wanna suck my cock, be my guest."

"I would."

"Here." He scooted back, leaning against the headboard, ditching the condom. My bed had a cheap frame made of painted metal tubing. I watched Badger adjusting, getting some welt or other aligned with a rung. He reached out and grasped the end posts, looking like Christ, muscly and passive, awaiting my worship or punishment. He looked obscene as well, in the best way. Soft black hair between his legs, flushed skin, ready flesh. I dropped to my hip and elbow and took him in my hand. He smelled good. And cock had never smelled good to me before. He smelled male and wild and . . . angry.

"Tell me what you like," I said, then lowered my mouth to him. He sighed, a perfect, filthy sound. He tasted nice, not as potent as he smelled, a touch sour from the rubber and its lube. He tasted just how he should—like fucking, not romance.

"Lemme feel your teeth," he murmured. "You don't have to hurt me, just let me feel them."

I gave him the faintest graze, trying to gauge what I was comfortable with myself. But any intimidation I felt dissolved the second his moan reached my ears. Power. That was what I tasted in the wake of the nerves. The power to make him feel good in his unorthodox way, and the power to overrule my own noisy brain and just *do*. Trust him, and trust us, and trust his ages-old relationship with pain instead of taking notes and drawing assumptions from my judgments and insecurities.

I felt the sweet, dirty weight of his hand on my head, his fingers trembling in my hair. "Yeah."

It lit me up to know he felt good from what I was doing. And liberating to know he could experience sexual excitement without acting out some victimization scenario.

"Fuck. Good."

The trembling turned to coaxing, gentle requests I gladly granted, taking him deeper, sucking harder and giving him the occasional graze of my teeth. I'd never enjoyed this act, not for more than a fleeting moment, and those typically only when I'd felt I was doing a good old sexy *Cosmo*-worthy job of it, more relief than pleasure. But this was all different. I'd asked for it. And it was infinitely easier than hitting him. This thing I'd always dreaded was suddenly so simple. Piece of cake. Piece of freaky, slightly fucked-up cake. Delicious.

"Suck me. Please."

I did as he asked, caught off guard each time he angled his back, savaged his injuries, and thrashed.

He might've been thinking . . . Well, I didn't need to know what. Something that kept him hard, if the pain wasn't enough. I didn't care if it was me in his head anymore. It was me here in reality. My mouth, my patience, my willingness.

His hand left my head to hold his cock, his thumb and first finger wrapping tight around his base. Tighter than I'd ever have done for him. Soon I felt his blood pounding against my lips, his skin hot and swollen. His hand shook faintly, and his breath was stilted and shallow. Wrong and scary and goddamn hot.

"Fuck. Please . . . Please."

I strained to stare up at him as his entire body shook, back arching against the headboard, hand clamped tight to his cock, the other rubbing frantically at his throat, back and forth, back and forth. A moan rose from him, so deep I felt it humming in his belly. He bucked beneath me, hips seeking my mouth or his back seeking pain. Then—

"Adrian."

Some swearing, some grunting, but I was stuck on my name, caught like a sweater on a nail, two and a half syllables pinging around in my ears and head. When he came, I swore I was coming myself, lost in some non-physical orgasm deep in my brain or wherever emotions live. Triumphant, I tasted him, a flavor I'd almost forgotten, vulgar and sweet.

I held him in my mouth until he went completely still, then swallowed and relocated beside him, my back against the headboard, only our hips touching. It seemed cold suddenly, but I didn't care. I felt awake. Vibrant. Violently conscious.

He cleared his throat. "That was . . ." Something overcame him, and I waited patiently while he found his words or his breath.

"That was the most normal sex I've ever had. The most normal sex I've had and actually managed to come, I mean." He stared straight ahead as he said it, and his tone told me it wasn't a tease or a good-natured slight against himself. He was shocked, barely believing what he was saying. He was in awe, something I'd never imagined him capable of experiencing. Such a quiet, reverent emotion.

"I'm glad," I murmured.

He turned to me, shifting to nuzzle my neck. The position made it awkward, so I urged him to join me in lying down. When we did, his face found my throat again, pure bliss. A long, hot exhalation steamed against my skin.

"Are you okay?" I asked.

"I'm . . . I'm confused. And surprised. And happy, I think. I'm not sure. I don't remember what happy feels like."

I had to smile at that. "Well. Good." I stroked his hair and tried to downplay what I was feeling myself—rising, soaring euphoria. Love, God help me. Or the closest I'd ever felt to it.

Lying there with Badger, or Isaac, it looked nothing like my parents' steady, companionable love, or like Amanda's easy romance with Derek, like nothing I'd ever seen in a movie or read about in a book. It was homely and broken and faulty, and wonderful.

Then I felt something extraordinary. I felt Isaac's breathing go shallow and slow, his body turning heavy and slack as he fell asleep against me.

I didn't care if my pinned arm went numb or I got no rest that entire night. I only wanted him to stay where he was, content against me. Spent and careless. I grazed my hand over his head for ages, taking in the subtle, personal smell of his hair and scalp and breath.

In time I nodded off, a fretful rest disrupted easily and often as reality intruded, but each interruption reminded me of the wondrous, wonky man adrift against me.

I woke in dozy fits, and a deep melancholy overtook me now and then as I wondered who she'd been. Isaac's mother. What woman had let this boy go, into the hands that had abused him beyond my comprehension?

Whoever she was, I wanted to hurt her. And I never wanted to hurt *anyone*. Only opiate withdrawal had ever made me want to physically attack and injure another person. That, and now this. This warm, damaged man, who'd arrived in this fleeting state of peace by nothing short of a miracle. The attachment I was feeling surely made him no better for me than another fix.

But then again, he felt so very, very good.

18

The next morning, I woke first. It took me a second to figure out why my arm was numb. It was Badger's arm, it turned out, curled around my middle. Mystery solved, I relaxed back against his warm body. It was Sunday, I realized. I was having dinner with my family, and I would tell them about my new job.

I wondered what I'd do if Badger magically asked me to do something with him that evening. Would I blow off my folks to be with him? I hoped not, but I wasn't honestly sure. One thing was certain—I couldn't invite him along.

Through the cracks beside the blinds, I saw it was just growing light.

Oh, shit.

I slipped from his arms and shook his shoulder. He made a sour face, one so adorable I thought I'd explode, and then his eyes opened, blinking.

"I think it's pushing seven," I said, aiming my breath away from his face.

"Oh, shit."

"Your bacon's going to burn."

"Yeah, and my grandma's going to assume the worst."

"Don't get grounded," I teased, but he was already up and searching for his clothes.

After the sex—the relatively normal sex—this wasn't how I'd pictured our parting going. I'd hoped it would feel softer, maybe tender, maybe hesitant or nervous. I'd envisioned more cuddling, that was for sure.

I studied his welts as he dressed, hoping he'd think of me when they pained him. Christ, what weird romance was this that I'd gotten myself tangled in?

I tugged on corduroys and a sweater while he was using the bathroom, then tailed him when he strode past to the kitchen to get his shoes on.

"Thanks for coming over last night," I said.

"Sure. Thanks for having me." Not the poetry I'd been hoping for, but I had to remind myself who exactly I was trying to flirt with.

"I guess I'll see you sometime."

He finished strapping on his holster and looked me in the eyes. "Guess so."

Kiss me, I thought. *Give me a sign that it's okay to get my hopes up and blow this all out of proportion.*

"I'm out of town tonight, having dinner with my family," I said.

"Good for you." He zipped his hoodie and held his handlebars, staring at me a long moment.

"Yes?"

"Can you get the doors for me?"

A psychic shoulder slump. "Sorry, sure."

We trundled down the steps and into the damp, cold morning air.

"Ride safe. Tell your grandma hello."

He nodded and slung a leg over his crossbar. "You take care."

I waved as he rode away, faking cheerfulness with every fiber of my being.

∘ ∘ ∘

I was over the angst by the afternoon. Mostly.

I toggled between a few defensive explanations for my anti-boyfriend's coldness. He wasn't a morning person . . . though he'd been borderline playful that other morning in his own room. Maybe he didn't like waking up in other people's beds. Maybe he really had been stressed out about being late for breakfast, worrying his fake grandmother. Whatever. Could be any or all of those things.

My phone blooped at four forty-something, and I set down the iron I'd been using to press a dress shirt for work—*ooh, work*—the next day. I tugged the cord from the wall and nabbed my phone from the bed, checking the text from Amanda. *Downstairs when you're ready.* I texted her back that I'd just be a couple minutes. I changed into a dress and cardigan and boots, grabbed my purse, and locked the apartment behind me.

She smiled and flashed her high beams when I emerged from the building, and I waved as I pulled the door shut. I jogged over and plopped into the passenger seat. We gave each other a half hug, and she started the engine.

"Sorry to rush you. The appointment was really quick."

"No rush at all. How do they look? The invitations?"

She stopped at the lot's exit and offered me a look, a grin of dopey, ridiculous happiness.

"That good?"

"They're so awesome. And it feels extra real now," she added, turning us into traffic.

"Can't wait to get mine in the mail."

She laughed. "Yeah, right. You're going to help me address them, sucker. You won't want to see another 'antique cream' embossed envelope ever again in your whole life by the time I'm finished with you."

"When's that happening?"

"I was hoping I might con you into a sleepover the weekend after Thanksgiving."

"Cool. Sounds fun."

We were quiet until she merged into the bustle of Centre Street. "So. What have you been up to? Oh, look what I bought." She nodded toward the back seat, and I contorted myself to peek in a paper shopping bag.

"Champagne?"

"Sparkling cider. To toast you at dinner."

"Aw, thanks, sis." I pursed my lips to suppress an urge to start blubbering. Who in the heck was I these days?

"You excited about starting tomorrow?" Amanda asked.

"Kind of, yeah. More excited to have some income on the horizon."

"I'll bet. What else is happening?"

"Found my Halloween costume. Are you going to Mom and Dad's this year?"

"Oh, yeah. Wouldn't miss it. What's your costume?"

"Flapper. Or, like, glamorous Twenties Hollywood woman."

"Ooh, good one."

"You should see my dress. It's like a goth exploded in a sequin factory."

She laughed.

Suddenly my mouth came out with, "I've been sort of seeing someone. Sort of."

I watched her blinking madly, eyes on the cars ahead of us but clearly wishing she could shoot me a look. "Really?"

"No, not really. Just sort of."

The light ahead of us turned red, and she finally got a chance to stare at me, an excited little mischievous smile curling her pretty lips, which required no lipstick to look that pink. Lips not included in my DNA.

"Wow," she said. "Where'd you meet him?"

"Just around. Downtown."

"What's his name?"

Was there harm in telling her? Unlikely. "Isaac."

"Ooh, Adrian and Isaac . . ." The light turned green.

"Don't get excited. He's not my boyfriend. He's weird, so I'm not holding my breath that he's up for anything as normal as a boyfriend-girlfriend scenario. Which I'm probably not ready for, anyway."

"What does he do?"

Oh, fuck. "He's, um . . . It's complicated."

"What, unemployed?"

"Not exactly. He's in . . . law enforcement. Kind of."

"Kind of. Sort of," she teased. "Did you meet him at camp? Does he live in Canada, so I can't meet him?"

"Shush. He lives in Somerville, with his grandmother. He's a bicycle enthusiast."

"Lives with his grandma? That's sort of cute."

"'Cute' isn't really the right adjective for their relationship. Anyhow, I'm seeing him. Ish. But he's tough to get a handle on. Like I hung out with him last night, and it was really nice. And sort of natural. Sort of romantic, and he's not a romantic guy. Then this morning he was different. Grumpy and short. Not quite rude, but . . . cold."

"Well, he's a guy. How long have you been seeing him?"

"Jeez . . . I've been seeing him regularly for maybe two weeks."

She snorted. "Well, of course he's being all hard to read. Guys always do that when they're not sure where things are going with a girl. He's probably starting to have feelings for you but doesn't know how to feel about it. Derek did that to me."

"Yeah?"

"Sure. Some guys are scared of feeling stuff strongly, or getting attached to people. He's probably just spooked. If he really likes you, he'll get over it."

Huh. He certainly was a strong candidate for having issues with feeling stuff or letting himself get attached. "Maybe. But he's not like a normal guy."

"So you said. How so?"

Oh damn, why'd I invite that question? Maybe because I was aching to talk to someone about Badger. "He's just . . . There's no way to explain it without making him sound unstable."

"Is he unstable?" She shot me another look, a leery one.

"Kind of. But not how you're thinking—he doesn't do drugs. He doesn't even drink. He's just emotionally . . . I dunno. He's intense."

"Intense like passionate artist, or intense like stalker?"

"Neither. It's hard to explain."

"Clearly." She edged us into the chaos of Route 9.

"But I like him." I held my breath as I realized what I was about to say and how true it was. Exhale. "I like him more than I've ever liked anyone."

"I can tell."

"But he's so weird, I don't think I should bother hoping it'll turn into anything normal. Or 'real,' if that makes any sense."

"Is he, like, emotionally unavailable?"

"Not even that. I'm sure this is going to sound really dumb, but it'd be like trying to date an animal. I think he likes me and cares about me, at least on a sort of primal, gut level."

"Okay . . ."

"He says stuff sometimes that makes me think he really likes me, in his own way. But it really would be hard to make something out of it. Oh, wait. Here. It'd be like dating a homeless person."

Yet another face.

"Exactly. And as sad as my life is—"

"Ade."

"Shush. As sad as my life's gotten in the last three years, I'm still a part of regular society. He's more of an outlier."

"What are you talking about?" she asked with a confused laugh. "Are you leaving something major out of this explanation? Oh my God! He's incarcerated, isn't he? Doesn't drink? He's *kind of in law enforcement?*"

My turn to laugh. "No, he's not in prison. He lives with his grandma, remember? But that's a good analogy, too,

I guess. He's just . . . It's not an option." Saying it solidified the fact in my mind, a reality check I'd been needing.

Funnily enough, it didn't make me sad. I couldn't picture Badger as a part of any normal-ish life I might enjoy, and I didn't want to. Domestication would ruin everything I liked about him. I wanted a stray, when I thought about it. Not a pet. Not even a rescue pet. I'd just keep putting food out for him and enjoy his companionship when it graced my stoop.

"Sounds very interesting," Amanda said.

"That's a word for it." *Try also: perplexing, exciting, ill-advised, ridiculous, orgasmic . . .* "But don't tell Mom and Dad. I know that whatever it is, it's good for me. But if I try to explain it to them, they'll just infer all kinds of red flags. I want to let them enjoy the job news."

"Good idea."

"But thanks for listening. I haven't had a chance to talk to anyone about it yet."

She glanced at me and bit her lip.

"What? The sex?"

She nodded rapidly, such a dork. "Yeah. How's the sex with this mystery man?"

"It's, um, kinda freaky."

"Freaky how?"

"No comment. It's just freaky."

She sang me a couple bars of "Superfreak" until we both started giggling.

"Trust me," I concluded, and switched on the radio. "You don't want the details."

o o o

We made it to Lincoln earlier than we were expected, and as the car crunched down my parents' long gravel drive, I was excited to be home. Early meant we'd get assigned jobs in preparing dinner, which I'd always loved. I hoped I'd get to whip the potatoes. My dad had always said I did that job better than anyone. Plus, I'd get to lick the beaters.

Wiggy, my parents' ancient cocker spaniel, came tottering around from the back of the house, and we paused to rub her ears at the front step. Amanda rang the bell, and I sniffed my hand. "Jeez, she stinks worse every time I come home."

"I know," Amanda said quietly, as though Wiggy might overhear and have her feelings hurt. "And she's incontinent now, apparently."

"Ew." I wiped my fingers on the siding.

The inside door opened, and my dad's broad frame filled our view. He scowled at us like we were Jehovah's Witnesses.

"We don't want any," he said through the glass.

We pouted mightily, as we always did. It felt nice to be back to these dopey routines. So nice I felt tears welling.

Amanda pulled the door open, and my dad stepped aside to let us in. My mom set upon us, and hugs were roundly exchanged.

"When's Derek getting here?" I asked Amanda.

"Any time now."

Damn. I'd been hoping maybe he couldn't make it. Not that I didn't think he was a good guy. Before all the Vicodin stuff, we used to make each other laugh. Since then . . . Well, I was guilty until proven innocent, in Derek's book. He wasn't suspicious, not quite, but skeptical. He kept me at arm's length these days. Literally. We didn't hug anymore, possibly because he was worried I might use the opportunity to pick his pocket.

"You both look great," my mother said, rubbing her hands together like we were on tonight's menu. "Especially you, Ade. You've got a real glow about you."

"Well, it's cold out."

Amanda shot me a meaningful glance. I shot one back that said, *Ix-nay on the oyfriend-bay.* She rolled her eyes, and we followed my parents toward the kitchen and attached dining room.

My dad had the Patriots game on in the den, and he stood in the threshold, half watching it, half pretending to listen to us.

"Smells great in here," I said, breathing in that awesome roast-aroma. I spotted the boiled potatoes, steaming in their sieve in the sink. "I call potato duty." I got to work with the butter and pepper while Amanda fished a sample wedding invitation from her purse to show us. "It'll be trimmed, obviously."

"Oh, it's so elegant," my mom said.

"But not *too* elegant," I concurred. "Not snobby." I tried to imagine my own invitations, in some totally fucked alternate universe. *Samuel and Shirley Birch request the honor of your presence at the wedding of their daughter, ex-con recovering pill addict Adrian Birch, to vigilante sociopath Isaac . . . something or other. Please RSVP.*

The chime of the doorbell tore me from the thought.

"I can't believe he still rings the bell," my mother said as Amanda jogged off to fetch her fiancé. I imagined Badger standing there in his place. *Guess who's coming to dinner!*

Amanda reappeared with Derek in tow, and we exchanged polite smiles.

"Hey, Adrian. You look nice."

"Thanks, Derek. You look very pretty yourself." That won me a smirk, a tiny taste of our old levity. Good. Maybe my big news over dinner would snowball the diplomacy.

"What needs doing?" Amanda asked our mom.

"Ooh . . . Shave carrots for the salad, please."

"On it. Dad's watching the game," Amanda said to Derek, who was wearing a Pats tee, and she gave him a nudge of permission to leave the women to their cooking.

Jeez, what would Badger do in Derek's position? I couldn't imagine him watching football with my dad. Or volunteering to help with the meal. Maybe he'd go out back and stick a rag in his teeth and play tug-of-war with Wiggy. She'd like that. And she'd been a part of the family *way* longer than Derek. Her opinion mattered as much as his.

"So what's been going on, honey?" my mother asked.

I glanced up to make sure she meant me. "Oh, stuff. I have some news, actually, but I'll save it for dinner."

"News? Like job news or romantic news . . . ?"

"You have to *wait*, Mom," Amanda said, then added haughtily, "unlike some of us."

"You two forget that the womb you shared belongs to me," my mom said, pretending to be cross. "I shouldn't have to be kept in the dark like the men around here."

I wrecked her chances at grilling me further by switching on the noisy electric beaters, and we sat down to dinner at six thirty.

"So," my mom said, passing me the salad bowl. "Adrian has news, or so I'm told."

My dad's brows rose. "Oh?"

I nodded, doling lettuce onto my plate. "I, um, got a job. I start tomorrow morning."

Dad dropped his fork with a clatter, for dramatic effect. "Honey, that is fan-*tastic* news."

"Oh, Adrian!" My mother clapped.

"Yeah, congratulations," Derek said, sounding perfectly genuine, if mildly surprised.

"What kind of job?" my mom asked.

"Copywriting, and maybe a little bit of graphic design, like package concepts. It's for a luxury cosmetics company in Brookline. It's not the most satisfying work, writing ad copy to sell rich people face cream—"

My dad waved his fork around. "This is no economy to get idealistic in, Adrian."

"I know, I know. That's why I took it. But it's full-time, in-house, with good benefits and a pretty okay salary. More than I made at that ad agency."

"Well, that is just wonderful news, honey," my mom said, all glowy, which made me glowy. "If I'd known, I'd have made a good dessert instead of that store-bought pie."

"Oh, wait." Amanda left the table to fetch the sparkling cider from her car. A minute later wine glasses were found and there was a pop, and suddenly we were toasting me. The five of us hadn't toasted since Amanda and Derek's engagement, and it felt nice to be the daughter having a fuss made of her. Made me feel fizzy and special, like the cider.

"You guys are doing Halloween, right? Trick-or-treaters and all that?" I asked.

"If we didn't, we'd get egged into lower property values," my dad said.

"Did you want to come this year?" Mom asked, clearly in favor of such an idea.

"Yeah, I would."

"You know we're always happy to have you," she said.

Almost always, I amended, then caught myself being gloomy and gave myself a kick in the ankle.

The rest of dinner passed way too quickly, interrupted now and then when my dad or Derek jumped up to see why the football fans on TV in the next room were cheering. A big deal was made of me, enough that I began to feel embarrassed. I steered the topic to wedding plans, which carried us through dessert and coffee. All too soon Amanda and I were bundling into her cold car in the dark . . . though I was warm inside, a sensation I wasn't used to taking with me, leaving my parents' place. Not in recent years.

"Sorry you have to drive me all the way back," I said as I buckled my seatbelt. "The next train's not until ten thirty."

She craned her neck, backing us down the driveway. "Shush. Even if there was a train right now, after you mess around on the subway it'll be, like, ten by the time you get home. And I'm sure you need your beauty sleep."

Yes, sleep. Because I was bound to rest so easily, with my first day looming and, no doubt, the business of lying awake wondering if Badger might turn up and prove to me that his brusque departure had been an exception, not the rule.

"I hope . . ." I stopped myself.

"You hope what?"

"I hope Derek will forgive me, sometime. If I keep *not* screwing up, you know?"

"He's forgiven you already."

"I dunno about that. But in any case, I wonder if he'll ever start treating me like he used to, when you guys were first dating."

She sighed, neither annoyed nor despairing, just tired. "He knew the old you—the *real* you—for maybe six months, before everything happened. Then he knew Mr. Hyde for two years. Give him time. He'll get to hang out with the real you again, and just like the other you eclipsed his good impressions, the new good impressions will eclipse the bad stuff."

"Maybe."

"Just be patient, and go easy on yourself."

"It must be stressful," I said glumly. "Having to defend me all the time. That must be exhausting."

"Oh God, no. I could defend you all day long and never get tired."

I smiled at that, unseen in the darkness.

"And it's not like he's ever made me feel like I had to choose a side. If he had, I'd have told him it wasn't an option."

"You were way too good to me, back when I was a psycho."

"You were never a *psycho*, Ade. You were addicted to painkillers. It can happen to anyone, scary as that is."

"Still."

"Well, of course I was good to you. How were you going

to get better if all you had to come home to when you got clean was a bunch of angry jerks making you feel bad?"

"Enabler," I teased.

"I was not. Mom was the enabler. She let you live with her."

"Yeah, true."

She laughed, a sad little noise. "Imagine if we'd had an intervention."

"Oh, God. That would've ruined the living room for me. How humiliating."

"We would've done it, though, if we had to. We talked about it."

I shuddered at the thought. How god-awful humbling. "Getting roughed up by a Macy's security guard was all the rock bottom I needed to hit. I really ought to figure out who that was and send him a thank-you note."

"Actually, you should. An early Christmas card, when you get your one-year chip. Who knows—if things don't work out with your abnormal non-boyfriend, maybe you'll hit it off."

"Yeah, right." Still, it was a nice idea, sending a note. Awfully nice.

19

No Badger that night, no shock. I waited up, but not for ages. I needed sleep, after all. I had someplace to be in the morning.

My first day at work was sort of a throwaway. I was set up in my very own office, of all things, with a computer and printer and window, and I passed the morning figuring out the e-mail system and flipping through our existing catalogs and other promo materials. Then Lani took everyone out for a lazy, gossipy two-hour lunch.

There were only four people in the office—me, Lani, Dana the front desk girl, and a nearly mute fiftysomething named Sandy who was our accountant-slash-HR person.

After lunch I spent a couple hours brainstorming product names with Lani—more an exercise than a vital assignment, but it was okay. *I* was okay. I had a job.

The day after was a more typical workday. I got my first real assignment, writing catalog copy for a line of body mist stuff, six different smells—sorry, six different *infusions*—that Lani lined up on my desk so that I might sniff them and infuse my senses, and hence infuse a Word doc with elegant prose designed to sell them for seventy dollars a bottle.

Mainly they infused me with an almighty headache, and instead of hiding inside my now pungent office, I ventured outside in search of lunch.

Two doors down from our office was a deli that did sandwiches and pasta salad and things like that. I pushed the door in with a jingle and looked around. New places made me nervous, places where I didn't know which counter was for ordering and which was for paying. I figured it out and waited in line, watching one of the aproned guys behind the display case take orders and make sandwiches.

He looked really, *really* familiar, and I racked my brain. Not from school—he was probably in his mid-thirties, too old to have been in my class. Oh fuck, I hoped I'd never done anything degrading to him for pills.

Then it hit me. He looked exactly like Al Pacino in *Dog Day Afternoon*. Rangy and dark, but with less Seventies hair. Not quite handsome, but not *not* handsome either. I stole looks at him until it was my turn to order.

"Um, coffee, please?"

He smiled, the tiniest bit annoyed. "You order coffee at the register. You want a sandwich?"

"No, thanks. Sorry."

"You sure? They're good."

"I'm sure they are, but I just want a coffee, thanks."

"Your loss."

I smiled awkwardly and shuffled off to get in the other

line. I grabbed a big waxed-paper-wrapped oatmeal raisin cookie from a basket on the counter and got a coffee—a nice, normal old drip coffee, one-size cup, no foreign words to pronounce. I took my drink and cookie outside and took a seat on the bench before the front windows, content to catch a chill instead of asphyxiating in my office-cum-perfumery.

After ten minutes the deli's door jingled open, and Al Pacino took a seat on the far end of the bench. I kept my eyes on the passing cars, pretending to be lost in my thoughts, since the guy made me inexplicably shy.

A gentle version of the cab-hailing whistle old men excel at turned my head. Al Pacino had an unlit cigarette at the corner of his lips and a lighter in his hand. "You mind?" he asked, cigarette jumping.

I shook my head.

He licked a finger and held it up, testing the breeze. "Switch places with me."

I obliged, shifting my cup and cookie and purse down to his end so he could sit downwind.

He lit up and stowed the lighter in one of his apron pockets. After a minute's silence he said, "I hope that's not your whole lunch."

I chewed and swallowed and offered one of those apologetic frown-smiles. "It's got raisins."

He shook his head, faking motherly disapproval rather adorably.

"Is that *your* whole lunch?" I countered, nodding at his cigarette.

"Appetizer." He squinted thoughtfully into the distance beyond my shoulder. "You smell like something."

"I smell like about twenty things right now. Pears and cucumber and lilies and rose water and spearmint . . ."

"Like, um . . . Shit, what's it called? Those flowers everyone has in their gardens, kinda rusty-colored, and they smell like tomato plants?"

"Marigolds?"

He snapped his fingers and pointed at me. "Marigolds."

"Yeah, those too. You're good," I said. "You should have my job."

"You sell perfume or something?"

I shook my head. "Ultimately, yes, but not the way you're picturing."

Al Pacino raised an eyebrow and sucked on his cigarette.

"I just started work, just over there, two buildings down. I'm a copywriter for a cosmetics company, and I have to write catalog descriptions for all these different body spray things. So I spent all morning spritzing them and trying to figure out how to make them sound amazing."

"Fun."

I shrugged, officially relaxing in his company. "In theory. But have you ever been dragged into a Yankee Candle shop?"

"Oh, right. That'll give you a headache."

I nodded.

"So sell me something," he said. "Sell me that cookie, Ms. Marketer."

I looked at it. Normally such a demand to perform would have clammed me up, but this guy put me at ease. After another bite of my cookie I ventured, "This is a European-style oatcake, infused with virgin black molasses and sun-dried Tuscan grapes. And it's a great source of antioxidants and fiber, spelled F-I-B-R-E."

"Wow," he said, nodding. "That is some world-class bull. I hope they're paying you a shit-ton. Spelled T-O-N-N-E."

I laughed. "More than I deserve."

"We should hire you to rewrite our menu. Say our tuna salad is, like, imported albacore paired with a French egg-essence reduction or some fancy shit. Charge people twelve bucks a sandwich."

"Ooh, that's good. Doesn't sound like you need to hire any outside copywriters." After a minute's silence I came out with, "Did you know you look exactly like—"

"Al Pacino from, like, nineteen-seventy-five."

"Yeah. So exactly that you're sick of hearing it, I guess."

"I get that a lot from old guys."

"I've watched *Dog Day Afternoon* at least five times with my dad," I said. "He's an old guy."

"What's your name?" Al Pacino asked.

"Adrian."

"Hey, like *Rocky*. Another classic. *Adriaaaan*," he fake-shouted, staring wildly at the sky.

"My dad's old-guy friends are always yelling that at me," I said dryly.

He leaned over and offered a hand. "I'm Ray."

We shook, and my shyness returned. I was pretty sure he was out here to flirt with me, which felt mildly scary but mostly nice. Nice mainly because he was probably too old for me, so I knew I had a diplomatic reason to turn him down, should he ever ask me out. Plus, in some ways he reminded me of the real reason I'd turn him down—harsh Boston accent, faint whiff of cigarette smoke. A little taste of the Badger.

"I better head back to work," I said, crumpling my cookie wrapper.

"Back to the bullshit mines."

I smiled at that as I left him alone on the bench.

I smiled to myself, too, because someone had tried to flirt with me. That hadn't happened in ages. Maybe it was true what they said about women in lust giving off some irresistible pheromone. Maybe whatever I was feeling for my screwy love interest trumped my scrawny, spooky packaging and made me seem interesting. Or maybe Lani really was on to something with those stupid body mists.

° ° °

No Isaac that night, nor the next night, not for the rest of the week and beyond. Though I was tempted a couple times to go after him, I resisted.

I did my level best to focus on work, but I felt sad, knowing his welts were fading more and more the longer we stayed apart. I didn't want to lose what little momentum we might have had, romantically, but I also didn't want to look too clingy and desperate, so I concentrated on my job, or told myself I was.

I settled into my new routine, and even if it wasn't especially fulfilling, I was all right. No super-late nights so far, though Lani *was* a pain in the ass, just as I'd known she would be.

Because there were so few of us in the office, I got a very large share of Lani's abrasive, micromanagerial attention. Her criticism was confusing and hard to wrap one's head around, like a turducken—disapproval wrapped in flattery wrapped in a patronizing smile. I wished she'd just tell me what she didn't like so I could fix it without having to dig through all the layers of gentle, misleading criticism.

But at any rate, I downgraded Lani from self-absorbed taskmaster to well-intentioned annoying person who was signing my checks. Even if the job got worse, I wouldn't quit. Quitting isn't in the repertoire of the meek. It requires far too much action and impetus.

Aside from the paychecks and insurance, the best perk of my new job was Ray.

He worked Monday through Friday, and he always seemed to be taking his smoke break when I was taking my cookie-and-coffee break, a charmingly transparent imitation of coincidence. Even when it was rainy or cold, I ate lunch on that bench to escape Lani's niggling. And yeah, okay, because I'd quickly grown attached to Ray's easy company. It wasn't an adequate substitute for Badger's attention, but it was nice for what it was. Made me feel special and interesting for a half hour at a time.

I guessed Ray probably liked me if he was constantly deigning to hang out with me, always careful to situate himself downwind. I liked him back, if tentatively. He wasn't striking like Badger, but he had an interesting face. Intense brown eyes, pensive mouth.

Ray made sandwiches and party platters to supplement his weekend gig as a bicycle mechanic—yet another connection to the Badger that made me like him. I gathered that he was a sort of middle-generation punk, one who'd quit caring about dressing the part ages ago, genuinely more interested in the music and politics. He was the sharpest, nicest breed of underachiever, one who'd opted out of the American cult of corporate-type success but opted out of disenfranchisement as well. He just worked and got paid and seemed to keep his life free of all avoidable responsibilities. In his time off, he did what he wanted. He made it look so easy.

The morning of my second Tuesday at work, I packed up all my Halloween stuff and brought it with me, excited to see my family. Lani found out my plans and decided to let everyone go at three, so I got to catch an earlier train to the suburbs. Pretty cool of her. Disingenuous as she usually came off, Lani was actually really, truly generous when it came to personal matters.

My mom picked me up from the Lincoln train station dressed as a witch. She always went as a witch. It was the same costume she'd had since Amanda and I were about eight. She always did it up good, though, with the creaky, creepy voice and everything. God, it had embarrassed me in high school. Now I almost couldn't wait for Amanda to pop out a kid so Mom could mortify the next generation.

My dad was sitting in a chair beside the front steps as we pulled up, wearing a Patriots sweatshirt with the sleeves cut off, plus a headset microphone and a whistle strung around his neck.

"Trick or treat," I called. "Bill Belichick again? You're so lazy."

"Heya, honey. Happy Halloween. How's that new job treating you?"

"It's good."

He stood, and I hugged him. We chatted until a car came down our long driveway and a mom emerged with three small kids. My dad blew his whistle authoritatively, then took up his post with a huge popcorn bowl of candy —good stuff, no Smarties or Tootsie Rolls—and I went inside.

It was a cold Halloween, and my costume was a shitty choice. But I liked it. In the guest room, I changed and got my accessories in place—long strands of pearls, cheap black satin gloves I'd found in Chinatown, a sequined strip of elastic I'd sewn together for a headband and into which I'd woven a pair of peacock feathers. A ton of eyeliner and mascara and gray, glittery shadow, dark red lipstick, a fake birthmark. I slid my big ring onto my gloved finger and adjusted my fishnets, liking my outfit. I didn't ever dance when there were witnesses present, but before I left the guest bathroom I attempted a little Charleston. Not bad.

Amanda arrived at six dressed as Alice, of Wonderland fame.

"No Derek?" I asked as we hugged in the front room.

"He's working late, and then I think he just wants to go home and hand out candy and be in bed by ten. You look awesome, by the way. Nice job."

"You, too."

"You'll be ready to punch me after a few hours of my bad British accent. I was practicing all week, driving Derek bloody mad. Oh, and I had this awesome plan to tie little tags around all the candy bars that said 'Eat Me.' But he said that would weird the parents out."

"Party pooper."

"So instead . . ." She reached into a paper shopping bag and pulled out an old glass bottle with a *Drink Me* tag, corked and filled with eerie, cloudy liquid.

"Nice. What is that?"

"Fresca."

We loaded up on cookies, then stood around outside for the first hour of darkness, when the majority of the kids arrive. I was a bit unsettled when not one but two of our former classmates turned up with small children. Jeez, I'd gotten no closer to marrying and spewing forth offspring than I had to heading the space program. Though I wasn't jealous. I was sure some women must get all moist at the thought of taking their children to the same houses they trick-or-treated at as kids, but I wasn't one of them. Amanda was welcome to the gig, if she wanted it.

The only downside to Halloween was the masks. I eyed the little Iron Mans and skull-faced monsters dubiously, unnerved by the gap between the plastic and the sheen of their eyes.

Thanks, Badger.

I was relieved when the stream of candy-seekers slowed to a trickle and we all went inside to spend the rest of the evening taking turns on door duty and standing around the kitchen table, eating veggies and dip and chatting about Halloweens past.

At eight I said, "I better change and get ready to catch a train."

"Oh no, no, no," Amanda said, waving like I was insane. "I'll drive you home."

"You sure?"

"Of course. It's about time I headed out, anyhow." She turned to our mom. "Are there any Butterfingers left?"

Once Amanda had her booty stashed, we said our good

nights to my parents and headed out. We were both suffering from sugar crashes and screaming-child fatigue, so it was a quiet drive. I fell into a gentle melancholy, thinking about Badger. About Isaac, the most fearless, confrontational man I knew, basically hiding in his apartment, lights off to stop the doorbell from ringing.

As we neared my usual exit, my mouth came out with what my head had already decided was a terrible idea.

"Could you . . ."

"Could I what?"

"Could you drop me in Somerville instead?"

20

"This is where your homeless man lives?" Amanda asked, pulling up in front of Barbara's house. "Looks pretty empty."

"It's supposed to look empty. But wait for my text before you drive off."

"Of course."

I gathered my coat and the bag that held my work clothes, and we said good night. I could hear the far-off whoops of drunken Halloween enthusiasts, wild as coyotes.

Feeling like a trespasser, I pushed up the heavy gate latch and slipped into the side yard. As I skirted the house, I glanced up at the windows in case he heard and was watching, debating whether or not to attack whoever was infiltrating the property.

It's me, I tried to tell him, in case the pull wasn't enough.

But I felt it. I knew he was home just from the purpose flexing my leg muscles, drawing me to him.

I padded up the metal steps in my flats, praying I wouldn't trip over my dress and kill myself on his fire escape. A faint glow shone through the drawn curtains, its promise making my breath go shallow as much as the climb. I knocked on the door, and it swung in instantly, Badger standing before me in flannel pajama pants but nothing else, Glock at his side.

"Trick or treat?" I offered, eyeing the weapon.

"We don't do Halloween."

"I know. I just came to see if you were home. Do you feel like hanging out at all?"

"Yeah, sure. Fine."

He stepped aside and let me in. God help me if I wasn't allowed to stay the night—I hated riding the subway late at the best of times, to say nothing of riding it among the wasted, noisy jerk-offs who'd turned Halloween into an orange-and-black St. Patrick's Day.

I tapped out a quick, reckless text to dismiss Amanda and shut off my phone.

The first few minutes of being alone with Badger were always awkward, as he wasn't much for greetings. Not a hugger. Not a small-talker.

He locked the door and wandered back to the lamp-lit bed, which had clutter spread all over it, books. No, albums, I saw as I crossed the floor—photo albums, a half dozen of them. Suddenly more intrigued than shy, I joined him on the mattress.

He arranged a couple snapshots beside some other ones, slid a photo of a wedding from one slot in an album and replaced it with a picture of a beach. I stared at the people smiling for the camera. A young woman in a bikini steadying a fat toddler holding a sand pail.

"Are these of your family?" I asked.

He shook his head. "My grandma's."

Barbara's, I corrected in my mind. His bizarre insistence on pretending she was his relative, when he knew *I* knew she wasn't, was beginning to creep me out. Though it creeped me out far less than some other things I knew about him.

He shuffled photos around on the bedspread, fussing and rearranging.

"What are you doing?"

"Putting them in order." He consulted the back of one, squinting for a time stamp.

"Ah. She asked you to do that?"

"Nah. Just something to do while I'm hiding inside all day."

Oh, how badly I wanted to draw him into a conversation, ask why his seemingly random time-filler task was this—not a puzzle, not a book. This, which had everything to do with obsessively spying on and ordering someone else's family and history.

How badly I wanted to analyze him. But he was so beyond that, such an exception to every rule, a language spoken by exactly one man, no chance anyone could ever interpret him. I wondered how many shrinks he'd been sent to as a child and decided, *probably a lot*. Enough that I'd do him the kindness of not being the latest of many to waste their time trying to figure him out.

"You probably don't have many photos from when you

were a kid," I said softly, picturing my own. Every costume, every Christmas, every family vacation, safely preserved for when memories got lazy.

He shook his head.

"What about of your mom?" Barely a whisper.

"My mother was an opera singer," he said, utterly deadpan. "Contralto."

His reply didn't even annoy me this time. What did the lies mean, though? That she was dead? Died in childbirth, maybe. Something awful. Or maybe "awful" to him would mean that she'd merely left him, sent him off into all that abuse—*good luck, kid*. Who were all these fantasy mothers—the immigrant, the contortionist, the opera singer? The same lies he'd told to classmates, perhaps, embarrassed by her absence at plays or fund-raisers or ice cream socials.

My heart broke for him. Not with the painful, ugly, splintering snaps I'd felt when he'd told me about the molestation stuff. Slow and silent, a deep, smooth crack.

"Are any of these already organized?" I asked, tapping the albums.

He handed me a binder from the end, with a pattern of faded roses on a dark blue background. I opened it on my crossed legs and flipped pages. Ancient photos of young men in military uniforms, stately women posing with their hands in their laps, their hair perfectly rolled, sepia cheeks and lips painted pink, faces painted flat beige. I tried to guess which child could be Barbara, but it was pointless.

"Do you have any baby pictures of yourself?" I asked.

His head snapped up, and his stare lingered. It wasn't a

glare, but it was aggressive, aggressively searching. Finally he left the bed. I feared he might walk to the door, hold it open and demand I leave. But instead he went to the same chest of drawers where he kept his condoms, and from the shadows came the soft rustles and scrapes of a box being rooted through. He returned carrying a card and winged it at me. Its corner jabbed my palm as I caught it.

It was pale aqua, with *It's a boy!* spelled in a motif of blue blocks on the front. After roughly three decades in a careless man's possession, it should have been sun-faded and bent, but it wasn't. He'd tossed it at me, faking apathy, but he'd stored it with care.

I opened it, and there he was.

The photo was small, its corners tucked into slots cut in the paper. Isaac was even smaller. Like an alien, with a scrunched-up red face and tiny preemie tubes trailing from his nostrils. The details had been handwritten in cursive on the appropriate lines. Isaac Belov.

Isaac Belov. Isaac Belov.

January eighth, said the line for the date. He'd be thirty-one next year. Eleven-eleven in the morning. Three pounds, one ounce, seventeen inches. *Welcome to the world, little one!*

I shivered and looked him in the eyes.

"What was the deal with your mom?" I asked point-blank. "Seriously. What was she? Any of those things you told me?"

"She was a crack addict."

I blinked. I nodded.

"Same as I was," he said, "for the first few months of my life."

I stared at the photo, and after a few breaths I began to cry, tears rolling hot down my cheeks.

"She died ages ago," he said. "When I was three, off in my millionth foster home."

I wanted to hug him. I wanted him to hug *me* . . . I wanted a hundred things I couldn't demand or expect from this man, suspended in my own unmeetable need for contact.

"Hence my amazing grab bag of behavioral disorders," he added quietly, then rubbed my back.

The touch felt so nice, so necessary, I cried even harder. His warm palm stroked in slow circles over the bare skin between my shoulder blades, exposed by the deep vee of my dress. I laughed at the sheer volume of tears I was managing to produce, and sniffled loudly. "Sorry."

I felt his shrug more than I saw it.

"I was small, too," I said, my voice sounding weird, all clogged with snot. "My parents didn't even know I was in there, hiding behind my sister. Not for months."

"You still hide behind her?" he asked.

I laughed. "Yeah, sometimes." I turned to look him in the face. "Sorry you didn't have anybody to hide behind."

His lips twitched, and he shrugged again. "You get dealt whatever you get dealt."

I glanced down at the photo and nodded. My nose was threatening to drip, so I closed the card and handed it back, excused myself to the bathroom. I stared at myself in the mirror as I washed my hands, my ridiculous eye makeup streaked, making me look like a glamorous raccoon. I tidied it with a piece of toilet paper, then headed back into the chilly, dark hall.

He was organizing photos again, and I crawled across the mattress to sit behind him. He let me wrap my arms around his bare waist and rest my cheek against the nape of his neck. I breathed in his smell, memorized the flex of his arms and stomach as he continued to sort.

He was so deeply screwed up, no one person, no well-intentioned woman, stood any chance of being enough to make up for everything that had happened to him. Especially not one as unremarkable and flawed as me. The thought made me feel helpless, and I squeezed him tighter.

"Don't feel shitty about it," he said.

"It's sad. I can't help it."

"If either of us should feel sad, it's me. And I don't, so you definitely shouldn't waste your time being all upset or whatever."

"I'm allowed to feel badly for you."

"But I'm not that baby in the photo. I'm some guy living in an old lady's attic."

I sighed, knowing that explaining empathy to him was a pointless exercise. Might as well explain algebra to a goldfish.

"Before all the stuff with the pills," Badger said, "what defined who you were to yourself?"

I pondered it. "I guess being artistic. Sometimes that was it."

"What about the other times?"

"Well . . . being not-my-sister. Being the dud twin, because she's really pretty and cheerful and—"

"Jesus." He shook his head, then shuffled around to face me. "What's with you, always dragging yourself down to whatever your lowest point was?"

"What?"

"You haven't used in how long? But you still walk around all guilty, like you just scored. When do you just fucking forgive yourself and move on? And start doing the stuff you want to be defined by?"

"I'm trying to. I got a job."

"But in your head you're just a recovering addict, aren't you?"

I didn't reply. I honestly wasn't sure.

"Do you look at me and see a crack baby or a kid who got molested?"

"Not constantly. But, I mean, they're parts of you. In the background."

"But when you stare right fucking at me, what do you see?"

"Some guy. With a lot of issues. And a bike." Some guy I was in love with, for reasons I couldn't comprehend.

"Right. Because that's exactly what I am. So start looking at yourself for exactly who you are on a given day, and quit seeing stuff you're not, like an addict or a fuckup. You let your accomplishments fade pretty fucking quick, I bet. But you drag your screw-ups around like a fucking body bag. Jesus, it must be exhausting being you."

"Sometimes."

He laughed. Nothing he'd said, as terse and callous as some of it had sounded, broken down into individual statements . . . He wasn't being mean. He was just being himself, saying what he thought and trusting me not to be hurt. Or not caring if I was. Or not understanding that anyone *might* be hurt by the truth.

"So right now, you're an oversensitive girl who showed

up at some asshole's place because for some reason that's totally beyond me, you care about me. That's what you are, right now, right?"

Nail on the head. "I guess."

"That's exactly what you are. So knock it off, thinking you're still the same person who ripped off your family or did whatever else you did to get your pills. The only bearable thing about being human is that you can change, the second you feel like. Get it through your head that you changed, and cut yourself some slack before you fucking choke to death from all the apologies lodged in your throat."

I stared at his chin for a long moment and swallowed the instinctual *I'm sorry* I'd been poised to offer. "Okay."

"Good." He turned back around to his sorting. I tucked my feet beside his hips, but I hugged my knees instead of his waist. The welts I'd given him were long gone, but pale pink stripes crisscrossed his back. *Usually when I get off, I'm whacking the hell out of myself with a belt or an extension cord.* Was this evidence of that? If it was, had he been thinking of me?

I gave one of his stripes a poke. "Does that hurt?" I asked, unsure if I was hitting on him.

"Barely."

"That's too bad."

"You look beautiful," he murmured.

The remark threw me. I began to dismiss it, to remind him it was silly, just my Halloween costume. This wasn't me, not really. But I shut my mouth.

The fact that he'd said that when he couldn't even see me . . . My heart warmed. He was so firmly rooted in the present, it told me the thought had been on his mind, lingering, and though it was totally irrelevant to anything we'd spoken about, he'd chosen to say it. Maybe he *had* thought of me, when and if he'd jerked off.

I scooted closer and hugged him, resting my head on his shoulder.

We sat that way for ages, and if life had simply stopped, frozen where it was for the rest of time, I'd have been perfectly happy. But since life comes with the annoying baggage of momentum, I knew the thought was delusional. It wasn't even a pretty delusion. But his body felt warm and strong, and his skin smelled so familiar now.

I parted my lips, once, three times, maybe five, until the words finally tumbled out. "I'm pretty sure I love you."

He turned, a sharp movement followed by perfect stillness. I held my breath and studied his profile, the lashes obscuring his downcast gaze. He seemed to stare at his own shoulder, and I waited what felt like an hour for his reply.

"I got no idea what to do with that."

The words fell like bricks between us, heavy and tangible . . . but dropped, not thrown. I held on tight.

"You don't have to do anything with it," I whispered. "I just wanted to tell you."

He swallowed. "Nobody's ever said that to me before."

I turned that idea around in my head. "Never? Not even, like . . ."

I'd wanted to say, *Not even your family?* But that was foolish.

"Not that I know of. I mean, I haven't ever given anybody any reason to."

"Well, don't do anything with it."

He turned his head a bit farther, staring at my neck. "I'm supposed to say it back to you."

"Says who?"

He shrugged, bonking my chin so I bit my tongue. "Movies."

"I don't expect you to say anything. Just be honest with me, or say thanks, or . . . or don't say anything. I just wanted you to hear it."

"I won't ever love you back," he said.

It wasn't a slight, ugly as the words were. It was a fact, impersonal and blunt. "That's okay."

"If I was capable of it," he said, "I'd want to feel that way."

"That's nice." It hurt, but for Badger this was practically a sonnet.

He dropped his head. There was a soft laugh in his voice when he asked, "Why?"

"Why did I want to tell you?"

"Why on earth would you love me? What have I ever done that would make you feel whatever that feels like?"

"I don't know." Why is rain wet or snow cold? It just is. If it wasn't, it wouldn't be what it was. "What did I ever do that made you want to take me all the way to that bridge in Winchester when I was upset?"

"I dunno. You're a nice person."

Was I? I didn't really think I was. I wasn't an actively *bad* person anymore, but I didn't do much to further society. "I guess. By some people's standards."

"You are. But I'm a shithead. I'm the last person anybody should love."

"I don't think you get to pick. People either make you feel that sort of thing, or they don't."

He shook his head. "Well, you've got awful taste."

I laughed softly. "Yeah, maybe."

"I'm not ever gonna make you happy."

I wasn't sure what to say, but he went on.

"You make me feel something, here and there, when you're around. That's all I might ever want from somebody, is for them to fill a gap, or make me feel something from moment to moment, because that's how I function. In chunks."

"I know."

"You're complicated, cupcake. You think about stuff. A lot. You worry about stuff that's already happened, and stuff that's going to happen, or maybe might happen . . ."

I nodded.

"I'm never going to be enough for somebody like you. And I don't mean that, like, I'm not good enough. I'm just not *enough*. I'll never care enough, or need you as much as maybe you might think you needed me."

My stray, I thought afresh. Turning up for scraps, then wandering off again. To him I was perhaps a convenience, the sex and company a welcome perk but one he could survive just fine without. Whereas to me . . .

But I wasn't the only one who'd changed since our magnets had drawn us together. He'd told me he'd felt happy, that time in my bed. That he saw me in color in a world full of gray. I wasn't determined to change him, but I wasn't willing to believe that feeling love—for me or for anybody—was beyond his ability to learn. It all felt very corny, like a bad screenplay. Corny and honest.

"Can I sleep here tonight?" I asked.

He turned again, enough for our eyes to meet. "Sure."

I left his warmth and headed back to the bathroom, scrubbing my face clean of eyeliner and glitter flecks and lipstick. When I returned to his room, he was still organizing photos, and I felt him watching as I changed from my dress into the undershirt I'd been wearing earlier. I joined him again on the bed, settling beside him and yanking his covers up around me.

"You can keep doing your sorting," I said. "I'm probably going to just go to sleep."

He didn't reply, and eventually I lay down and burrowed deeper beneath the comforter.

I closed my eyes, and for a while the albums seemed to reabsorb his attention. But then his weight left the mattress, and I saw him carry the binders to a table by the door, the covers cleared of photos. I moved over, and he joined me under the blanket, our legs locking at the knee, my face tucked against his neck.

"You warm enough?" he asked.

I nodded. I slung my arm over his ribs and squeezed him.

"Did you want to kiss or whatever?"

I wasn't honestly sure. Between his baby photo and his lukewarm reception of my love proclamation, I felt naked and sore, like my skin had come off. I didn't feel sexual, and I didn't feel much like sexualizing him. "Do you?" I countered.

"Yeah, sure."

That changed my mood, knowing it was what he wanted. I backed away and stared at his face a few moments. Watched him blink, studied his nose and eyebrows and mouth, realizing he really was handsome, now that

I wasn't afraid of him. I touched his ears and jaw and pressed my lips to his. My thighs hugged his tighter.

Between kisses I asked, "Where did you get your pajamas?"

"My grandma gave them to me."

Of course. It was impossible to imagine Badger strolling into Sears and picking out something as wholesome as sleepwear. Of course they'd been a gift.

"For Christmas?"

He nodded, eyes trained on my mouth.

"Did you give her anything?"

"She hates presents. I just do shit around the house when she tells me to."

I kissed him again. Then again.

It wasn't like me to kiss men. To get kissed, sure. To passively accept and to pretend to enjoy lest I ding some fragile male's ego, and to downplay my enjoyment if I was really into it, since being openly turned on had always made me embarrassed.

What a waste of womanhood I'd been.

Would I go back to that, when my non-relationship with Badger—with Isaac—inevitably ended? I kissed him deeper, in case my days of being this woman were numbered. With Isaac I played tourist in someone else's body, someone I liked better than the girl I knew myself to be.

Maybe he makes you the best Adrian you can be, said the Amanda voice in my head.

Maybe. But it didn't change the fact that this slightly better version of me required batteries—Badger-shaped ones—and that I wasn't *her* without *him*.

Tension rose in my center, curling my fingers against his

neck, tightening my insides. He was kissing me back, and his noisy nose-breaths were absurdly sexy, announcing a change. I stroked his bare chest and pictured him naked, pictured him below me with those mean eyes watching. I reached around and clawed his back in long, slow strokes. His thigh pushed deeper between mine, hips moving to draw his hard, clothed leg against my panties.

We kissed like fucking had never been invented, and this was the nastiest dish on the menu. A cold hand slid beneath my undershirt, and he palmed my breast, callused skin rasping, fingertips glancing. I suddenly became a very lousy kisser, gasping against his mouth. *More*, I thought.

"More," my mouth supplied. Whoa. My mouth never had the balls to say shit like that, especially if I was asking for something that only I'd be taking pleasure from.

He rewarded my scrap of bravery, sliding his hand down my stomach. His thigh made room, and those rough fingers slipped inside my underwear, finding my clit. Finding me wet. My face heated, but from arousal as much as embarrassment.

Two fingers slicked my clit, and he rubbed me—light grazes, as though he'd watched me by myself, taken notes on what I needed. Like he knew the things I'd never ask for in words.

A breath warmed my mouth, a harsh sigh like he'd been hurt.

I moved, angling myself against his fingertips, hazarding small thrusts. He held his hand still as I moved against him in tiny strokes, my sounds drowning out his. The pleasure was a craving, a physical longing potent as hunger demanding food, a chill demanding warmth. I kept my eyes open, studying his face. It looked as it had that night we'd had sex in my bed, eyes narrowed and mean, lips parted and flushed.

"Are you turned on?" I asked.

"Sort of."

I ran the back of my hand across the front of his pants, finding him soft. But he was aroused, mentally. Emotionally? Maybe that was a wish too far, but mentally, yeah. He was turned on in some way that had nothing to do with his dick or with wanting to come. Fascinating. I could've spent the next decade with this man and probably only hoped to understand a single percent of who he was.

"You wish I was hard?" he asked.

"Kind of. Maybe. But as long as you're enjoying yourself, I guess I don't care." Who needed a stiff cock when they had two raspy fingers taunting their clit? Getting Isaac hard was, well, hard. It demanded both physical and emotional stamina. His erection was a trophy, and in a selfish way, I was proud I knew how to claim it. I had the key to his rusty-ass lock, and what other girl in this city could say that?

"Before me," I asked, moving my pleasure to simmer on a back burner as I indulged my ego. "When was the last time you were with anyone? Sex-wise?"

"Since before I lived here. Three years, I guess."

"Was it good?"

"It did the job."

I wanted details. Had she beat the crap out of him, some perfect lady-freak? How had they met? "Were you the— So you weren't doing what you do now, back then. With the paintballs?"

"No. It was before that."

Oh, how I glowed.

It was better than unwrapping my and Amanda's much-pleaded-for Nintendo 64 that jubilant Christmas morning, knowing *I was the only woman who'd ever fucked the Badger.* That smug thought was as sweet and gooey as frosting.

Then I panicked, wondering how old that made his condoms.

I'd better start packing a couple, just in case. I wondered if I could ever get him there. Get him off while we were screwing. Without choking him, that was, perhaps with the paintball welts.

Nosy questions begged to be asked. I held back the ones whose answers could hurt my feelings and replayed what he'd told me, looking so dumbfounded that other night. *That was the most normal sex I've ever had.*

I fidgeted against his fingers, and the pleasure sucked me down into my body, out of my head. His breaths darkened to moans, and I watched him fucking me in my mind's eye. I pictured his face as he came, still inside me, the thought a match flicked into a puddle of gasoline.

"I'd love to watch you come. When you're inside me."

A pause. "You'd have to hurt me."

"I know." He'd like that. Maybe someday *I'd* even like that.

"We can try sometime."

I nodded, lost in my visions of his strained face, of his strained body jammed hard against mine as he released. My own climax gathered against his fingers, hot and needy.

"Adrian."

"I'm going to . . ."

And I did. I gasped and mewled and rubbed against his fingers. I bit back three dangerous words and replaced them with a cuss.

My hips stilled, and he drew his fingers away. My bones had gone soft. I shifted, pressing my mouth to his neck, breathing him in.

It was all so backward, my being with someone who could take or leave his own pleasure. That had been me, after all, in all my sexual encounters, too bashful to make demands and too embarrassed to even come for real in front of someone. Not that Isaac was bashful. And not that he backseated his pleasure to be deferring. Still, I'd never been the greedy partner before, the spoiled one. It felt nice.

He toyed with my hair, pushing it back from my neck, and the attic's cool air caressed my flushed skin. Again, the words begged to be said. No. I'd said them already. Saying them again wouldn't change the fact that I didn't get to hear them in return. But it felt as though saying them again might open a valve in me and lessen the pressure threatening to burst through my heart's muscly walls, crack my ribs, split my skin.

It was unfair that there wasn't any simple thing I could do to reciprocate the pleasure. Isaac was right on that count, in so many ways—I wanted far more from him than he did from me. He was a houseplant, and I was an infant. One of us was content to exist with the bare minimum of care, the other an endless source of unarticulated needs. I shifted closer, wanting to absorb more of whatever fucked nutrients he gave off, the ones that had me thriving as I hadn't in years.

At some point I fell asleep—fell hard and fast and

deep, not waking for what seemed like hours. It was pitch black when my eyes opened, so it had to be earlier than six thirty. Still, I needed to go home and change before work. I realized Isaac wasn't next to me, and the anxiety sharpened.

He didn't have an alarm clock or phone to consult, so I left the warmth of his bed to pad across the cold, gritty hardwood and root through my bag for my cell, my way lit by the distant light of the open bathroom door down the hall. I turned on my phone. Thank goodness—barely three in the morning. I put it away and went back to the bed.

Water ran in the bathroom. He must have woken me, getting up to have a pee. I tucked myself back in and waited for his return. Would he curl himself around me when he got back under the covers? I hoped so.

But he didn't return right away. I lay there for fifteen minutes or more, hearing nothing from the hall.

It would've been dumb to get up and check on him if it turned out he was in the midst of something . . . private. And nothing pleasantly private like masturbation, since surely that act was far from silent, the way he needed it.

I waited ages, a half hour or more, until curiosity became concern. I abandoned the warm covers again to venture down the hall toward the light from the half-open bathroom door. I crept slowly, waiting for a peek to make sure he wasn't on the can, doing anything that I had to admit the Badger probably wouldn't hesitate to do with the door open.

The toilet tank came into view, as did his shoulder and his face in profile. I frowned. He was turned the wrong way. Another step and I saw it all, something far more private and disturbing than him taking a shit.

He was still dressed in his flannel bottoms, crouched on the closed lid of the toilet. One elbow was braced on the tank, his arm striped red with cuts. The other hand drew a fresh line with a razor blade, his fingers perfectly steady, body still as stone, face placid. He looked hypnotized, and I was afraid to move or speak lest I startle him, make him gouge himself. Soon enough, I joined the trance.

Some of the lines were near-invisible, others pink, others beading with tiny, dark droplets. He went slowly, so slowly that the cuts at his shoulder were dried maroon, the freshest ones scarlet. His attention was locked on the process, surely just how I looked, lost in one of my collages, my own neglected blade therapy.

For minutes on end I watched, until finally he glanced up between lines, staring right at me with nothing behind his eyes.

I hadn't surprised him.

He'd known I was there all along.

I edged closer to lean in the door frame. He went back to his ritual, painting a ribbon of red down his forearm, all the way to the bone at his wrist, then set the razor blade on the porcelain. His ribs jumped with a tight breath, hands suddenly trembling. His Nyquil had worn off, and whatever anxiety had driven him to this returned. He flipped around, sitting on the lid and shutting his eyes, features tight with some unpleasant emotion. The man who'd rubbed my back and made me come was gone. Isaac was gone. He'd abandoned me with a wild animal in a mean old lady's bathroom.

"You okay?" I only needed to whisper, it was so quiet.

He said nothing.

There was no turning back, no retreating to bed to pretend I hadn't just walked in on something awful. I slid down the frame and sat cross-legged in the threshold, the floor cold against my bare thighs. I felt the wetness from what he'd given me before I'd fallen asleep, embarrassed by the sensation.

His cut arm was facing away from me. I was grateful for that.

"Should I leave you alone?"

He raised his chin and met my gaze, blue eyes empty. Then he blinked, and some of their glassiness seemed to leave. He stood, stepped to the sink, and opened the cabinet behind the mirror. I watched him set a bottle of rubbing alcohol on the tank and unwind a few squares of toilet paper from the roll before taking a seat once more.

He folded the tissue into a wad and uncapped the bottle.

"You haven't done that in ages, have you?" *Tell me it's not because of what I said.*

"C'mere." He wasn't meeting my eyes anymore, attention solely on the toilet paper as he doused it with the alcohol. His invitation wasn't kind.

I shuffled closer on my butt, the chemical smell sharp, jarring as a loud noise.

Badger opened his knees, the mechanics of his request clear, its purpose not. I sat between his spread legs and put my hands to his shins, waiting.

He brought the dripping tissue to his shoulder, touching it to the top cuts. He twitched and made a noise, a pained grunt. As he inched the paper down, his other hand cupped his dick. I looked back and forth between the two spots, unsure how to feel about either. I watched him grow unmistakably hard behind his bottoms and swallowed, awaiting orders, praying maybe they wouldn't arrive.

He paused to toss the wad of toilet paper away and prepare a fresh one. Clear liquid snaked down his arm, gathering blood, splashing silently to the white tile floor in pink blossoms. I held my breath. He pulled his pajamas' drawstring free, edging closer. I didn't want to do what he was going to ask, but I knew I wouldn't say no. I'd left my spine out in the hallway, sent it clattering to the floor the second I'd spotted blood.

When he pushed his waistband down, I wasn't horrified by what he was demanding. It scared and unnerved me, but it'd be a lie to say my body didn't rouse from its sheer wrongness.

"Suck me."

I got to my knees.

Bad memories flashed, vague scenes of things I'd done or thought perhaps I'd done in the service of scoring pills. Blurry snatches that were neither memory nor fabrication, moments from a life I'd neither lived nor imagined. Shame stung my cheeks and soured my middle but warmed me between my legs, the way your body reacts when you stumble across someone else's gross kink, out there in the Internet ether. That repulsive flavor of arousal.

I took his head in my mouth. He tasted sweet and primal like blood, but soured by the chemical stink. As the alcohol wiped his skin clean and sterilized his vice, I felt filthy.

The tiny room filled with his sounds, groans and gasps brought on by the burn in his arm or the pleasure in his dick, or both together. Or neither, maybe just the wrongness. I tried to stay separate from this sickness, because I suspected that to him, I was a convenient, hot, disembodied mouth. Which felt worse than any other aspect of this scene.

He held my head, and though he didn't force me, the trembling weight of his hand tightened my throat. What an idiot I was to feel upset. This man had shot me in the leg the first time we met, stalked me to my NA meeting, made me choke him to the threshold of consciousness, coerced me—if unintentionally—into a dozen things I'd never wanted to do.

What an idiot I'd been to have forgotten those earlier transgressions or to think I'd changed him from the man who'd initiated them. To think I'd found the real him, the Isaac behind the Badger.

My jaw hurt. I gagged. Snot clogged my sinuses, and tears stung my eyes, but even if he'd let my head go, I wouldn't have stopped. Maybe that made him my cutting. My hideous distraction. If only they made rubbing alcohol for the cuts I was slashing across my heart.

A final, fresh wad of tissue, a final, fresh wave of that awful smell, and I knew it'd be over soon. His arms and legs shook, and his cock was hard as bone. His noises grew wilder, until the pleasure and suffering were as indistinguishable to my ears as they were in his fucked-up brain. He didn't say my name, the way he'd muttered it in bed. He didn't say a word. He went silent, and his hand and hips came together, forcing his dick deep, beyond gagging to a bruising punch at the soft wall of my palate. So deep I didn't taste a drop of his come.

Still, I didn't jerk my head away. I sucked sloppy breaths through my dripping nose and counted the milliseconds until his hold went slack. When it finally did, I sat back on my heels, my eyes burning, my face so hot that the tears slipping down my skin felt cool. He let his pants ride up, hiding his softening cock.

"Get the fuck out."

The words landed with such a heavy slap, I tipped back, landing on my palms.

Out of this room? Out of your attic?

Get the fuck out of his life, suggested my tiny, under-developed voice of logic.

I got to my feet. I closed the door behind me. The floorboards were ice beneath my bare feet, and I went to my bag and dug around in the dark for my pants. I tugged them up my quaking legs, unable to fathom that I'd worn these to work the previous day. I dug out my sweater and jacket and slipped my feet into my shoes, made sure I had my phone. My Halloween dress and accessories were somewhere nearby. I abandoned them.

You look beautiful.

Fuck you, Badger. Or Isaac. Whichever man had let me cry over his birth, then punished me for it. Because that's what that had been, unmistakably. It seemed my precious little fixer-upper masochist wasn't without a sadistic streak.

Fine. Let him have it.

Let him fall asleep and dream of plastic Halloween masks and every other ugly thing that got him stiff.

Twice he'd made me cry tonight. What an idiot I'd been to waste those first tears, feeling badly for him, thinking he'd ever been the baby from that photo.

How pathetic that I'd told him I loved him, and that I'd ever believed I did.

I fumbled with the lock, descended the fire escape with a frantic, clumsy slowness, scared of falling. I made it to the damp ground, slimy leaves sticking to the bare tops of my feet in their flats.

Shit.

Dawn was still two hours away. It was cold and quiet, and the subway wouldn't start running until after five. I had no cash for a cab, and with my first paycheck still pending, I didn't even have enough in the bank to make it to JP.

I got as far as fishing out my phone and selecting Amanda's number, but I couldn't pull the trigger. She'd been too happy about me supposedly stumbling my way into a romance. Hell, *I'd* been too happy.

Somerville was cold and dark, and my feet were already tingling. An hour I had to kill. The longest hour of my life, I bet, save the first one I'd spent locked up. How awfully nice it would be to be home in my bed, brain going fuzzy from a dose of Nyquil, head slipping free from my shoulders like a balloon.

Better yet, Vicodin.

I could be happy, a pink ghost floating thoughtless above this pain for a few hours, free of the burdens of my downer memories, my weary body.

But I wouldn't.

I was apparently still the kind of girl who'd get on her knees and let someone fuck her mouth in exchange for her drug of choice. My drug was nearly six feet tall now, clad in a striped jacket instead of an orange bottle.

But it still didn't love me back.

That hadn't changed.

21

I wound up wandering around for an hour, slower and slower as my cold shoes drew and lanced blisters at my heels.

I wasn't the only one waiting for the subway to wake. Among the low-income women with inhumanely early commutes were scattered still-drunken partyers, but a long night had left them largely silent. They huddled in clusters by the vents, clad in silly, short-skirted getups. I studied their pasty, shivering legs, their smeared makeup and the wigs tucked under their arms. I was sober and dressed for work, but really I was the worst of anyone, the bloodiest, most crumpled train wreck.

Just after five, a T official unlocked the station doors, and I shuffled in behind the rest.

I imagined ridiculous things during the trip home.

Badger, waiting for me in the laundromat parking lot,

having pedaled like a demon to beat me there. He'd wonder why I'd left.

"I only meant you should get out of the bathroom," he'd tell me.

I'd hold strong in my anger, because the way he'd said it, and the act it had followed . . . I wasn't blowing it out of proportion. He'd crossed a line. I'd let him, but he'd crossed it.

I emerged on Green Street after six, the sky still dark. It had begun to drizzle, and as I limped homeward, I pictured Badger at my door, bike leaning against the building. We'd spend perhaps two minutes playing the I-didn't-know-you-were-upset game, and then he'd bow to my reason and sensitivity and apologize. But I wouldn't cave so easily.

I'd tell him I wanted time apart—only not worded so cheesily—and make him sweat. Plus, we really should take some time apart. He was right. There was no good reason for me to love him, apart from it occasionally and briefly feeling awfully good. My love for him wasn't anything I'd wish on my sister or a friend.

But in my imagination he put a cold, damp hand to my jaw, held my face, and kissed me, soft and sincere in the moody streetlight and misty rain. I melted in the moment, but when I pulled away I found the strength to say, simply, "Goodbye, Isaac," and I went inside my building, shutting the door on him. Roll credits.

I'm such a moron.

I held my breath as I reached my block, and I was actually surprised to find no one waiting for me. Suddenly I was cold, tired, and wet, bleeding from my heels. I opened my door and collected my junk mail before trudging up the steps. At least a warm shower was waiting to greet me.

I left the bathroom door open, just in case the doorbell rang (see: *moron*). It didn't, but the steam set off my smoke detector, and I had to scramble through my bedroom naked with shampoo dripping down my back, wet feet picking up lint from the carpet. I climbed onto a chair and flashed anyone who might've happened to glance up at my kitchen window, steadily going deaf as I fucked around and spilled the horrible demon device's batteries across the linoleum.

By the time I reprised my shower, my mood was too foul to be appeased by mere hot water.

I bandaged my blistered heels and dressed, unable to believe that I'd done the same yesterday, that I'd worked on Halloween morning, that I'd seen my family before the ugly crap that happened at Badger's. That I'd told him I loved him, cried over his baby picture, come against his fingers.

I spent my pokey commute trying to make sense of it all. Such a pointless exercise, searching for logic in that man's actions. Was it as simple as impulse-control issues, his beckoning me over and being so rough, and his harsh dismissal? It didn't feel that way. The head he'd demanded had felt more like a punishment than a sex act, and if he'd spoken any words during those excruciating minutes, surely they'd have been, *This is what you get.* That's what his tone had said to me. This was what I got for trying to get close to him.

Maybe he had split personalities—Isaac and Badger, like my Adrian and Mr. Hyde, only mental, not chemical.

Maybe I loved Isaac. Maybe in time my affection could excise Badger, if not tame him, or send him into exile behind all the junk piled in that fucked-up mind.

Then again, it was Isaac who'd made me cry and come, but it was Badger who'd made me feel alive.

As the Green Line trolley rattled up to the street at St. Mary's, I decided we all had split personalities. We've got the one we actually present to the world the majority of the time. Then we have the other one, the one who unleashes terrible barrages of disgusting vitriol at the people who piss us off, only in our heads, and fucks whomever it feels like, exactly when and how it wants. In our heads. I bet we all had a Badger in us, an impulse to hurt and punish. We just had some component that kept it caged in exchange for living in civilized society. Isaac's cage door must've dropped off its hinges. His animal came and went as it pleased.

I got to work on time, but considering how I'd woken, what had happened, and the fact that I'd now made two long subway journeys, my body thought it had to be the afternoon. No such luck.

Mercifully for me, Lani was running errands for much of the morning, and I was free to click and type my way through some e-mails and draft a product description, zombielike. Probably zombie-quality prose.

The three hours leading up to lunchtime felt like ten, as if the clock were going backward. I usually took my break at one, but when the computer told me it was quarter of, I decided, *fuck it all*. I pulled on my jacket, grabbed my bag, and headed back out into the gloom.

As I entered the sandwich shop, I was greeted with the usual "Adriaaan."

I smiled weakly, barely meeting Ray's eyes, and got in line at the register. I was tempted to take my coffee and cookie to the office, but Lani would be back any moment with several hours' backlog of interruptions to lay on me, and Ray's company was far less likely to make me snap than hers. The bench it was.

Ray still hadn't asked me out, but he'd asked me *along* on occasion. He was going to a punk show that weekend —what was I up to? I should swing by, if I wasn't busy. His neighbor was having a party. A bunch of people were going to the Cantab for drinks. Things like that. Things that involved alcohol and socializing, activities I wasn't much good at . . . or didn't want to get too good at, in the case of drinking. Though a couple of times I nearly went, even got so far as dressing up before chickening out. And sure, part of that chickening out had been the idiot hope that maybe that would've been the night Badger came back.

Ray had even offered to build me a bicycle when he heard I didn't have one—just casual, in passing. I feared someday I'd show up for my cookie break and he'd be waiting, bike propped against the bench with a bow on it.

Or maybe not. Maybe he wasn't angling to bone me. Maybe he was just that nice. Maybe I reminded him of some fuckup pity chick he used to know, some broken girl he'd lost to a tragedy. I knew Ray as deeply as I wanted to, as deep as I could handle.

I paid for my lunch. I still wasn't sure I wanted any company that day, even company as undemanding as his. But five minutes after I settled on the bench outside with my cookie and coffee, he took his place on the far end and lit up.

I was in such a foul mood, I knew I'd better force myself to be friendly or else I'd risk snapping at him if he spoke first. As little as I knew him and as pathetic as it might've been, Ray was the closest thing I had to a friend—or the closest friend who hadn't shared a womb with me. After all, we spent close to three hours a week talking, and he was good for me, I thought. Steady and constant. Somebody who'd miss me if I stayed home sick. The last person I wanted to be snippy to.

I offered a weak, cursory smile, then turned my attention back to the traffic.

He smoked and snuffed two butts before he finally spoke. "Can I ask you something?"

It proved a relief, this invitation to vacate the stuffy recesses of my head.

I nodded and met his eyes. "Sure." *Ask me out. I could use the flattery.*

"Are you okay? You seem pretty . . . worn out."

"Don't I always seem that way?"

"No, not really." He lit a third cigarette. "Usually you've got, like, a little smile, just behind your lips."

I blinked, thinking about it. I supposed I had. Because behind the facade of my boring life, I'd had a rather intriguing secret, a doomed but interesting sex life, an atrocious, fascinating love interest. I'd had unknown run-ins to look forward to until that morning.

It occurred to me then, too, that Ray had only ever

known post-Badger Adrian. I wondered if he'd met me before I met Badger, if I'd have seemed any different afterward. Noticeably happier and more awake once I got tangled up with that psychopath.

"Um, yeah, I do feel worn out," I said.

"Halloween party?"

"No, not really. Just went to my parents' place in Lincoln to pass out candy. But I . . ."

Jesus, should I tell him? Ray had never flat-out asked me if I was single or told me he was single himself. I suspected he liked me the way I liked him, as someone to fill a lunch break. Or in my case, someone to bother putting on mascara for in the morning. I liked his attention, though my heart wasn't exactly up for grabs. It had been spoken for by a man I now knew could care less, and too banged up to hand over. Plus, the two-dimensional non-relationship I had with Badger was likely all I was qualified to take part in. My nicotine patches. My training wheels.

"But you what?" he prompted.

I took a deep breath. "I'm seeing a guy, and he was kind of a dick last night." Oh yeah, *kind of*.

Ray made his face exceedingly stern and carefully tucked his cigarette between two fingers before punching his palm. "You want I should straighten him out?"

I laughed. "Thanks, but no. Nice of you to offer. He's just . . . weird. I don't know how to handle him sometimes. Most of the time."

"Dump him."

"I don't think I can. We're not even a couple."

"Quit seeing him, then."

"I should."

Ray smirked. "But you won't. I can tell from your face. Is the sex, like, completely off-the-wall?"

I smiled wanly.

"Sorry, none of my business. I just make the sandwiches."

I shrugged. "It's all really . . . weird. And probably not healthy for me." But when it felt good, it felt *so* good.

"We've all been in one of those. Or a few."

"He's not abusive or anything." I remembered the choking, the paintball he'd shot me with, the horrible minutes spent kneeling on his cold bathroom floor. Oh fuck, of course he was abusive. Duh. But I also remembered sitting under the bridge with him, kissing him, bandaging his hands.

"He's kind of unbalanced." I wanted to add *Not dangerous or anything*, but that would just have been a lie.

"I've never met him," Ray said, "but I can tell you right now, you can do better."

"I guess."

"You guess, but I know."

"How old are you?" I asked.

"Thirty-four. You?"

"Twenty-seven."

His eyebrows rose, and he blinked.

"What? Did you think I was older or younger?"

"Uh . . ."

I laughed. "That must mean older. Don't worry, my feelings aren't hurt. How much older?"

"My age, I thought. No offense, though. I hope."

"I'm not offended, I promise. I have old-looking eyes," I offered, trying to give him an out. He was right. I did look older, the way forty-year-olds who've had a tough life look like they're pushing sixty, a bustedness that goes beyond wrinkles and gray hair.

"It's not even how you look," Ray said. "You just *seem* older. You talk slowly, like your brain's busy all the time, like there's not enough juice left over to make your mouth go fast."

I smiled at that, thinking of my mouth as a slow-loading web page, my yammering brain hogging all the bandwidth.

"You're not in a rush," Ray added, "like people usually are in their mid-twenties. I dunno. You seem real mature."

I shrugged. "I've never been very bubbly. My grand-mother said I have an old soul, whatever that means."

Ray nodded, seeming to agree. He sucked his cigarette down to the filter and crushed it under his heel, blowing his smoke into the brisk breeze.

My stomach had unknotted over the course of having this conversation. Relaxing to have *any* kind of meaning-ful, deepish conversation with a man. A handsome man, I decided just then, with rather soulful eyes. I willed myself to develop a crush on Ray, a proper one, but there was an ominous, stripey obstacle standing in the way. Maybe someday.

"I better get back to work." I stood and popped the lid from my coffee cup, stuffing the cookie wrapper inside and sealing it back up.

Ray smirked.

"What?"

He pointed to my cup. "You always do that. You always do exactly that when you're done with your lunch."

"Oh."

"You also eat your cookie from the outside in."

I blushed, flattered he'd noticed. "I like the center the best. It's the chewiest part."

He stood, smiling deeper. I wished the man I sort of loved could look at me like that, finding me adorable for such innocuous, silly reasons. Sigh.

"I'll see you tomorrow," I said, and tossed my trash in a bin.

"Bet you will. You have a good rest of your day."

"I'll try. You, too."

"Get some sleep," he added. "Don't waste your time worrying about any assholes."

If only.

22

Badger didn't show that night.

He didn't show the night after, either, nor on Friday, not any night that weekend, though I won't lie—I waited up. Not until three, when I knew his vigilante shifts ended, but midnight, sure, until my lids grew heavy and betrayed me.

Funny how my priorities had shifted. To think that a month and a half ago, I couldn't wait to be asleep.

The next week at work, I caught myself daydreaming about him. When I wasn't obsessively trolling the Boston Badger Watch site, that was.

I Googled Isaac Belov, of course. It took me a couple days to realize I could, and even longer to ignore the part of my brain that said I really didn't want to. I really shouldn't.

Don't be a stalker.

Let's just open a new browser tab . . .

He'd grown up half a decade before me, a teenager in

a time just before every school event got uploaded to the web, so I didn't get many hits—not for "Isaac Belov Massachusetts." I found his name amid a couple lists for juvenile offenders, and once in a no-longer-existent PDF of a newsletter from the grocery store he had apparently worked for. But nothing in the way of details. Also nothing that told me he'd killed or sexually assaulted anyone, or anything similarly heinous.

A search for "Isaac Belov Badger" produced nothing that linked him with his alter ego, so it seemed his secret truly was mine to keep. The second I finished that search, however, a paranoid thought gripped me, and I glanced frantically around my office, terrified the CIA or somebody might be monitoring Badger-related web searches.

I told myself I was being a spaz and to get a grip. But just to be safe, I then Googled a dozen variations of "badger pest extermination," like that might throw the feds off the scent (see again: *moron*). No black-clad SWAT guys rappelled through the window, and eventually my pulse dropped back to normal.

Did he feel bad about what had happened and the way he'd dismissed me? I doubted he was capable of it. Though he had apologized to me before for making me choke him. Still. Didn't strike me as likely.

Worst of all, if I confronted him about being such a creepy shit to me, would he even know what I was talking about? Would the poster child for impulse-control issues even remember that he'd ordered me to get the fuck out, and my sudden obedient flight, or had those dissolved from his brain the second a new stimulus arrived?

That was the worst thought of all, the one that told me maybe things weren't ruined.

That first Badger-free weekend, I'd bought a cheap DVD player to replace the stolen one. I'd gone on a film jag, one with a focus so opaque I hadn't even spotted it at first. *Greystoke, The Enigma of Kaspar Hauser, L'Enfant Sauvage.* Basically, anything featuring a feral lost cause. Even the schemes I came up with to distract me from thinking about Badger reeked of obsession.

But the theme ran out quickly, and I found myself stretching. *Good Will Hunting* had the Boston factor, the orphan factor, but it was bound to take far more than the love of Minnie Driver and the warm, fuzzy counsel of Robin Williams to fix my outcast. Though it did make me cry a bucket, especially that part where Matt Damon leaves Minnie all crumpled and heartbroken in bed, right after she tells him she loves him. I wished I had an offer to study medicine at Stanford, so maybe Badger would deign to chase after me.

An even further reach was the Disney version of *Beauty and the Beast,* though I watched with such intent, you'd have thought there was a test directly following the credits. I wondered if I had what it took to reform my own personal prickly, reclusive sociopath. Probably not. Belle exceeded me in both her charm and measurements.

I turned that one off a little after eleven on Wednesday night, now a full week since I'd last seen my sadistic love interest. The news was on, and as I folded a pile of laundry, a headline hiked my chin from the task.

"The Badger strikes again, and this time, the shot was heard

all the way on Beacon Hill," the studio anchor said, and then it switched to a male reporter standing in a dark park.

"That's right, Jill. Though it wasn't hard to hear that shot from Beacon Hill, because it happened right here on Boston Common, within view of the State House. The city's now in-famous Badger—the anonymous, self-styled vigilante on a bi-cycle—allegedly shot one of his trademark white paintballs at a woman walking her dog, right where I'm standing now. The victim? Governor John Truro's twenty-four-year-old daughter, Ashley Truro. She was struck in the arm by the paintball. Though she wasn't badly injured, she was taken to Mass General as a precaution. The governor had this statement."

The shot changed again, to the man in question sitting behind a wide desk, the seal of the Commonwealth behind him. *"This nonsense has gone on long enough. I'm angry not only on behalf of my daughter, but for the daughters and sons, mothers and wives and loved ones of everyone in this city. I'm going to be personally working with the Boston and Cambridge police departments to make sure this nuisance is brought to justice."*

Back to the reporter in the Common. *"But the Bad-ger isn't seen as a nuisance by some Bostonians. Though his methods are illegal and arguably dangerous, many of the Hub's residents agree with his ethics. Until now, his attacks have always followed a breach of law or decency—a punish-ment doled out to the seeming bullies among us. But Ashley Truro maintains she did absolutely nothing to provoke this morning's assault, and the governor's office suspects this latest incident can only beg one question—Has the Badger gone political? In downtown Boston, I'm Gene Cristoff."*

I gawked at the screen, jaw clenched, a pair of socks trembling in my fists.

The Badger, gone political? That was the stupidest thing I'd ever heard. They might as well speculate he was half-dolphin, it was such a ludicrous idea. I shoved the socks in a drawer and slammed it.

I wondered what the governor's daughter had done to earn her paintballing, because I goddamn *knew* the bitch was lying. I hoped she'd been wearing a really nice, expensive, impossible-to-clean coat. And I hoped she didn't have a welt. That would've made me jealous, as welts had become like roses between Badger and myself, the ugly, tender red blooms we exchanged on special occasions. Or had.

Twitchy and pulsing, I switched off the TV. The theme from *Beauty and the Beast* played on a loop in my head, undermining my angst.

In earnest, I began to worry.

Would the reward go up, and did anyone aside from me know anything about the Badger worthy of the payout? Someone from the grocery store he'd worked for, maybe, if they might recognize his face or bike from the blurry photos. Whomever he bought paintballs or spare tires from. Some other Boston Badger Watch enthusiast, someone who wanted to get paid, not merely to bone their shabby hero. Someone who hated what he did as much as some of us delighted in it. There certainly were types like that. I rolled my eyes at their message board rants daily.

At noon the day after the news story, I left the office and buttoned my coat against the drizzle and jogged half a block to the sandwich shop. Ray was busy making someone's order, but we shared a smile while the girl at the register rang me up for my coffee and cookie.

Five minutes later the door jingled open. I heard the snick of his lighter and smelled his Camel, glanced at his scuffed old boot as he crossed his legs.

He nearly always let me speak first. Sometimes it felt like he was testing me, knowing I ought to get better at engaging. Other times it was more like respect, as if he understood I simply didn't want to talk some days.

"Feels like winter already," I finally said.

"No kidding."

I turned, and he looked as tired as I felt. "How was your morning?"

A shrug. "Usual. Yours?"

"Usual." I took a bite of my cookie, mulling things over before I spoke again. "Have you heard of the Badger? The guy with the paintballs on the bike?"

"'Course I have. Everybody in the cycling community knows about him."

"Oh. Do they hate him or love him?"

"Both. Some hate him for giving us a bad name—like we need any more shitty press. But I think most of us are pro. I'm pro. All the younger kids are pro. Makes the place a fuck of a lot more interesting."

I nodded. "I'm pro, too. Did you hear on the news that he paintballed the governor's daughter?"

Ray laughed, then coughed from the smoke. "Not surprised. I'd like to meet that guy, just to try and get a handle on what the fuck his deal is."

I balanced my cookie on my knee and warmed my

palms on my paper cup. *I've banged the guy*, I thought. *And I have no clue what the fuck his deal is.* "There was a reward before, but I bet it'll go up now."

"You got some thing for this guy?" Ray teased me.

"It's just an interesting story, I guess."

"True."

We sat without speaking, me lost in worry over my ex-never-really-a-boyfriend's future, Ray thinking about who knew what.

At length he asked, "You, uh, ever get out to Harvard Square?"

"Not a lot, but sometimes." *Until recently, I used to pass through the station, en route to throwing myself at a border-line abusive man incapable of ever requiting my feelings.*

"I'm pretty sure I'll be at Charlie's Kitchen, upstairs, tomorrow night. There's a New Wave show that's supposed to be good. You should come along. If you're free."

"Oh, thanks. I, um . . . Shit." I looked him right in his eyes. "Can I tell you something?"

He smiled, and I caught a glimmer of disappointment there as he sensed my pending rejection. "Go crazy."

"I'm not really into the bar scene. Or drinking. Or anything even remotely exciting."

"That's cool. You can just tell me 'no.'"

"Well, you're a nice guy, so I'll level with you. I'm a recovering pill addict, so I have to kind of steer clear of all that stuff."

He did a nice job of nodding politely and pretending not to be shocked. "That's cool. I'll quit asking you, then. Sorry if I made you uncomfortable."

"No, nothing like that. Just thought I'd clue you in to

why I never show up when you're nice enough to tell me about parties and shows."

He leaned closer, speaking quietly. "Can I ask what? What you used to do?"

"Vicodin, and whatever else was lying around. For a couple years, and I've been sober for eleven months."

He nodded. "My older sister had a heroin problem. For ages. It's no fun."

"You're telling me."

"Eleven months, though. Well done."

I shrugged the compliment away. "Anyway. I've never had trouble with alcohol, not by itself, but I wouldn't put it past me to make some trouble, so . . ."

"Say no more."

"Oh, and you know . . . No one at my work knows, so . . ." I waved my cookie between the two of us.

Ray pulled an invisible zipper across his lips.

"Thanks."

"Do you go to meetings?"

I nodded. "I do. Though I'm kind of overdue." Quite overdue. I really needed to pull my finger out and find a new sponsor. My old one had relapsed on oxy and disappeared off the face of the earth back in August. And I really ought to make an appearance that night, in case my Thursday crew were worried about my absence. They'd be happy to hear I was still drug-free. Just addicted to the twisted excitement of my certifiable ex-fuckbuddyship.

"So you must steer clear of guys who drink and all that," Ray said, not especially smoothly. Pretty adorable.

"I really ought to steer clear of guys, period."

"Oh." He stared blankly at the cars passing by us.

"I'm such a mess, I'm not qualified to handle a relationship." Not a decent one, anyhow. I'd done a bang-up job fostering a dysfunctional mindfuck of a romantic diversion. "Especially since I'm just getting over my . . . whatever I had, with that guy I mentioned. I'm feeling like kind of a screw-up at the moment."

Ray's face was tough to read, but I thought I could guess what he was deciding not to say. He liked me, screw-up or not. He held the words back, either because none pithy enough arrived or because he didn't want to make me uncomfortable. Or because my pill issues really did give him the pause they frankly ought to.

"I appreciate it, though," I said. "You inviting me to do stuff. It's nice to . . . I dunno, get invited. To be somebody anyone even wants to invite. But I'm just finding my feet again. Like I'm treated, you know. I'm stitched back together. But I don't want to fuck anything up until I actually feel healed. I don't want to rip my stitches out."

"You should get one of those head cones," Ray teased, eyes crinkling as he surely pictured such a thing. "But say no more."

I finished my coffee and cookie and made a methodical show of removing the lid and stuffing the wrapper into the cup, Ray nodding along to tell me yes, I was following the correct procedure. He made a noise like an air lock closing as I sealed it with the lid, and I laughed.

I stood, wishing I could stay on the bench all afternoon,

with Ray making me feel like a normal girl. "I guess I'll see you tomorrow."

"Guess you will."

"Have a good day."

"You too, kid."

23

I went to NA that night, desperate to vacate my house and my head. And also to listen to people's stories and to try to figure out if what I had for Badger was a new addiction or not, in case I ought to be more worried about it.

By the end of the meeting, I'd decided that since it wasn't interfering with my ability to hold a job or threatening any of my personal relationships, I was probably just plain old lovesick, not love-addicted. I left feeling good about my recovery, having realized I'd be getting my shiny twelve-month chip in a couple weeks. It took the edge off my mopiness and reminded me that as blah as I felt, I was worlds better than I had been this time last year.

It also kept me out late, so when I got home there was no time for movie watching or overthinking, just sleep.

The next morning at the office, I felt off. Not quite sick, maybe pre-sick. An uncomfortable sensation in my stomach that I tried to blame on too much coffee. At one-fifteen I wrapped a draft of a product description, saved it, and bundled up against the cold.

"Anything from the sandwich place?" I asked Dana, winding my scarf around my neck as I passed by the front desk.

"Nah. Thanks."

"I'll be back in forty or so."

"Cool. Don't forget there's a meeting at two."

"I won't."

Middle still not happy, I headed down the stairs and out into the blinding sunshine. Cold, but hardly any breeze.

Feeling especially shy, I didn't scan the people behind the deli case, just headed for the basket that held the cookies and grabbed the roundest-looking one.

"Adriaaan!"

Ray was assembling someone's sandwich, and I flashed him a tight smile. When my turn came to pay, I ordered a coffee I really didn't need and set my cookie on the counter.

"Saw your buddy the Badger this morning," Ray said to me over the register girl's shoulder.

My churning stomach flipped inside out. "Oh yeah? In Brookline?"

"You didn't see him," the girl said. "I did. And yeah, he rode right past, maybe an hour ago. I wonder if any of our customers got paintballed." She grinned and wiggled her brows at Ray, like they must've had a few regulars they wouldn't have minded seeing splattered.

"Yeah" was all I could think to say.

"That's three twenty-five."

"Oh, right." I scrambled for my wallet, then slipped outside so the next person could pay.

I shivered even as the sun heated my hair. Another week or two and I'd have to start eating lunch at my desk or inside the deli, though frequently there weren't any free tables at that time of day. I'd miss my little flirtation sessions with Ray. Though at the moment I could barely picture his face—the one I'd smiled at a mere minute earlier.

I scanned the road, wondering if the counter girl really had seen Badger. Snotty as the thought was, I liked to imagine I was the only one who really could recognize him, really ID him. Except when my stomach churned anew, I felt it for what it was.

The pull, only different.

The pull gone sour.

He *had* been here an hour ago, right when I started to feel weird. Had he come for me? Did he even know where I worked? He did, yes. Sort of. I'd mentioned my office was a couple blocks past the theater. Even if he hadn't remembered that conversation, the hook-in-the-guts could have led him here. The latter seemed more likely. It struck me as un-Badgerish that he might do something as purposeful as remember where someone worked.

But those questions paled beside the uncertainty of whether or not I wanted to see him.

If he was looking to apologize . . . Oh God, I'd be so fucked. I'd forgive him before the words were even out of his mouth.

I wasn't certain I *wanted* to forgive him, or even to be apologized to. I wanted to be the kind of woman who didn't hand out endless strikes, who drew a hard line and gave a man hell if he crossed it. I was suspended between the woman I had been and the one I wished I was. Before, I'd have mumbled an apology after he told me to get the fuck out, beat myself up the whole journey home for wrecking things and professing my love. I'd never have let myself be angry at him. But this new stopgap Adrian had been angry, and if she'd had just a bit more in the way of boundaries, she'd have stood up and glared at him and hit him with an irate *"Excuse me?"*

I wound up feeding most of my cookie to a pair of pigeons, marveling that I'd ever thought Badger was their spiritual brother. Pigeons were skittish and needy and social. Pigeons were gross, but generally gentle. Badger was—

Ray sat down beside me. I hadn't even heard the door tinkle.

"Any Badger sightings?"

I shook my head, realizing I was glad about that. I might have secretly wished he was trying to find me to apologize, but as hard to interpret or predict as he was, I didn't think it was likely. The pull didn't feel good anymore. Now that we were upset with each other, it felt nothing like magnetism or gravity. It felt the way rotting food smells. *Danger. Get away.*

Ray lit up, and I turned to watch him. I never stared at anyone—I kept my eyes averted at all times on the subway. If I was ever given one of those observation tests where a stranger bursts into a classroom and pretends to mug the teacher, and all the students are asked to describe the assailant, I'd fail miserably. I could ride the T for a half hour with the same forty people, and when I got off, I wouldn't be able to pick a single one of them out of a lineup, not unless they were maybe wearing really interesting shoes. Maybe.

But I studied Ray, memorizing his face. His dark eyebrows and the little scar on his forehead, his crow's feet and the flat, diamond-shaped bit on the bridge of his nose. I wondered what it would feel like to press my fingertip against that spot.

He swiveled his gaze to mine. "I got something on my face?"

I felt too tired and ill to be bashful. "Just looking at your nose." A narrow nose, very unlike the strong Eastern European-style one I'd been studying from so close until recently. His chin was sharper than Badger's, lips thinner, but always ready with a wan smile. I willed myself to have a crush on him.

"What about my nose?"

I pointed. "Just that little flat part on the bridge. I was wondering what it felt like."

He leaned forward, and in a moment of goofy boldness, I reached out and rubbed the spot. Felt just how I'd expected. Nice that a man could feel predictable.

Ray sat up straight. "Happy now?"

I nodded. "Mystery solved."

The door jingled beside us, and one of the girls who worked the register stuck her head out. "Jen has to go home. Something about her dog."

Ray made a face, one that told me that whichever of the counter girls Jen was, she had to go home often, and for consistently spurious reasons.

"Can you take over getting that party platter order put together?"

Ray stood with the weary huff of a much older man and snuffed his barely smoked cigarette on the sidewalk. "Watch out for badgers, kid," he told me, and disappeared inside.

And I did watch. Oh, how I watched.

I ate my cookie slowly, eyes jumping from one lane to the other, scanning for gray and yellow as my brain scanned my stomach for spikes in queasiness.

If I saw him, if he was looking to apologize . . . I'd be cold. I'd nod and accept his courtesy, but I'd make it plain I was done with him. I'd be equally cold should he turn up acting like nothing bad had gone down. No point playing the I-shouldn't-have-to-tell-you-why-I'm-upset game with that sociopath, but whether he could comprehend why or not, he deserved to see me pissed. I should have let him see it the second he told me to get the fuck out, but he'd been the angry one then.

My stomach turned over, officially pickled from the caffeine. I stood to chuck my half-drunk cup in the bin, and holy fuck—

There he was.

Just standing astride his bike at the edge of the alley between the sandwich shop and the building next to my building.

I stared at him.

He stared back.

There was *nothing* in those eyes that told me I meant anything to him. His expression was as cold as that first night I'd stopped him on the bridge, and I felt acid boil up from my belly, heat flood my face.

Come here to intimidate me? If he'd been a more conniving, self-serving person, I'd have assumed that glare was telling me to keep my mouth shut about his identity. But I knew him better than that.

Maybe that glare was demanding, *Who the fuck was that guy whose nose you just touched?*

None of your fucking business, you maddening, crazy prick.

I stared right into his eyes, and I dropped my cookie wrapper on the ground.

Go on, I dare you.

For seconds on end, we were frozen. I threw my coffee cup on the sidewalk. The lid popped off, and the last few swallows trailed toward the street.

I double-dog fucking dare you.

The Badger did nothing.

I turned with what felt like a rather smart flip of my hair, faking cool over-it-ness with every fiber of my being as I strode past him. I held my breath, waiting for the paintball. I really liked my coat, but it would be worth having it ruined for a chance to just keep on walking, not even a flinch to acknowledge the pain.

I waited for the *pop*, the *thwack*, and I reached the door to my building.

Nothing.

I punched in the key code. I mustered the superhuman will to not look behind me. The door hissed shut, and the lock clicked as I trotted up the steps.

My anger ebbed when I reached our office, and I felt awfully guilty for littering.

I felt awfully confused by what had happened—or rather, not happened. Had he spared me by way of apology? Because I was special? Or was it some harsher estimation, my not even being worth correction?

"That was quick," Dana said. "Have a good lunch?"

I blinked. "Oh yeah, fine."

"Lani said we should meet in the break room."

I nodded, unbuttoning my coat. Right, yes. Work. Meeting. New product brainstorming.

"You feeling okay?"

I snapped to attention. "Um, yeah. I'm fine. My stomach's just sour. Too much coffee, I think." I pictured the last of it, splashed across the concrete.

"I've got Tums," Dana said, already rooting through a drawer.

I accepted the tablets and chewed them on my way back to my office. The mint might help the stale coffee taste in my mouth, but it would do nothing to fix what ate away at my insides. I remembered an old battery I'd found in my room growing up. I'd left it on a sunny windowsill for ages, until when I'd gone to pick it up weeks or months later it had corroded, eaten through the casing and right into the wood. That was my relationship. Once the thing that lit me up and propelled me places, now it had burst its container and was chewing at the edges of my brain.

I nodded and *mmhmm*ed my way through the meeting. It was less a business discussion than a show-and-tell, Lani passing around exciting new prototype dry oil spritzers hot off the plane from Damascus or somewhere. One of them was actually really nice. Smelled like lemon and warm spices and trees. Smelled like winter giving way to spring, earthy and warm and wet. It smelled like how I'd like the new Adrian to smell, and I'd campaign heavily for it to become a real product. *Metamorphosis*, we could call it. I pictured my old self, a half-shed husk still tripping me up. Still, I could see the woman emerging. Could see her throwing her coffee cup on the sidewalk.

When I left the office at five, Badger was long gone. So was the pull-turned-rotten and my discarded cup, but I found the cookie wrapper and lid and tossed them in the bin before heading for the subway.

I grabbed dinner at a wrap place and wound up talking to Amanda on the phone for two hours, a whole lot of soothing nothing, wedding details, job details, a brief admission that my never-really-a-relationship was officially over and how okay I was about it. She was the only person I knew deeply who took me minute by minute, forgave my past transgressions, witnessed me changing without making a big, humbling deal of it. She treated me like a work in progress and didn't make me feel as though my becoming a different, better person was anything to be surprised by.

We hung up around nine, and I watched a movie on TV that had nothing to do with wild children or reforming delinquents.

I woke in the dead of night from a nausea that had nothing to do with needing to vomit.

That great wrongness in my gut, not pain this time, just unsettledness.

You're pregnant, my half-asleep brain declared. But of

course I wasn't. I hadn't had my period in almost three years, so unless it was the immaculate kind . . . and I was no Mary.

With a bolt of clarity I sat straight up, covers falling away, cold air hugging my torso. I got to my knees and shuffled to the windows, jerking the cord for the blinds.

He was there, standing in the parking lot with his crossbar between his thighs, in the streetlight, staring up at my window. I stared back, frowning. My stomach settled, but I told him with my face, *I don't know what the fuck you're doing here.* I hoped he wasn't stalking me, as sickly flattering as the idea was.

We stared at each other for no less than two minutes, then I mustered the affected nonchalance to tug on the cord and lower the blinds. As if he could see through the walls, I curled back up under my covers, pretending to go back to sleep. I barely breathed, wondering if the bell might ring. It didn't. After maybe two more minutes, I heard a faint, insectlike noise. His chain as he glided away, off into the night.

24

The next morning I lay in bed for a half hour before my alarm was due to go off, desperately trying to guess whether he'd really shown up. I peeked out the blinds, but there was no cookie wrapper this time, no evidence that our interaction had really taken place. Just a photograph snapped in my mind's eye, and I didn't trust my head one bit where Badger was involved.

And for several days, things stayed quiet. Too quiet.

I'd been checking Boston Badger Watch at least once an hour at work, but there hadn't been many posts since the incident with the governor's daughter. In fact, for three days running, there hadn't even been any credible sightings of him riding around. The usuals on the message boards where I lurked were getting nervous, and theories were running wild.

He'd been arrested, people speculated. He'd been snuffed by the cops, paranoid dingbats surmised.

He'd retired. He'd been hurt. He was taking the movement underground . . .

Every idea made me nuts, every person who seemed to think they could guess what their little hero was up to.

You're all such idiots, I longed to post.

If anyone knew the Badger, I did. If anyone could guess what had happened, I was most qualified, and these strangers' certainty in the face of my utter ignorance boiled my blood.

My breaking point came on a Monday afternoon, following four days without a single viable sighting on Boston Badger Watch. That was a deafening radio silence from a man who spent hours a day causing near-constant mayhem, and it had me scared. No sign that he'd been arrested either, which scared me more. Was he hurt? Or worse? Had something happened to his grandma-landlady?

At quitting time, when Lani and Dana came by to bid me a good night, I said I'd be working a little late on some copy. Though that copy consisted of a message to the BBW webmaster.

Since I was still paranoid about unseen government surveillance, I opened a throwaway e-mail account for the task. I clicked on the BBW CONTACT US link and typed my message.

Hello. I'm writing out of curiosity, to ask if the blog is down, as there haven't been any new sightings posted in several days. Any info would be appreciated. Keep up the good work.
—AB

I opened a document and went through the motions of

working, drafting a product blurb, deleting it, writing it again with different adjectives. I thought I was being overly hopeful, checking my new inbox a mere half hour after hitting SUBMIT, but to my shock there were two replies. One was an automated message receipt. The second e-mail had followed only fifteen minutes later. I opened it with my pulse racing, feeling high and complicit.

Thanks for your enquiry and concern, AB! No, the site is up and running as usual, though it appears that perhaps the Badger is not. We haven't received any recent sightings from the news or the citizenry. Perhaps Boston's most beloved hero / despised nuisance has taken a much-deserved holiday. We here at BBW trust that he'll return soon, and when he does, we'll be the first to tell you about it.
Cheers,
BBW Admin Troll (also an AB)

The news dogged me all the way home. I was tempted to go to Somerville, but Badger didn't regularly return to his belfry until late at night, and I didn't want to bother Barbara, as she seemed the type to rise before the sun and go to bed shortly after dinner.

I couldn't remember exactly what time we'd eaten breakfast at his place, but I guessed it was about seven. I set my alarm and rose at five, dressed for work, and took one of the day's earliest trains into the city, then out to Davis Square.

I got lost in his neighborhood and had a moment of panic that Barbara's house might be like a ghost ship, or that Badger was some strange, ethereal being and I wouldn't be able to find the place unless he led me there himself . . . But no, there it was. The streets just all looked alike.

Upstairs to Badger's attic, or use the front door? If something really were wrong, I didn't want to find out by stumbling across it. Or who knew—stumbling across some other broken-ass woman loitering in his lair. Some woman so compellingly fucked in the head that she'd seduced him off duty for four whole days. Shudder.

Front door, definitely.

I rang the bell and listened to the elegant old chime. I scanned my body for the pull, but all I felt was queasy. A noise from inside, then nothing. I rang again. A movement in my periphery turned my head, and I saw Barbara's face sandwiched between a window frame and curtain in the front room. We made eye contact, and she scowled, busted. Her face disappeared. A few seconds later the front door opened.

"Yes?" she asked.

"Hi, Barbara. I'm Adrian?"

"You asking me or telling me?"

"We met a couple weeks ago, at breakfast?"

"Yes, I know. I'm old, not stupid."

Her grumpiness relaxed me, a sign that all was as it should be. "Is B— Is Isaac here?"

"He better be. Come in before I catch my death or burn my breakfast."

I followed her inside and shut the door on the cold morning breeze. "I haven't talked to him in a while. I was starting to worry."

"He's sick," she said over her shoulder.

"Oh, dear." Yet my heart soared. He wasn't dead or screwing another girl.

I tailed Barbara into the kitchen, where she busied herself at the stovetop.

"He's got the flu or bronchitis or something."

How surprisingly human. I wondered if my absence had somehow made him ill, like a nutrient removed from his diet. The narcissistic notion made my insides smile.

"He's always getting bugs in the winter," she added, waving a hand like she was shooing her own irritation. "Takes such awful care of himself, out on that bike at all hours, in all weather. But since you're here, you take his oatmeal up. Save my old knees the trip."

"Sure."

"Don't expect any thanks. He's been in a real mood. Here's his tea." She turned to hand me a mug, then doled oatmeal into a bowl and added a spoon. She handed that to me as well, and I pretended it wasn't burning my fingers. She draped a napkin over my arm.

"Um, thanks."

"God help you," Barbara said with another dismissive wave, and turned away to putter.

I juggled the bowl and mug and my purse up the carpeted stairs, through the seemingly unused middle floor's handsome rooms, to the steps in the back. I wondered what she'd meant about him being in a mood and how much that mood might have to do with me. My defiance outside the deli, or how I'd dropped my blinds between us.

I kept my eyes off the bathroom when I reached the

top floor. All the doors were open, and my hands were occupied, so I wasn't sure how to go about announcing myself. I paused in the hall at the threshold of his room.

"Hello?" I called, probably not loud enough. Nothing. I thumped the door frame with the toe of my shoe. "Hello?"

After a pause, my greeting was met with a limp "Yeah."

I stepped inside, finding Badger in bed. The covers hid his bent knees, and he was hugging them with his bare arms. He looked god-awful. He looked as he always did—harsh, lean, severe—only like an unflattering filter had been laid on top, making it so much worse. His assassin eyes could've belonged to an eighty-year-old. The curtains were drawn, and it felt like nighttime.

I crossed the floor. "Hi." I kept my voice neutral. I wasn't here because I felt affection for him, I told myself. I was here because I'd been worried. I was here for my own peace of mind.

"I came by to see if you were okay. I hadn't seen you in a while."

"Sorry. Didn't know I was supposed to be checking in with you."

Ow. "That, and there haven't been any sightings of you for a while. Of the Badger."

"I'm sick. The Internet can take a fucking breather while I'm sick, can't it? Aren't there some hilarious videos of people breaking their necks falling off trampolines they can use to fill the dead air?"

"Probably. Uh . . . I heard you assaulted the governor's daughter."

"Did I?"

"Apparently. In the Common, not quite two weeks ago?"

"I assault a lot of people in the Common."

"She was wearing a bright pink coat." I'd seen a shot of it on a news blog, the arm ruined with a huge white paint-turd.

His gaze went distant. "Right . . . that lazy bitch who didn't clean up after her yappy little rat-dog." He smiled, more rue than mirth. "Oh yeah, I remember that."

"The cops are, like, crazy pissed now."

"Good for them. I'm sure they love an excuse to ignore the real crime going down over in Roxbury and Dorchester. Merry fucking Christmas."

"Anyway. Be careful. Barbara gave me your breakfast." Like he couldn't see that. "Where would you like it?"

"Wherever."

"Okay." I set the bowl and mug on the bedside table beside a tall stack of paperbacks. I glanced at the top cover. Crime pulp, at least fifty years old.

"Her dead husband's got hundreds of them," he said, noting my attention. "Only thing in the house to read aside from puzzle books."

"Huh. I . . ." I'd been about to offer to bring him some other fare, but it wasn't worth my breath. I stood clasping my hands at my crotch. "I hope you feel better soon."

Being back in this room, seeing Isaac again sans costume . . . I wanted to touch him. I wanted to crawl across the covers and hold him, but I could feel the barrier separating us, real and unwelcoming as barbed wire.

"Do you need anything else?"

"Don't you have to get to work or something?" He was as brusque and cold as he'd been that first time on the bridge, same glare as when he'd found me in Brookline.

Same way he'd been that morning after waking up at my place. These mood swings weren't a figment of paranoid interpretation. He really was an asshole, just as he'd always claimed.

"Yeah, soon. I start at nine." My words dripped with Old Adrian, Adrian of a month ago.

"Then you should probably go."

"Yeah, I guess so. Feel better."

I wanted to run—across the floor and down both sets of steps, out into the cold morning air. But I just smiled and walked away, quiet, calm, cringingly polite.

"Wait."

I turned, gut filling with dread, head with dizzy hope. "Yeah?"

"Take this." He leaned over to hold out a bowl and spoon and crumpled napkin, damp with yesterday's soup.

"Sure." I took it, face sore from forcing the smile.

You're welcome, my brain prompted.

He grabbed the book from beside him on the bed and opened it to a dog-eared page, done with me.

And then I left him, for good.

25

All through the workweek, a war raged in my guts between the two Adrians, pre- and post-Badger.

The old Adrian was poised to wallow and lament, to second-guess everything she'd said to him and beat herself up for ruining the happiest few weeks in her recent history.

But the new Adrian, the one Badger had fostered with his kindness and later his cruelty, was filled as much with annoyance as regret.

Fuck him, if he was continuing to be a dick just because I'd tried to connect with him like a normal human being. That's what he was, after all—the human part, if not the normal. Fuck him if something I'd said made him skittish, made him want to drive me away. Fine. Away I'd stay.

Fuck, fuck, fuck him.

But I was still relieved when he resumed his duties and the BBW news began flowing again. He was okay, and it was time for us both to move on. Hell, he probably already had moved on. Probably hadn't given me another thought after I'd disappeared down the hall with his dirty bowl.

On Friday morning, I woke with blood between my legs.

It would seem I finally had enough meat on my bones to menstruate. Luckily I still had a travel pack of tampons stashed away in my cabinet. Good. All very good. I was healing. Unless this was all evidence of something inside me bleeding out. All that sourness in my middle, eating a hole in some important organ . . . But no. I'd felt the ache in my back yesterday and blamed it on my shitty posture. I had my period. Felt goddamn good.

On Friday afternoon, I made a decision.

Earlier in the week I'd asked Ray how the show had been at Charlie's Kitchen, and he'd told me it had been postponed until tonight. I'd go.

I had no urge to drink or otherwise self-medicate, so it felt like a harmless impulse. Lift me out of my stagnation, let some band fill my head up with noise, too loud to let me think for an hour or two.

After work, I went home and got changed immediately, before I could chicken out. It left me with quite a bit of time to kill, sitting around my apartment, questioning my ensemble, perfecting my eyeliner to a level no one would be able to appreciate without a microscope. But I wanted to look as pretty as possible, because goddamn it, I was going to go hang out with someone capable of noticing. I'd borrowed a prototype body mist from the office and I spritzed marigold essence between my modest breasts.

Charlie's was odd, a second-floor bar that felt like a

basement. The usual tables had all been taken out to make room for the band. The crowd was thick, and the jostling people seemed so young. The two or three times I'd been here, I'd been as young as them, early twenties. Funny how just those few years' difference made me feel like a separate species.

I scouted for Ray's more seasoned face, not finding it. I felt dumb and alone and conspicuous, and I wished I could order a drink, a real drink, find some kind of purpose in being here. But I bought a Diet Coke instead, a prop to help me pass for someone who belonged in a place like this.

Stay a half hour. It had taken nearly an hour to get here, on top of the three I'd spent getting ready and anticipating, so I couldn't just suck down my soda and run home.

Two songs in, a headache hatched behind my eyes. Air met my tongue as I sucked the last of my drink, and I replaced that distraction with a willful stabbing at my ice cubes, trying to look cool and blasé. I let my gaze drift around the crowd, and a jolt righted my spine and drew my back from the wall. Ray.

He was at the edge of the crowd on the other side of the room, also watching, nodding his head and looking disengaged. A woman next to him leaned up and cupped her mouth and said something right into his ear. He did the same to her, and she turned away, disappearing between the bodies.

I was torn. Relieved I had someone I could talk to, but scared maybe I'd proved a highly replaceable date. Not that he'd ever asked me anywhere explicitly as a date . . .

I didn't get any more time to worry, because just then he spotted me. After a second's blankness he smiled and strained his face and mouthed, *"Adriaaan."*

I mouthed "Hey" and tried to control the smile of relief hijacking my lips. I made a little motion, the hand signal for "Should I come over there?"

He shook his head and turned away, lost in the crowd.

Half a minute later he muscled through the bodies nearest me, preceded by the beer in his hand, arriving at my side just as a song ended.

"Hey, you." He gave me a quick half-hug, and though we'd never shared contact beyond a handshake and a nose touch before, it felt natural.

"Hey."

He said something, but a new song had started, and I couldn't hear.

"What?"

He leaned close, enunciating loudly in my ear. "Didn't think I'd be seeing you here tonight."

I shook my head and shouted, "Me neither, but I got bored."

"Cheers to that." We tapped glasses, and his gaze snagged on my empty drink.

"It's just soda," I bellowed.

He nodded. "Gotcha." He glanced in his own glass. "If I knew you were coming, I'd have skipped the beer. You know, solidarity."

I smiled. "That's sweet, but I'm not sensitive about it."

For a song or two we watched the band, and I wished I'd had more practice at this stuff. Was it bad or good to feign apathy at a New Wave punk show?

The air between us grew thick, solidifying with every minute's conversational lag. Afraid it might harden to a full-on wall, I tugged his shoulder so he'd lean in, and I asked, "Are you here by yourself?"

Ray shook his head. "I'm here with friends," he said in my ear. "But I'm a third wheel, so you make me feel way less pathetic."

I smiled at that. "Ditto."

"You like the band?"

I bit my lip. "Good, um . . . energy."

He laughed. "I think they suck. But the guys who are on next are great. Me and their drummer work on bikes together sometimes."

"Oh, cool."

"You smell really good," he shouted.

"Thanks."

Ray was dressed differently, in jeans and classic black Adidas sneakers, a worn-out old fitted bomber jacket. No apron, no mustard smears. It occurred to me that I only knew Ray from one very specific, limiting angle. It made me wonder what other personal details I was missing. Tattoos, maybe. Which albums got the most play from his CD changer or turntable or iTunes. How his sheets smelled. That final idea warmed me, and the idea that I could have such an idea warmed me deeper.

I studied us in the mirrored wall behind the band, thinking we looked pretty all right. I could pass for that girl. Maybe in a few months, I'd *be* that girl. Maybe he could be the right sort of guy. Ragged around the edges, which I liked, but kind on the inside, and not a danger to my sobriety.

The din lulled me. I nodded to the band's ruckus, let it rush into my ears and brain and through my veins instead of tensing to keep it at bay. I let Ray settle inside me as well, let his company loosen me the way a drink might've.

After a few songs he leaned in to shout, "You having a good time?"

I nodded. "Yeah, I am. Thanks."

"Follow me," he said, piquing my curiosity.

We edged our way to the rear of the bar. There weren't any free booths, so we loitered near the bathrooms.

"My ears needed a break," he said, leaning against the ATM. Something behind me caught his eye, and he raised a hand to wave at some acquaintance before turning his attention back to me. "I'm glad you came out."

"Me, too."

"Sure you don't mind me . . . ?" He held his glass up.

I shook my head, charmed by his worry. He was concerned he was making me uncomfortable, drinking a beer in my company. Why had I ever pined for a man who had practically choked me with his cock on his alcohol-stinking bathroom floor?

Ray's eyes narrowed. "You okay?"

I blinked and banished whatever anxiety had hijacked my face. "Yeah, sorry. Just spaced out there."

The opening act wrapped, and we joined the applause. I asked Ray about his friend's band while they were setting up and gathered some details about him. I found out he'd grown up in Quincy, went to school here in Boston for electrical engineering but dropped out after two years, when his sister's heroin addiction rocked his family.

"How long was your sister, you know. . . active?"

"Eight years."

"Wow." I wondered if I might've had the power to wreck my family that badly, if I'd gone on that long. "And she's been sober for . . . ?"

His dark eyes swiveled skyward as he did the math. "Six years. Well, five and a half, since she had a brief relapse after her last rehab." His gaze dropped back to mine, and he smiled.

"I guess I'm lucky I only put my family through two years of that," I said. "And that I haven't relapsed."

"You do sober living or any of that?"

I nodded. "For six months, earlier this year. I was, um . . . I was court ordered to. Did your sister?" I asked, hoping I'd distract him from asking about my embarrassing record and finding out I'd been incarcerated.

Ray shook his head. "That was her worst enemy, for the start of her sobriety. She never thought she was 'one of those people.' She didn't think it was fair that she had to give up her old friends after she got clean, or her boyfriend who she thought she could, like, save from himself. Hence the relapse. Since then she finally came around and said, 'Fuck those assholes,' thank God."

"Sorry," I said. "You know, on behalf of what some of us put our loved ones through."

Ray shrugged, gaze drifting away from mine. "It's not like you choose it."

The main act started their sound check, and Ray touched my shoulder, coaxing me to head back toward the stage. His fingertips were firm, guiding but not bossy.

The band started up, and so did the audience. The music was far more punkish than the opening group, and

I got jostled and elbowed and deafened from all angles, anxiety spiking and shortening my breath. Ray seemed to sense my panic, and he muscled us closer so we were in the front and stood behind me with a hand softly on my waist. I went deafer still, but whatever body parts were flailing behind us, he took the impact.

A half hour into the set, the band took a beer break. I felt drunk from the noise and the crowd, hoarse from shouting, exhausted from the energy swirling in the room. I turned to Ray, breaking the warm, damp point of contact between his palm and my side.

"I think I might head home."

"I'll walk you down. I could use the air."

I followed in his slipstream and made it to the stairs with only one sharp whack of a gesticulator's pint glass to my head. We clomped down the steps, sliding into the cold night air.

"I'm getting too old for this," Ray said, rubbing his ears.

I smiled at that, and I got my coat buttoned. "Me, too."

The bustle outside felt like nothing now, the smell of the congregated smokers fresh as a spring day after all the human and bar aromas marinating my nostrils. The streetlights seemed brighter than normal, my rising breath like magic and the whole world sharper, the way it sometimes feels after a rainstorm or a fast, stiff drink.

I glanced at Ray, suddenly shy. "Thanks for telling me about this. It was good for me to get out of the house. And my little routines." My safe little lonely pen. I rubbed the bump on my head.

"You okay?"

"Yeah. Just got clocked by somebody's glass on the way out."

He cocked his head, mouth dropping open. "What? Who?"

"I dunno. Some guy."

"What'd he look like?"

I laughed and clapped Ray on the arm. "It's fine. It was an accident. Thanks, though."

He sighed.

"Seriously. I'm fine."

"You taking the train?"

I nodded.

"C'mon. I'll walk you." He offered his elbow, a gesture that would've been corny coming from a more upstanding guy but was rather endearing from a washed-up punk.

"You should stay and watch your friends play."

"They'll still be on in fifteen minutes." He held his elbow higher.

I linked his arm with mine, feeling pretty. I walked differently, as though I were playing the part of someone charming in a movie. It felt nice. *Ray* made me feel nice, even if he'd never make me feel electric the way only one man I knew of could.

"Got any exciting plans for the weekend?" Ray asked.

"Not really. Sleeping in. That's about it. Maybe work on some projects."

"What kind of projects?"

"I do some illustration stuff in my spare time. Or I used to. I want to get back into it."

"Like freelance?"

"No, just for me." I'd started a piece a couple days earlier but lost steam as I'd neared the halfway point, as I often did. Fear of failure. Fear of success. Fear of having my distraction end.

"How about this?" Ray said. "On Monday you bring whatever you're working on to lunch, and show me. Then if you don't get anything done, I can guilt-trip you about it."

"The stuff I do is really hard to move. But I'll take a photo and show you that."

He looked down to smile at me. "Deal."

How odd to be hanging out with a man this . . . pleasant. Who either actually, truly cared about me as a friend does or was at least courteous enough to put on a convincing show to that effect to get in my pants. The latter possibility didn't even bother me. I could stand to be reminded what wooing was supposed to look like.

"So," Ray said, squeezing my arm with a flex of his. "Do I dare assume you and your not-a-boyfriend are officially over?"

I wasn't sure I was prepared to welcome an official advance, but fuck prepared. "That's a safe assumption, yeah."

"So maybe you're in the market for a date or something? Dinner someplace, sometime?"

"Sometime, maybe. I'm still not sure if I'm qualified to be doing that stuff, but you can ask, I guess. This," I said, jangling our elbows, "is about all I'm ready to handle."

"So this is a date?"

"Kinda feels like one." Wow, I was *flirting* with someone.

"Does it kinda feel like I should try to kiss you when we reach the subway, or is that kinda too forward?"

"I'm not sure."

"Maybe I'll try and find out."

"Maybe you will."

My heart raced as we waited for the Walk sign. The beats turned to thumps as we crossed to the square and slowed to a halt under the Out of Town News awning, out of the flow of meandering human traffic. Ray let my arm go, tucking his hands in his pockets and standing right in front of me. His jacket smelled faintly of cigarettes, but I didn't mind. His kiss would probably taste of beer, but I doubted I'd mind that, either. He was flavored with soft vices, an angel compared to the masochist I'd been canoodling with of late. I smiled up at him.

"Yes?"

"You're supposed to try to kiss me."

He faked surprise. "That's right. I forgot."

"My train could be pulling in at any moment," I added, pretending to check a nonexistent watch.

"Wow, no pressure. I forgot how this works, exactly."

"You sort of turn your head . . ."

He turned his all the way to the side, presenting me with his ear and sideburn.

"Not quite that far."

He faced forward. "How?"

"Kind of more like . . ." I rose on my toes and angled my face. "About there, only with your nose going the other way."

Ray quit teasing and kissed me. Right on the mouth, lips closed but soft. His hands held my ears, feeling warm, engulfing my head in echoes, and I touched his sides, holding his jacket. We didn't make out, but I let him coax my lips apart to flirt with his, a very nice kiss caught in the taunting, sexy middle ground between chaste and dirty.

If I hadn't been so ruined, Ray's kiss would've left me floating, would've had me calling my sister the second I got home to say I'd just had the best kiss of my life. But the smell of tobacco on his skin reminded me of someone else, and the gentleness of the moment only highlighted the aggression I'd first come to tolerate and ultimately to miss. Being with Badger these last few weeks was like drinking seawater, and everything after him tasted bland and sterile.

I touched Ray's neck, searching for a spark but not finding one.

I broke away after an enjoyable—if not rousing—half minute. Ray ran his tongue over his lower lip, then smiled at me in a distinctly wolfish manner.

"That was nice," I said.

"Agreed."

"I better catch a train soon, though."

He nodded, then put a hand on my upper back. We walked to the entrance. "Hope you enjoy sleeping in tomorrow. Don't forget, you owe me some proof that you worked on your art stuff on Monday."

"Or there'll be hell to pay, I'm sure."

"Or there'll be a mysterious absence of oatmeal raisin cookies," he clarified.

I gasped. "That's extortion. I'd starve to death without those. They make up, like, a quarter of my diet."

He shook his head. "All the more imperative I convince you to come out for dinner sometime."

"Maybe."

Ray gave me a little poke on the cheek with his knuckle, then turned me by the shoulders and pushed me toward the stairs. "Have a great weekend, kid."

"Enjoy the rest of the show," I said, then headed into the station, not looking back.

26

The Red Line was quiet, just a few hyper college kids' noise to tarnish the pleasantness Ray had left me feeling. Not the dynamic pleasantness of a possible impending romance, but a calm one, like relief. Relief I'd just had a normal kiss with a normal man. That I was capable of attracting one, and someday of finding one attractive in return. It felt so nice, I told myself to be careful not to lead him on in the coming weeks, greedy for a hit of his easy normality but unable to reciprocate the affection.

I switched to the Orange Line and got stuck waiting ages on the platform. A noisy cluster of teens halted nearby, talking loudly, pushing one another in that limply aggressive way males do when they're at that age, that age when the pressure to prove you're a man must be so suffocating. They were annoying, whistling at a girl farther down the platform until she wandered off, eyes on her texting fingers. It only seemed to rile them more.

I wanted to move away too, but doing so would mean passing them, making it clear I was intimidated. Better to pretend I couldn't give a hot shit. Better not to feed their belief that they were worth being offended or intimidated by.

My cheeks burned hotter with every endless minute, but finally the train squealed to a stop before us. I'd gone to the very end of the platform because usually those compartments were the emptiest. But now it meant I was stuck in the same car as these noisy assholes. Whatever. Good practice honing my apathy skills.

I took a seat, and to my dismay they congregated in the door just across from me. Why hadn't I brought a book to read? Brought my iPod so I could drown these jerks out?

"Aw, dude, this train fucking stinks," proclaimed the fattest of the annoying teens, pulling his shirt collar up over his nose and lips. In truth, it did smell. But come on, it was the T. What did they expect?

"I can see your roll," his cohort said, pointing at the flesh exposed by the kid's hiked-up hem.

The fat one let his collar go and smoothed his tee. "Fuck you." He said it again, in that strange mix of bored and threatening, right up in the other guy's face.

"And your breath stinks."

"Stinks like your mom's pussy," Fatty replied, then backed off, sounding theatrically bored.

I held my breath, but the other kid didn't take the yo-mama bait, just hissed a dismissive *pssshhhh.*

Good answer, I told him, and glued my eyes to the boots of the woman sitting across from me.

The kids went quiet for a few stops, or quietish, the fat

one muttering hip-hop lyrics, using a Burger King cup as a microphone. This was relative peace, and my clenching muscles softened.

"Yo, what happened with that chick, man?" one of them eventually asked the quietest, skinniest, third member of the trio. "The one with the ass?"

"Janelle. I dunno, dude. She won't return none of my texts, so fuck her, I guess."

"You wish you had," Fatty said. "Wish you fucked her. I woulda."

"Yeah, right. Like you could ever hit that shit."

"I'd try, man. Unlike you. Why'd you give up, huh? Faggot."

"Fuck you, dude."

"Fucking faggot," the fat one repeated, and kicked the skinny one's sneaker.

"Don't fuck with my shoes, dude."

"Faggot," his friend chorused, then said it again in a loud singsong.

"Jesus Christ," someone said. "Shut the fuck up."

Mentally I began applauding them. Then I realized, *Sweet fuck, that was me.*

I'd said that.

My head jerked up. Where in the holy hell had that come from? *Shit shit shit.*

The noisiest, cussiest, fattest teen of the three turned. "Fuck you, bitch."

"No," my mouth said, still on its terrifying autopilot. "Fuck you."

"Yeah," the older lady seated next to me chimed in, addressing the kid. "Shut the fuck up so us hardworking people can relax. It's goddamn Friday." Someone across the aisle joined our cause, adding a spirited if unimaginative "Yeah."

The train wailed to a halt at Jackson Square, and thank *God*, the kids were getting off. If I'd been stuck with them for another stop, I bet I'd have fainted dead away from the adrenaline. Or else worried myself into an ulcer, terrified they'd get off when I did and do something awful to me, make me run and cry to the nearest T employee and prove how cowardly I really was.

"Fuck you, you ugly bitch," the worst of the kids said as he was leaving. He whipped his cup at me. The lid came off, and cola and ice splashed my lap and the legs of the woman next to me. I shot him an unseen look that said, *Whatever. Look at me caring.*

The doors slid shut, and I could suddenly feel my heart, pounding like a jackhammer in the vicinity of my ears. I brushed the ice from my skirt and felt a piece slip deeper in my boot, melting. But I'd sooner leave it there than admit my discomfort. I turned to my neighbor. "Sorry about that."

She shrugged. She was about fifty and looked like she'd seen worse in her life. "It was good you told them off. They probably never get told off at home. Not like my boys. They'd never try that bull, no way." She shook her head in an unmistakable lament against those teens' mothers.

The train went back to normal—and train-normal in Boston is depressing. It meant no one acknowledged the outbursts further, everyone pretending there wasn't a puddle of watery cola—and what smelled distinctly like rum

—snaking its way down the car. Feet relocated to avoid the stream, but other than that, it had never happened. I bet when I woke the next day, I wouldn't fully believe it had happened myself, not unless I fished my sticky tights and skirt from the hamper to confirm.

My soda-splashed neighbor and I both got out at Green Street. When we reached the exit, she bid me a good night, and I apologized about her pants again, then bid her a good night, too.

It seemed way colder than it had an hour ago, back when I'd been kissing Ray. My neighborhood was quiet and deserted, and my stomach was sour.

A shower would feel good. Warm me up and wash the bar smell from my hair and the drying sugar off my thighs. The idea chipped through the nervous crust that the annoying teens had clad me in, and underneath I found I actually felt good. I'd flirted with a suitable man. I'd stood up not only for myself but for a train car full of strangers. I'd done the thing I used to not even want others to do—to make a scene, no matter how much a scene demanded to be made.

By the time I was a block from my place, fresh energy had flooded in to crowd out the bad feelings and exhaustion. I'd stay up late and work on my half-finished illustration project, I decided. Stay up until one, two, three, maybe later, make tomorrow's sleeping in feel all the more earned.

Then as the badness lifted and my guts unknotted themselves, I unearthed another sensation. A funny pull just above my female machinery.

Oh, fuck.

And there he was, standing with his bike in the shadows to the right of my door.

Where were you that morning after you kicked me out, asshole? That's when he should have been waiting here, not now.

I fished out my keys when I reached the parking lot, acknowledging Badger with eye contact but not inviting a conversation.

"Adrian."

I opened the exterior door. "What do you want?"

"Hello to you, too."

"Yeah, hello." After a quick glare, I turned away to unlock the inside door and collect a flier from the mat.

"Where were you?"

"Why do you care?" I asked, pretending to be interested in news of an upcoming street sweeping.

"I'm just asking."

"What do you want?"

"Our stupid magnet-thing brought me here, so you have as good a guess as I do."

"Well, I don't have *any* guess. I was having a very nice night, not worrying about you at all. Especially nice, since apparently worrying about you just gets my head bitten off."

He made the briefest condemning face, just enough to tell me he knew why I was pissed. "Can I come up?"

"Why?"

"To talk to you."

I laughed, a smug little huff, and shook my head. That shit on the subway still had me buzzing, and goddamn, it felt good. Must be the feeling cokeheads were always chasing. This little sedative addict finally saw the appeal.

I started up the steps. At first I didn't hear him behind me, but by the time I flipped on my kitchen lights, there it was—the thump of his shoes on the stairs and of his tire bumping the walls. I crossed my arms and watched as he leaned his bike against my fridge.

"Lock the doors."

He shot me a look but obediently disappeared back down the steps.

My high deepened, ringing itself in pleasure as I realized I had the upper hand. He *actually* cared that I was pissed. Hell, maybe I was finally speaking a language he could understand.

"You smell like booze," he said when he returned to the kitchen.

"Someone threw a drink at me."

Something sharp flickered in those eyes, gone in a breath. "Can we sit down or something?"

I looked to my tiny dining area, one of the chairs still covered in carefully arranged strips of paper. Which did I want more—to keep my project in order or to keep Badger out of my bedroom?

"Fine. Grab that empty chair." I unzipped my boots on the front mat and headed to my room, sitting cross-legged on the bed with my back to the wall. My tights felt stiff and gross, but fine. Matched my mood. I switched on my reading lamp. Badger set my kitchen chair before the bed and took a seat, knees spread wide, elbows on his thighs, hands dangling between his legs. His eyes looked dark and dangerous, but alive. I hadn't seen life in that stare in a long time.

"I'm glad you're not sick anymore," I said flatly, making my annoyance plain. "And you're welcome, by the way, for my stopping by to make sure you weren't dead."

He sighed, all traces of apology leaving him. "When're you gonna figure out that I'm not some stray you can fix if you just feed me and love me and pat my fucking head?"

I flinched, because he'd snatched the metaphor straight out of my mind.

"I'm not a stray," he said. "I'm. Not. Right. In. The. *Head*." He jabbed his temple, and the bump on my own head seemed to throb. "I'm fucking rabid and mangy, and I'll piss all over your carpets if I stick around long enough. I'll take what you give me, but I'm not nice, Adrian."

"Why'd you push me away?" I asked, narrowing my eyes.

He blinked at me. "'Cause I don't want you to get bitten. And that's what's going to happen if you stick around me long enough. And because it's obnoxious, knowing you want to fix me."

"I never wanted to fix you. I like you *because* you're . . . defective."

"Bet I make you feel real normal and upstanding, don't I?"

I shook my head, confused. "Why are you being such a dick? What'd you even come here to talk about?"

"I *am* a dick. Why you gotta keep inventing chances for me to disappoint you, huh? Why are you even surprised?"

Because he'd changed. That was why. He'd changed, and I'd seen it, and now he was going back to how he'd been, back to the man who'd shot me in the leg.

"Who were you with?" he demanded.

I blinked, blindsided.

"Who. Were. You. With," he repeated, slow and patronizing. I pursed the lips that Ray had kissed only an hour earlier and wondered if Badger was animal enough to smell his rival on me.

"Who was I with when?"

"You fucking know."

I rolled my eyes. "A friend."

"Kind of friend you fuck?"

I sat up straighter. "So what if he is? How in the fuck is it your business, anyway? Why do you even care?"

"I didn't say I care."

"Then why ask?"

"Something's all fucked with our magnets, and I bet it's that guy I saw you sitting on that bench with."

"Our magnets have been fucked since you made me suck you on your bathroom floor, you creepy dick."

"Thought you liked that," he said, gaze moving to the side, to my headboard. "You practically begged me for that once."

"Fuck you. You know that was different. Different in every fucking way."

He leaned back, crossing his arms over his ribs, the leather strap of his holster peeking at me from the open vee of his half-zipped hoodie. "So what does this guy make you feel, huh? All soft and squishy? Does he get hard from just sniffing your cunt and having boring old normal sex?"

My slap landed before "sex" had fully fled his lips, before I'd registered crawling across the bedspread to deliver it. Damn, there went my charade of apathy. He smirked, then opened his mouth to show me the slick red spot where he'd bitten his tongue.

"You haven't, have you?" he asked, grinning. "You didn't fuck him. How come?"

I glared poison at him.

"Not enough of a fuckup to get you wet, is that it?"

"Your being a fuckup never got me *wet*. Kissing you did. All the nicer stuff we did. You know, you don't get to come over here and talk to me like this. Not when the last two times we saw each other . . ." I paused, remembering when he'd stalked me on my lunch break. "The last *three* times we saw each other, you treated me like shit. I didn't even want to see you the last time. I came over because I actually was worried about you."

"You're wasting your time worrying about me."

"Yeah," I said, nodding vigorously. "Yeah, I was. And I'm wasting my time talking to you now. A few weeks ago I was stupid enough to think I could care about you. That you'd maybe even be capable of *letting* me care about you. So let's just agree to leave each other alone, okay?" Get some days between us, let me earn my one-week Badger chip, one month, a year . . . Get me clean from this filthy habit.

"Yeah," he said. "Fine."

But he didn't get up, and I didn't order him to. We stared at each other for a long time, eyes darting. We took each other in, trying to make sense of what on earth was strung between us. I wondered if we were meant for something. If I needed him. Maybe I'd needed him to make me this person, the woman capable of being this angry.

But if so, what did he need me for? I'd brought out some softer version of him, but only for a time. Now Isaac was gone, and I hadn't changed Badger for the better, not in the long run. The connection we'd shared was gone, like an organ graft that hadn't taken.

Our gazes dodged, then slowed, then finally settled, and we stared each other right in the eyes. He looked as wild and untouchable as the first night I'd spoken to him. Sadness settled in my belly, and I let myself mourn Isaac, the man I'd fostered and enjoyed so briefly, then driven away. I scooted closer, sitting at the edge of the mattress to stare at him close up. I squinted, searching for a glimmer.

"You're different," he said, and somehow I knew exactly what he meant.

"I kissed another guy."

"He's not good enough for you."

I leaned back a few inches. "Like you'd know him enough to say. And like *you* were ever good enough for me." Though he had been, from moment to fleeting moment.

"Does he make you feel what I do?"

"What, like in my gut?"

"Alive, or however you put it. Awake."

"He makes me feel like he actually cares about me, which is more important."

"So he doesn't, then," Badger said, and his mean grin narrowed my eyes. "He can't make you feel what I can."

"There are things more important than our stupid, arbitrary pull. Like the way a person treats you. *Consistently* treats you. Maybe he doesn't make me feel all . . . whatever you do. But he also wouldn't kick me out of his house before the subway's even running, just because I had the gall to care about him."

"Do you? Care about him?"

"I don't love him, but yeah, I care about him. He's a good guy. If I could, I'd love him."

"But you can't."

I took a sharp breath and shook my head. "Probably not. Not yet," I qualified, not wanting him to believe he'd wrecked me. Not wanting to believe it myself.

I stared at Badger's mouth, that well of callousness and occasional kindness, of hateful words and pleasurable caresses. I pictured his body, bare and lean, man stripped down to his most essential bone and muscle and scar tissue, devoid of excess. Would I ever be able to have sex with another man and not think of this one? Maybe. Maybe in a year or five or ten, in that future life where I'd be capable of loving someone like Ray. Maybe I'd look back at all this and remember it like a hallucination, blurry and wild, never real. Good riddance.

My lips parted to answer the question he'd asked minutes ago. "I never fucked him."

I moved, or maybe Badger moved. I'm not sure. But somehow he was on the bed, me kneeling, straddling his lap. It was movie-lust, the kind I never believed happened in real life. An attraction and need so potent, your face collides with a man's and your mouths commence to hate-fuck. Something I'd never find with Ray or anyone else, not from any amount of good intention or wanting.

I scraped his scalp as hard as I could, and he groaned into my mouth. Something in him opened, flowing into me, our pull gone bright white to weld us together at an unknown, unseeable joint. The pain slackened him, and I knew he'd tell me whatever I wanted to know.

"Why were you such a dick to me?" I demanded.

"I can't stand being seen when I'm sick."

"Before that. Halloween. In your bathroom."

"Can't stand being seen when I'm weak. Stuck inside or doing sick shit to myself."

I bit his lip and felt his erection brush the crease of my thigh, hard as the gun strapped to his ribs. "How was you cutting any sicker than making me choke you, or anything else you asked me for?"

"Just is."

"Why'd you make me . . ." I couldn't bring myself to say it again. "In your bathroom."

"I didn't *make* you do anything."

"You had to know I didn't want to." Even as I said it, I slid my hand between our bodies and cupped his cock. "You know every other thing about how I work."

"I was pissed. I wanted to hurt you, for seeing me how you had."

"That's a real shitty thing to do to somebody who was only worried about you."

"I don't want anyone worrying about me. I don't want anyone loving me or expecting anything from me, or being pissed off when I don't feel shit back."

"I never was." I squeezed. He gasped.

"You would be," he muttered, voice shallow. "Sooner or later. I know you think you see something in me, like there's some light on inside, if you could just unlock me. But sooner or later, you'll just want to take a baseball bat to the door, you're so frustrated. And there's nothing inside, okay? Just whatever rescue fantasy that's got you so wet, thinking you could fix me."

"Fuck you. I'm not trying to fix you." I'd wished I could, sure. But I never presumed I actually had what it took.

"Just stay away from me, like you said, and you'll be a lot happier." Even as he said it, our bodies squirmed closer, and we tipped onto our sides, thighs wrestling.

"It'd be easier to stay away from you if you'd quit coming after me," I cut back between deep, hateful kisses.

"That thing that used to feel good between us feels shitty now."

"I know." Still, I squeezed his cock tighter. *Like you fucking hate it*, my memory coached.

"Feels worse every time I see you. I want it to keep feeling bad until it goes the other way, and we repel each other."

Try "repulse," I thought, feeling the icy bathroom tile under my knees. I searched for an analogy, for two materials that came together, reacted in some glorious, effervescent process, only to combust with prolonged exposure. Too bad I'd paid so little attention during chemistry. But that's what we'd been, substances that had burned bright for a moment, then eaten straight through the dish, spewing poisonous, sulfur-stinking smoke.

"You're an asshole," I told him, then bit his lip again, hard.

"Like I ever promised you I wasn't."

"How come you're not a shithead to your quote-unquote grandma, if you hate people seeing you all vulnerable—sick and homeless?"

"'Cause she and I make sense. We use each other. I get

why she wants me around, to guard her house and fix stuff and bring her groceries in exchange for someplace to live and food to eat. I don't know what it is you want from me, because I haven't given you shit, except for fucked-up sex you don't even really like, and maybe a project to keep you busy so you don't have to do your art or whatever makes you happy."

I bit his lip again. "I don't want anything from you. I never did."

"That's such bullshit." He kissed me, deep and nasty, a hot breath from his nose flaring against my skin. "What am I to you, really? Just the newest bad habit that keeps you feeling dirty? Just the latest cinderblock you're tying your ankles to?"

"Fuck you."

"Why'd you have to even say you loved me, anyway?"

I frowned. "I wish I hadn't now. But I thought it was true. I just wanted you to know."

"You just wanted to feel special—the only person who was so royally fucked that they'd care about me."

"Tell yourself whatever you want. I said it because I felt it. Past tense. You're just terrified of hearing it for some reason, and now you're trying to scare me off so you'll never have to hear it again. Don't worry. You won't."

He didn't reply, just stared at me, nose to nose, his eyes hard and empty.

My hand went still against his cock. "What are you so afraid of, from people seeing you weak? Because of all the shit you went through as a kid? Why does my loving you scare you so fucking much?"

"Just don't say it. If nobody loved me when I was little,

way before I was a douchebag or a criminal, why in the fuck would anyone feel that way now? Or if they do, how fucked in the head must they be?"

I moved my hand to his side. "You don't get to choose that. People just make you feel stuff. Anyway, the guy you are right now . . . I'm not in love with that guy." I wasn't, was I? Whatever. "The guy I was dumb enough to think I loved, I haven't seen him since right after I came, on his hand, in your bed. Then I fell asleep, and he hasn't been back since. I liked him, a lot. The guy who took me to that bridge and showed up unannounced to kiss me on my bed, and told me stuff about himself."

"Sounds dreamy. Bet you'll be prom king and queen—"

"I don't love you. I loved whoever that other guy was. And I'm not willing to put up with *this* you anymore, on the off chance the nicer one might turn up and hang out for a few hours and get my hopes up." I huffed. "Where did he go, anyhow? What'd I do to make him go away?"

His eyes darted mightily, not quite rolling. An expression more sheepish than annoyed. "I got no idea what you mean, about me being two different guys. But I dunno. Maybe you used him up or something."

Maybe I had. Greedily sucked down all the soft, sweet, sticky flesh and left myself with this. I squinted at his chest, picturing a gnarly peach pit where his heart ought to be. But it wasn't true. I'd felt a beat there once, under my very own palm, heard it with my ears and borrowed its rhythm.

He took a ragged breath, shaking his head. When he spoke, he sounded a hundred years old. "What in the fuck do I make you feel, aside from crappy?"

"You? The guy in my bed right now? Alive. And pissed off. Things I don't feel very often—not sober. And that other guy, the one I liked . . . He just made me feel nice. And accepted. And hopeful, I guess. Or deluded." We were silent a moment. Then a question begged to be posed. "What do I make *you* feel?"

His gaze dropped to my throat. "You used to make me feel calm. Now you just make me feel worse. You make me want to cut myself for the first time in ages."

"That's a horrible thing to say."

"Yeah. Well, it's a horrible thing to feel."

Though the Adrian of a month ago would've apologized, my lips had no trouble holding the words back now. "Is that why you cut, because it makes you feel calm, like I used to?"

"No. It makes me feel numb."

"Numb from what? What do I make you feel that you need to stop?"

He raised his chin and looked me straight in the eye, his expression promising cruelty that didn't arrive. "Confused," he said coldly. "And helpless."

That final word softened me in a way nothing else he'd said had even come close to. It was honest, I thought. Beyond fact to genuine emotion. Human. A dangerous glimmer.

"Helpless how?"

"Helpless like, if you stick around, eventually I'll disappoint you."

"And if you act like a dick and scare me off now, you're doing me a favor?"

"Doing both of us a favor. Whatever we got between us,

it's infected. We're making each other worse the longer we let it fester."

Jesus. I hadn't expected him to describe our romance as a brittle, dying rose or anything, but what a disgusting metaphor. "So by being a dick, you're lancing it?"

"Sure."

I blew out a weary breath. I untangled our legs so I could roll over, leaving the bed to shut myself in the bathroom.

I stared at myself in the mirror. The liner beneath my eyes had bled tiny veins into the lines in my skin, and my brown irises looked black. I looked bruised, and wondered if I was dying from the inside out, the rot inching closer to the surface every time I saw him.

A strong, violent urge ordered me to cut all my hair off. I took the scissors out of my cabinet. I opened and closed them and stared at myself, breathing deeply until the impulse faded.

I looked at the fingers gripping the handles, at my nails. They were overgrown, and I snipped my thumbnail, snipped twice, cutting a vee out of it, leaving it pronged like a snake's tongue. I studied it. I did the same to the next three fingers and shaped my pinkie nail into a single point. Digging them into my palm, I thought, *Here's your going-away present.*

I glanced at the toilet.

Fucking go for it, Adrian. Go nuts, bitch.

If this was our last time stroking our magnets together, no sense pulling any punches. I'd debased myself before for a fix. The time had come to be the one debasing.

I ditched my tampon.

My claws nicked my other palm as I washed my hands. I switched off the light and headed back into the dim room.

He was right where I'd left him, propped on one elbow, something resembling trepidation casting a shadow over his eyes.

I crawled across the bedspread, the nails of my left hand catching on the cotton. He let me straddle him and unzip his jacket, spread it open and yank it halfway down his arms. My claws raked the bare skin below his T-shirt sleeve, and his eyes widened, irises rolling back. I unsnapped the strip of leather that held his Glock in place and eased the gun free. Holding it by the barrel, I said, "Put the safety on."

He did something that clicked. Satisfied, I set it on the chair beside the bed, set it as far away as I could reach so he'd know it was playing absolutely no part in the otherwise most-fucked-as-possible sex I intended us to have.

My skirt was caught between my legs, and I tugged it loose, hugging my thighs to his, finding his dick still hard behind his fly.

"What are we doing?" he asked.

"We're going to screw one last time before we never see each other again."

He neither yeaed or nayed the idea, but his body went slack in a submissive, receptive way that told me he was A-OK with my plan. I stared down at him, almost wishing he could stay as he was, in his hoodie, wearing his holster, so there was no doubt which one of him I was fucking. But I couldn't claw the crap out of him with his clothes on. I eyed the tidy scars on his arm.

"What?"

"Get your jacket off."

He did, freeing himself from the sleeves and wrestling it out from under his back, unstrapping his holster and tossing it to the floor. I kept my eyes off his cutting marks. Those belonged to Isaac, and I was done fucking Isaac. I didn't want to care about the human side of the man in my bed, though he became harder to dismiss as the Badger's trappings were shed.

I moved to the side and stripped my top, ripped my tights to hell with my talons as I got them off, ditched my panties and skirt. He took the hint and peeled away his T-shirt, unbuckled his belt, shed his jeans, leaving his underwear as I'd left my bra. We came together in a melee of cold legs, grabbing hands, needy mouths. I dragged my modified nails from his hip to his shoulder blade, and he sucked a breath like a death rattle. I hadn't seen him surprised since we'd accomplished the so-called normal sex in this bed weeks ago. So much white around those blue irises.

We ground our bodies together, my savaging touch keeping him hard. I could feel wetness between my thighs, and I knew it wasn't anything so pretty as arousal. I broke our middles apart enough to check, finding his gray shorts stained dark along the ridge of his cock. His expression shifted as the realization dawned, brows drawing tight and nostrils flaring, lips parting.

I pressed my claws into his neck, drew my sharpened thumbnail across his throat. His eyes shut, and he shuddered, a hand drifting down to palm his cock, maybe to marvel at how hard he was, maybe to feel the damp blood there. I drew a line back and forth across his jugular, and he shook like I was hypothermia. I realized then, there was no dichotomy—no Badger versus Isaac. Isaac is just Badger when he's helpless, docile and declawed. The man I'd loved was one I'd created. He was the Badger, reduced. Diminished, maybe. Maybe I'd fallen in love with my own power, with being the only one who could domesticate this feral wretch.

With a bossy application of pressure and points, I urged him to move down the bed. He did as instructed, and I lay back, not especially turned on by what I was demanding but high on the trip.

He didn't need further coaxing. I shivered as his tongue lapped me, suddenly unsure who was being demeaned. His mouth wasn't the hesitant tool of a man coerced. He gave head like a starving animal, and I went soft and receptive as carrion, hesitant to take or admit to pleasure in the act. *Let him have this*, I thought, dragging my nails across his scalp. When I watched him leave for the last time, I knew it would feel like he'd eaten my heart straight out of my chest. He might as well know the taste of my blood.

But his lapping tongue began to draw my middle tighter. It began to feel good, and that couldn't happen. He didn't get to make me come, not like this, not on my back. No more proof he was special, able to accomplish what other men never had.

"C'mere," I muttered, raking his shoulder.

He rose to his hands and knees, a gingko-leaf fan of red at each corner of his lips, the pure crazy in his eyes hotter than any sensation his mouth had given me. My core clenched as he edged up the bed, straddling my knees, thighs, hips. He stared down at me, threats growling from every harsh shadow of his body.

I had a red line all around my middle from the tights. I didn't care. Didn't care that I was bleeding, or sticky from the cola, or that my face looked ugly from the anger blazing in my eyes. It was time to make a bad decision, one with minimal risk but steeped in a deep vat of stupid.

"Fuck me."

As he got between my legs, I clawed his shoulder hard enough to break his skin. He pushed his waistband down to free himself, then sank deep, the friction erased by my blood, his spit, the spiteful arousal gripping my body. His flesh slapped mine, and our hip bones clashed like antlers. I raked his arm and back with my left hand, rubbed myself with my right. I watched his pale cock grow streaked with red and listened to his frightened breathing, and I came harder and faster than I ever had in my entire twenty-seven years, so hard it hurt.

Pressing but not choking, I held his neck. His back arched, and he came after a dozen violent thrusts, nearly the full weight of his body jamming his windpipe against my palm.

No names were uttered. No gasps admitted awe in the ferocity of the sex or satisfied relief in its wake. He collapsed beside me, chest rising and falling, eyes on the pebbled texture of the plaster above.

I lay still, filled with visceral ugliness—in my head, behind my ribs, slicking the insides of my thighs. My sweat cooled, and my skin went clammy, and I left him.

When I returned from the bathroom, he was sitting up, leaning against the tubes of my headboard.

I smoothed my hair. "Get the fuck out."

Only the slimmest second's hesitation rewarded me, and then he was up.

I watched his flexing back as he righted his blood-stained shorts and pulled on his pants, his right-hand side scratched to hell. *Where's your precious rubbing alcohol now, asshole?* I hoped the lines would linger, and I hoped they'd make him miss me. Not because I wanted him to come back. Just to make him suffer.

I hoped he'd get home and look in a mirror, remember exactly who'd given him his red wings. Tongue the dried blood and get a hard-on from it, knowing he'd never earn that or anything else from me ever again.

He donned his shirt, buckled his holster and replaced his pistol, zipped up his jacket and cinched the hood. He shot me a dark look and left my bedroom.

I didn't need to hear him leave. Just let him be gone. Let him be the habit I walked away from before I hit bottom.

I shut myself back in my bathroom and clipped all my nails to the pink, filed them cleanly. I took a shower and washed the tackiness of the soda from my legs, the stickiness of my blood and Badger's come from between my thighs. I shaved my armpits and legs. I shaved my pubic hair clean away, getting dizzy from the steam as I cleared the blades between endless strokes. I didn't stop until I felt smooth and exposed and alien, free of him.

When I shut off the water, I missed its din. I toweled my body and brushed my wet hair, found a tampon, wiped the fog from the mirror and picked up my haircutting scissors.

I didn't hack it all off. That impulse had passed, and Badger didn't deserve to make me regret anything come morning. Instead I combed out the front and cut bangs straight across at the eyebrow. I tidied the line, liking the change.

If it had been earlier, I'd have laundered all my bedclothes and cleaned my entire apartment, rearranged the furniture. Make it all different, unrecognizable, so any ghosts who might turn up looking to haunt would think they'd gotten the address wrong and leave me in peace. As it was, I put on pajamas, locked up, poured myself a glass of water, and turned off the kitchen light.

Though my bedroom still smelled of sex, it didn't dog me the way I'd thought it might. I felt careless and detached, but not numb. Nothing tugged at my limbs and forced me to raise the blinds and seek his stare. I curled up beneath my covers and shut my eyes.

Sleep would come easy, not because I was exhausted but because I was calm. My middle was placid for what felt like the first time in weeks. I'd yelled at strangers. I'd hate-fucked my grubby former idol and sent him off into the night from whence he'd come. Though the memory of what had happened in Harvard Square felt hazy, I'd let a man who actually deserved to kiss me do so there in the crisp, thin, winter-smelling air. And maybe someday I'd deserve him back.

Though I wouldn't hold my breath.

27

By the morning, Ray's kiss felt like a dream, the stamp of its proof scrubbed clean from the back of my hand, as forgotten as the songs I'd paid to hear.

But there was far too much evidence of what had happened afterward to pretend Badger's visit had been a figment. I straightened the line of my bangs with the naked-feeling tips of my nail-less fingers and filled the tub with cold water so I could soak the bloodstain from my bedspread.

The weekend passed too quickly, gobbled up with housecleaning and the rearrangement of my meager furniture, with countless errands and the fussy shuffling of tiny scraps of cut paper against illustration board.

I felt out of sorts in my skin, unnerved and exposed from where I'd shaved, as though I were missing more than mere hair. The pull was gone, utterly, and though in its wake was peace, I had no clue how to sit with the sensation. I'd gotten so accustomed to searching myself for his disruptive gravity, I felt suspended.

Monday dawned, and I was awake, dressed, traveling underground and resurfacing, sitting at my desk.

I didn't want lunchtime to arrive. I didn't want to have to see Ray, but I wouldn't *not* show up like usual, because if he really did like me, that would be cruel. I knew too well how crappy it felt when you were excited for someone to show, only to be let down.

It was an icy-cold day, and I was grateful for it. It could explain why I might not find the balls to hang out on the bench after I fetched my coffee and cookie. My stomach gurgled as I shrugged into my coat. I felt like someone had asked me to care for their goldfish and I'd messed up and killed it. I'd let Ray kiss me, and it had been wonderful, but I'd crushed the moment and its memory. Or worse, I'd let Badger do the job. I knew I didn't owe Ray anything, and that if I'd led him on, it had been in the most minimal, well-intentioned way. Still. I'd gotten rusty at doing the hurting. Funny how badly it hurt.

As I descended the steps to the first floor, I hoped Ray would be busy. Maybe I could get away with a friendly smile, and my hat and scarf would tell him why I wouldn't be eating my cookie on the bench. I could cool his hopes gently.

But stealthiness was not in the cards.

"Adriaaan!" Ray was already on the bench, a coffee cup in one hand, cookie in the other.

My middle tied itself in knots, but I smiled as warmly as I could. I paused as a car pulled onto the street from a back parking lot. Peering down the alley, I found no

Badger. I should have known. There was no hook in my guts, only acid. I stopped in front of Ray, glancing between each of his offerings.

"How did you know?" I teased. It felt nice, actually. He still made me feel charming in that easy way. I hadn't ruined *everything*. "You didn't have to do that."

"I didn't get a chance to buy you a drink or pay your cover last night, so think of it as a retroactive gesture of my chivalry." It could have been a lofty statement, but his accent chipped the soft edges off the words.

"Whatever it is, thanks." I took the coffee and got settled with a couple feet between our hips.

"I like the bangs. They suit you." Ray made his face fall, faking worry. "Unless some crazy person assaulted you on the way home and stole the front of your hair?"

"No, that was all me."

"Well, it's nice." The season's first snowfall had begun, tiny white flakes only clinging for a moment to his knit cap before they disappeared. "You got home all right, then?"

I nodded and sipped my coffee. Had he asked one of the register girls what I take, or did something about me just scream *black coffee*? Still, the perfect amount of sugar. "Someone on the subway threw their soda at me, but other than that—"

His brows flew up. "What?"

"Just some stupid kid. He was being a noisy jackass, and I told him to shut up, and that was his witty retort, I guess. Anyway, I got home fine. Just a bit stickier than I'd planned." It was *after* I'd gotten home that things had gone so perfectly fucked. Badger's cock flashed across my mind. Badger's eyes, Badger's pained face in the soft light of my reading lamp.

"That sucks. Sorry, kid." He held out the cookie.

"Thanks."

"And here I was hoping you'd spent the whole ride home composing poems in your head about how awesome I was."

I smiled at that—a small but genuine smile. Goddamn, I wanted him to be enough so, so badly. Maybe in some other life . . .

Though in some other life there would have to be no Badger. And with no Badger, there might not be the Adrian that Ray seemed to like. There certainly wouldn't be an Adrian capable of bitching out hoodlums on the MBTA. No Adrian brave enough to meet a sweetly shameless thirty-something guy for a show at a bar, not the one who'd flirted with him under the Out of Town News awning. Maybe no version of Adrian that Ray would find so compelling. Just the same old cringing, mousy apology fount from a month or more ago.

"You are pretty awesome," I said. "And how nice that you're so modest about it."

"No sense hiding the obvious," he said with a smirk. "You bring me a photo of what you worked on?"

"Oh, crap."

He smiled, shaking his head.

"It wound up being a weird weekend. Tomorrow, maybe."

"Tomorrow, if you value your cookie supply."

"Promise."

He crossed his legs. "So."

"So?" I took a bite of my cookie.

"So, can I ask you out? To dinner or something? Any-place but this dive," he added, hooking a thumb at the deli's front window.

I pursed my lips and felt crumbs there. I licked them clean as I pondered my reply. Ray's face fell for a fraction of a breath, and then he hitched his mouth into a tight smile. "Not yet, huh?"

The "yet" let me breathe, took me off the hook. "No, not yet. I don't want to lead you on or anything, but it's such a sloppy time in my life. I'm just finding my feet with a lot of stuff. It doesn't feel right, I guess." *I don't know what I'm capable of anymore, and you're too nice to be the one who helps me find out.*

"I'm not asking you to be my girlfriend or anything. Just to hang out. You know, and kiss."

"Hanging out and kissing sounds nice . . ."

"But?"

"But I'm all messed up still, you know? I know it sounds simple, the way you're offering it, but my head's not good at making *anything* simple just now."

He nodded. "I do know."

He knew about how addiction fucked with people's heads, anyhow. He didn't have the first clue how psychotic vigilante masochists short-circuited one's sense and best intentions and lady-plumbing.

"Anyway," I said, "don't leave the light on for me, but thank you. Really. For even wanting to ask me out. I feel so wrung out, I can't believe anybody would want to. So thanks for making me feel ask-out-able."

"I think you're a lot more together than you give yourself credit for," Ray said, channeling my sister.

I shrugged. "Try living inside my head for a couple hours." I smiled, but guilt dragged down the corners of my lips.

"Awww, don't look sad." He leaned over to give me a highly platonic, fortifying rub on my upper back. "It's not like I'm in love with you or anything. I just have a crush on you. It's not terminal. Quit looking like you feel bad."

"I feel a little bad." I paused until the urge to tear up had passed, then looked him right in the eyes. "I wish I felt ready for that stuff."

Ray took his rubbing hand back, clasping it with its mate between his knees. "You will be, someday. Be nice if that someday was a few weeks from now so I can ask you out again." He wiggled his eyebrows at me, a harmless gesture, no pressure.

"Maybe," I said, limply.

He could've come up with any excuse then to go back inside, his true plans for me wrecked now that I'd turned him down. But he slid the cigarette pack from his apron pocket and propped an ankle on his knee, getting comfortable. I watched his hands, pale skin against ragged-hemmed, black fingerless gloves. I watched his darting eyes, irises deep brown in the weak wintry light, flakes dissolving on his eyelashes, his cheek. He was like a crush I might have on a film character. Better from afar. Only possible from afar. Safe that way.

"Where'd you get your scar?" I asked him, tapping my own forehead when he glanced my way.

He touched the spot. "Fell off my bike a zillion years ago. Eighth grade."

So normal. So nice. So much less fucked than Badger's

corduroy or cigarette pit or masturbatory welts and whippings. Why couldn't I just fall for this man? Then I conjured my sister's face when she'd realized—after days of self-inflicted guilt and agony—that she hadn't misplaced her engagement ring. So, no. I didn't deserve a man like Ray yet. I still had penances to pay, smudges on my soul to buff clean before I could leave the old Adrian behind.

But a thought perked me up. Thursday was payday, and I'd done the math. My rent was current now, and this check would go toward utilities and a credit card payment, groceries, hospital installment. My next paycheck, or maybe the one after that, would fill my account enough to finally pay Derek back for the first engagement ring. I'd prove I was redeemable, and that I deserved the second and third and fiftieth chances his future wife had granted me. And with the paycheck after that, I'd buy myself a new computer. Merry Christmas.

"I better get back to the office," I told Ray, flexing my stiff fingers. "Thanks for lunch."

He nodded, grinding his butt under the heel of his boot. "Stay warm."

"You, too."

28

The pull didn't return.

Badger didn't return, either. The stain came out of my bedspread after two washings, and my pubic hair began to grow back, prickly and itchy, and I vowed never to do that to myself again. I missed my nails, now stuck moving tiny bits of paper around with tweezers in their stead as I plugged away on my project.

I still liked my bangs, at least. So did my family when I saw them for the holiday. I ate turkey and stuffing and felt genuinely thankful, then spent Friday addressing invitations for Amanda, who couldn't use a calligraphy pen to save her life.

I tried to stay outside myself, but I didn't stop thinking about Badger, not for a minute. The way we'd said goodbye had been too perfect to ruin by seeking him out. But I watched the news religiously and followed his movements on BBW with a stalker's fervor once the next workweek rolled around.

He'd been busy.

If I'd hurt him, he was taking it out on the citizenry of Boston and Cambridge.

Usually, a bustling day on Badger Watch amounted to five or ten legit-sounding sightings, mostly of the "OMG the Badger rode by me on Boylston!" variety, plus one or two reports of actual vigilantism. It seemed people who got paintballed didn't really want to make a thing of it. After all, who would advertise the fact that they'd had their clothes ruined, especially when so many of us would infer they'd done something to deserve it? But in the week following my and Badger's breakup—if that was what it had been—at least twice as many sightings got logged, and way more reports of paintballing.

On Thursday, the reward went up.

Boston Badger Watch announced it in a post on the home page with a Photoshopped wanted poster that rendered Badger's police sketch as an etching, the details set in a playbill font on a yellowed parchment background. Very clever, I had to admit, but I resented them making a feature of it. The fewer people who knew about the price on his head, the better, in my opinion. I wanted him out of my life, but I still wanted him free and active, bringing the kind of justice to the streets that I could sink my teeth into. Property damage aside, I believed the city was better with that freak on the loose.

So I fired up my fake e-mail account and wrote to the BBW webmaster again.

Hello. Thanks as always for your informative and entertaining website. I'm writing out of concern, however. I know the site neither supports nor condemns the Badger's activities, but many of its followers, myself included, consider themselves pro-Badger. I'm writing to request that you remove the post featuring the wanted poster. As a Badger supporter, I worry it will needlessly advertise the fact that there's a reward available for information leading to his capture. Though I believe it was created to mock the authorities' efforts, I feel a better protest would be to ignore the crackdown altogether. Just my two cents.

Keep up the good work,
AB

As I reread it, it sounded fussy, and I doubted very much it would reap results. But to my surprise a message showed up in my inbox two hours later.

Greetings once more, AB.

I can appreciate your concern about the poster. It was created and submitted by a fan of the Badger, as a rib against the police, as you surmised. Though it seemed like harmless fun at first glance, after thinking about what you said, I've decided to remove it, for the reasons you detailed. And also, because it behooves me personally to keep BBW as neutral as possible, and hence not give the authorities any reason to try to ascertain the identities of those who run the show.

Thank you for your vigilance, citizen.
The other AB

P.S. We could use more of your sense on the message boards. Do feel free to join in the lively discourse.

I smirked. No, thank you. The people who got into flame wars in the posts' comments were loudmouthed know-it-all nutballs, of both the pro- and anti-Badger camps. So no, I didn't join the discussions. I did, however, stumble into a pen pal relationship with the webmaster.

I replied with something to the effect of, *Thanks very much for seeing sense and removing the wanted poster. Don't hold your breath on me popping up in the trenches, though . . .*

And he or she replied with, *Well, I can't fault you on that. After all, I just lead the troops into battle and watch them destroy one another in five thousand characters or less . . .*

To which I quipped, *Playing God, are we?*

And so on and so on. I didn't see the Badger, and thankfully I wasn't really pining for him for a change, though I was still obsessing . . . just a bit more socially than before.

Then on a Wednesday morning, after a week of us bantering back and forth via e-mail several times a day, I arrived at my desk to find a new message from the other AB, with a link.

Hello again, O rare possessor of common sense. Since you're now my go-to authority on what's innocent, neutral fun and what's a red flag wagged in front of the feds, I was wondering if you might weigh in on this little gem, programmed and submitted by a nerd even more enterprising than yours truly. Personally, I love it, and I'm DYING to post it. But I'd appreciate your more balanced opinion. AB

I clicked the link, which brought me to a BBW page I'd never seen before, presumably one not discoverable through a general search. I laughed aloud.

It was a game designed to look old-school Nineties, à la Super Nintendo. Its rather intriguing title, *Spot the Badger*, was splashed above a pixelated Boston skyline, a blinking PLAY button hovering beside the Hancock building.

Grinning, I got up and quietly shut my office door, then clicked PLAY.

The game's only objective was to correctly spot the Badger as he zoomed across the screen on a bicycle. To be the correct Badger, the blocky figure's jacket had to be gray and black, his bicycle yellow, and his shoes orange.

Cute. And if anybody could spot the Badger, it was me.

The first level was easy. A digital cyclist glided across a 16-bit rendering of a city street, complete with a T stop sign in the background. I didn't click, because he wore a green jacket. Another rolled by and I ignored it, because of his blue bicycle. My finger got itchy and I clicked the next figure too soon, just as I realized his shoes were purple. The game made an angry noise, and one of three circles in the upper right corner turned into a white splatter.

The next round was pretty much the same thing, only faster. I played until I lost on the third level, then closed the tab and went back to my e-mail.

Well, I wrote, *that certainly is . . . awesome. And it doesn't depict the police, or paint the Badger in a bad or glorifying light. If anything, it's a tribute to the website. I say go forth and post! Maybe the message board trolls will get addicted and quit sniping at each other for a few days.*

The other AB replied, *Yessss! Fist-pumping!! I was hoping you'd say that. I'll post it this afternoon. But don't get your hopes up about a reduction in infighting. I'm going to build a widget to display people's scores by their screen name, so if anything, they'll be even more belligerent! Thanks for beta testing.*

As it happened, *Spot the Badger* took off. Took way the fuck off.

I checked before leaving work that night, and the top twenty scores list was already filled up, fifteen of the slots occupied by the same three names—all major message board wags, one of them a pretty funny commenter, the other two exceedingly annoying. The antagonism had risen to a new level. I played a round of the game myself, earning nowhere near a top score. But it was addictive for a few minutes at a time, something to do while one waited for real Badger news to arrive.

I imagined a world in which there really were this many striped-hoodie-wearing bicycle vigilantes, hundreds of targets, hundreds of pieces of hay in the stack keeping the police from nailing their needle.

My hand froze on the mouse, and I blinked at the screen, colored graphics blurring as an idea took shape, quick as a chemical reaction. Its implications thrilled and terrified me, but I fired up my e-mail before I could talk myself out of it.

AB, I typed. *Feel free to be skeptical, but I'm wondering if you might be interested in meeting for coffee. I've had a Badger-related brainwave that might just eat a hole through my skull if I don't bounce it off of someone. I'm free tomorrow or Friday evening after 5:30, anywhere near a subway stop. That is, if you even live in Boston.* There was nothing to keep him or her from running the site from afar, and judging from a "colour" here and a "vandalise" there, I suspected the other AB wasn't homegrown. Still, worth a shot. I signed off with my real name and phone number, as a show of good faith to convince AB I wasn't a cop looking to interrogate him or her about the Badger's whereabouts.

I had to wait until the next morning for a reply, by which time I'd decided my idea was madness. I was nearly hoping the other AB wouldn't be willing to meet, sparing me the humiliation of explaining my crazy scheme. No such luck.

Adrian, huh? I guess I'll never figure out if you're a guy or a girl unless I agree to meet up, now will I? 5.45 tomorrow at the Starbucks across from the Park Street stop. I'll be wearing a red sweater. Oh, and I'm male, in case you had any bets placed.

Dying of curiosity,
Alec

29

It was gusty and cold and dark the night I was to meet with Alec. My mind raced all the way to Park Street, heart in my throat as I mounted the station steps back into the wind, right on time for my rendezvous.

Alec's e-mails had all been funny and clever, but I really had no idea what to expect, aside from the fact that he'd be wearing a red sweater. It turned out to be a red-and-gray argyle sweater, and Alec turned out to be a rather adorable nerd.

I spotted him across the coffee shop, face aglow from the silver MacBook open before him on the table in the corner. Christmas decorations sparkled behind him beneath the track lighting. He suddenly looked exactly how I thought he should.

I crossed the room and steadied my voice. "Alec?"

He looked up, seeming surprised. "Adrian?"

I smiled and took a seat.

We gave each other a once-over, and just as with Ray, in another life—the life I might've been living if I'd never met Badger—I could have developed quite a crush on this man. He was pale and slender, with a pronounced Adam's apple, slightly overgrown mousy brown hair, stylish glasses. A bit tall, I guessed. A bit charmingly awkward, I hoped.

I shed my coat and gloves, and we shook hands. "Thanks for meeting me."

"Thanks for asking," he said, proving himself English. "Good to know my silly little blog's got fans."

"Well, I think it's the Badger who's got the fans, but it's a cool site."

"Cheers. Way more fun to work on than my day job."

"Which is?"

He grinned and shut his computer. "Back-end interfacing for data transfer optimization."

"I see."

"Thrilling, I know. Did you fancy a coffee?" He nodded toward the counter.

I eyed his empty cup. "Good idea. And can I get your next one? I'd have bought your first if I'd gotten here faster. Green Line."

"Nonsense." He stood. "What would you like?"

I fished my wallet from my purse, but he slapped my wrist charmingly when I tried to hand him a five. "Okay, then. Just a small coffee. Black with one sugar."

I unwound my scarf and stowed my hat while Alec fetched our drinks. It felt weirdly like a blind date. And I felt weirdly as though I was doing something wrong by being here, same as when I'd kissed Ray. But I was here for Badger, in essence. He wasn't my boyfriend, and I borderline hated him now, but here I was, for him. A petty bit of me hoped he'd ride past the window and see me. Serve him right.

Alec returned with two fresh cups, my coffee and a tea for himself. He sat and bobbed the teabag up and down, up and down, finally meeting my eyes without actually raising his chin. *Quite long eyelashes*, I thought idly. Quite pretty hazel-gray eyes.

"So," he said crisply, so very, very English. "What can I do for you, mysterious Adrian?"

"Well, I'm a fan of the Badger. Obviously."

He squinted pensively at me. "You're not alone. What exactly is the appeal, for you? I love hearing people's arguments on the topic."

As much as I trusted his like-mindedness, I couldn't tell him the extent of my . . . *enthusiasm* for Badger. Or my involvement. The reward made honesty too dangerous. "He avenged me when a car broke my wrist in a hit-and-run."

Alec's eyes widened.

"I'm not used to being stood up for," I said. "I dunno. It just . . . resonates."

"Exactly. I wish I had the knackers to do what he does, instead of just running a website about it."

"I bet it takes a certain kind of personality disorder," I said with a smile. "I sure as heck don't have it."

"Me neither. I grew up a massive comic book geek . . . and I still am, frankly. I loved how the heroes all had these mild-mannered facades, nobodies by day, arse-kickers at night. I had the nobody part down . . ."

"But not the ass-kicking?"

"No. Hardly anyone does in the real world. Except this guy who's brought us together, it would seem. So what's your top-secret plan, then?"

"Well, you know the cops are cracking down, of course."

"Of course. The reward just went up to ten grand this morning. I reposted the news myself." He bit his lip. "I post everything, actually. I'm the *only* person behind the site, truth be told."

I blew out a long, anxious breath. "Ten thousand dollars is an awfully big enticement."

He smiled thinly at me. "Oh, okay. Wait. Are you here to do a deal with me in exchange for some kind of insider info? Or are you here to threaten me if I'm thinking about going after the reward myself?"

I started. "Oh, God, no. Neither. Well, maybe the latter, but I'm not very good at threatening people."

Alec laughed and seemed to relax again, if not completely. "That's a relief. I'm not interested in either option. I don't need money badly enough to tattle on the closest thing this city's got to a superhero."

"Good. Well, I'm here because I was hoping to sort of . . . recruit you, I guess. Or team up with you."

He raised an eyebrow. "You've got me intrigued. And nervous. Go on."

"Now that there's a price on his head, he needs to keep his identity a secret worse than ever. And the video game gave me an idea. I thought maybe we could stage a sort of underground rally—well, not a *rally*. That sounds too political. A meetup."

"Okay . . ."

"Buy dozens of cans of yellow spray paint or yellow masking tape to do people's bikes, and encourage them to buy black-and-gray hooded jackets. I found some online that could work, and they're not expensive." I pulled the printout from my bag of the web page with the garment in question. "Or they could bring black hoodies—everybody's got a black hoodie, right? And we could tape or paint gray stripes onto those as well . . ." I gave him a look, asking to be told whether or not the idea was completely psycho.

"You want to turn Boston into one big game of Where's Wally for the police?"

Assuming that was Waldo's cousin across the pond, I nodded. "And the populace, who'll call in all kinds of mistaken reports." I grinned, high on way more than the caffeine. High on the complicity sparkling in Alec's eyes as he considered my idea, his face reflecting my own excitement, my sense of purpose. He liked the idea. He liked it more than he was prepared to admit.

"It doesn't have to be huge," I said. "Just enough to annoy and discourage the police. I mean, they can't arrest anyone for wearing a certain jacket or riding a yellow bike, right? So I was hoping to get you in on it, since you're the information hub. And I was also hoping you might consider posting some fake sightings."

"To throw them off the scent."

I nodded. "And remove some real ones that might actually be useful, or change the details."

He nodded slowly, eyes on the printout. "Maybe. That's never been what the website's about, though. It was always about data. It's never taken a stand, pro or con."

"But you're obviously pro."

He looked up. "Obviously. But not explicitly."

"Well, things are changing. He's not just a nuisance or a local eccentric anymore—he's like public enemy number one. A frigging *terrorist*," I whispered.

Alec sighed, gaze on the paper. "I'll be honest with you, I'm intrigued. But the stakes are high for me if I come off looking like I'm trying to impede justice. I'm anonymous now, but the authorities could still find me out. I'm here on a work visa, and I'd rather not give anyone a reason to revoke it. I'll have to think about it. I was afraid to even meet you here, in case you were, like, undercover." He entertained me with a couple seconds' over-the-top shifty eyes, miming how paranoid I'd felt when I e-mailed him and Googled Badger's real name.

"And you don't think I am now?"

He shook his head. "No offense, but I looked you up."

My heart sank.

"Seems you're quite the subversive yourself," he teased, and I was suddenly almost proud of my screw-up credentials.

"So you'll think about it? I know maybe only four people might show, no matter how hard we push it. But I'm friends with a guy who's plugged into the grungy side of the Boston bike scene. He might be able to help, getting people to come. It's worth a try, right?"

"I think maybe it is. I'll *definitely* think about it. Just give me some time to be cautious and weigh the danger against the brilliance."

"Not too much time," I said. "The reward keeps getting bigger, and the police keep getting angrier."

"And the Badger keeps getting more reckless, it would seem."

"Can we meet again, on Sunday maybe?"

He nodded once, twice, slowly. "Somewhere near here? Somewhere big and noisy."

"Jacob Wirth's?" I nodded in the direction of the bar in question.

"That'll do nicely. I'll need a stiff drink."

"Great." I sat back in my seat, positively vibrating. We chatted about other stuff while we finished our coffees, and I found out Alec had moved here from England four years ago to get his master's from MIT and stayed on for his current web developer job with one of the major financial firms. In his spare time he ran long distance and enjoyed pub trivia, tapas, and the X-Men.

"All the best villains are actually heroes, if you look at them from the right angle," he told me. "Like Magneto. In their minds, the best villains believe they're truly righteous. It's the heroes who are dark and doubtful and conflicted."

Oh, what a lovable dork he was. I tried very, very hard to force myself to speed-develop a crush on Alec, to no avail.

We finished our drinks and bundled up, standing in the brisk wind outside the café.

"Well, thanks again for meeting me," I said, and we shook gloved hands.

"Pleasure, Adrian. I'll see you on Sunday. Two o'clock?"

"Two's perfect. I won't bring any cops if you won't."

Alec put a hand studiously to his heart. "Not even a meter maid."

"Great. See you then."

I headed for the subway, tempted to dance myself through the crosswalk on Tremont. But no, stay calm, stay cool. I was a freedom fighter now, an underminer of authorities, a protector of protectors. I was high on the idea, shaking with excitement, just as I'd surely have been shaking with terror had I gotten wrapped up in this scheme only a couple months ago. But I knew if Badger was put away, a chunk of my newfound ballsiness would go with him. So underground I would go, and viva la stripey revolution.

30

By Sunday afternoon, Alec was on board. In fact, he was positively beaming as he approached me in a corner of Jacob Wirth's, the place bustling with lunchtime tourists and theatergoers.

He set a beer beside my coffee.

"Hey," I said.

"Good afternoon, co-conspirator." After he shed his elegant coat and put his bag down at the far end of the booth, he took a seat across from me. He'd told me in an e-mail the day before that he wanted in and that he'd already begun planning. *Plotting*, I think he called it, actually. I could see gears ticking behind his hazel eyes.

"So, we're a go?"

He nodded, something happy and devious playing at the corners of his lips. "Looking back, I can't believe I had to think about it for a second."

"With your work visa and my record to consider, thinking is probably a wise course of action."

"It's worth the risk," he said. "Plus, for all we know, no one will show up. But the more people who do, the smaller targets we become as individuals." He opened the leather bag beside him and drew out a gray-and-black-striped zip-up.

I laughed. "Nice."

"H&M," he said, glancing at it. "Very fortuitous. And if we have our way, they'll sell out by next week."

"So what are you thinking, venue-wise? And recruitment-wise? And when?"

The details fell into place over several refills of our respective drinks and via e-mail and phone calls the next couple of days—plans for the meetup, as well as our plans to stay as anonymous as possible.

We decided the best base of operations would be my old college, MassArt. Art schools are natural breeding grounds for half-baked activism, and a stream of young people congregating with spray paint cans and tape, wrecking their clothing and bicycles, wouldn't raise many eyebrows. Alec used the website to recruit two like-minded mixed-media majors, who promised us a large classroom in which to assemble the following Saturday evening.

"Saturday," I repeated to Alec on the phone on Wednesday. I spritzed a bottle of lemongrass and clover body mist above my desk, trying to choose between "verdant" and "evocative" for the catalog blurb. What the fuck—stick them both in there. "Seems like short notice."

"So are students' attention spans. Quicker the better. Get them in while they're still excited. Plus, for all we know, Mr. Badger could get nicked tomorrow, and this little prank will turn into a protest outside the State House. Which, frankly, I wouldn't prefer. Our plan sounds like far more fun." There was that new note in Alec's voice again, one I hadn't detected at our first meeting at the coffee shop. Something mischievous and very slightly sinister. Some part of him was getting off on all this, the criminality of it, the plot. He felt like the thing he worshipped so much, I suspected—a mix of hero and villain, a spreader of chaos. It was fine by me, him taking the wheel. This one brainwave aside, I wasn't built for leadership.

"So six o'clock?" I asked.

"Yes. Until whenever. I've arranged to keep us both anonymous."

I perked up. "Oh?"

"The guys who've arranged to get us the room, they're spreading the word. They look like the point people, and I'm not advertising it overtly on Badger Watch. I've posted a couple messages under pseudonyms about the event, but I've made it sound as much like a silly dress-up party as possible to keep the naysayers from taking it seriously, blowing it out of proportion to the authorities. But apparently these two guys from your old school are plastering the local hot spots in fliers, and texting and posting it to social media."

"Excellent. I've still got to talk to my friend, the one who knows all sorts of shady local cyclists."

"Yes, do."

"We need someone to read out some prepared ground rules," I reminded him. "We have to make sure the people who show up don't think they're supposed to imitate the

Badger, not beyond wearing a striped jacket. I'd hate for someone to get arrested, taking it too far. Because of us."

"I've already drafted a list."

"Ooh, you're good."

"I'll e-mail it to you. I've got to go now," Alec said with a regretful sigh. "Reality intrudes."

"I'll talk to you later."

"Later, Adrian."

At one o'clock I fetched my cookie and coffee from the deli and went out to the bench, nervous. I wanted to invite Ray to the Badger meetup, but caught up in the snowball of it with Alec the past few days, I'd lost all perspective. Neither Alec nor I were in our right minds when we got going on Badger-related nonsense. I was afraid Ray would point out some terrible, foolhardy downside and make me want to take it back, now that I was neck-deep in the thing.

The door jingled, and he took a seat, rubbing his hands. He fished his fingerless gloves from his apron and pulled them on, then lit his cigarette.

"Any more Badger sightings around here?" I asked him.

He shook his head. "Nah, nothing that exciting. I bet she never even saw him to begin with. I bet people think they spot him all over the place, call the cops and waste their time."

I smiled. I couldn't have asked for a more perfect segue. "The false sightings are about to get a lot worse," I said quietly.

He picked up on the scheming in my voice and narrowed his eyes. "Oh?"

I swallowed. "On Saturday, at MassArt, there's going

to be a meetup. People are going to bring their bikes, to paint or tape them yellow. And they're going to either buy striped hoodies or bring black or gray ones and paint the stripes on." I bit my lip.

His smile was tight, and I couldn't place its message. Disapproval? Amusement? "You going?" he asked.

I nodded.

His smile deepened, and I realized he was teasing me. "You groupie, you."

"I think it'll be fun. I hope a lot of people go. If they could get, like, a hundred random, fake Badgers riding around the city, maybe the cops'll decide it's more trouble than it's worth, responding to all the calls."

"A hundred sounds ambitious."

"Maybe, but who knows? I guess we'll find out."

He licked his lips, holding something back.

"What?"

"You just surprise me. You don't seem the type to welcome trouble, you know?"

"I know."

"Aren't you worried the cops'll get pissed and harass you for walking around, obstructing justice or whatever?"

"Yeah, a little. But they can't charge me with wearing a striped jacket, can they?"

"No, I guess not."

"And no one's planning on, like, getting paintball guns or imitating his actual crimes. Just, you know. Where's Waldo?"

That earned me a laugh. "Right. Somehow I doubt the police will enjoy the game, but okay. I could see how that could be fun."

"You want to come with me?"

His smile drooped. "Shit, I dunno. What would I be doing? Wearing a hoodie and painting my bike yellow?"

I nodded, waiting as he pondered it.

"The thing I don't like is, I don't want to get stopped by a cruiser and get patted down for a weapon before they're convinced I'm not him."

A good point. I hadn't been worried about that myself, because my gender instantly acquitted me. Girl Badgers—and black and Asian and portly Badgers and so forth—might enjoy instant visual immunity, but the skinny white guys who deigned to turn up would have to relish the thought of being wrongly hassled by the police. I wondered what sort of weirdos would show and realized their motives might not mirror my own so tidily.

"Well, it's Saturday night at six at MassArt, in the South building. Third floor, I think."

Ray stared thoughtfully at the street for a long time before glancing at me again. "If I go, will you let me take you out for something to eat after?"

"Like a date?"

"Yeah, like a date. Like Charlie's. No pressure or anything. No expectations."

"Maybe. I plan to be there pretty late, though, helping out."

"Late dinner, then."

I nodded. "Okay. Deal."

His smile returned, and we shook.

"Bring your pro-Badger cyclist friends. As many as you can muster."

When I got back to my office, a package was waiting for me at the front desk. I'd had it delivered to work, since I was never home to sign for things. It was soft and squishy inside its plastic envelope.

"Clothes?" Dana asked.

"Yeah."

"Anything special?"

I shook my head. "Just a jacket."

"Let's see," she said brightly, clearly eager for a distraction.

"Um, let me see how it fits first. I, um, I'm always weird about trying stuff on in front of people." *Good save, self. That totally sounds like you, you cagey spaz.*

Dana sighed, then laid her forehead on the desk. "This is, like, the day that won't end."

"Try week."

She righted herself. "Any good plans for the weekend? Oh God, that's so depressing. It's only Wednesday."

I smiled and excused myself to my office, not eager to lie about not having anything special to look forward to.

I didn't open the package right then. I took it home and let it stare at me from on top of my dresser until Friday evening, when I finally slit the plastic open and pulled the hoodie out.

I laughed. It was like I was holding Badger's shed skin. I slipped my arms into the sleeves and zipped it up, looked at myself in the mirror. It wasn't quite right. The stripes were too narrow, the cotton too new and clean, no drawstring for the hood, no soft frays on the cuffs. But who besides the Badger's number-one groupie would ever know that? Somehow, I'd turned into Alec. I bet he nudged his companions at the movies, pointing out all the Hollywood inaccuracies of his favorite heroes' and villains' costumes and casting.

I wore the hoodie while I heated some soup, willing myself to relax in it. I half expected lights to flood the kitchen as a helicopter hovered outside, busting me for conspiracy, perversion of justice, pathological romantic obsession.

I'd be terrified the first time I wore my Badger-skin jacket out of the house. Best that I got used to all this peripheral stripiness.

At six I turned on the TV and settled on the bed with my soup. The news didn't waste any time in making me slop scorching broth and noodles over my calves.

"Boston's infamous Badger crossed a new line this afternoon—"

"Ow, motherfuck."

"And this time, it was a thin blue line. For the story we go to John Greely downtown on Tremont Street."

A reporter stood before a taped-off crime scene. A police cruiser was ten feet behind him, a parking meter jammed into the socket where one headlight ought to be. A bunch of officials milled around it taking pictures.

"The so-called Badger, Boston's hotly debated bicycle vigilante, is known for his rap sheet. Vandalism, reckless riding, evading arrest. But now it seems he's decided to add another crime to the list—assaulting an officer."

"What?" I asked my TV.

"At approximately four thirty this afternoon, the Badger shot the driver's side windshield of the cruiser right behind me with two white paintballs. The vehicle was operated by

Officer Frank Drew, who swerved and struck a meter, as well as causing minor damage to a parked car. No one was injured, but expect strong words in a statement from Boston's chief of police later this evening. Back to you, Kathleen."

Oh, fuck. This was bad. This was *so* bad.

We couldn't hold the meetup, not now. Who'd find Badger sympathetic after that, aside from people who simply hated the police out of principle?

I abandoned my soup and dialed Alec, plucking the noodles from my pant legs.

"Adrian," he said cordially after a single ring.

"Hi, Alec. Did you see—"

"The news? Of course. I *am* the news," he said cockily over the sound of typing. "This narrow vein of it, anyhow."

"I don't think we can do the meetup now. It's getting too polarized, don't you think?"

"Self-defense," he replied, but nerves flattened his tone. "A witness said so. But we couldn't call the meeting off if we wanted to. I'm not the information hub on this one—posters and word of mouth and Facebook and texts are. People will come, whether either of us does. And I'm going. I can't *not* see what we might have started."

"But he's way worse a villain now. He assaulted a police officer."

"He assaulted a police *car*," Alec said. "And some of us don't mind him being a villain. Some of us prefer it."

"I don't think I can go."

"Why did you want to make all this happen in the first place, Adrian?"

"To get the heat off him."

"Now more than ever," he countered.

"Now more than ever, he doesn't need to piss the cops off. Neither do we. What if this actually goes somewhere? I don't want people getting arrested because of my stupid idea if the police decide it's obstruction of justice or—"

"Adrian?"

I took a deep breath. "Yeah?"

"It's too late, sweetheart. It's started. The car's rolling down the hill, because you and I pushed it. Nobody's steering, but everyone's watching. Myself included. I'm not missing whatever happens when it really picks up speed. And I suspect somehow that neither will you."

"What if—"

He made a loud, distinctly British shushing noise. "Whoever shows up, they're not robots, and you didn't program them. You didn't coerce them or order them, and you don't control them. Anyone who turns up, you seduced them, that's all. Your idea seduced them. No one need know it was you. No one *will* ever know it was you." His voice blipped out a second. "Sorry, I've got a call I need to take."

"Alec—"

"I'll be there tomorrow with the rest of them. And I bet you will be, too."

And he hung up on me.

31

Alec was right. I did go.

I was a nervous wreck the entire train ride, though, and was glad it was cold so I could wear my coat over the jacket, barely bold enough to let the striped hood drape from under my collar.

The lock on the building's main door was duct-taped flat, and I went inside, followed by a young guy on a bike, a plastic Walgreens bag of who-knew-what dangling from his handlebar. I led the way up to the vast room, where I was pretty sure I'd taken freshman-year Form Study. What I found waiting there took my breath away.

So many people.

At least fifty, and it wasn't even six yet. There were hooded sweatshirts draped everywhere, cans of spray paint, bikes leaning against every surface, jugs of wine and Solo cups, several iPhones set up in portable speaker docks.

Apparently my stupid little idea made for quite the party, and I nearly wished I could take credit. But only nearly.

A stripe-clad Alec dodged his way to me through the crowd, a can of paint and a foam brush in one hand, a tangle of white particle masks in the other. A big-ass smile on his face.

I waved, biting back my huge grin at the sheer number of bodies we'd managed to mobilize. "Hey."

"Glad you decided to come."

As promised, we didn't greet one another by name.

I looked around demonstrably. "This is more people than I'd *ever* guessed we might get."

"It's not even magic time yet."

"How many do you think it'll wind up being? A hundred?"

"Easily. I have to hand it to you, this idea's got legs. Who knew so many people would care enough to shell out fifteen bucks to buy a hoodie, or show up on a Saturday evening?"

"I thought you did," I teased.

"Well, I was optimistic. But insanely so, I reckoned." He shrugged. "Apparently we're just the tip of the iceberg."

"He's the closest thing we've got to a social revolutionary."

Alec laughed at that. "Him and you."

I blinked, taken aback. "No, not me. I'm a chickenshit." Or I had been. What I was wasn't so clear anymore.

Another laugh, and Alec spread his arms, waving them around the room—all these people I realized anew that I really was responsible for bringing. All this effort. I blushed.

"My cyclist friend probably deserves some of the credit, too," I said, deflecting. There were plenty of people of Ray's more seasoned, grungy ilk milling amid the student-aged horde. "I wonder if he's here yet."

Alec stooped to murmur, "You know we can only do this once."

I nodded, relieved to hear him say it. "We can try to keep it going online, anonymous, but you're right. The novelty will only keep for so long. Somebody'll want to cash in on the reward. Thanks," I added. "For sticking your neck out for this."

He shrugged. "Makes obsessively tracking the blog's traffic pretty boring by comparison, so thanks for the thrill."

"Who's reading out the ground rules?"

"Some guy named Todd, one of those two initial students I got in touch with. He's volunteered to emcee, whether he understands the potential consequences or not."

My happy bubble deflated a bit, as I realized my little —now big—lark wasn't completely innocent. But Alec was right. They weren't robots. They wanted to be here, and this Todd person probably relished the role of figure-head. He was welcome to it.

Alec and I wandered around, checking out the projects people were setting up. Someone had brought dress forms from the fashion department, for ease of sweatshirt-paint-ing, and there were hair dryers for speeding the drying process. They'd thought about this—really thought about it. The biggest table was stocked with bike-modification stuff, yellow spray paint, yellow masking tape and blank police ribbon for those who didn't want to alter their rides permanently.

At five after six, a speaker hummed to life, and the conversations quieted. A skinny young guy with a fire-engine-red beard climbed onto a work table with a mic.

"Hey, everyone!"

A mass "Hey" in reply, plus a "Woo, Todd!" scattered here and there.

"Thanks for coming. This is awesome. So, I'm not really in charge here. I'm just Bosley, and even I don't know who Charlie is."

I shot Alec a smarmy look, which he mirrored.

"But I think you all know why *you're* here. We're going to leave tonight as a small army of fake Badgers, to confuse the police and keep Boston's best vigilante since the seventeen hundreds free to do what he does best."

A ton of people whooped and clapped their agreement. A bolt of resentment zapped me as I realized they felt some attachment to the Badger. They didn't have the first fucking clue what being attached to him felt like. Only I did. But they were here to help him, whether their admiration was personal or rueful or trendy, so I tuned out the angst.

"There are some ground rules that our anonymous organizer has given me," Redbeard said, unfolding a paper. "Rule one, if you take part, you must imitate the Badger in appearance *only*. No homegrown justice, okay, guys? You can waste police time, but do it peacefully. Don't give the cops any reason to arrest you. You're all free to wear whatever kind of hoodie you want and ride a yellow bicycle, but don't get aggro, okay? Be cool. Don't be idiots.

"Rule two's the same idea. If you do your bicycle, be careful to adhere to traffic laws. Again, don't give the cops any reason to hassle you.

"Rule three, if anybody asks you why you're doing this, deny, deny, deny. Tell them your mom bought you your jacket. Tell them yellow's your favorite color. Or just ignore them. Don't engage with any haters, no matter how heated they get about the Badger. This is a purely visual protest, got it? Don't be idiots. That's your mantra."

Alec leaned in to whisper through the next rule. "My manifesto was a bit more eloquent than his delivery."

I nodded. Alec's code of conduct had read like a founding document. "The message is the same. Whatever drills into their heads not to fuck things up."

Bodies were still coming through the doors, and I spotted Ray when he arrived, along with two other guys and one girl, all wheeling bikes. I waved, but he didn't see me.

"So," Todd said in summation, "what's the most important thing to remember once we're all out there in the streets, after we leave here?"

"Don't be idiots," everyone chorused.

He clapped once. "Awesome. Let's get to work."

Todd hopped down from the table, and everyone dispersed, heading for work stations to get busy on the arts and crafts projects I'd anonymously assigned them. My hoodie was done, and I didn't have a bike, but I'd brought an old pair of canvas sneakers to paint, a detail I didn't expect anyone else to bother with. I tried to find Ray, but the crowd had grown too thick, so I grabbed a spot at the corner of a table and got my shoe-modification operation set up. It turned into rather a hot offering, and all told I must have turned twenty people's Chucks and Keds and espadrilles orange, until I ran out of paint.

I tossed my savaged foam brushes and empty paint tub, set my still-drying shoes on a radiator, and went in search of Ray. He seemed to have been doing the same, and we finally found each other in a corner near the wine station.

"Hey, you." He gave me a hug, then said, "Oh, fuck," and backed off. He seemed to scan me for any paint that might have transferred from his freshly striped sweatshirt.

"Don't worry. I came prepared to get messy."

He looked around us, the room heaving with what I guessed was over a hundred people. Maybe a hundred and fifty.

"Just look what you crazy kids have done," he said.

"You, too—you and whoever you got to come."

He nodded. "Quite a few. I underestimated the Badger's popularity among my scumbag peers."

"Did you do your bike?"

"Just wrapped the frame in yellow tape. I wasn't bad-ass enough to actually paint the thing. Though I am pretty much airborne from everyone else's fumes. People are seriously into this."

"I know. It's way more than I'd expected to show."

"What about you? You find yourself a bike?"

I laughed. "Oh, no. I'm afraid of biking in the city."

"You're afraid of biking in the city, but you're not afraid of joining a couple hundred strangers to piss off the cops?"

Joining? Try organizing. "Seems that way . . . but I didn't expect all this. Do you know what time it is?"

Ray fished a phone from his pocket. "Quarter after eight."

"We could probably take off soon. Let me just check with another friend."

I found Alec and said goodbye, fetched my dried shoes, found my coat and then Ray. "Hungry?"

"Yeah, just gotta grab my bike."

We stopped by the door, and he took the lock off his tube and wheel. He had a cool canvas bag set up behind his seat, almost like a tool belt, with grommets and leather straps.

"That's awesome," I said, inspecting a compartment and finding some sort of wrench set.

"I'll tell my sister you approve."

"Oh, she made it?"

Ray nodded. "Keeps her busy."

As we descended the stairs, Ray's bike propped on his shoulder, I said, "The stripes suit you."

"You, too. Just glad they're not black and white, so we don't all look like convicts, huh? That'd be lousy foreshadowing."

The comment reminded me of my own stint in a correctional facility, and I fell quiet, worried my prank might land someone else in a similar situation. Ray noticed. He set his bike down as we reached the exit, and I tugged on my hat and gloves.

"I say something wrong?"

I pursed my lips and shook my head. "No, not really."

He rubbed my arm. "C'mon, what'd I just fuck up?"

"You're fine, really. I was incarcerated once, is all."

"Oh Jesus, I'm sorry."

I laughed at his wide eyes and open mouth, his face pure, horrified apology. "No, I'm not insulted. I just hope no one here tonight gets arrested because of . . . because of taking part. That's all. And I'm tired. Don't worry about it."

He looked skeptical.

I gave his shoulder a slug. "Seriously. It's fine. Our uniforms were purple, anyhow."

He sighed, admonishing himself. "Very smooth, Vitale."

"That's your last name?" I held the door for him to wheel his bike through.

"Yeah. What's yours, anyway? That's sort of bad, if this is our second date and we don't know each other's last names or phone numbers."

"I know where to find you," I said with a smile, idly wondering if we'd kiss again or not after said second date, wondering if that was what I wanted. "My last name's Birch."

"Birch." He nodded sagely, brow furrowed with exaggerated pensiveness. "Possibly my favorite tree."

We agreed on Indian food and hiked through the cold to Kenmore Square. As we stepped into the spangly, gaudy-elegant greeting area, I prayed I didn't reek of spray paint. A hostess seated us, and papadam and sauces were delivered and fancy metal water cups filled. We scanned the menus for a couple minutes, then set them aside.

I reached for my purse. "I have something to show you."

Ray leaned forward on the other side of the table.

I took my brand-new medallion from my wallet, much fancier than my wooden nine-month chip, some kind of heavy gold-tone metal with maroon enamel. I handed it to Ray.

He smiled, turning it around in his fingers. "One year." He looked up, face full of a deep, somber happiness I'd seen my sister wear from time to time, the kind you can't fake. The kind you earn the hard way. "Dinner's on me, then."

"You—"

"Shush." He pressed the token, cold from my bag, between his palms. The waiter came by, and we ordered, and when Ray handed my chip back it was warm. I slid it in my pants pocket to keep it close.

"So is it easier at all? After a year?"

"It is. For me, anyhow. The less screwed up my life is, the easier it is. You know, the less I have to want to run away from, the farther away all the terrible memories get. My first three months were the hardest . . . but once my family started acting like they believed in me and my shame started fading, it got a lot easier." I paused, then reached out and gave Ray's forearm a squeeze. "Having your family behind you makes a ton of difference."

He nodded. "It's tricky, on our side. You want to be supportive, but you don't want to enable anyone. You want to be tough-love, but you don't want them to think you're giving up on them. It wears you out."

"I bet. Eight years," I murmured, remembering what he'd told me at Charlie's. "I did plenty of damage in my two years. I mean, I stole my twin sister's engagement ring."

Ray winced. "Yikes."

"God knows what else I might've done, if I'd kept using."

"Well," he said, holding out his water for me to toast. "Here's to you never finding out, huh?"

"Indeed." I clacked my cup against his.

Our samosas arrived, and we moved on to lighter topics,

rehashing the meetup, theorizing on what, if anything, might come of the project.

I'd noticed before that there are certain people in one's life who are just exceedingly easy to feel charming around. Something complementary about their personality or style of conversation brings out the best in you, makes you more likable, more clever. Something in their face tells you they like what they're seeing, and as with a flattering mirror or a rose-colored light bulb, you like yourself more, too. Ray did that to me. He drew out the best version of my true self, made me nicer, softer, funnier. I'd be a moron to recognize that and not try to make something of it.

So why was I so hung up on a man who made me feel nothing but desperate and obsessive and confused?

Maybe because with Ray, I didn't have to try. I'd be so accepted as I was, there'd be no onus to change, no challenge. Badger did nothing but challenge me, and I'd be delusional to believe I wasn't a stronger person, courtesy of his psychotic tutelage. He was a shove forcing me into the cold outside world. Ray would let me stay in, bring me hot tea, give me permission to hide where it's safe and dry and warm, familiar, where I was less likely to relapse.

Though Ray also wouldn't talk down to me or borderline rape my mouth, or drive me to vindictive, sadistic sex acts and frequent insomnia. Kindness wasn't a *bad* quality, after all.

Choices, choices.

We finished our meal, and Ray paid.

"Thanks. That was delicious." I checked my phone. "It's almost ten. I better head home. It's been a long week."

"You taking the subway?"

I nodded.

We bundled up and hurried down into the warmth of Kenmore Station. An outbound B train pulled up to the platform, one that would carry Ray home to Allston, the opposite direction from where I was headed.

"Thanks again," I said.

He waved the train away. "I rode here, remember? I'm just down here keeping you company."

"You paid two sixty-five to stand around with me?"

He shrugged.

"That's silly, but thanks."

He wanted to kiss me, I could tell. And I wanted to kiss him, too, or at least I wanted to *want* to kiss him.

He pursed his lips, gaze flicking from my eyes to my chin to my cheek.

"Go ahead," I said with a smile.

He did. He kissed me softly on the lips, just like Harvard Square. It felt good. I let him take it a bit further, to the shallow end of making out, before a loud clanging drew our faces apart and an inbound train squealed to a halt.

"Figures this would be the one time the T actually shows," he said, and ran his tongue over his lower lip.

"I guess I'll see you on Monday."

"Guess you will."

"Thanks again for dinner, and for coming out." I eyed his hood, peeking from under his bomber jacket. "Don't be an idiot."

"You, too." He gave my shoulder a squeeze as the train doors opened and chimed. I waved and left him on the platform.

It was a busy night, and there weren't any free seats, so I held the bar. I waved to Ray again as the train hissed and lurched. He smiled and turned away to leave, and we were gone, off in opposite directions through Boston's grimy viscera.

32

It all happened So. Fast.

So fucking fast.

I woke late on Sunday morning and putzed around my apartment, replaying everything that had happened at MassArt, giddy. I made several too many cups of coffee and did laundry, wrote Christmas cards for the few people I hadn't totally screwed over or alienated. I had hoped to slip a large check into the one addressed to Amanda and Derek, for the ring, but my bank account wasn't quite there yet. Soon, though.

At one I settled on the floor of my bedroom with my latest project and turned on the television, delighted to find they were playing *White Christmas*. I'd watched that movie at least twenty-five times with my mom and sister. I knew the lines by heart.

Just as the drama with the rug and the landlord was going down, my phone buzzed on the kitchen table. I hopped to my feet and dashed to the next room, finding Alec's name blinking on the screen.

"Hello?"

"Adrian. Have you seen? Have you *seen*?" He sounded delirious, like an ecstatic drunk.

"I guess not. Seen what?"

"The website! Oh my God, it is *brilliant*."

"We've got fake sightings coming in, then?" I sat with a smile, picturing the angry faces of the police dispatchers stuck answering endless phone calls claiming to know the Badger's whereabouts.

"Not only that, but it was on the news this morning."

"What, the rally thing?"

"The movement itself. Do you know how many more imitators this will inspire? Every mildly fed up wannabe cynic in this—no offense—rather terribly cynical city is going to want in on this. This is fantastic. This is Christmas, two weeks early!" He sighed like he'd just met the girl of his dreams and kissed her good-night on her front step. "And you would not *believe* how many fans his Facebook page has."

His what, now? "Well. That's encouraging. And a little scary. I hope no one goes out and buys a paintball gun or antagonizes the cops. You know, antagonizes them outside of wearing the uniform and going about their peaceful business."

"Not our problem," he said. "All we ever did was give them the idea to play dress-up."

"Yeah, but it'll make the cops hate the Badger even worse, if things get chaotic. And it could get the stupider imitators arrested." I frowned as I imagined their future job searches, marred by a record as mine had been. Guilt wriggled in my stomach, muscling the giddiness aside.

"You worry too much," Alec said crisply. "We're standing in the way of misguided justice, to keep the most ethical man we know free to do what he does best."

"I wouldn't say he's ethical, per se."

"He avenges rudeness and petty crime," he countered. "What more could you want in a vigilante? He's not even filthy rich like Batman. Though I'd happily be his butler, if he were in the market."

"I just hope we're not unleashing a small army of criminals, you know? If they start tagging stuff, or defacing police cars, or getting too ballsy once they put that jacket on. Costumes do things to people." I remembered the distant baying of drunken Halloween wolves, and my own lack of inhibition all the times I'd slipped inside Mr. Hyde's chemical skin.

"You're worrying far too much, Adrian. The smart people will just go about their business, not causing any trouble aside from wasting police time. And the dumb ones, well, they'll deserve whatever they get."

"I don't—"

"Go to the website and check it out. Utterly brilliant. Bloody Christmas," he murmured, and I could hear typing in the background. "Just be happy. This is what you wanted, and it's succeeded beyond either of our expectations."

"I know. I don't have a computer at home, but I'll try to get to the library today."

"Don't have a computer?" he repeated, faking astonishment. "You adorable Luddite, you."

"I got burgled a month ago. Anyway, I'll have a look."

"See that you do. It'll *make* your day. You've gone positively viral, darling."

Ah, no wonder I felt so queasy.

I headed to the library shortly after we hung up, and the news was alarming, if thrilling. The prank had made all the local news sites and blogs, with dozens of different pictures of fake Badgers out in the streets, alone and in pairs, on bikes and on foot, one even manning the drive-thru at a Dunkin' Donuts in his striped jacket.

The smart ones did as directed and denied allegations that they were dressed as the Badger—*Who's the Badger?* Others said yeah, they were, they liked what he stood for and wanted to show support. Bad move, since they took heat for impeding the police's efforts to bring a wanted felon to justice. Still, no one had been arrested. Though the police hadn't yet processed the bizarre situation enough to respond with an official statement.

On Monday at work, I saw Ray as usual at lunchtime. He offered me a smirk as he sat down and lit his cigarette.

"No hoodie?" he asked me.

I shook my head. "Not to work. It's kind of a story now, and I don't want to upset my boss, if she knew I was involved. I highly doubt she's in the Badger's fan club."

"Ditto. I wore it around town over the weekend, though. Told my sister about it. She laughed her ass off. Said she'd go online and try to find herself one."

"That's good. I just hope no one gets arrested."

He blew out a jet of smoke. "Someone already did."

My heart sank. "Did they?"

"Heard it on the radio, like, half an hour ago. Some BC

student. Got all hotheaded when the cops stopped him and started asking questions."

"Oh, no."

Ray shrugged. "Bound to happen. I just wonder who it'll demonize—the resister or the cop."

I nodded.

"Still, nice to see Boston all riled up. People around here can be so apathetic. Nice to have the city on its toes over something that doesn't involve the Yankees."

I nodded again, not paying a hundred percent attention.

"You all right?" Ray asked.

"Oh, yeah. I'm fine."

"Going to assume you're distracted by really heinous, filthy sex thoughts about me," he teased.

I sat up straighter, surprised. It was the most forward thing he'd ever said to me, flirtation-wise.

He laughed. "That got your attention. So, this is when you say what a lovely time you had on Saturday. At dinner."

"Yes," I said, sounding very prim and formal, still on the alert from his comment. "I did have a lovely time."

"So can I ask you out again?"

"Let me ask you first," I said, channeling the new, assertive version of myself. "And I promise I will. I just need to do things on my own timeline." I *would* ask him out. I'd be dumb not to. Ray was my methadone, the steady prescription that might one day free me from my far more destructive Badger habit.

"Deal," he said. "Lemme know when you're ready, and I'll cook us my mom's manicotti and rent whatever movie you want."

"That sounds nice." Far nicer than being dragged into

the woods and made to shoot sex triggers onto some pain-freak's bare back, then getting ditched in the morning without so much as a goodbye kiss.

I looked forward to accepting Ray's invitation to get spoiled, and for a brief moment I imagined exactly how good he might be at oral sex. My cheeks burned, so I blinked the thought away.

I crumpled my cookie wrapper, stowed it inside my cup. "I better get back."

33

Snow fell through the week, accumulating, then melting, turning to ice in the frigid evenings, all as my silly little prank grew, sprouted legs, and charged off on its own errands.

The car Alec and I had nudged down the proverbial hill kept on rolling, pushed along by more and more excited strangers, hundreds of them. On Monday there'd been the one initial arrest. Three more on Tuesday, eight on Wednesday. By the time I met Alec for a drink at Jacob Wirth's an hour before my NA meeting, Thursday's tally had reached ten.

We needed to touch base. I needed to tell him I was done being a part of what I'd started. It wasn't a prank anymore, and I wanted out. People were getting heated and polarized, and the reward had risen to twenty-five grand. I'd never meant to inspire an army of imitators and tar the Badger with conspiracy on top of resisting arrest, assault with an illegal firearm, vandalism, reckless endangerment . . . No way he'd get bail now. He'd be off to jail, with a far worse sentence than he'd ever earned from punishing litterers.

My stomach was violent all week, sending me scrambling to the bathroom every half hour. Lani worried I had a virus. She'd told me to stay home if I wanted, but I didn't. Work was an ineffective distraction, but the only one I had.

My coffee was delivered just as Alec arrived at the bar.

"Pint of Guinness, please." As the waitress left, Alec shed his overcoat, revealing his stripes. My own jacket was folded inside my coat, wadded on the bench beside me. I'd grown less and less comfortable being seen in it, and cowardice had little to do with it. Intuition had told me, *This was a shitty, selfish idea. Listen to me, for the first time in your life.*

Alec took his seat, grinning at me.

I mustered a weak smile in return. "You look pleased."

"Oh, I ought to be. This is all so exciting, don't you think? Hey, you're not wearing your jacket."

"No, it's too warm in here."

"I got turned away from a restaurant yesterday for wearing mine," he said, glowing.

"It's, um . . . it's surprising, everything that's happening."

"Isn't it, though?"

I sighed heavily, surrendering to the weariness and worry. "It's more than I bargained for. People are taking it way too far."

"You're *still* stressing yourself out about that?"

"There's already been, like, twenty arrests."

"Twenty-three, as of this afternoon. And arrested, not

charged. There's nothing *to* charge anyone with. The more the cops overreact, the worse they'll look." He waved my concern away. "Every group's going to have some troublemakers. By and large, people are doing exactly as we'd hoped. Twenty-three people arrested out of perhaps, I don't know, five hundred out there wearing the stripes now? More? A very tiny minority."

"Twenty-three people in *five days*. And some of them didn't do anything to deserve it. They just got picked off by the police for incitement or whatever they're calling it."

"Oh, Adrian." He reached across the table to pat my hand, his posh accent making it all the more patronizing. "You live to fret, don't you?"

I imagined him taking me out to dinner one day, us trying to date, me like something he'd picked up from the pound, another amusing project to make him feel godlike. No, thank you. Bad enough that I'd ever tried to play the reformer myself.

"Every war's got casualties," he went on, then pouted as his stout arrived, clearly annoyed I wasn't sharing in his festive mood. "This whole Badger thing's given me the weirdest bicycle fetish," he added, changing tack.

"Well, I'm sure my friend Ray's got some eligible lady-cyclist friends, if you ever need any matchmaking done."

He laughed, looking perplexed. "Darling, I think you've got me figured wrong."

I offered a blank look.

"I don't fancy women."

"Oh." I cocked my head. Funny how that had never crossed my mind. His Britishness must have jammed my gaydar. "Oh, sorry."

"Don't be sorry. I'm not."

"No, of course not. I just assumed, you know."

"That I wanted to fuck Wonder Woman, not Superman?"

I smiled and nodded.

"Neither," he said. "Too squeaky-clean, the pair of them . . . Oh my God." His eyes went wide. "Look. Look look look." He pointed behind me out the windows, and I craned in my seat to see a young man passing in a striped hoodie. Alec thumped on the glass. The passerby turned, spotted his brethrenly stripes, then raised his fist in salute and grinned. Alec returned the gesture. Fucking Christ, did we have a hand signal now?

I shook my head. "Weird."

Alec settled back down and sipped his drink. "Anyhow. I'd much prefer to fuck the Badger over any made-up character. Same as you."

I started. I'd heard him wrong for a second, thinking he'd used "same as you" to mean he knew I had indeed fucked the man in question.

"Oh, come on," Alec said, giving me a skeptical look. "Like you haven't imagined it. Unless *you* prefer Wonder Woman?"

"No, I like men."

"Well then, don't be coy."

"No one even really knows what he looks like," I muttered.

"I always picture him like a slightly younger Michael Fassbender," Alec said dreamily, then sipped his beer. "Probably wishful thinking."

I held back my urge to correct him. The Badger looked like the Badger. He looked like Isaac Belov, a whacked-in-the-head, white trash dead-ender from due south of here, whose face I'd studied with my eyes and hands and lips for hours at a time. He was fucked and he was beautiful, and he wasn't Alec's to fantasy-cast in some masturbatory comic book film adaptation.

"Plus, he's probably nuts," I added, deflecting.

"That doesn't put me off, somehow." Alec's gaze lost focus, mind hijacked by thoughts I didn't care to guess at.

My skin crawled. Had I been naive, assuming Alec had started BBW unmotivated by a desire to keep tabs on a man he was actually hot for? Oh God, was there Badger fan fiction out there? Would there be, now that I'd unleashed the horde and called yet more attention to him, made him some cult hero, a martyr figure, an idol? A *sex* symbol?

Creepy.

Plus, if he was anybody's, he was *mine*. Or had been. How dare Alec have a reel of speculative sex tape in his head involving the man I'd mistakenly, briefly loved? A man he didn't even know, not outside of stalking him with the aid of a clever website and hundreds of like-minded strangers.

"I better head out," I said, digging my wallet from my purse. Alec still had two-thirds of a beer to drink, but I was done with him, and done with my untouched coffee.

"So soon?"

"I'm meeting my sister to go Christmas shopping." The fib was more than dumb—it was shameful, because I was using it to keep from telling him I was doing something equally worthwhile and productive. But he'd professed an infatuation for my sort-of ex, and I didn't relish reminding him how screwed up I was, not when I was feeling so high and holy and scandalized.

"I'll talk to you soon enough, I'm sure," Alec said, openly perplexed by my flight.

"Probably." If I deigned to take his calls after this unsettling talk. "Enjoy the rest of your night."

"You, too."

o o o

NA was the answer to a prayer I hadn't articulated.

It grounded me and banished the competitive, defensive emotions fluttering in my chest. It reminded me I was just another dented human like everyone else in the circle. I wasn't special, not any more special than any of my fellow attendees, and that was a relief. It's never safe for an addict to feel too separate, too vindicated. Too above it all.

Fuck Alec, I thought as I bundled up and headed for the stairs. Fuck him and his stupid hero-worship fanboy website. Fuck this whole movement I'd started, only meaning to be helpful. It was so *like* someone like me to find a bright and blazing purpose outside of themselves to obsess about. I should've been fixating on the small things. Being a good worker, being a good sister and daughter. Not being such a damn good moth, circling Badger's glow and slamming myself into the glass trying to reach him.

I tugged on my hat as I stepped into the dark, cold night, flipped my striped hood out from under my coat collar. I went to fish my T pass from a pocket when someone jerked my arm, hard.

Give them your purse! my brain screamed. Then my mind

went blank and my eyes went wide as I found Badger's blue ones boring straight through me.

Better or worse than getting mugged? No time to wonder.

His hand tightened. "We gotta talk." I'd grown so used to Alec's posh accent, Badger's scraped like a cheese grater. He was in civilian dress, an anonymous coat and knit cap, no bike. He jerked my arm again, tugging me away from the corner and back toward Downtown Crossing.

I tried to wrest my arm away, but not wildly enough to draw attention. "Let go of me."

He didn't. Afraid to give anyone reason to call the police—like anyone here would ever get involved when they could be minding their own business—I let him lead me over the lumpy, icy cobblestones. He steered me gruffly down Winter Street and into an alley, poorly lit and infinitely sketchy, and pressed me against a wall in the shadows. He jabbed me in the sternum. "What the fuck, Adrian?"

I smacked his hand aside. "Quit being a psycho or I'll scream." And I would've. I had it in me.

He stepped back a pace. "What the fuck are you doing, with all this shit with the people on the bikes with the jackets?" He grabbed my hood and shook it.

I slapped his hand away again. "How do you know I had anything to do with that?"

"Because I know. Same as how I know when you're within half a mile of me. I just know."

I crossed my arms over my middle. "Fine. But Jesus, don't be pissed off. Everyone's doing it to help you, to keep the cops off your back." I wished they weren't now, but I wouldn't tell him so.

"Good for them, but not for you, you retard. Last thing I want is to have anything to do with you getting arrested again."

I stared at him, utterly irate. "Don't call me a retard. I was trying to help your cause."

He sighed loudly. "When are you going to fucking realize I don't have a cause? I have a fucking mental disorder. When are you going to quit treating me like a hero?"

"I'm treating you the way I treat you. I like what you do. I wish I was more like that, and this was my attempt to help you."

"Well your little copycat army is a dumb-shit way to go about it."

Agreed. Thank you, hindsight. "Since when did you care about creating a scene?"

"It's not the scene. It's you, behind the scene." Footsteps echoed from Winter, shoppers or late workers crunching past on the sidewalk salt. "Fuck. This is going to turn into some long-ass talk, isn't it?"

"I dunno."

"You were so much easier to bully before," he muttered. "Come on. We'll go to my place." He grabbed my hand, but I yanked it away, leaving him holding an empty glove.

I snatched it back. "I'll go, but don't jerk me around like a toddler."

He grumbled something I didn't catch, probably relamenting my freshly grown spine.

I followed him to Park Street Station, and we didn't exchange a single word until we got off the train at Davis.

"So was it your idea?" he asked me as we began the walk to Barbara's.

I buttoned my coat against the wind. "Yeah, I suppose it was."

He shook his head. "Ambitious. I'll give you that."

"I didn't know it'd get so . . . popular. I'd been hoping for maybe fifty people. Not the better half of a thousand or however many there are now."

"How'd you do it?"

"I reached out to the guy who runs the website, the one that tracks all your news and sightings, and he recruited some students, who recruited way more students. It wasn't supposed to turn into all this. Nobody was supposed to get arrested. I only wanted to frustrate the police so they'd get discouraged and you'd be harder to find. It's gotten out of hand."

"No shit."

We finished the walk in silence, Badger not breaking stride when I half-fell on a patch of black ice. I recovered and jogged carefully to catch up as we neared Barbara's house. We entered via the rear stairs, and I didn't realize exactly how cold I'd been until we stepped inside. The smell of the place wound around my body, nostalgic, as though I'd visited here ages ago, not a couple weeks.

Badger switched on the bedside lamp, and I shed my coat. I looked around, waiting to feel surprised by how foreign or familiar the space looked after my absence, but nothing profound claimed me beyond the scent. I saw his epically trendsetting hoodie draped over an old velvet chair by the dresser, holster hung on a drawer pull. He'd come out to seek me, naked and unarmed.

I spotted something else hanging nearby—my sequined Halloween dress. He'd taken the time to put it on a hanger along with the necklaces and hook it over the closet door-knob. Whatever that might mean, he was welcome to it.

He took a seat on the edge of his bed and pushed off his sneakers. "What do I have to do to talk you out of this shit?"

"Into not wearing this?" I asked, ditching my coat and plucking at my stripey sleeve. I was eager to give it up already, but fuck him. Let him beg. "I dunno. Ask me nicely. Tell me why I should stop."

He rubbed his face. "Because you're asking for trouble, and I know you. Trouble and you don't get along. Last thing an addict needs is chaos in her life, or some screw-up to set her back and make her miss her pills. Or lose her job. Remember last time you fucked up and lost a job? It's too fucking cold to ride you all the way to Winchester now."

"I'm a *recovering* addict." I said it in a cocky voice that would've earned me some majorly pitying looks from my group, had I ever had the nerve to pull that shit in their presence.

"Recovering ain't the same as recovered," Badger said, and rightly so, but being contrary felt so awfully nice just now.

"Just ask me to stop," I said. "Just ask me like a normal, concerned human being, and I will. I'll stop."

"Stop," he said.

"That's an order, not a request."

Badger rolled his eyes so vigorously his whole head joined the gesture. "Fucking semantics."

I stepped closer, crossing my arms over my chest. "You can't do it. You can't just be nice when someone asks you to. You can't say 'please' unless you're begging somebody to beat an orgasm out of you, can you?"

His eyes narrowed, telling me I was right. I wondered what other phrases he couldn't utter. "I love you," certainly. "Thank you," perhaps. Civility and affection and respect belonged to a dialect he'd never been taught. But if I'd managed to teach myself how to tell aggressive strangers to shut the fuck up, he could learn to ask nicely.

"Just fake it," I said. "Write it down and read it off a piece of paper. 'Adrian, please stop fucking around with those Badger imitators and wearing that jacket.' And I'll say, 'Okay,' and you'll say, 'Thanks,' and I'll say, 'You're very welcome, Isaac. Thank you for asking me so politely—'"

"Jesus, shut up."

I wandered to the other side of the bed, flopping down on my back across his rumpled covers. "I did all that for you," I muttered, and sat up halfway. "Why'd you assault that police car, anyway? Was it self-defense?"

"'Cause I didn't want him to follow me."

I lay back down.

Why was I here? To find out if he'd ask me to stop what I was really quite happy to stop? To take care of unfinished business, to understand our magnets, to fuck him one final time and wreck my fabulously vindictive *other* final goodbye fuck?

"Why am I here?"

He sighed, annoyed. "Like I know. I tried to stay away from you, but here you fucking are."

"You didn't try that at all. You came by where I work, you showed up outside my apartment. Now this."

"Couldn't help it. It's your fucking voodoo suction non-sense, *making* me show up."

"Fuck you, acting like you don't have any free will."

Another sigh, and he lay down, the crown of his head a couple inches from mine. "I've known since forever that I'm nuts," he said. "Because I got told all the time, and labeled by shrinks and special needs teachers and foster system case workers. But I never felt like, yeah, I'm crazy. Not until I met you. Not until you did that calm shit to my head, made me sober just long enough to realize what drunk felt like."

I held my tongue, not wanting to say anything that might banish the softness that had crept into his voice.

"Why do you have to keep making me into something I'm not? Somebody worth caring about or saving or fucking campaigning for? All it does is make me even more of a shithead—which isn't a small feat—when I prove to you I suck. Just accept that I suck."

"You don't always suck. Sometimes you didn't suck at all, when you rode me to that bridge, and that day we played hooky. And when we . . . you know. After you made me shoot you."

"Why can't you fixate on the part where I *made you fucking shoot me?*"

"Sometimes I do." Not often enough.

His words hardened. "What the fuck is your problem? Self-esteem issues? Maybe you actually *like* when I disappoint you. Is that it?" His body was agitated—I could hear his clothes rustling against the covers with each jerky gesture. "You get off every time I prove that yeah, you know what? Adrian does deserve shittiness in her life. Look at this piece of shit, of course she'd get mixed up with him. She's a real fuckup, just like she always suspected. That what you finger yourself to? Banging the biggest douchebag on both sides of the Charles?"

"Jesus," I muttered. "Shut the fuck up."

I turned my head enough to see that he was smirking. Something softened in his expression.

"Why'd you have to do all this shit, all this protest bull?" he asked. "I mean, I could give a shitting fuck about those however many hundred other people, but Jesus, you, too?"

Don't tell me I'm special. Don't you dare.

"Isn't it bad enough I wreck your personal life? You wanna get arrested, doing this for me, so then I'm responsible for you losing your job and messing up your record? Huh?" The final words were quiet, and he reached over his head and wound a lock of my hair around his fingers and tugged gently, a chin-chuck quality to the gesture. "Give up on me, Adrian, for fuck's sake."

I stared up at the ceiling. "You make it sound awfully easy."

"It should be. Anyone else in the world would have no problem walking away from me."

"Not Barbara."

A breath hissed from his nose, but he knew what I'd said was true. Two people cared about him. One enough to feed and house him, the other to be fool enough to have fallen in love with him once.

"What is it with you people, caring about someone who's only a jerk to you?"

"You're not a jerk to her. You run errands for her and keep her safe. And you were nice to me, more than once. Not as often as you were an asshole, but enough. Some of us choose to focus on the human parts of you. Maybe it *is* foolish, but it's not something we can help. Same as you can't help doing whatever your impulses tell you to."

"Whatever. You're both masochists."

"Oh, right," I said through a laugh. "So says the cutter who needs to bleed before he can get hard."

A pause, and then he laughed, too. A quiet, grudging sound.

"Do you love me?" I asked him.

"I don't love anything. Or anyone. It's nothing personal. It's just not something I feel. Same as how people who're color blind don't see red or whatever."

"How do you know, if you've never felt it?"

"How does a woman know she's never had an orgasm before she has one?"

"That's way different. Love doesn't feel like that, all violent and spastic." Not always. Not when you're doing it right, surely. "It's more than just some physical sensation that happens in you. It's lots of things. Sometimes you don't even know you love someone until you think about it real hard and decide you do."

"That's stupid. You don't get to decide emotions. You just have them, like weather. If you could pick how you felt, everyone would just choose to be happy all the time, the sun always shining."

"Well, sometimes you can pick. Or some of us can. I guess the rest of you are just stuck feeling whatever other people's actions *make* you feel."

"Guess so."

I sighed to myself, and neither of us spoke for several minutes. I listened to our breathing as it slowed.

"I guess I'd say I loved somebody," Badger mumbled, "if, like, I'd volunteer to die for them. Like some crazy person with a knife is going to stab them unless I take their place. Maybe that's what love is, when you can't feel anything to prove it's there."

"Maybe. Who would you die for? Anyone?"

"I dunno. I'm shitty at imagining stuff."

"Your grandma?"

I heard him shrug, covers rustling around his shoulders.

I wouldn't bother asking if he'd do that for me. Why invite a fresh punch in the gut?

"You love all those other recovering addicts down in your little Thursday-night basement jamboree?"

"No," I said. "Not love. Not the way I love my family. I care about them and wish them the best, and I'd go out of my way to help them, but I wouldn't give my life for theirs."

"You said you loved me."

"I did. I said I *thought* I loved you, anyhow."

"So what if some guy had a knife to my throat?"

I pondered it, really and truly and deeply for a full minute, and then I lied. "I'd put myself first."

"Good."

"Yeah, good."

After a long silence he asked, "What happened to your hair, anyway?"

"I wanted a change."

More silence, and I sat up. "This is headed nowhere. I'm going home."

Badger sat up, too, something uncertain tensing his mouth and brows.

"No," I said. "I'm not going to stop being a part of your little resistance movement. Not until you ask me to, and say please." I went to my things, zipping up my hoodie, waiting.

But he didn't ask. He didn't say a word. He sat on the edge of the bed and watched me get my shoes on, my scarf, hat, gloves, shoulder my bag. I tucked my coat under my arm, hoping he'd think I'd be bearing my stripes proudly the entire journey home.

We stared at each other a long time, and I finally opened the door. Still nothing from his mouth, so I spoke for both of us.

"Goodbye, Isaac."

I shut the door quietly and descended to the yard, and I didn't cry. Not even close.

34

"Wait," I said. "A what, now? A rally?"

"Indeed." Glee danced in Alec's voice, and I wished I hadn't taken the call.

I stood to shut my office door, then sat on my desk. "A rally for what?"

"To demonstrate solidarity against the police and their campaign of unfounded aggression," he said, like a recitation. "Sundown in the Common on Tuesday, until whenever."

"That's before people are even out of work."

"Exactly. Plenty of witnesses, and just in time for the evening news."

"Did you have a hand in organizing this?" I asked.

"I may have." I could picture him, buffing his nails on his lapel, feet propped on some stately mahogany slab. "Tell me you're coming."

"I'm working."

"But you've got a doctor's appointment that afternoon, surely?" he ribbed.

I sighed, rubbing my temple. "I don't know. It's gone farther than I'm comfortable with."

"It's a peaceful rally. Five hundred or a thousand Badgers telling the police we're fed up with the arrests and the misdirection of their attention and our tax dollars. I've been brainstorming slogan ideas for signs with Todd. Todd's the guy—"

"I know who Todd is." Redbeard.

"My favorite one is, 'Two-thirds of Boston's murders go unsolved. Get your priorities straight, BPD.'"

"That's very . . . Anyhow, I'm not sure. I have to get back to work." Get to work worrying, that was.

"I'll e-mail you the list, if you want to lend us your art skills, make up some signs?"

"I'm not sure," I repeated. "I have to go now."

"Very well. But I know you . . . I'll see you Tuesday."

You don't know the first thing about me. You don't know who put the last notch in my lipstick case, fanboy.

"If I can find you in the teeming throng, that is."

"Bye." I hung up before he could even return the sentiment.

Had I done that to him? Made a reckless riot inciter out of the cautious nerd I'd met at Starbucks that first night? Felt like I'd given an uptight, goody two-shoes college freshman her first cocktail, the one that had turned her into a binge-drinking turboskank by winter break.

The thing was, I agreed with the spirit of the rally. It was getting us back to what the seedling prank had been about. Frustrating the authorities so maybe they'd quit wasting time and tax dollars demonizing a guy who shot paintballs at litterers and bad drivers. I was tempted to go, to linger at the periphery and keep out of trouble, see the fruits of my idea, mutated and monstrous as they'd become. I'd ask Ray what he thought of it.

"Wow," was what he had to say that afternoon on the bench.

"Wow like, 'Wow, what a terrible idea,' or wow like, 'Wow, that sounds awesome, count me in?'"

He pursed his lips. "The latter, I think. I mean, it's true. It's ridiculous how much energy the authorities are putting into arresting kids when there's way more important stuff falling through the cracks. The police should be above getting drawn into vendettas against college students and some guy with a paintball pistol."

"Do you think you'll go?"

He shrugged. "Maybe. Probably. I get off at three, so I don't know why I wouldn't. Nothing more exciting going down on a Tuesday night. You going?"

I turned my cookie around and around. "I don't know yet. I'm tempted."

"You're, like, one of the original hundred people from that first meetup. You should totally go. Tell your grand-kids about it someday, when the Badger goes down in history as Boston's Jesse James or whoever."

"I get anxious in crowds."

"I'll go with you. Keep the jostling masses at bay."

"And I'd have to lie to get the afternoon off, if I wanted to be there on time."

He smirked. "Heaven forefend."

"What if I got arrested? I could lose my job. And it

took me forever to find a job, because of my old record. Which my boss doesn't even know about."

Ray's face fell. "That's not an awful point."

"So I don't know. I want to, but the stakes are high. If I did go, I'd have to play it safe. No hoodie, no pissing off the cops, no sign waving."

"You could go as a spectator," Ray said. "Just being there bodily helps get the point across, without you announcing your loyalties."

"I guess."

"You guess right. Being cautious is all well and good, but if you use it as an excuse, let it get in the way of you doing stuff that means something to you, then it's just cowardice."

I flinched at the word in the same second I committed to a decision.

When I got back to the office, I hung up my coat and knocked on Lani's door.

"Come in."

I smiled weakly.

"How's that rebranding sketch shaping up?" she asked brightly.

"Oh, pretty good. I'll be ready to show you by the end of the day."

"I can't wait. But what can I do for you?" she asked, leaning on her elbows, brows drawing together in a decent imitation of maternal concern. "You still feeling under the weather?"

I was, actually. Sick in my stomach and heart. "Yeah, still."

"You need to go home?"

"No, but I probably need to see a doctor soon." Perhaps a psychiatrist.

She nodded sagely. "Your health comes first."

"If I took Tuesday afternoon, would that be okay?"

She shook her head, filling me with both disappointment and relief.

"Oh. All right."

Her smile was wry. "Take *all* of Tuesday off, Adrian. Get some rest, get yourself checked out. Do you need a referral? My best friend's nephew—"

"No, no. I have a doctor," I lied.

"Right, well—" Lani's phone rang, perfect timing.

"I'll let you take that. Thanks for giving me Tuesday."

She waved the thought away, and I backed out of her office as she picked up the receiver.

Decision made. Tuesday it was.

35

I wished I hadn't accepted the full day off, in the end. All I spent the hours leading up to Tuesday's rally doing was worrying myself sick and pacing my apartment.

Ray met me at the edge of the Public Garden at quarter to four that afternoon. He was across the road, sans stripes, leaning against a streetlight pole and smoking when I emerged from Arlington Station. I studied him as I waited for the walk sign, pretending he was my boyfriend. Would my parents like him? Amanda would. She liked nearly everyone, staring through their packaging with her sky blue eyes and straight into their souls. Some people see only the dog turds, but Amanda always focused on the grass. And there was a lot to like about Ray, I reminded myself as I crossed the street. Maybe I'd get him a Christmas present. Better yet, make him something, art or baked goods. Heartfelt but not too loaded. Oatmeal raisin cookies.

"Hey," I said, poking his arm.

He turned and smiled. "Hey yourself. You see?" He nodded toward downtown, and past the garden I could just make out Boston Common in the dying daylight, enough to spot the white squares of poster boards and discover there were more bodies than normal milling about. Far more.

"Well."

"Wanna go see what you and your crazy friends started?"

I nodded, girding my spine. He offered his elbow, and we linked arms, heading off in the direction of the rally.

Holy.

Fuck.

Shouting grew coherent as we reached Charles Street and the river of cars that separated the two parks. People were chanting in the distance, the action seeming to be centered at the far end, nearer the State House.

I read signs as we passed. There were more neutral ones, like *Keep Boston Beautiful—Leave the Badger Alone!* Some a bit less innocent: *BPD wastes taxpayer $$$ trying to lock up Boston's most concerned citizen!* And far harsher sentiments, such as a cartoon of a police officer with a rainbow of actual paintball splatters shot at the image.

And of course, because this was Boston, a stick figure accepting a stack of dollar bills, X-ed out with angry red lines. *DON'T SNITCH*, it warned.

"People really take this shit personally," Ray said.

"You're here, too," I reminded him.

"Yeah, and if I was still twenty-five and perpetually pissed off, I'd be screaming my lungs out, I'm sure. Guess age really does mellow you."

For some, maybe. Seemed I'd waited until now to let

myself get angry. Or to have met someone worth the energy of getting angry at.

I wondered what Badger would make of all this. If he'd be among the stripey cyclists by the end of the night, annoyed beyond reason by what people were doing on his behalf. Maybe he was already here. Uneasy, I slipped my arm from Ray's and stuffed my hands in my pockets, pretending they were cold.

Flashing police lights joined the chaos as we mounted the hill halfway across the park. We paused to admire the scene. A police barricade had been set up, plastic saw-horses and hazard tape to keep the crowd contained so they didn't wander beyond the bounds of the Common. The officers I could see seemed stoic enough, talking into handsets, standing authoritatively with their arms crossed, waving at people to tell them to keep back, be cool.

Ray nudged me. "How many, do you think?"

I tried to estimate the number of bodies congregated in the shadows of the buildings. "Five hundred?"

"Not bad."

"And it's still early."

"How you feeling?"

Humbled, I thought. Proud. Sick. "I'm not sure. Surprised."

"It's pretty cool," Ray said. "Cool that we're riled up over more than sports or parking spaces for a change. I wonder if the actual Badger's out here someplace."

"Me, too. Is it okay with you if we just hang out up here for a while and watch what's happening?"

Ray nodded. "We can hang out up here all night, if you want. You want me to grab us some coffees or something?"

"Actually, yeah. That'd be great." Great until I had to pee, but I didn't think I'd ever wanted something warm and distracting in my hands so badly.

"Black with one sugar," Ray said, not a question. He let me give him a couple bucks and left in search of drinks.

I zoned out, watching people emerge from the subway in uneven swarms, checking how many made a beeline for elsewhere and how many joined the swelling crowd.

Local TV crews gathered. Cars honked more than usual, workers eager to get home to the suburbs, annoyed by the groups dashing across Tremont Street. More signs marched past, some making me smile, some making me cringe. Che Guevara with his hat replaced by a striped hood. *Oh come on, you guys.* The Badger avenged *littering.*

Still, at least they cared. They could've been home where it was warm, playing video games or updating their Facebook status, but they'd chosen to come here. *Let them believe the Badger is theirs. They're probably no more delusional about it than you ever were.*

Eventually Ray returned with two steaming cups and something lumpy under his arm. I held our coffees as he unfurled the mystery purchase, unrolling a new fleece blanket so we could sit on the frosty grass.

Ray blew on his drink through the hole in the lid, dark eyes on the action. "It's getting big."

I shed my gloves to cup the hot paper in my palms. "I know. It's really something."

"I bet whoever thought all this up is shitting themselves."

"I bet you're right."

The sun had set and taken my rational brain with it, my body pulsing with pure emotion. It was probably the adrenaline, maybe the promise of caffeine, but I was high, looking down from above it all, disembodied. The world seemed profound, the way it tends to at dusk, and I drank in the results of my whim. I registered a rare glimmer of connection to something bigger than myself, and I said a prayer that this would actually work, make things easier for Badger. I was done wanting to hurt him for having hurt me. We were as even as we might ever hope to get. Good luck to him, doing his thing, living his life, obeying his impulses. If he was smart, he'd just swap jackets and repaint his bike.

Someone at the front of the main crowd had a bullhorn, leading a chant that went on for ages. *"We are gray. We are black. We're bringing Boston's justice back."*

Despite the shouting and the sign waving and the police presence, things were peaceful. It was a carnival, not a war zone. My curiosity was sated, fear largely subdued, faith in my city's collective common sense restored.

I glanced at Ray long after our coffees had gone cold.

"You thinking of heading out?" he asked.

I shifted my butt on the hard ground, cheeks numb. "Yeah, pretty soon."

"You hungry?"

I shook my head. "No, thank you. I'm too bushed. Some other night."

This had been my goodbye-to-Badger party, because tonight I knew I didn't need him anymore. We were done, and I had mourning to do, back in the warmth and safety of my apartment. I'd watch the footage on the news later and see this spectacle for what it was—public domain, like the man it celebrated. I'd strip away his extra dimensions and love him the way everyone else did, with detached amusement. I'd root for him, perk at news of his comings and goings, but I wouldn't care anymore. I couldn't. I didn't have the stamina.

Ray stood and offered his hand, hauling me onto my frozen legs.

"I'll walk you to the—"

A sound cut him off, the unmistakable pop of a gun. My heart pounded, throat closing.

"Paintball," Ray murmured, not sounding convinced.

"I hope so."

It didn't matter. The crowd surged, its center contracting like a sphincter nearest the front, its edges dissolving as the smarter people ran. I felt Ray's hand on my back.

Not Badger, I prayed. Just some imitator moron who'd get hauled off to jail for pelting an officer, or maybe just somebody's paintball rifle that had gone off by mistake. *No one hurt. No one hurt.*

Ray tugged at my arm. "C'mon. Let's get out of here before people go batshit."

Too late. The human lake turned choppy, signs sinking to the bottom to get trampled as people panicked and jostled.

"Stay behind the partitions," commanded a police megaphone. *"Stay calm and stay put."*

Ray tugged at me again, and then a second pop cracked through the thin winter air, and panic gave way to chaos.

"Adrian, come on."

But I couldn't. Someone was shooting, and that meant somebody else could be getting shot. Badger could be either of them, unlikely or not, and I couldn't go without confirmation. Plus, this was my party. Who was I to run, leaving everyone else to clean up the mess I'd made?

I yanked hard, frustration flushing my skin, but Ray's grip only tightened. I whipped my head around and laid a glare on him, cold enough to drain the blood from his face. His hand went slack, and I got away, tromping down the hill even as others fled behind me.

"Adrian." Ray followed, voice jumping with his footfalls. "Seriously, think about your record. Think about your job. Don't do anything stupid."

Don't be idiots. Too late.

More pops as we crossed the grass, different ones, and soon after I smelled something odd. Misty plumes curled up into the darkness beyond the streetlights. My eyes stung, and the capillaries inside my nose tingled. I heard Ray mutter "Fuck" as more people broke from the throng to run from the tear gas.

"We don't want to use force, but we will," said the voice of authority. *"Disperse calmly before anyone gets hurt."*

Wrong thing to say. Shouts erupted all over, a discordant chorus to the tune of "Then quit throwing fucking tear gas canisters at us!"

Then I felt it. The pull, real as a punch in the gut.

Badger was here, somewhere in this sea of dark stripes and anger, perfect camouflage.

Everyone was shoving, pulling, shouting, kicking. A living wall of flesh, but I'd knock every last motherfucker down myself if that was what it took to make sure Badger hadn't discharged a shot, or worse, taken one. I made it to the eye of the storm, got my breath knocked out by a shove, my ear boxed by an elbow. "Fuckers."

A clearing opened, and I paused to get my bearings and blot my tearing eyes and nose on my sleeve.

"Adrian!"

It was Alec, waving from a few yards off. I dodged panicked bodies to meet him, Ray lost behind me somewhere.

"Jesus," I said, at a loss for anything else.

To my horror, he grinned. "Amazing, isn't it?"

"Has someone been shot?"

"It's paintballs. Up into the air. Harmless."

"No, it isn't!" I waved my arms around at the chaos, accidentally whacking a teenager as she dashed past. My apology was lost in the shouting.

"Let the cops overreact," Alec said. "It'll only make them look worse."

"They're tear-gassing us!"

Alec shot me one of those twee, pitying looks I'd grown to hate and put his hands on my upper arms. I could smell whiskey on his breath from some celebratory flask. "Everything's—"

Someone slammed into him from behind, and he shoved me by mistake, sending me sprawling to the ground on my back with a yelp.

Then Ray was helping me up, but the pull hooked me so hard I never registered standing. So hard, it felt like a vice clamped to my belly, squeezing my air out. Ray was shouting at Alec, but I blocked his way when he tried to advance on him.

"He didn't mean to," I said. The pull again, tugging at me, jerking. I whipped around. Two blue eyes glared from the shadow of a hood fifteen paces away, anonymous to everyone except me.

"You're okay." I said it to myself, relief inflating me like the oxygen I sucked into my lungs. He was okay . . . but he wasn't. Hatred burned in his eyes, surely aimed over my shoulder at the man he thought had pushed me. I shook my head. "No." The cops were too close.

But he was already striding straight past me, bound for Alec. *Don't let him smell the booze.* I grabbed his arm to hold him back, but he wrenched away, and my frozen fingers slipped from his jacket. I dashed to get between him and Alec, but he shunted me aside. His hand disappeared inside his hoodie.

"Don't! He didn't push me on purpose!"

Alec's eyes went wide as he realized he was the target of this crazy-eyed man's advance.

I grabbed Badger's sleeve again, but a flash rearranged my head, pain so sharp my body didn't let me feel it until after. I heard Ray shout and looked to my right to see a cop, one holding a baton I vaguely understood must have just struck me in the temple.

Time slowed.

I touched my head and felt wetness, sticky red on my fingertips as I drew my hand away. Motherfucker.

"Motherfucker," echoed a low, cold, deadly voice.

It was a cut, not a laceration, but I caught Badger's eyes as I glanced up from the blood, and I'd never seen that look. Pure liquid nitrogen, freeze-and-shatter. His hand went to his jacket, and I shook my head.

"No. No no no."

The pale skin of his hand disappeared, reappeared, a white point fled a black barrel with a pop, and the cop who'd hit me cupped both hands over one eye, baton jettisoned.

Time sped.

Badger charged and knocked the cop to the ground. Another appeared, and a Taser lit the chaos in bright, dancing light. Badger fell back. I heard his head thump the hard earth. I lunged, but too late. Another flash from above, but no voltage this time—an invisible strike that bounced Badger's chest.

I was on him before I'd given my muscles the order. My fingers found his zipper, his hood's drawstring, found heat pulsing there, wet and thick. "No."

Someone leaned in, but my shriek ripped the air in half. "Get the fuck away! Get a paramedic!"

It was another cop, and he retreated a pace, turning his efforts to keeping the greater crowd at bay. Shouts volleyed, summoning medical personnel from wherever they lingered. Ray was at my back on his knees, faint as a ghost. He hadn't run, as Alec had.

My head pounded where I'd been whacked, heart pounded from fear. Badger's wound steamed in the dry winter air, blood smelling of rust and life, smelling bright red. Noise fogged the world around us, screams and shouts and sirens, but I heard his words as clear as if we were alone in his room once more.

"Hey, cupcake."

My arms shook, and I held him tighter to still them, speaking against his neck. "Hey."

"You look real pretty."

"Jesus . . ."

He sucked an ugly, wet breath.

"Does it hurt?"

"Nah. It doesn't hurt. Feels like falling asleep. Like that bridge, all echoey."

No, no no no. He couldn't . . .

Even as I thought it, I registered the heft of my coat, collecting what he hemorrhaged.

"Don't. Don't fall asleep. Just hang on, and there'll be a medic."

"It's okay. It feels good."

My chest clenched, strangling my heart. "Don't. Don't."

"You take care."

"Fuck you. Don't say that. Don't go."

"This isn't—" A wheezy gasp cut him off, followed by a sucking sound that told me his lung must be filling. He coughed, and I felt blood spatter my cheek. I held him tighter, thick heat trickling down my forearm, collecting in my sleeve.

His breathing grew shallow, and his taut limbs went slack. The pull began to fade, gravity surrendering, like maybe we'd float up into the black sky if not for Ray's hand on my back, pinning us to the earth.

"Sorry," Badger sputtered, sucking air. "Sorry I can't. Say it."

"I don't care. It doesn't matter. You can say it some other time. Or don't. Who cares? Shut up and keep breathing." He wasn't leaving me. Even if he thought he was, I'd be damned if he'd go out apologizing.

"Don't." I grabbed his face, pressed my ear to his lips. His breath was thin, scraped raw and tinny like an old recording. I kept squeezing, my entire body a tourniquet. The smell was pungent, earthy and vital. Behind it I located his latest cigarette and the scent of his skin, the man I'd tasted all those times we'd kissed. Then, like it had been sucked down the drain in a final, raspy slurp, his breath stopped. His lungs stopped. His heart stopped.

"Adrian." Ray, at my back.

"No. No no no no no."

The pull cut me loose, but I held his body like an anchor, afraid to drift off on the December breeze, off with the tear gas clouds, off with the sweet heat of his blood.

No one had held him when he came into this world, but I clung and cradled long after he'd left it.

When the paramedics dropped to their knees at my sides, I let them pull me away. My hair stuck to Badger's blood-tacky jacket, and they made me kneel a few paces away as a stretcher was set up.

"Adrian."

I turned to stare up at Ray.

His eyes were wide, dark irises fish-darting in pools of white, flitting from the ground to my face, back and forth, back and forth. He had to grasp now what had kept me at arm's length, even as our mouths had occasionally come together. The first of many to realize exactly who'd become the inaugural casualty of this battle.

"We have to go, Adrian. Now." His eyes darted again, to the police, I could only guess. To something on the horizon, threatening my future.

My nod was like a seizure, continuing as he helped me to my feet. He dragged me, stumbling, the first few paces as I craned my neck for a final glimpse, but Badger was lost behind a wall of medics.

The hard, grassy earth rose up to punch my feet with every step, and I let Ray wrap my wet body in the fleece blanket at the top of the hill. There were lights—streetlights and strobing red and blue from the distance, sweeping beams from news or police helicopters, camera flashes. Ray spoke ceaselessly, his voice as sweet and meaningless as birdsong, and he kissed my temple, the only place where the blood he'd taste would be my own.

36

My name is Adrian Birch, and I used to be nobody. An apologist, a coward.

Then I met a madman on a bicycle and I lost my mind, lost my way, got my heart broken and my head rewired, and woke from a nightmare of my own design, fear gone like an ex-lover I'd never spread my legs for again.

How Ray had gotten me home, I didn't know—the subway, the bus, on foot, a cab . . . I only knew where I ended up. He'd taken my bloody clothes and steered me into my bathroom, turned on the shower for me, later swabbed and bandaged my temple.

He never asked me about Badger. Not once the entire night. He tried to stay awake with me but passed out fully clothed on the end of my bed around four, while I sat up, hugging my knees and shaking, watching TV in case the next news update would pronounce a miracle.

It never did.

Badger's identity was surmised by his possession of the infamous Glock, a police-issue training weapon, it turned out, not something you could just waltz in and buy from a store. What had been a tragic accident one moment was tantamount to assassination the next, and the city went insane.

And the next morning, I was in the papers. Sort of.

There was a flash-harsh camera phone picture of Badger on the ground, my hair fanned across his chest, only my ear and a sliver of my profile showing. Ray's forearm and hand were in the shot as well, his fingertips lost behind my coat collar. It was the cover story in the *Globe*, the *Herald*, the *Metro*, the *Phoenix*. I became an anonymous, iconic any-girl, a horrified, grieving disciple clinging to her grungy martyr, his naked face finally revealed.

His identity as the real Badger was announced, civilian name uncovered through fingerprinting and released officially nearly a week after his death. But it spread long before that, and who knew who'd recognized him from the photo—an old schoolmate, maybe a coworker from the supermarket. It didn't matter. Isaac Belov became a somebody to hundreds of thousands of people, spread so thin there was nothing left to get hold of.

Alec got his fifteen minutes, going on the radio and TV as a Badger expert, which, to be fair, he was. My blood boiled when I first heard, but he spoke with a fan's genuine reverence, and he never implicated me in any of the organizing. He'd been obsessed with the Badger a full year before I got hit-and-run, after all. His grief looked nothing like mine, but I conceded that he'd earned it. Bet he wished he'd earned that splatter he'd had coming, too, gotten marked by his precious antihero.

The two cops—the one who'd lost his eye to a paintball and the one who'd shot Badger—had their fifteen minutes as well. Worshipped like 9-11 first responders by the anti-Badger populace, hated by the mourners. I turned off the TV whenever they came up, unable to blend my guilt and rage into something that didn't feel like evisceration.

There was no funeral for the Badger, not a proper one. There was a massive candlelight vigil that reconvened every night for two weeks, Boston Common aglow with thousands of flames, then hundreds, then dozens by the time Christmas arrived, and finally just a handful, lit by the homeless who slept on the grates outside Park Street Station.

I didn't hold a candle with the crowd. My grief was sometimes black and bottomless and quiet as a quarry, other times a violent gale, a deafening echo rising in waves, pushing and sucking with no end in sight. I didn't want to share it. I didn't want it folded into the greater whole, swallowed or diluted.

I hadn't lost the same thing they had. I'd lost a man in the same moment they'd lost a character.

I'd felt his hot blood pool in my coat sleeve, warming my elbow. The two of us surrounded by hundreds of people, only me truly knowing that it was him, the real Badger, bleeding out on the stiff winter grass.

All those copycats, they'd found out from the news or from a tweet, or a text message starting with "OMG."

Fuck them.

They had no clue who'd been lost. Only two people I knew of in the entire world came anywhere close to knowing who was gone, and the burden of being one of them, being one of two women capable of grieving his death as that of a human being . . . It hurt like nothing I'd ever conceived of. Like my marrow had turned to acid, chewing my bones to chalk and splinters. Like my heart was wrapped in concertina wire, tight enough to pierce, and tight enough to keep the blood inside so the suffering stretched out before me, endless.

After two weeks passed—after the candles burned down, their fire gone and their wax puddled all over the park, confusing the pigeons—the skin of my heart began to close over, swallowing the barbs and keeping them safe. Keeping them deep. Keeping them sharp, so should that muscle ever decide to beat for someone else, it would sting.

After two weeks I mailed a pair of letters. One to Derek, finally, with a check for a thousand dollars, which I'd hoped to send sooner. Delayed or not, the act felt like I was dropping far more than a thin envelope into the box. Felt like a ten-ton anchor slipping free from my neck. The second was a tardy Christmas card that I sent to the downtown Macy's, attention: the security guard with the cornrows who'd been working on December fourteenth the previous year and had busted a skinny, tweaky woman for trying to steal a red handbag. I thanked him for my rock bottom and my current sobriety and wished him a happy holiday.

After two weeks I decided I wanted a bicycle.

I'd texted Lani that I was ill and didn't listen to any of the messages she left. And after two weeks without speaking to anyone, without showing up at my office or taking anyone's calls, I woke early and returned to work.

Lani was equally surprised and relieved by my reappearance, but she welcomed me back in the wake of what she must have feared was stomach cancer or a pregnancy. I didn't lie, just told her I'd been sick, and it seemed to be enough. She was a good boss. I vowed to quit finding her annoying and to work harder.

I fetched my cookie and coffee, and Ray joined me silently on the bench. He smoked three cigarettes before I spoke. My voice came out weak from disuse.

"I want you to build me that bike."

"Okay."

"A fast one."

"Sure. Give me 'til next Monday."

I nodded.

Boston wouldn't be easy to ride in. Unpredictable traffic, construction, narrow streets, one-ways, pedestrians, sporting events. It was no place for the meek.

But I wasn't meek. Not anymore.

That weekend I went to an outdoor store to buy paint-balls, white ones. The guy behind the counter said, "Sorry, we can't sell white ones in Middlesex County. There was this guy . . ."

What color, then? Yellow? Yellow like his Schwinn. Yellow like my belly in some previous life.

But in the end I left empty-handed, because that was never my path. No bicycle, no paintballs. No cheap imitations of who he'd been. Never my path. It had been his, and he was gone. Gone to where there was no pull, no gravity, no impulse.

37

Someone once told me, you'd have to be a retard to know what you love doing, and what you're good at, and not do it.

What was I good at?

I was good at my artwork, and I promised myself I'd keep doing it, do something every single day until I got a show at the same museum that had turned me away when I failed my pee test. Maybe by then I'd know who I was. Really know. Maybe by then I'd be able to kiss Ray or someone like him again, and truly feel something.

But that was a selfish goal, and I wanted more. I wanted to help, the way Badger had arguably helped, even if his altruism had been little more than a side effect of his greater mission to punish.

I didn't want to punish people, no matter the outcome. I didn't want to be Badger. As bold as he'd made me, I couldn't ever be him. I had too many marbles, too many filters.

In NA they liked to talk about service, about doing the right thing for the right reason. Badger's reason never would've been right for me. If I made the world nicer, with less trash on the ground, less apathy, less rudeness, it couldn't be through violence.

So I ditched the vigilante aspirations by New Year's, quit researching paintball pistols.

Instead I bought two handsome wooden walking sticks —one straight, one with a curved handle like an old-timey umbrella. I went home for the weekend, and my dad took me to the hardware store. We squirreled ourselves away in his cold toolshed for a couple hours, and he showed me how to drill a tidy hole in the bottom of the curved stick and screw in a spike, about four inches long, and he soldered a strip of metal around the hole, just for looks. He also helped me spiff up a metal grabber-thing, a pooper-scooper. We removed the mechanisms from the original aluminum tubing and attached them to the second walking stick, the straight one.

The Grabber and the Stabber, we named them.

For the cost of materials, Ray's sister, Erica, made me a bag, a sort of quiver with shoulder straps. One diagonal sleeve for the grabber, a crosswise one with a steel cup in its base for the poker, a loop at the hip to hold a sack. I bought new boots, the same brown as the quiver's leather trim.

I was ready. I even knew my first patrol route.

"It's community service," I told the T official who stopped me, wanting to know what sort of poles I was intending to waltz onto the Orange Line with strapped to my back. Getting around would be easier once my bike was ready. But I showed him the Grabber, and luckily he didn't ask to see the Stabber.

"I'm a recovering pill addict," I told him without apology. "It's a penance."

His eyes narrowed. I showed him my twelve-month medallion, and he showed me his fifteen-year keychain. He let me board.

I resurfaced at Davis. It was warm, in the low fifties. Finding trash to pick up wasn't difficult, and the normally twenty-minute walk to Barbara's took me nearly three hours. Along the way I filled five and a half plastic shopping bags with soggy old gum wrappers and receipts, innumerable coffee cups and spent subway tickets, impaling them on my poker and drawing them off in thick bundles. It was the most laborious of labors, but through mindless repetition came Zen, I'd heard. Plus, it was a Sunday. I had all the time in the world.

No one asked what I was doing. No one saw my stabbing at the trash as criminal or mock-worthy or even curious enough to inspire conversation. The trash left the ground as unnoticed as when it had been jettisoned, and I imagined myself negating not the litter itself, but the laziness behind it. Combating apathy with intention. Not one person thanked me, but I didn't mind. Like Badger, I was doing this for me. A selfish act best left ignored, lest it be mistaken for goodwill and praised.

My one-woman parade reached Barbara's as the sun was setting, and my trash-stabbing palm was worn raw, the pads of my fingers blistered. They'd thicken soon enough.

I pressed her bell with an achy thumb and listened to the chime.

Did she even know what had happened? As far as she knew, had he simply gone missing? I shivered. Maybe she was like me, linked to him through some strange intuition. Had some part of her gone dark three weeks earlier, blinked out the second he'd bled out?

I was surprised when she answered. She opened the front door, and I saw a Christmas tree behind her, tasteful white lights, just a few presents beneath it.

"Happy New Year," I said.

"It's you." She stared at me a moment, looking exhausted. "Well, come in."

"Thank you."

"He's not home," she said coolly, stepping aside.

"I know."

I followed her into the den and slipped my quiver from my stiff shoulders, leaning it in a corner next to an umbrella holder.

"What's that, then?" she asked, eyeing it.

"I'm picking up trash. It's a poker and a sort of pooper-scooper thing."

She nodded and shut the front door. "Better you than me. You want tea?"

"Yeah, okay."

I trailed her into the kitchen and sat at the table while she filled a kettle and set it on a burner. I watched the icicles dripping outside the window, looked around the room, trying to decide how familiar it felt.

"Your tree looks nice," I said.

She kept her eyes on the mugs she gathered. "He put it up."

I should have guessed. "How are you doing? With him gone, I mean. I know it's been a while." Did she know he was dead? Perhaps she thought he'd merely moved on. If so, I wouldn't correct her. I wished I believed such a thing, myself.

"I'm fine," she said. "I'm not the one dressed as Robin Hood, picking up garbage like a convict."

I smiled weakly at that. "Do you need any groceries or anything? Any chores around the house?"

"I've got someone delivering from the store again. They do a god-awful job. Always screwing up my order. *He* never screwed up my order," she added in a grumble.

"Well, if you ever need anything done, I can leave my number."

She didn't reply right away, just tore open the envelopes and set a tea bag in each cup. "I know he's dead, you know."

My heart thumped, punching my ribs. "Oh?"

No answer.

"I think it was kind of my fault," I said after a very long lapse.

She finally met my eyes, her rheumy blue ones leery. "Kind of your fault?"

"What happened. That he was there."

"You tell him to assault an armed police officer?"

No, I hadn't done that. I shook my head.

"'Course you didn't. Nobody ever told that boy anything. He just did as he pleased."

"I just—"

"You just nothing," she snapped. "He did what he does. You were only unfortunate enough to be there when he finally crossed a line."

"Did you always know . . . You know. What he did? Who he was?"

She nodded curtly. "I read the papers."

"Did you ever talk to him about it?"

"No. We kept out of each other's business, aside from making sure the other was fed and safe."

She turned to fuss with something on the counter, and I sighed silently to myself. When the kettle whistled, she filled the mugs and set my tea before me on the table. "I miss him," I said, eyes on the steam curling out of my cup.

"Bet you do."

"Bet you do, too."

"Yes, I do. We may be the only ones," Barbara said. "Only ones who really knew him as more than just a sensation on the news, or some crazy person wrecking their clothes or cars."

"As an actual man."

"Very sad, broken, angry man," she agreed.

We sipped our tea in silence. Then she told me, "He's somewhere better now. He wasn't meant for this world. Not this time around."

Brewing tears tightened my throat, and I simply nodded.

"You staying for dinner?"

"I dunno."

"You know how to play canasta?"

"No."

"Well, I'll teach you. You'll come around on Sunday nights, and we'll play canasta and have dinner, and if

I need something done, I'll maybe let you do it. More respectable than collecting other people's trash."

"I like collecting trash." I didn't like thinking about the careless people who'd left it where I found it. I liked imagining it had always been there, and I was merely helping it find its way to where it needed to go. A steward of the misplaced. "But okay, that sounds fine."

"Good," she said matter-of-factly. "I'll be needing help getting that Christmas tree cleared out of here. Goddamn men, always leaving me with their goddamn Christmas trees."

It took me a few moments to notice, but Barbara had begun crying, quiet and calm. I didn't try to console her. Instead we drank in silence, and then I took our empty cups and washed them in the sink. By the time I was done, her face was dry, lips steady.

"We're having ziti," she announced. "If you don't eat meat, you're shit out of luck."

"I eat meat."

"While I get it ready, you're going to read the *Hoyle's* and learn the rules of canasta, so by the time we start playing I don't have to explain every last little thing to you."

"Sure."

She led me to the den and handed me a paperback of card game rules from a drawer and two decks strapped into one tall stack with rubber bands. I studied the guide and tried to play two hands at once, to practice. But I was distracted by the cards that Badger had touched and shuffled and dealt, the ones whose corners he'd helped soften.

Eventually, she called me to the kitchen, and we ate without speaking before retiring to the den.

"Cut," she said, presenting the deck she'd shuffled. I did. She dealt our hands and flipped over the top card of the stack. I fumbled my way through a few hands, losing them all but starting to understand the strategy.

"Quit throwing away your twos," she said, handing me back the wild card I'd once again discarded, having forgotten it was special. "Last time I give you a mulligan."

"Understood."

"He was awful at canasta, too," Barbara said with a sigh. "Couldn't read a meld to save his life."

"Maybe he let you win."

She made a noise. "Charity wasn't in that boy's genetics."

No, I supposed not. Not pity or forgiveness either, not any impulse that required empathy and self-awareness. Nor, I suspected, was the attention span and focus required to excel at canasta.

"I think he really cared about you," I offered.

"Same as a dog loves its owner. Same as any animal loves the hand that feeds it. Surprised I never got bitten, like the saying goes. You did, though, didn't you?" she asked, eyeballing me.

I nodded. "A lot."

"You cared too much, and you let him see it. You let him see your fear. Animals hate that."

"He wasn't an animal."

She nodded, gaze on the hand she was arranging. "He was. And there's nothing wrong with it. I like animals. Like them better than people." She sighed mightily, then muttered something.

"Pardon?"

"Badger," she said. "Of all the comparisons. Terrible creatures. We don't even have them in New England."

"I think it was only because of the stripes. What would've been a better fit, do you think?"

"Something loyal," she said, laying two kings and a two on the table before her. "Something that only bites when it's bitten. Or when its master's bitten. Nothing as dirty as a badger. Filthy animals. You'd think he didn't have someone to wash his clothes for him and offer him a hot shower."

I was quiet, still unsure exactly how I'd bitten him to deserve all those times he'd bitten back.

"I was going to leave him this house," Barbara said, glancing around the room.

"Really?"

She nodded. "Had my will changed and everything. It always surprised me, how easily he settled into this place. Like he'd been waiting his whole life to belong somewhere."

"Huh."

"I lost him to you, a little bit." She laid down her entire hand and set a red three on the discard pile.

I folded my cards in defeat and sat back in my chair. "How so?"

"He was different after he met you. Punchier."

"Oh."

"I think he loved you," she said.

"Maybe. In his way."

"He loved you as much as he was capable of loving anyone. After you two met, he never settled down. Always like a dog whose master had gone out, when you weren't here. Like he was pacing even when he was standing still."

"He said I made him feel calm, once."

"Probably you did. Probably made him nuts when you weren't with him, when he wasn't there to know you were safe."

It sounded nice, but I wasn't sold. "He drove me away in the end." He'd driven me to drive him away, anyhow.

"Of course he did. Probably couldn't stand feeling all that for someone. I don't know who his family is, but I know they weren't close. I always bet maybe he had a father walk out on him, something like that. That same sort of thing that kept him pacing outside the door in his mind, waiting for someone to come home. Waiting to feel missed."

A father, no. A mother. Other people due to return, their sick and selfish affection not welcome. "Something like that," I agreed.

"Are you pacing," Barbara asked, "now that he's gone?"

I shook my head. "I was at first, but not anymore. Not now that I'm keeping busy. Are you?"

"No. I know where he is now. I'll miss having someone to worry about, but I won't miss the worrying." Her gaze moved to the tree. "Get that box," she said, pointing to one of the wrapped presents. "My back doesn't like when I bend over anymore."

I fetched the one she'd indicated, a garment box, narrow and pliable. I went to hand it to her, but she waved me away. "Sit down. Open it."

"Was it for him?"

She nodded.

I tore the paper aside. It was from Macy's. I raised the lid and spread open the white tissue, half expecting to find the purse I'd tried to steal for pill money. But it was a plain sweater, merino or maybe cashmere, red as deep and rich as strawberry sauce.

"You should have that," she said. "I've got no use for it."

I stroked it. "Thanks. If you're sure."

"Sure I'm sure."

I would wear it, oversized though it was. I'd wear it until the cuffs unraveled and the armpits were pilled and threadbare, until my quiver straps chewed the weave to cheesecloth at my shoulders. I folded it neatly and hugged it to my chest. "I better get home soon."

"Yes, I suppose you better."

"I'll come by next week." With a gift of some sort. A puzzle compendium, maybe.

"You do that. You need a lot of practice with canasta, that's for sure."

I nodded.

We stood, and she touched my upper arm, steering me toward the door and my things. "You'll be way better than he ever was, though. If you work at it."

"Good."

"Next week I'll make meat loaf. I'll need you to bring some broccoli. The stuff they deliver is terrible, always the worst they have, I'm sure, like some stupid old lady like me can't tell. So get two big stalks from somewhere decent. And not shipped all the way from Chile or some other ridiculous place."

"Okay."

"And don't you dare show up without a proper coat on.

You young people think you're invincible. Invincible until you come down with frostbite and lose a toe."

"I won't." To show her I was obedient, I pulled the sweater over my head before I shrugged into my quiver.

She looked me over. "You're a stick. We'll have to do something about that. I'll make cookies. Fatten you up."

I nodded.

We said goodbye, and I headed back out into the brisk winter breeze, Somerville a different world than when I'd arrived. Sunny before, now dark and frosty cold. My entire adulthood felt like that—dark nights giving way to merciful dawns, back to dusk, the flux of seasons, bad following good, good following bad, black chasing gray in endless stripes. Would the black ever fade, I wondered? Would the gray ever bleach to pure white? Would I ever wake as fair as my sister, the gleam instead of the shadow it cast?

Whatever. Like anyone fucking knows.

There was no poetry worth finding in me. Poetry only ever led to drinking problems, anyhow. I was a twenty-seven-year-old girl stumbling toward womanhood with a pike and shit-scooper strapped to her back. I'd met a man, let him cleave the apathy and apology from my spine, got pushed away half-healed and taught to push in return.

He'd hurt people for littering, never once picking up a discarded cup or scratch-off ticket. Maybe he'd left those for me. A wealth that would keep me busy indefinitely, until the day came that I no longer needed its distraction.

I paused at a trash can to empty the scraps rustling at my hip.

Maybe a year from now, I'd be sipping sparkling cider at my own opening in a little gallery someplace. My parents would be there, Amanda and Derek, maybe Ray. Maybe a year of slicing and fussing and reassembling strips of paper would show me who I was, all those bits and pieces joined to reveal a more fascinating whole.

I made it to the Red Line platform without interrogation. I flexed my savaged hand and waited for the train that would take me home to my more civilized projects. It would hurt, holding the X-Acto, but nobody ever promised that art felt good. What growth came of staying comfortable, after all?

The train trundled up, and I boarded. My muscles ached as I took a seat on the hard bench, begging me to let them rest when I got home. But I wouldn't. No rest. No sleep.

I'd stay up until eleven, midnight, one o'clock, hunched over an illustration board, because what had sleep ever done for me, really?

CREDITS

AUTHOR	C. M. McKenna
EDITOR	Ruthie Knox
COPYEDITOR	Kelly Lauer
PROOFREADER	Beaumont Hardy Editing
COVER ILLUSTRATION	Grace Mutuku
COVER DESIGN	Book Beautiful
INTERIOR ART	Grace Mutuku
INTERIOR DESIGN	Williams Writing, Editing & Design

ACKNOWLEDGMENTS

This book is for Ruthie, who was there at its conception and mopped my sweaty forehead through the delivery.

With thanks to my agent, Laura Bradford. I knew it was true love when you agreed to take this one on.

Thanks also to Sarah Frantz, and to every friend who read this story, years before it found a home—Bobbi, Charlotte, Shari, Amber, Mary Ann, and likely others. You kept the Badger fires burning.

Though you'll likely never read this, thank you, Brian, for being my Ray when I needed one.

Thank you to the closing months of 2011. You treated me bad, but I couldn't have written this book without your discouragement.

And thanks finally to Boston. I miss you.

Brain Mill Press would like to acknowledge the support of the following Patrons:

Noelle Adams

Rhyll Biest

Katherine Bodsworth

Lea Franczak

Barry and Barbara Homrighaus

Kelly Lauer

Susan Lee

Sherri Marx

Aisling Murphy

Audra North

Molly O'Keefe

Virginia Parker

Cherri Porter

Erin Rathjen

Robin Drouin Tuch

ABOUT THE AUTHOR

C. M. McKenna, writing as Cara McKenna and Meg Maguire, is an award-winning author of more than thirty-five romances and erotic novels. Her books are acclaimed for their fresh voice and defiance of convention. A recent transplant from Boston, she now lives with her husband in the Pacific Northwest, where people make a startling amount of eye contact. You can find her online, at www.caramckenna.com, or on Twitter at the handle @caramckenna.